SNA

Bedu Lim

For
Shakuntala Gune and Beda Lim

The Chinese Babies

SNAKE WINE

A Singapore Episode

By

PATRICK ANDERSON

KUALA LUMPUR
OXFORD UNIVERSITY PRESS
OXFORD NEW YORK MELBOURNE
1980

Oxford University Press
OXFORD LONDON GLASGOW
NEW YORK TORONTO MELBOURNE WELLINGTON
KUALA LUMPUR SINGAPORE HONG KONG TOKYO
DELHI BOMBAY CALCUTTA MADRAS KARACHI
NAIROBI DAR ES SALAAM CAPE TOWN
© *1955 Patrick Anderson*
First published in 1955
by Chatto & Windus, London
Reprinted 1980 by
Oxford University Press Kuala Lumpur

ISBN 0 19 580455 4

Printed in Malaysia by Sun U Book Co. Sdn. Bhd., Kuala Lumpur
Published by Oxford University Press, 3, Jalan 13/3,
Petaling Jaya, Selangor, Malaysia

CONTENTS

Part One

CHAPTER

A LONG TIME ARRIVING

PAGE

9

A Sequence of Letters: Autumn, 1950

Part Two

QUEER CAMPUS   73

January—June, 1951

1 The Keys of Ah Ting   75
2 Down Orchard Road   89
3 The Cannas on the Campus   115
4 Matins with the Monkey God   133
5 Buying a Monkey   141
6 Profile of a City   151

Part Three

SQUIRE OF SUNGEI TENGAH   165

June—December, 1951

7 I move to the Jungle   167
8 The House   182
9 The Silence of Ah Tum   201
10 The Chinese Babies   215
11 The Balcony   224

Part Four

EPILOGUE IN BLUE AND WHITE
STRIPED PYJAMAS   251

Spring, 1952

ILLUSTRATIONS

*

1 The Chinese Babies   *Frontispiece*

2 'the small curving river which slips down through Chinatown'   *Facing page* 48

3 'below the crossed flags of laundry hung on poles from the upper windows'   65

4 Tamils also lived in the village   160

   a gibbon's black disgruntled face, a Malay's broad pleasant one

5 'a ghostliness out of its very solidity, as it glimmers at you from its palms'   177

6 'with sampans in the rushes and black mud shining through the mangrove roots'   240

7 'a crazy world of flaring lamps, far too much beer, and children whose business it was to flirt with Europeans for money'—the Beggar Woman here tried to get me a Boy   257

   'children began to invade the House'

PART ONE

A LONG TIME ARRIVING

A Sequence of Letters: Autumn, 1950

The Verses on pages 219 and 220 are taken from COLLECTED POEMS by C. Day Lewis and from COLLECTED POEMS by Dylan Thomas published by Jonathan Cape and the Hogarth Press, and J. M. Dent respectively.

In the Persian Gulf . . .

THERE'S a kind of voluptuous sadness to being cooped-up for weeks and weeks, without responsibility, as though if one were content to remain a child, or a sentimental half-man, one need never land at all. A mixture of *Peter Pan* and *Outward Bound*. In the dining room (two sittings) we're as greedy as children over our curries and Bombay duck; food is as important to us as it ever was in nursery days. In the bar we drink and drink, and yet never seem to get drunk. We're always a bit bored, a bit feverish, anxious for any excitement and yet lulled by the enormous sunny routine. Life is happening somewhere else and the nearest we can get to it is the sense of our own collective motion, which unseen sailors control: the mild expert hum of engines and ventilators, the mild melodramatic swirl of water from the bows. The stewards, several of whom cultivate an hermaphroditic appearance with peroxided hair and long (surely darkened?) eyelashes, regard us with maternal half-contemptuous eyes, bandage us with cynical address. Well, but not too well. For who amongst us has paid his own passage?

I must keep up these letters. A first voyage to the Far East is not to be sneezed at. Or notes. But already we've been at sea so long that I've lost count of the days. Time is no longer a tyrant but something you digest like a good meal during an endless summer afternoon, suspended in a vacuum of opalescent haze. If it re-establishes itself at all, it is as the pre-war Thirties when the going was still good. And, anyway, it is far too hot to write in my cabin. I spend much time in the bar (gin sixpence a tot, beer the most expensive drink), watching our long sad wake, lacy at the edges, quilted satin in the middle and on closer inspection faintly dirty, as though I were indulging in an invalid's bedroom farewell. It is with a narrow and *disciplined* glamour that we draw away from England.

Two things give me the confidence to imagine that I am a man of the world and an experienced traveller: the phrases uncoiling inside my head and seeming more and more apt as drink succeeds drink; the timeless solitude in which, with no immediate preoccupations, I can flatter myself with the facts of my private existence until they acquire a beautiful if fatuous significance. How astonishing to be thirty-five years old! How extraordinary to be an adopted Canadian, especially when this involved a 'professorship', however minor, at McGill University in Montreal! And how intoxicating this new freedom is, sailing away to take up a reasonably senior post in the English Department of the University of Malaya! A month ago I was so desperate for a job outside Canada that I even dickered with the post of travelling salesman for an educational publisher in the Manchester Area. Or a temporary position at a very small grammar school in the Cotswolds....

Image follows image but each crystallization makes one by contrast more passive and pleasantly amorphous, no more than a cavernous womb, until one's fourth or fifth drink puts an end to the day's writing. The Mediterranean? A polished blank, like the hall at an airport, all chromium and glass with here and there a view of North Africa in tasteful monochrome. Port Said? A town scratched out of khaki sand-paper, full of pimps, corner-boys and flies, seizing one with a sort of truculent impropriety. Suez? The water turns to syrup, flecked with sulky yellows and mauves, and mountains bulge in the haze, like something in Monet, crumbling and slithering with light, restoring themselves again in huge hallucinatory shadow. Various islands? I should have suggested analytical cubism but someone beside me said, 'My God, exactly like a plate of potato chips!'

Approaching Penang . . .

Aden was far better than I had expected. The setting is all hot savage rock in the midst of burning blue sea with the town itself like a huddle of dilapidated farm-buildings in which a musical-comedy company is having a picnic. The police look extremely smart and there are a few government buildings gleaming with efficiency, and some shops and hotels along the front, but just behind this everything is precipitous, dusty, full of children and goats. You have only to walk ten yards to get away from the tourists, but none did except myself, and I was filled with a ridiculous sense of innocence and daring as I accumulated Arab and Somali boy-guides, visited mosques, watched wayside letter-writers and theologians, pushed by youths shrouded in white muslin, who stared at me with kohl-brightened eyes. I made sortie after sortie, crowing with excitement.

Back on board I got a drink and stood with it at the rail, listening to snatches of conversation: 'Good-bye, old chap. Not long till you get your leave. Be sure you enjoy it. . . .' 'Sorry to have missed Fergie. Tell him we'll soon have the bandits licked. . . .' 'Such a darling little brooch but of course I wouldn't stand for his asking a price like that. Sheer robbery. . . .' 'It's a *positive* oven. I can't see how they stand it. Singapore's marvellously green, at least.' The rocks twisted themselves, burning, into the sky. Presumably up there, too, would be goats. Athleticism of flame and ash. Then the Governor of Hongkong, who is our principal passenger, came grandly aboard.

Tropical life is in full swing. Fu Manchu, the government official who shares my cabin (more about him later) heaves himself into a mess-jacket and cummerbund for dinner while I try to ring the changes on white coat and black trousers, the top part of my linen suit and black trousers again, or all black, or on one occasion black on top and white below—each of these changes has, I suspect, its faint romanticism. But most of the day people are taking clothes off, not putting them on. First Class nudity is

restrained, the women's bare shoulders a freckled martyrdom, the men comfortable rather than stylish. Most of us
reveal an unhappy whiteness as we lie under the awnings.
Our bodies belong to the Expressionists and Realists, not
to the Italians or Poussin. We are hurt by them. It is incongruous that we should offer them to the sun. They
blush with sun-burn or prickle into rash. And in a way
they are more sexy like that ; they require darkness and to
be comforted. Different from those Americans I used to
meet on the transatlantic boats who looked as though life
came clearly and easily to them, with the controlled
ebullience of a milk-shake, the blondness of cereal, the
open-air idylls of clam-bake and barbecue and the Fourth
of July. Not, of course, that it did.

Below, for the small sloshy pool is on the Tourist Deck
and principally occupied by their class, the scene is far
livelier. The pool is indecently tiny; people bathing in it
have the look of being caught at their baths; women tend
to balloon, as though they were vegetables growing there;
men grow lean and passionate, savaging the water, or lie
back with brick-red faces and idiot grins, and now and
then peer down in a satisfied manner at their heaving
forms; the water becomes tufted with armpits and spread
with hairy chests and bandanas and bosoms. (I once un-
dressed and got to the edge of it but I just couldn't go in.
Sometimes I take a small boy to the brink where one of the
elder little girls looks after him.) Nevertheless, and this is
the funny part of it, it is at the end of the day, when the
water has been splashed and spat out and sweated into for
hours and hours, that His Excellency takes an occasional
swim. Twilight is falling and most of us are in the bar,
which overlooks the deck aft so that the Governor and his
lady can be seen by us as they hustle down to the pool,
she all a-glimmer with the gay duty before her, so that
little wisps of graciousness and embarrassment detach
themselves from her presence, he marching solidly ahead
a noble and yet curiously modest and endearing figure.

We wait for the two splashes. Having heard them, there is a faint nod of satisfaction throughout the room. We can go on with our drinks.

As for the passengers, let me describe my own table first. Respectability is represented by a small neat clergyman with the appearance of a benevolent but unobtrusive egg and the extraordinarily Trollopian name of Dr. Flower. He is an Australian Bishop. His wife, whom he refers to constantly as My Pet, is equally dignified. They perambulate the deck together, hand in hand. It's odd to sit opposite them at meals, suppressing the two or three double brandies inside of one, while they rather charmingly attempt to give the appearance of not being at the Palace table without, of course, betraying their faintly saccharine dignity. Some glints of alcoholic wildness do get out, especially when talking to my other companions, and I notice the discreet evidences of personality they manifest in return; he susceptible to the drier kind of joke and expressing a polite interest in academic subjects, she revealing a frankness and common-sense behind her mask of reticence. I shouldn't be surprised if she had once been a nurse. As for him, perhaps his *egg-ness* is cautious rather than unobtrusive, and what he shines with is not benevolence but a gentle superiority; the tension is egg-shell thin—crack it and there might be nothing. But it's impossible without violence to get beyond the double (and paradoxical) barrier of their tactful reserve, and their air of being very much in love in a Yardley's lavender, parasol and cricket flannels, Love's Young Dream sort of way.

Two of the other people at the table are definitely not the Bishopric type. One is an enormous rancher from South America, supposedly Swiss but resembling far more an Aztec god; a good-looking tough of the Richard Conte variety who wears Hawaiian shirts and ties of Amazonian luxuriance, and grins and grunts out of a proudly maintained adolescence which he assures me has never faltered despite the ministrations of a series of negro housekeepers.

If he has succumbed to their sultry blandishments it has only been as animal necessity, to be regarded afterwards as a joke and soon forgotten with the aid of guns, fists and the problems of driving a recalcitrant labour force. The other fellow is a commercial traveller. He is a middle-aged man, softly and whiningly embittered, and the trouble seems to be that he has some Indian blood. He does all the things that one reads about in Kipling: protests his British background over-much, moans about the untrustworthiness of the natives, is reckless in conversation and then becomes sour and depressed, occasionally makes off-colour jokes with an air of unhappiness, not as though he enjoyed them but as though they were a passport into a more egalitarian world, a democracy of lust and disgust—and all this happens under the mildly disengaging tilts of Bishop Flower's bald head and Mrs. Flower's oceanic eyes deepening and chilling until finally one hears 'Shall we go up for our coffee now, My Pet? . . .' 'As you say, darling. You will excuse us, won't you?' No wonder some of us are beginning to call him Tarbrush.

More important is my cabin mate. He's a high-up official in the Hongkong government, a vast man with narrow blue eyes and a large moustache who speaks apparently perfect Chinese and has a Chinese wife and adopted daughter. He looks remarkably like Colonel Blimp but these oriental affiliations have earned him the nickname of Fu Manchu.

When I first got into my cabin he wasn't there. In fact he didn't come in while I was unpacking. I put my new clothes away, tenderly loosening the white sharkskin dinner-jacket from its tissue-paper and rather incredulously surveying sports-shirts and shorts, and then I arranged the books I bought that last day at Foyles and Zwemmers on the shelf over my bunk: *Coleridge On Imagination*, *Poetry and Humanism*, the Oxford Book I should have owned years ago, and the Joyce Careys. They looked, I thought, exceedingly impressive. When I next returned to the cabin I saw that Fu Manchu had been sampling them. 'Like to borrow one or two of these' he said gruffly as he steamed away over his dinner clothes. 'Of course,' I answered. 'By the way, I'm afraid I snore. . . . '

The next morning I woke to find him already shaving at the end of the little passage that leads to our only port-hole: a badger in his burrow. 'Got to be careful or I cut myself. Skin's as thin as paper. Japanese internment no good for the skin.' Very soon the casual grunts as we banged about developed into conversation. Nowadays Fu Manchu is often awake when I come in late at night and we have midnight talks of a boyishly bookish kind. His striped pyjama jacket open and his mountainous belly a-quiver, his voice takes on a tender gravity as he speaks of the beauties of Hongkong or the intricate charm of Chinese poetry, or questions me about Lawrence or Joyce. He is one of those men who combine fierce common-sense with a good deal of emotional *naïveté*. You'd think such qualities would only support dullness in a colonial servant. Not a bit of it. His often contemptuous common-sense operates in the opposite direction. He is an eccentric and a rebel—and makes rebellion seem orthodox. And his *naïveté* is part, I think, of his near-artistic scholarly nature. My response is to make him into a father although he tells me that he is only three or four years older than myself.

By now Fu Manchu and I have had several set-piece conversations, less personal than those which take place later at night, on tropical fruits, tropical fish, etc., and I have been delighted with hosts of unfamiliar names and occasional flashes of brilliant colour. These sessions are sometimes terminated by Mrs. Manchu, a woman of such vivacity, whose diffident 'Excuse?' has given way to flurries into the cabin in order to rub her husband's back, for he has developed lumbago. 'He reads too many books,' she tells me. 'He is very clever. Always he is reading books.' To which his response is to chortle over her in an uninhibited way. They spend much of their time at Bingo, for which she has a passion, or at conversation (she has a whole aviary of small talk) and they are always accompanied by a Chinese Y.M.C.A. official called Dr. Boon. Now that the weather is hot all three sport fans.

I seem to have acquired a girl-friend called Susan: an odd name for so commanding a woman. Susan Hitchcock. During the first few days I kept passing her on the deck. She always walked by herself and I suppose that I thought her a practised voyager; tall, in slacks, with a thick tangle of very dark curls over a lean, shadowed face, she had very much the air of a lioness. However, our eyes met with increasing frequency. Hers were large and brimming. Then one night I noticed her watching me over the Bingo (I wasn't playing but was at the table of the Fu Manchu threesome; Madame ecstatic over the game, the two men so excited about their variant memories of a Chinese poem that Dr. Boon actually went out to send a cable of inquiry to his wife in Singapore) and when I quite consciously detached myself and went into the bar, she followed me. She was wearing something old but obviously good in black: not a dress such as other women wore but a *gown*. She had a weary and jaded femininity, I thought, a sort of trembling and suppressed fierceness which was very attractive. I complimented her on the dress (by Worth she told me, but old, old) and I soon found out that she had theatrical connections, her son by her first marriage goes to Rada; diplomatic past-history; Bloomsbury and Scotland. Rather an expensive taste in drinks, together with of course, 'My dear, I'm so desperately poor. It's beastly to be poor, isn't it?'

Since then our affair has progressed rapidly and has done a good deal to restore my self-confidence. At night, on the boat deck, we have long talks. 'I do hope the East will not hurt you too much,' she says as she leans urgently over the rail. 'You will find it so cruel, so terribly cruel. The people are beastly to animals and the poverty is loathsome and there are so many temptations to abandon one's standards and become sort of sodden and corrupt. Darling, you won't let that happen to you, will you?' And she turns breathlessly towards me, eyes tawny in the moonlight, one snake-like curl whipped out by the wind, like some classical heroine, statuesque and marmoreal, but at the same time incongruously nervous in her light fluttering clothes, themselves both glamorous and shabby. 'I see you as someone', she goes on, 'essentially fine and sensitive and able, but you mustn't let your sensitivity betray you into becoming wounded and silly. You must follow your true self and have a solid respectable career. You must always wear good clothes and be dignified as you are now.' She encourages me, compliments me on my brain and (thank heavens) appearance and—I don't think I'm being disloyal by saying this—broods over me passionately. She *broods* rather than acts, because a good deal of the time she is intensely conscious of what other people think, and is capable of the most infuriating vacillations. 'I didn't mean to meet you,' she will say. 'I planned to have a complete rest during the voyage. I don't know if you are good for me. . . . No, but of course you are good—only I'm so tired and there's so much to do with little Toby and I'm so anxious to meet Rupert (that's her husband) but at the same time I don't know . . . he writes charming letters but he's been a beast.' Nevertheless she seems very fond of this American of hers, an ex-paratrooper now in business in Rangoon.

Mornings are quite virginal. We smile affectionately first thing but don't meet. About eleven I discover her in a deck chair, knitting with every appearance of domesticity. I get her a drink. We talk mostly of impersonal things, or of the past. From time to time we look in on the childrens' cage. Now and then we squabble over cigarettes. After luncheon I sometimes visit her in her cabin and help to try to persuade Toby to go to sleep. Her cabin is on an unfashionably low deck but it has two portholes and is very close to the sea; it is full of light reflected from spray and of the waves' rush and clamour. Toby has his drink of soda-water, a bottle of Gordon's emerges from the clothes' cupboard, the door is (probably) left ajar. Promised passion shivers and tinkles into nerves: lyrical bits and pieces—syphons, dinky-toys, lipstick, kleenex. Susan goes to bed in her slip and I repair to my own cabin to lie smothered and dripping. At night, though, we dance in a state of mounting tension until Susan begins to vacillate over whether or not she should go up to the boat-deck for a last look at the moon on the sea. Will it be too cold, or too windy, or too dangerously romantic? I remain flattered and passive and light a cigarette. . . .

Our association has had some effect on the other passengers. It has brought into prominence a Mrs. Bootham from Scarborough, a prosperous Yorkshire-woman who is travelling to Singapore with an odd intelligent gauche daughter called—yes, really—Elvira. Mrs. Bootham is sensible and nice. She is enjoying a release from conventionality and takes up towards us the role of a sort of Wife of Bath. She thinks me a gay dog and Susan a sophisticated representative of the *demi-monde*. Mrs. Bootham's newly-acquired sapphires sparkle conspiratorially at us. Elvira bestows on us a wry blush: we are something she had in sociology at Leeds.

At Colombo I eventually found my Indian poet, late of Bloomsbury. It was a complicated business because I had decided to go ashore with the Aztec god, who looked even bluffer when on dry land and began to show boyish yens towards girls and gaiety. All this was held up by my hunt. We took a rickshaw to the Galleface Hotel, my friend kicking up a frightful fuss about the price, and then walked back under an incipient thunderstorm along the edge of the beach with the rollers pounding in our ears. We next tried a taxi and drove far out of town in search of a club the Poet was said to frequent; the driver deserted us in order to make inquiries in the dim intricacies of the suburbs and, while he was away, the rain began to crash down; finally we arrived at what looked like a beachcombers' shanty and here one of the two or three lugubrious inhabitants told us of a man we might telephone. Back in town and ten rupees poorer I did this to learn that Kumar's hotel was only a few streets away. 'Want a little boy?' was whispered from the shadows to the disgusted astonishment of the Aztec god as we walked there. An entrance hall piled with rubble. Stairs to a sort of barrack at the back. A thin corridor dividing a series of wooden hutches, some with padlocked doors. Our guide was a blotch of rags, a sidling wheezing bit of chiaroscuro with a hoarse voice, reddened eyes and no English, who now indicated that we should knock on the first of the doors; we did so and after a pause it creaked open; a portly man stood in the door-slice, almost completely naked, a great bland belly the colour of olive oil and a fuzzy chest imparting curious dignity to a sad slapdash face; the third door on the left, we were told, and I could see my Aztec god didn't like it, wanted champagne popping not this sombre poverty of unpainted wood, where a gold tooth was a highlight and the shadows were rags. Someone grunted behind the second door when I knocked, I opened it, and found myself staring down at books by John Heath-Stubbs, David Gasgoyne, Keith Douglas and the T. S. Eliot symposium, freshly elegant amongst the cigarette butts and litter—and up at their owner, unshaved and more than a little drunk: Kumar of the midnight fights and angry attempts at lechery, of whom it is said that two friends of his, going as far away from Charlotte Street as they thought possible, to some entirely remote and undistinguished sea-coast town, woke on the first morning to hear the maid of all work singing as she swept the passage

> *O where, O where*
> *Is my Kumar gone?—*
> *With his hair like a golly-wog's*
> *And no clothes on.*

Kumar greeted me with his characteristic succession of powerful blue-jowled grunts and high-pitched laughs and chuckles. He has a way of finding things entirely new, surprising and delightful. So it was 'What on earth are you doing here?' for a long time. (He, by the way, seems poor and disgruntled. He writes a sort of loud jeering gossip-column for one of the local papers.) Meanwhile the Aztec god, who looked more and more like a rubber truncheon in his enormous rain-coat, bulked gloomily in the passage, disapproving of all the emotionalism. His emotions ran in a different direction and, having of course decided to make a night of it, we set about satisfying his desire for a girl. After a brief visit to a deserted club (it was then very late), Kumar took us by taxi to a mysterious area which I suppose must have been in the suburbs. I got the impression of a place so lyrically tropical that one could scarcely believe in it; the jungle steamed after the rain, there was water and a bridge, there were little houses latticed and shuttered; there was the cosiness of thatch and faded white wood-work, and something charmingly relaxed in the way the palm trees bent this way and the other and the sand comforted one's steps, and there was the intimacy of the heat and of the fact that people lay asleep all around. But it was still unreal, like a fantasy world in a big shop: Father Christmas's Court at Selfridges, perhaps, or a Caribbean beach for the display of bathing suits. Shouldn't I be afraid of snakes?

Kumar laughingly investigated various little houses and by-ways. However indifferent or hostile they might prove to be, the ease and immediacy of the scene was so great that to approach a house was like whispering in its ear or getting entangled in its hair-do. And they weren't hostile. A girl soon fluttered between the shrubs. Aztec god followed her, only to come back a few moments later with the protest that she was far too old. A man who is terrified of being fooled. . . . So eventually we hired a sampan and I took Kumar back to the ship, where you can

drink beer all night in the Dining Saloon. He had to sleep
on board in one of the deck chairs and next morning at
breakfast some of my friends were shocked. 'We've seen
your poet! We could smell him a mile.' And it must have
been a bit odd for them, all fresh and athletic on their
morning promenade, to come upon a long-haired corpse
with a hangover, and truculent as well. But he went ashore
like a lamb and was soon busy entertaining Susan and me.
Toddy-shops. Bazaars. Susan didn't altogether approve
of him. Too hysterical, she said.

One returns to the ship after these shore excursions
with a sense of renewed rather cloying peace; it is all so
settled here, so cosy, with its daily routines and little
cliques; the two overwhelmingly decent young men going
out for the first time to the Hongkong Shanghai Bank, one
of whom has carried his father's gift of a book on elephants
about for days and days—he undid its parcel, in fact, on
the way down from Southampton and it still appears
beside him as he sunbathes, next to his bottle of protective
oil, and signalizes his proprietorship of a deck chair, and
has its pages whipped over by the occasional wind,
'Oomba: A Trusty Friend,' 'Mother and Son,' all the
anecdotes of loyalty and wisdom together with something
laconic and stiff-lipped about amoks and rogues. Very
different, but just as much part of the scene, is an uncouth
young man about to take up a job as assistant-manager of
a rubber estate in Johore—the sort of young man one
would call really odious were it not for the fact that he is so
patently a sacrificial victim, and that his blundering blus-
tering concern over 'valuable jewels' he has been sold in a
bazaar and 'awkward customers' he has outwitted in the
alleys of Colombo and Bombay is so soon to be matched
against the communist guerills; so to the Boothams with
their sapphires and anecdotes of Scarborough, to the
Flowers reading *Kon-tiki* and bowing to the Australian
methodist family reading *Inside Asia* (for books, knitting
and children are the flags flown by the various clusters),

and to the nice young planter who has married a particularly mixed-up Eurasian (her various bloods so baffled
that you can't decide whether what you notice is her being
actually *coloured* or a sort of freckled, bruised, blushing,
angriness, or is it just *scrawniness*? to her)—anyway, she
roots him out of the bar and he is soon to be seen trund-
ling a pram round the deck.

I have made friends with Bert and Ed (the bartender
and smokeroom steward) and really enjoy talking to them
as much as anything. They can be quite caustic when they
want to. Often when I sit down at one of the bar tables I
am joined by Tarbrush. He seems to hate the East. All my
efforts to see it as exotic and glamorous are laughed sadly
away. There aren't enough white women and life is far too
expensive. What white women there are are either married
or unscrupulous members of the 'fishing fleet'. They get
their claws into you: if married, they want excitement; if
unmarried, security is what they're after. 'Oh yes, it's all
very fine for them. A nice bungalow, plenty of servants,
mahjong parties, dances at the Club . . . what more could
they ask for?' And Tarbrush spreads his puffy hands.
'Those bitches would just be trash at home. But it's the
man who pays for it, of course. Oh yes, they see to that.
And then when the kids are old enough, they take them
home and have a fine old time into the bargain. Who's to
know?' The naughty glint to Tarbrush's spectacles does
not hide the pale restless look in his eyes. 'When the cat's
away . . .,' he adds with mournful relish. If Susan suddenly
appears outside, he withers at once. 'Your friend Mrs.
Hitchcock is looking for you. I mustn't detain you.' But
Susan rarely comes in. 'After all,' she explains to me in one
of her gayer moods, 'I *am* a secret drinker.' Not that she
doesn't put away a good many Tom Collinses on deck.
She has her morning-look today, let's suppose: graciously
remote, a trifle bewildered, her eyes brimming without
a precise focus, her eyebrows raised, she is in search of
something—Toby who has escaped from his cage, Mrs.

Bootham who promises a recipe, someone with a pink
wool to match what she is knitting, cigarettes, the Shop.
'I'm glad to see you talking to people,' she says when I
join her for a moment. 'You can do that little man good.
It's hell for those half-castes when they're sensitive.'
I disclaim any altruistic motive. 'I'm just being sodden,'
I tell her, 'and talking about women in an earthy way.' 'But,
darling, how sweet! And right for you too, you monster. I'd
love to listen, but I can't. I'm hopelessly broke and I've got
to get the purser to cash me a cheque.' I can feel her eyes,
her whole fluttering presence, searching the air behind my
head. She trails over to the side of the ship and sniffs the
wind approvingly, her head thrown back. Flying fish pelt
away from the foam. What aggregate noun for them?—a
gaggle of geese, a wisp of snipe, a *fillip* of flying fish?

So I return to Tarbrush who tells me of his infinitely
careful marriage plans; he has arranged a marriage with
an *Australian* girl for Australians have the advantages of
(*a*) not being snobbish (*b*) being able to rough it and (*c*)
allowing, one suspects, a certain amount of subtle con-
descension on his part; she has been trained as a nurse
and this suggests that (1) she has no silly ideas about men
(2) she likes a good time but is prepared to pay her own
way (3) she knows about house-work; furthermore, she is
'definitely not a spring chicken' (it's odd to notice the
mixture of romantic ruefulness and business-world satisfaction with which he tells me this) and consequently both
an excellent bargain and, masochistically, no better than
he deserves. The whole plan is recounted to me in terms
of a potentially aggrieved money-consciousness but, all the
same, it *does* have its pathos, and even its tenderness. I
suspect he is quite fond of this 'young girl of forty' whom
he hopes will be 'a good pal'.

Other conversations are with planters, who tell me the
bandits would never have started if the British Government had paid the resistance units properly—and, of
course, with Fu Manchu, who has now translated a poem

of mine into Chinese. Yesterday there was a knock on my cabin door and in popped Polly, their vivacious adopted daughter, with the remark, 'Mummy say I stay here. Mummy and Daddy together in cabin. Locked door.' Endlessly I ask about the kind of life I can expect: the luxurious not very believable side, in which I shall yacht and ride and play tennis and drive an M.G. to exclusive clubs (Singapore is very snobbish, they say); but much more the native eastern part of it all, to which my dream world has been partially open for years and years, and which fills me with far greater excitement. All this focuses on the absorbing question of *what sort of a servant shall I have?* Shall I have a Malay, or an Indian, or a Chinese? And shall I be able, through him or her, to grapple with the country, understand it and love it? (Of course, romantically, I love it already.) All sorts of things inside me are waiting to expand. You could sum it up by saying that I want to look at Puritanism from *within the flowers*. I don't want to be spiritual or 'northern' with a sneaking suspicion that I am doing it because I can't get at the flowers. I want to be free. In fact, I want to flower myself.

So much for a *cri de coeur*. We are approaching Penang, which everyone says is lovely. Very soon now I shall experience what Conrad wrote about. . . .

October 20th

. . . Arrived yesterday. Very conscious of the problem of settling down and of whether I am as receptive as I used to be. Now that the frivolities are over, I am rather depressed with technical matters connected with unpacking, buying everything from cooking utensils to lamp shades and cushion-covers, and coping with the bad news about my salary: the money given me in London was an *advance* and not, as I hoped, my first month's pay. So I start in debt!

Arrival itself was exciting. On the last night, coming

down from Penang, there was a *sumatra*, one of those vivid enlivening storms R. talked about in London, not serious enough or long enough to be taken other than aesthetically, nevertheless the wind roared, the ship rocked, there were great wet flashes of lightning, a dark pool of rain spread over the dance floor and Susan, who has been even more timid and vacillating of late, rose to the occasion and we were the only couple to dance. Mrs. Bootham approved of the gesture.

Next morning all the Singapore contingent was busy packing and when you caught sight of them they had a new sealed look to their faces as though they (the women anyway) were in the process of putting on an efficient rather anxious charm. Chits had been called in so I had to pay for my drinks. I got the idea that Bert and Edward regarded me differently. 'The fun is over—you must land and become ordinary and drab.' Tarbrush had a beer with me and insisted on the insincerity of any invitations I might make as to our meeting in Singapore. As usual the East was no good (lack of women) with Singapore the worst city of a bad lot (lousy snobs . . . think they own the world) as well as desperately expensive (don't think you'll find it cheap to drink like you're doing now). As soon as I got ashore I wouldn't think of being seen with him (suppose I did ring you up and say who I was, you'd ask yourself what does that lousy bum want with me—that is, if you remembered my name). After a bit I went out on deck.

The sea changes near a port, even if still out of sight of land. Add a couple of buoys, a distant drift of smoke, a certain oily smoothness, and all the immensity becomes sad and industrial. The water looks muddy and shallow, and the ship dawdles, and people start talking about the pilot. All morning it had been like that, tepidly devalued, and as sad as breaking open a cocoon and finding inside the faceless earth-coloured pupa. But now we were really close in, gliding between tufted violently green cliffs with red bases. The opening to the harbour must be very narrow. I thought it remarkable to have such intense foliage so near to a city and began to get quite excited, although a voice inside kept saying, 'This isn't New York 1938. Your eye is more jaded and inward now. You are likely to pass through these straits without being really compelled.' So I went back to have another B.G.A. and felt more blasé than I should have done.

There was quite a long wait after we had docked as the Governor of Hongkong and his wife had to leave first. There were crowds of people in front of the go-downs (tropical word for big storage sheds) but my interest in various tattered and savage-looking labourers was rather mitigated by the fact that I had been told that these go-downs take the place of a real water-front with dives and bars—I imagine the differences of religion and colour prevent seamen meeting to have a drink together. Most of the Indians don't drink, and the Europeans must have to go somewhere else. Then R. and Dorothy came aboard and behaved with an uncomfortable briskness from the point of view of someone still immersed in the sentimental boredom of the voyage. There was also a photographer and two reporters; the photographer took a picture of me in the door of my cabin but I had to be embarrassingly quick and even sly in getting my statement across to the reporters, partly because everyone was ready to go and partly because I felt guilty that it was me they were photographing and not Dorothy. She is evidently celebrated here as an actress. It was a pretty florid statement, anyway.

By now it was raining hard. This gave a hint of desperation to our leaving the ship. We found R.'s car and drove to the Customs shed where the inspection was surprisingly casual—I could have had dozens of Sten-guns and hand-grenades in my luggage. We drove about five miles through a misted haphazard landscape (factories, bits of jungle and rows of yellow stucco shops, many of them arcaded), and finally arrived in what looked like 'the rolling park-like country' R. had said surrounded the university. I felt quite solemn. I realized I must take in everything I could, that this was the precious first impression I had been looking forward to so long, but what with the rain and the conversation in the car this was difficult. And I was solemn about the conversation, too, since I just have to get on with these people and (though they seem quite charming) they got brisker and brisker as they spoke out of their knowledge of the place, and their settled certainty, and their sense of having the situation well under control.

They told me that I was not to stay with them after all since, on returning from leave, they had been presented with a flat instead of their old house. A room had been taken for me at one of the big hotels but perhaps I might like to move directly into my own rooms; not a whole house, as R. had hoped, but part of one? Wanting to be obliging I said yes, of course. Their flat struck me as being very magnificent. It is in a large modern block fairly close to the university buildings and has an enormous balcony reminiscent of some penthouse in the movies. R. has some quite nice paintings—he paints himself but modestly does not hang his own stuff on the walls so I don't know how good he is but he is certainly modern—but even more endearing are his activities as a naturalist. The flat is full of aquariums, caterpillars gormandizing on large shiny leaves, and butterflies pinned up here and there, as well as occupying whole cabinet shelves.

It was still raining when I was conducted round the university; cream-coloured unpretentious buildings, with a sort of lyricism to them, standing on a rise above great sweeps of country; no academic Gothic or phoney Greek although admittedly there are two potentially unfortunate domes but these, true to the general good taste of the place, are flattened almost out of existence. R. has a nice corner office with green-shuttered doorways opening onto the exterior colonnade. A Cézanne hangs above his desk. He marched me round and introduced me to one or two people, whose names I didn't catch, and even to some of the students but I confess I haven't got the hang of them yet. My first impression was that they were pale almost to languor, and smiling almost to sycophancy, but I think I only met Chinese. I was rushed upstairs, architecture cool and rather grand, and popped into an office where the vice-chancellor rose to meet me and said, in a dry voice, 'Is this a present for me?' for I happened to be carrying a large brown flower-pot R. had decided to lend me. Later I found that this was only the acting vice-chancellor. Eventually R. took me to my house (I am still stupidly confused as to its exact position in relation to the other houses) but it is the middle one of a set of three, all simple yellow box-like shapes with jutting roofs and green shutters, surrounded by gentilities of very smooth grass and very clean gravel, and only some fifty yards from part of the university, though what part I don't know. My room, for alas! it is only one room although it can be divided into two, looked awfully bare; the bookcase had not yet been delivered but the rest of the *heavy furniture* was certainly heavy, and heavily impersonal—not hideous but none the less making demands on one's imagination, and probably also one's purse. The cane sofa and two armchairs are provided with uncovered cushions for only the bottom part, you must purchase the others yourself. I suddenly remembered the way I had felt going up for the first few times to Oxford, on a scholarship hunt or as a freshman: an obvious similarity, and then an even more important difference. Even at their most depressing (the Meadow Buildings in Christ Church) those rooms had been part of something complicated and close, as well as delicious hideouts for cigarette smoking and the absorption of one's first bottle of whisky, guiltily bought in the Corn and carried home under one's coat; here the more elegant bareness reminded me that I was older, less easily satisfied and still uncertain as to what it was to which I belonged.

We went out again after a brief look round during which I tried to hide my disappointment, for I had imagined an old rambling house and an untidy jungly garden. R. left me with a member of the English Department, name of Margaret Rutherston, a strange sensitive-looking woman who has, I understand, only recently taken up academic work after years of being a planter's wife. She has an anxious manner which seems to oscillate between feminine plaintiveness and helplessness and sudden bursts of decision, especially where tropical life is concerned, and I imagine that she now deals with university problems as she once dealt with her servants. This ambiguity extends to her appearance for her body is large and somewhat limp (she was wearing a blue silk dress, rather grander than the dresses I had so far seen) but out of this emerges a long neck and a small shingled head, its face almost colourless and dominated by a pair of very pale blue eyes. She looks dyspeptic in repose and when she smiles it would be somewhat wearily, or even languishingly, were it not for a certain intellectual voraciousness imparted to her expression by her prominent teeth. In fact she combines in her appearance to an extraordinary degree the tired middle-aged lady, the aesthete and the blue-stocking. I am told she had a brilliant university career and was at one time associated with the British Institute in Athens. Margaret immediately swept me off in her Hillman Minx to the Tanglin Club for tea. I had imagined fabulous luxury but the Tanglin Club might almost have been an extension of the university; it sat modestly at the side of the road, nursing a baby swimming pool on its lap, and inside it looked nice but worthy, with a reading room. Margaret sat firmly down in the midst of the emptiness and shouted, 'Boy!', after which she turned to me with the explanation, 'The Call of the East, you know!' These Boys, of course, are not boyish in the least but sometimes quite decrepit and alarming: very silent and with mask-like faces—a submissive blankness without real civility only emphasizes some queerness in their features: twisted eyebrows or a smile full of gold teeth. I

may be silly about this but I prefer to use the word *waiter*
rather than 'boy', and feel self-righteous as I do so.

   Margaret told me a good deal about herself. As she sat
pouring out tea, and questioning me on critics she had
heard I admired, I couldn't help noticing how, for all
her natural sweetness, she was somehow over-defined, as
though a clear thick line had been drawn around all her
movements. I put this down to her being a colonial woman.
During the war she had many adventures, escaping the
Japanese and ending up in India. She is a bit of a hypo-
chondriac, I feel; she is terrified of the rigours of an English winter and hopes eventually to retire to Western
Australia where, since she is a staunch Catholic, she can
live near a monastic community, listen to church music
and—this last phrase is essential—drink the monks' wine.
All the time I sat listening to her, I was wavering ridiculously between hope and despair, uncertain as to whether
this kind of gentle but somehow arid conversation could
last me for several years and wondering how easy it would
be to live in a place where the evocative cry *Boy!* with its
connotations of Ganymede, Giton and the interests of some
of my London friends, echoed from every corner.

   R. had arranged drinks for the early evening so that
I could meet the other members of the Department. These
consist of the following: Ellis Evans, a young Welshman
who teaches language and has a specialist's interest in
semantics; he has one of those Greek-Welsh-slightly
Jewish faces such as I often used to see in Anglesey, wavy
black hair, wears glasses and is angular and nervous. He
publishes papers in very learned magazines and, judging
from a talk I had with him today, feels rather cut off from
the world around him, since nobody even begins to understand his subject with its algebraic formulae. His wife is
buxom enough to be called Midge. She seems a very
sensible human sort of person, slangy and down to earth,
and much addicted to amateur theatricals. I was delighted
to find that Ellis and Midge lived for quite a time in Lon-

don, in a mews near Paddington, and that they knew a number of people from the Wheatsheaf and the Fitzroy (but not the Black Horse). We quickly made a nest of warm untidy Bohemianism, Midge's language grew rather violent and I began to sense some slight disapproval from the direction of Dorothy. As for R., he seemed more official now in an absent-minded withdrawn way: more anxious, in fact, to see that things were going well than to follow up any particular remark. The other new lecturer, who arrived here shortly before me, is a recent graduate from Cambridge (with a First) called Allan Painter. A vague benevolent man. Another member of the Department put in an appearance later. This was Mary Barker. She, like Margaret, is an old hand at the East: a fierce kindly soul; grey hair, keen blue eyes, loud voice in which academic dogmatism struggles with an innate humility, very lean. Wearing efficient green linen dress with white trimmings and plimsolls.

In the midst of all this Susan rang up from the Raffles Hotel. I was quite flattered to appear not completely lost or a stranger to the people present but I had the usual variety of reaction; I was conscious of having to move away from small-talk, however lively, to R.'s professorial telephone becoming sulphurous with the tones of Susan's voice and once again I was back in the freer atmosphere of the voyage, an atmosphere that could be seen as pathetic now. 'For God's sake come down and see me! It's hell here,' said Susan.

Margaret was driving Dorothy down town to a rehearsal so they gave me a lift. In the car they talked about taxi-burning, one of the techniques used by the local communists, and I began to feel more depressed. R. had told me that bandit activity did not extend to this island but apparently there have been numerous incidents: taxis and buses have been burned, identity cards stolen, handgrenades thrown into bars (one was thrown at the Governor, hit his thigh, bounced off and proved to be a

c

dud). Margaret said she felt safe in the university area, which is incidentally the fashionable district, because G.H.Q. was near 'and there must always be plenty of soldiers about'. When I left them the streets seemed all hot darkness and Raffles Hotel itself more clumsy than elegant. Susan's accommodation was off an upstairs gallery; you pushed through Shanghai doors into a dingy little parlour, and then through more doors into the bedroom where Toby lay asleep. Susan ordered double brandies, extremely expensive, and we spent an exasperating couple of hours together, trembling, cursing and sighing on the brink of romance. I got lost in my taxi on the way back, appeared to be crossing an open field, finally recognized R.'s block of flats and found him just about to put his car away. He re-directed me and I came home to this bare room.

Night was supposed to hold no terrors for me since R. had assured me that nothing poisonous was likely to be around, so I walked confidently into the bathroom only to find it occupied by the most enormous spider I have ever seen. After the hysterical time with Susan, the spider was too much. I went back to my precious little pile of new books of literary criticism, hesitated for a moment, picked up *Poetry and Humanism* and hurled it at the spider. Of course I missed. The spider shot across the bathroom with a dreadful fluid celerity. So I got one of my ties, wound one end over the doorknob and fixed the other to a chair. I fell asleep fairly easily, with a naked electric light bulb almost directly overhead—heavy furniture doesn't include lampshades and I was too nervous to put it out— and later in the night I was aware of hundreds of crawling things on the tiled floor beside me. These looked delicate and harmless and, since most of them were in pairs, I imagined that they were performing some kind of nuptial dance. Later I found out that they were flying ants attracted by the light. In the morning the floor was littered with their discarded wings. I felt quite peaceful with them, glad of a sign that I was in the tropics. Sleepily I listened to some strange bird noises and occasional splutterings in the tree outside my window.

In the morning I was woken by the sound of faint knocking. Looking up I saw a middle-aged Chinese woman in a white tunic and black sateen trousers, with her hair coiled into a bun at the back of her head and a perplexed grin on her brown seamed face, who was rapping on the wardrobe beside my bed. This was the *amah* whom the co-sharer of my house has put temporarily at my disposal. I understand that many of the Chinese are very superstitious about disturbing people in their sleep as they imagine that a sudden shock may permanently separate the soul from the body. One practice was to strew seed round the bed of the sleeper so that his soul might fly down to peck it, and thus enter his body again. The *amah* brought me early tea and some segments of pomelo. A little later she gave me breakfast of bacon and eggs. In the meantime she swept up the piles of ants' wings.

I had no idea what time it was; I could see nobody moving about from my window; the sunlight was very gay and strong, without yet being a glare, and I realized that the great moment had at last arrived, and that I must now make my first personal steps into the mysteries of the tropics. Yesterday had been entirely taken up by people and the rain had blurred everything. In Colombo also I had not been alone. I expected I don't know what beautiful and monstrous things for which I felt myself to have waited since the earliest days of childhood—parrots, cockatoos, dense trailing creepers, orchids and other flowers read about in books and usually described as fleshy and grotesque and, in the midst of the foliage and the steaming heat, wonderful brown-skinned people. I started to walk, first in the garden and then down the nearby road. The garden looked even neater than before; there was no lushness and nothing could possibly grow round you, envelop you and hide you from your neighbours. In front of their part of the house Dr W. and his wife had placed rows of potted plants but the space under my windows was bare hot concrete. The lawns were beautifully cut, with crescent-shaped and circular flower beds some of which were protected by chicken-wire, and there was quite a number of frangipani trees whose white and yellow, or white and pink, blooms lay singed and twisted on the grass like starfish. The various curves of gravel drive collected themselves together and climbed smoothly out through a big gap in the surrounding hedge, where two white curbs marked the entrance. This was only a few yards away but I took a long time to get there, because I was expecting something to beckon me and nothing did; I felt myself moving through and through my inhibition and nervousness; part of me seemed drained away already by the light and the decorum and the fragility of the trees and flowers. This was quite exciting but not in the way I had expected. When my feet felt the hot asphalt of the university road under them, I had the sensation that it was far more positive than I was. And how cleanly it bulged, with a steep bank of grass above it, and beyond the grass the yellow stucco of the arcaded buildings! Not a sound, not a person.

I turned to the right, walked down a hill and found that I was skirting the back of my own group of houses (Numbers Six, Seven and Eight) and then others at the top of a longer but gentler slope; R.'s block of flats was in the distance, to my left, but between it and me there lay a marshy hollow, with a stream and a row of very black dense palm trees—not the coconut kind—like palms in oilskin. Ahead I began to see big houses with verandahs and balconies perched up hills and round every house were the same scrupulously-cut green lawns, the same carefully-planned beds of canna lilies or shrubberies of bougainvillea. Some of them squatted like cliffs, others rambled on concrete stilts. All had separate servants' quarters, half-hidden behind clumps of banana. I liked the flat floppy banana plants, with their immense ribbed leaves

and improper purple phalluses, far more than the frangi-
panis.

Once more I turned to the right, suspecting that the
town (its most exclusive suburb rather) would begin if I
continued straight ahead. Besides, this road had a wood
on one side and looked as though it might get darker and
wilder. Vines hung from some of the trees, ferns sprouted
out of clefts high in the air, and the ditch was deep and
overgrown. Two large dusty black butterflies were playing
over some ferns. I had taken the right direction for I soon
came to the back entrance of the Botanical Gardens. At a
fork in the road the trees soared into a cliff (I think it was
my consciousness of these great trees in the distance that
had helped to draw me this way) and where the cliff ended
there was a gate and a path. I don't suppose I paused for
more than a moment but I was now more than ever
conscious of my expectancy, and of the feeling that whatever resisted or urged me forward occurred only within
myself. The road was now dark, although sprinkled with
patches of sun, and from the Gardens there came the
smell of damp vegetation. I've often read in books that the
jungle is 'sticky' and 'rotting'—read of 'fleshy' carnivorous
flowers and strange moths and the sudden brilliance of a
parrot against the gloom—and for a moment the Gardens
did suggest all that, but with the disqualification that their
effect would inevitably be to some extent contrived. But as
I entered them, and subsequently walked right round them,
without as yet exploring the actual forest, the adjectives
that came to mind were not 'wild' or 'corrupt' but 'charming', 'lyrical', in fact Shakespearian. They belonged to the
Forest of Arden, Prospero's island and *Twelfth Night*.

The path kept close to the trees, running in their
shadow, but on its other side the grass shelved away,
glistening with dew, and in this small valley there stood
all sorts of palms which burst out of the grass in fountains,
suspended themselves high in the air in floating showers
like those that rockets trail, or maintained a delicate

equilibrium between plumes gently pointed at the sky and plumes languidly bent towards the ground. Palms wrestled with themselves, fitted themselves with cogs and gears until they spun round in a sort of mad machinery, grew exhausted and buried themselves deep in moss. I looked at some of their names—I can remember one: *Borassodendron Machidonis*. There were trunks notched and bulbous, shaggy and slim, and about all palms there seems to hang an air of effort and decay; coconut palms have an eccentric elegance because they look so slim and spring from the earth at such odd angles, bearing aloft dead fronds as well as living, but many of the other species are so complicated that half of them seems dead all the time. It's surprising that more hasn't been written about them for they are certainly literary trees. As for this deadness, you find it everywhere in a land where there are no seasons. There is a touch of Autumn all through the year, stealing like a ghost amongst the foliage.

Once, as I was walking along the path, I heard a splashing in the boughs above me and thought of monkeys. I had decided that the moment when I saw a real not-in-the-zoo monkey would be the crucial one. But the splashing stopped and I could see nothing. After this I soon entered the more central part of the Gardens, where there was a grassy hill, a number of strategically disposed flower-beds, a small bandstand and an air of ceremony which the joyousness of the light still kept casual: from here you could wander down Liane Walk (!) into the jungle, or go and have a look at the lake with its bamboo-clotted island, or steam yourself in the orchid-house, or explore certain rocky gulleys full of giant ferns. Two things in particular caught my attention. One was an enormous tree, smooth and cinnamon-coloured, which shot up for about a hundred feet before breaking into feathery leaves; its trunk was beautifully flanged towards the base, the flange growing out of it like a fin and then curling round to make a smooth slender-walled niche, while ropes of creeper dangled down from above, twisted round each other and writhed in coils on the grass. Unquestionably this was a *jungle* tree—force and strangeness at last—and when I looked at it, or at other domed trees I came to later, I was no longer vaguely troubled by the slightness, or prettiness, of much that I saw around me. Admittedly this slightness was frequently odd, as when new leaves hung folded in rows from their twigs like bats or the closed wings of a grasshopper, or when a frond was seen to protrude large isolated black thorns—admittedly there was a good deal of grotesqueness about, flowers like Christmas tree decorations, crimson pom-poms, sticky chandeliers—but I didn't want to be just a *handler*. I didn't even want a mood, such as the rather theatrical lyricism of the place suggested. I wanted to be compelled. And this tree did, for the moment, compel me.

And then, before I came upon a single human being, I saw the monkeys. Perhaps because they were on the grass, and some distance from any tree, I found myself very slow to believe in them. There was simply a grey flash, a series of grey flashes, rather a long way ahead, and then the impression solidified into largish creatures running on all fours, not very attractively. I thought of dogs, goats, even rabbits, although I should have known they were too big and besides they had tails. Of course, they were monkeys. Yes, yes, how amusing and exciting, they were monkeys at last! There were mothers and babies and they all ran down to the lake to drink on all fours, lapping the water, and the mothers seemed to be attempting to wash the babies. Nevertheless I was disappointed. And for the first time since the Tanglin Club yesterday I began to feel lonely. What time was it? Should I be doing something? I began to walk back and as I did so I passed an Indian gardener. He was a young man, dressed in light brown shirt and trousers, and he walked with his head bent forward so that when he looked at me from under the tangle of his curls he appeared to scowl. He didn't salaam. I noticed how the thin material of his trousers flapped around his almost emaciated legs: how bony his chest was, how yellow his eyeballs, how flat and dirty his bare feet.

And yet I don't think I was really disillusioned. The Botanical Gardens are certainly beautiful—what's more they combine stretches of jungle with the parts I have started to describe. It's just that they're unexpectedly gay, charming, some word like that. But I understand that there are really wild places not far from here around the reservoirs, also mangrove swamps and coastal areas where the Japanese used to hunt crocodiles.

Tonight we are all invited by R. to a Chinese dinner at the Great World (an amusement park). I hope it will be as good as the truly wonderful ten course meal I had at Penang, *pièce de résistance* being a large already boned duck stuffed with almonds. . . .

October 24th

Although R. suggested very generously that I should have a period in which to settle down, I decided to begin lecturing as soon as possible. I met my first class this morning. It began at eight o'clock, an unbelievably early hour for me, which took me back to those days during the Munich crisis when I was hanging around the State University at Burlington, Vermont, eating 'blue plate specials' of frogs' legs with Greek engineers and joining in when the boys of the Sigma Alpha Epsilon fraternity-house sang their theme song about Sweet Violets. I remember how astonished and secretly contemptuous I felt when they told me that they had eight o'clock lectures. Then, too, I had suddenly and almost inexplicably arrived in a new country and felt exalted by loneliness.

The alarm went just before seven and I jumped anxiously out of bed since I have overslept twice these last few days due to the superstitious hesitancies of my *amah*. However I had plenty of time, strolled quite calmly down

the colonnade, hid myself in my dry little cave of an office
while I finished my cigarette, glanced at my notes. There
weren't many of them as this was one of those delightfully
introductory lectures where all that matters is personality,
high principles and the gift of the gab. Then I marched
into a dim medium-sized room, with sunshine and trees
glowing at the farther end and rank upon rank of expec-
tant faces, the men almost exclusively in white, the women
sedate and flowery. I soon found that I could get them to
laugh and that they are responsive to a new approach or,
better, attack, for I gave them everything I had got, even
to turning my back on them and writing things on the
board, which I hardly ever did in Canada. Once or twice
members of the staff passed by the open doorway (R.
included), and I hoped they were impressed, but everything is so open here that I must have been heard for a
hundred yards in every direction. I had time for part of a
cigarette before my first tutorial group arrived at my
office. In their gay clothes they might have been dressed
for a garden party. There were five of them, mostly
Indians, and at least I got them to talk, and indeed to
argue, which is one of the most important things in this
kind of work. I asked a man with a beard what he had
thought of my lecture and he replied, 'I don't know that I
altogether understood what you were saying because I was
too interested in the way you put it. I can understand how
you became President of the Oxford Union.' I suppose he
knew of this through some of the publicity I have been
getting. At the end of the tutorial I asked how I could
identify two students whom I understand to be very
valuable and go-ahead, Wang Gung-wu and Beda Lim—
one of them a poet, the other some sort of impresario. But
the descriptions weren't very clear.

My work here will consist of the following: a course of
lectures on Tudor, Elizabethan and metaphysical poetry
for the Second Year (the one I gave this morning), the
poetry part of a First Year Nineteenth Century course, and

a series of lectures—not compulsory—on modern poets.
I gave the first of these this afternoon. The room was
packed and extra chairs were brought from outside. R., by
the way, tells me that it is difficult to discuss metaphysical
poetry with orientals because they lack any sense of tension and paradox; they don't know what all the bother is
about and the Chinese in particular, being good material-
ists, are more likely to indulge from time to time in a
rather luscious romanticism, the literary counterpart of a
technicolour banquet, than to be interested in the wrestling of flesh and bone. Nevertheless I can see the attraction
in teaching them Elizabethan lyrics so early in the morning
when the world does look wonderfully new and one is
almost giddy with its unaccustomed freshness and promise.

I find that I have now accumulated a list of names on
my desk, all that is left so far of the various polite and
reticent figures who have been with me today, exotic
crystallizations of polished dark heads and alert eye-
glasses. The Malay names include *bin*, son of, *binti*,
daughter of; the Indian are long and wrangling; the
Chinese possess three quaint little monosyllables, the first
being the family name, the second common to all members of the same generation, and the third personal to the
man himself. I have been told, though, that all sorts of
more or less secret nicknames are used and that mothers,
in their desire to scare away devils, will often refer to their
offspring as Toad or Pig, even going to the extent of
making a male child wear an earring in its left ear so that
the evil spirits will think it belongs to the inferior sex. It's
just as well that Freud didn't do his work here. One can
only shudder at the Oedipal confusion of a child bearing the
inhumanly reticent name of Ng, admitted to his mother's
breast under the soubriquet nasty little snake, and presented to the world as some sort of hermaphrodite. . . .

The other piece of news is that I have hired a Boy,
whose boyishness is not purely professional, who is in fact
prodigiously small, young even to pathos and ferociously

efficient. It happened like this. Dr and Mrs. W. just failed to get me an *amah* and I felt I couldn't go on using theirs, charming as she was and eagerly as she provided me with banana fritters in the middle of the afternoon and fruit before breakfast. I was then told that there was a Chinese youth in search of a job about the place, his age in the region of seventeen or eighteen, and Mrs. W. suggested an interview. Ever since London, where my friends were so amusing on the subject, the idea of having a servant has been almost an obsession with me, as a symbol of luxury, a challenge to my imagination and tact, and an opportunity to get into direct relation with the East. After the scrawny or decrepit monsters seen so far, my romanticism turned towards Indians or Malays, though neither are employed to any extent at the university and Malays, Mary tells me, may suddenly grow melancholic and have to be shipped back to their families before they seize the nearest *kris*, scream horridly and run amok. A genuine Chinese youth would, however, be the sort of person I was looking for and I waited eagerly for his visit. Sooner than I had expected I heard the tinkling laughter of Mrs. W. and her two *amahs*, there was a knock on my door and through it appeared a very small schoolboy whom I took to be an outrider or advance agent of the candidate himself, especially when Mrs. W. followed him in a state of almost uncontrollable amusement. But this was Ah Ting, the putative boy. Not seventeen or eighteen by any means but, possibly, since the Chinese consider themselves one year old at birth, fifteen years old. He looked very neat and dignified, with a small confident smile. I noticed that Mrs. W. treated him in summary fashion, telling him to be clean and obedient, leading him to the kitchen and ordering him to scrub it out, and asking him how much money he wanted in a tone that suggested he deserved none at all. His answer, 'What you say, Sir,' was non-committal. I winced inwardly at being called Sir instead of the more romantic *Tuan* which the *amah* had always used. Mrs. W.

suggested that I buy a nail-brush and insist that the boy wash his hands and brush his nails several times a day.

Ah Ting, then, is now a member of my household, the first personal servant I have ever had, but I'm not at all sure which of us is really the master. I gather that he was previously employed for a short period by one of the high university officials, whose wife mothered him and dressed him up in a special uniform which included long pants. He has probably been made a bit conceited by his association with the Registrar's *ménage* but he certainly shows no signs of wanting to continue as an eighteenth-century blackamoor or grotesque. I rushed down-town to buy cooking utensils, some nice food and the necessary nail-brush, and also added some chocolate as a sign of paternalism, but without much success. For, when I dumped pots and pans, steak and a tin of mushrooms, etc., with something approximating to the air of a man who intends to live well, I only received in reply a long list of other requirements, delivered in a burst of items followed by a trailing series of afterthoughts. I had bought saucepans with metal handles and it was indicated to me that wooden ones would have been better. Buckets were needed, and brooms, and kitchen soap, and something called cooking-oil or, alternatively, *chopping* (presumably he meant dripping). So I produced the nail-brush with what was far from being a flourish, pointed at it, and explained its use. All Ah Ting gave me was a pained look. So later, when he came into the sitting-room with the tea, I offered him his chocolate. The result was quite unexpected and I still don't understand it: not dignified refusal but a real animal horror—he acted exactly as though the Cadbury's bar was going to bite him, moved backwards abruptly and shuddered. 'No, no, no!' he said.

The next morning, when he came to wake me, I pulled back the mosquito net to make a sort of arch through which I could drink my tea. Once again his remark was 'No'. A righteous, complacent, aunt-like 'no' this time.

He proceeded to gather the net from all round the bed into a twist or pigtail, whipping my face with its edge as he did so. His diminutive size prevented him from tossing it up on to the frame from where he stood. He had to place one surprisingly large flat foot on the edge of the bed before making his cast. A moment later all the four shutters were banged open and sunlight streamed into my room. The grass outside was noisy with hens; no one apparently can stop the servants from keeping them and they are the one ungenteel thing about the place. As a matter of fact, shutters play an important part in Ah Ting's life, and so do keys. He is eternally opening things up and shutting things down. The hour after luncheon gives him the greatest scope for it is then that he puts the whole place to bed and firmly locks me in, after which I hear the shuffle and click of his sandals on the concrete outside as he gravely goes home. He doesn't live here, preferring to stay with his father who is an old reliable Boy, and this of course is the lucky part of it since it means that I now have a spare bedroom at the back. His other passion is for lists which he often writes down on scraps of paper and leaves for me to find when I come home late at night. The childish writing and the opening 'Dear Sir' remind me of the little notes I used to get from my First Formers in Montreal, when they had excuses to offer about the weekly essay.

My relations with R. continue good, although I am more conscious of his withdrawn quality than before and of the perplexing way in which his various gifts and interests mingle together. It would probably be asking too much to expect that they should mount up, through simple addition, into a splendid total. There must be subtle subtractions and divisions. He goes off on a natural history expedition every Sunday morning, taking his daughter Susie, who has a mania for collecting fish, and often accompanied by the Director of the Raffles Museum. I went with them the other day. We drove to the farther of the two (or are there three?) reservoirs; not the pretty one at the back of the Golf Club, to which he has taken me already, but a wilder catchment area near Seletar. He was armed with a large butterfly net and a poison bottle, Susie had glass jars for her fish, Mr. Tweedie bore another butterfly net and I felt inadequate beside them, possessing nothing but my innocence and a lurking anticipation of snakes. We walked through overgrown jungle paths, with the bushes shabby around us and the spaces between the leaves filmy and dirty blue, for the day was grey and soft, and there was no question of brilliant colours and luscious blooms. From time to time R. would give some of the shrubbery a violent knock or shake and out of it would flutter some dusty bedraggled little creature which he declared to be an interesting specimen and, surprisingly often, rare. He also showed me pitcher plants growing by the path, with long green sacks and oval lids poised above their openings, and there were many sensitive plants, so many that I soon got used to the way they fold their leaves and bow their stems when you touch them.

After a bit Tweedie announced that the only way of penetrating into the real jungle was to walk on one of the irrigation pipes. This we did but I didn't like it: a narrow perspective through dense trees, a large iron pipe often ten or twelve feet in the air with marshy and muddy irregularities of ground under it, and one's feeling of intense silliness at getting giddy on top of something really so large but whose fat gross curve simply invited one's feet to deviate, and whose speckled texture swam before one's eyes. I walked much too slowly, had to confess that I wasn't enjoying myself on the pipe, and felt immediately that I was being a nuisance (neither R. nor Tweedie is a fatherly man, to whom one's inadequacy can actually be a virtue, and you know how some slight stupid social unease can open up vistas of lostness and shame). I had the feeling that R. doesn't bother about people much and that he wouldn't want to ask me again. After a mile or so on two different pipes, we dropped off into some unpromising looking ooze (it occurred to me that we could have alighted on similar places many times before) and here R. and Tweedie, smiling delightedly, plunged thigh-deep in mud and water, scooping out handfuls which contained occasional tiny fish. I followed Susie farther down the stream. The undergrowth fell back, the water grew shallow and sparkled over sand, a golden oriole flew out of a tree and I was suddenly back in the Forest of Arden atmosphere, which I have already described in my account of the Botanical Gardens and university campus. It was enormously peaceful, with the sun out at last and Susie catching raspberry-coloured fish with placidity, for she is not a little girl, she must be fifteen or sixteen. Then R. called me over to explore a much more exotic path than we had yet come to, perhaps because of the sunlight, and as we walked along it past dangling lianas and sprouting ferns, and all the mossy richness of life and decay and life again, suddenly a bright whip tightened before us, R. stopped abruptly, and there was my first snake. R.'s idea was that I should stop there to guard it and keep it amused while he went back for Tweedie; already he spoke of the snake with great affection, calling it a charming little creature; but I demurred to this and so he sent me in search of the others while remaining himself. I ran back and called, but my shouts were absorbed by the forest. No one answered. and in a few minutes R. appeared. 'Have you lost it?' I asked, half-disappointed, half-relieved. 'Oh no. It's such a nice little thing that I've brought it with me.' Sure enough he had a branch in his hand and on the branch, waving to and fro, body tightly coiled but head raised and often perilously close to his face, was the snake. We decided that the others must have started back and so we had quite a long walk, avoiding the pipe-line, and during this walk R. kept commenting on this and that plant, using the branch as a pointer so that the snake kept teetering in the air beside me. Tweedie was equally charmed with it, describing it as a viper. Endearments, which I am sure their wives would have given much to hear, were delivered in the snake's direction, and far from being killed it was reverently placed upon the nearest tree. For now they had spotted more sinister quarry: a large Dutch naturalist, in horn-rimmed spectacles and bulging shorts, who was investigating the foliage nearby. 'Wonder what he's up to?' said R. 'Always boasts that he has his private hunting ground,' said Tweedie. And few greetings could have been more coldly formal than those they exchanged.

Ah Ting is questioning me about dinner (whether I want *all* or *half* the potatoes and precisely how many pieces of toast should go with my bacon and tomato) so I must practise my arithmetic and geometry and stop. . . .

November 12th

. . . Social life has arrived, although not explosively. In other words two cocktail parties. And one dinner. Imagine first an immense number of cars, for everybody has a car here, and much of the talk is on the car market—it's expected to rise—and who has what on order, and the make one intends to take back on leave—I expect their subconsciousnesses are mechanically minded too, with Fiats wanting to be Vauxhalls, and Vauxhalls wanting to be Humber Snipes, and awful moments when one's younger brother announces, 'Mummy says I can have a Jaguar,' and nightmares in which one has to drive to Tanjong Malim, Kuala Lipis or Alor Star and finds one isn't sufficiently armoured. Imagine the sound of a car drawing up on gravel, brisk as a tree falling: hot headlights swinging into drives, sweeping across lawns (the clichés are full of power, indifference, fake glamour)—but add to this the concourse of Malay syces in the darkness below the bright windows and verandahs (satin-

2.
'The small curving river which slips down through Chinatown' (p. 54)

skinned young men with big lips and broad pelvises, reconciling somehow the floral and the ape-like, one's dumb loyal friend and the most treacherous dreaming, the most subversive frivolity . . . and old wrinkled men dwindling below their songkoks, which are a sort of fez, tarboosh or what have you)—and then don't forget the policemen who have come to protect some important guest and who stand listlessly about, their palms cupping the mouths of their rifles, attentive only to the orders of a Lieutenant d'Souza or Rodriguez or O'Hara, their Eurasian boss.

I don't suppose I have any right to generalize about the pattern here. My feeling is that the university keeps very much to itself, and that there isn't a great deal of mutual exchange within it, certainly not to the extent of prying into one's affairs and embarrassing one. Thus, though my flat is institutional *and* publicly situated, no one bothers me, my only callers are Margaret, Mary, Allan and R. Allan raps on the shutters before looking in; Margaret calls from a distance of some yards (e.g. 'Pat!—Are you decent?') for there is a certain tang to our relations; I might be naked, I might be indulging in some nameless artistic eccentricity; Margaret seems to take a motherly interest in me, but I flatter myself that she does this with emotional self-distrust as well as Catholic moralism; as for R., he is elaborately discreet, neither calls nor raps but speaks first to Ah Ting. R. and Dorothy don't know the W.'s, which augurs well for my being able to live a private life here. On the other hand it means that I am alone a great deal and too far from town to be able to obtain immediate distractions. I can't window-shop as in Montreal, or luxuriously humiliate myself by buying *Time*, or watch people in a drug-store, or quickly get a drink in a pub. My distractions are writing, oriental perversities with regard to the flat, and the bottle. Gin and Italian is now firmly established as my drink. Outside the university circle I have made friends with only one family so far, people called Topley, very lively and intelligent but also very occupied. And I have been promised an introduction to the novelist, Shamus Fraser, who teaches at one of the local schools.

Which brings me back to the cocktail party. The people are mostly university, then, including of course the Medical College; they have met before, and will meet again; their presence is partly functional, and so is the party itself which will follow well-ordered and long familiar lines; inevitably the result is a certain flatness, a certain dowdiness, together with a few privileged eccentricities (drinking too much rather than thinking too hard, talking too brilliantly or letching after somebody else). At the end one will reflect that Professor So-and-so was rather high, that the middle-aged Mrs. X was flirtatious and gay —one knows that her husband's status made her flushed full-blown attentions innocent and abstract—and that old Such-and-such always does this sort of thing remarkably well. Catering by the Singapore Cold Storage. Lots of *ketchil makan* (first word pronounced kitchy, at least by the Tuans and Mems: it means 'Little food' and I believe purists reverse the order of the words so that the adjective follows the noun). This quite frequently will consist of real caviare as well as all sorts of rococco contortions. And endless *stengahs*. For I believe one rarely gets cocktails at a cocktail party; I don't think one Chinese in ten thousand knows how to mix them and it is considered *infra dig* for any European to appear in a menial capacity. Most of those who meet at the party have long ago decided which people they want to entertain more privately, and there is said to be now, with the cost of living so high, a movement of recession among the senior people so that some of the younger wives complain that they have been misled by helpful letters urging them to come out with 'several cocktail dresses and at least two evening gowns'. A formal politeness might be the thing, if only somebody knew how to be formal; instead there is a flustered, slapdash *bon-*

homie (the wives tending to deserve the first adjective, the
husbands the second) beyond which, after his eyes have
boggled confessionally and her cheek-bones have flared
red, you sense a yawn, a remoteness at once complacent
and dusty, and remember that he is an important surgeon
or even a Dean. Yet you cannot be discarded. You cannot
for the most part be actively disliked, at least not by him—
his wife has greater freedom. No longer hugged now but
held rigidly at arm's length, you and he must rotate
socially through the length of your 'tour' for you are both
white, both colonials and both members of the same staff.
Furthermore, he needs you since he is unlikely to have a
social position of his own; his position depends on his
being linked to you, as your superior, of course.

There must be gossip, quite a lot of gossip really; sheer
fright before the strenuous shabbiness of it all (the
glittering, mincing irony of some of the provincial young
men, the positively Hanoverian queenliness of some of
their wives, with huge bright flowers crawling all over
them) impels me towards Midge or Allan so that we can
whisper in corners; or the failure of a good gay introduction to a relatively orchidaceous someone (who turns
out to be not the season's *femme fatale* but salaried and
institutionalized into knowledgeable aunthood in Radio
Malaya) causes me to drift in the direction of Dorothy
who wants me, I am told, to be the eligible bachelor she
thought I was in London. But this gossip cannot be
really dangerous because no one has a sufficiently large
following or a deeply-felt system of values. And then, in
the midst of all this, I find myself staring at a large tin
bath full of ice in which bottles are being cooled—notice
the unresponsive gawkiness of the Boys—and begin to
find everything dull to the point of brutality. I suggest to
Allan that we go somewhere else; he asks me where and I
answer, 'The Savoy'—realize that I have been overheard
and feel faintly ashamed for I understand that my
nocturnal activities are not always approved.

I have now discovered my own pub-round. Whether it is as good as the previous ones I can't really say as yet (obviously nothing is going to be anywhere so grim as the Montreal taverns with their sewage-coloured walls, icy draughts along the floor and buffalo-shaped men in heavy overcoats angrily brooding over their beer—obviously, too, one can't expect the Black Horse, Lamb or Cross Keys) but I am quite pleased with it. The odd thing is that all the advice given me on the ship, even that of the stewards, wasn't much use—perhaps because they preferred Hongkong and told me either about places to which only servicemen are admitted or relatively expensive bars associated with the big cinemas. For days I went around imagining that there was nothing in between the Shackles and Union Jack Clubs, and the Capitol Cinema or Adelphi Hotel. Or, rather, that if I looked hard enough and went down a sufficient number of back streets I should arrive at last at some darkly alluring, faintly sinister door and enter the smoke-filled room of my dreams, or at least of those dreams which have been prompted by the American movies—a place so ambiguously mingling shadow and light, brashness and intimation, gongs and whispers, that even the most peroxided of stewards would never have found it. And then I suddenly saw that I was being foolishly subtle. Every bar was of more or less the kind that I was looking for. Every bar was a dive. But this was due not to the calculation of a wicked proprietor, nor to the presence of different racial types, but simply to the great wave of servicemen which sweeps the town night after night. These ubiquitous servicemen make it difficult for one place to have a different or more exciting atmosphere than another.

I started off with the Singapore Bar which I entered at what I thought a most inappropriate time: half way through a hot afternoon. I had been shopping in and out of the white glare—not so much shopping as wandering restlessly about, amazed to find goldsmiths in rows, and violent displays of textiles in shop after shop, and places

selling exactly the same crockery in almost infinite series
—and I walked back for a long time in the sun, between
the meadow (*padang*) with the cathedral on it, and the
other meadow by the sea, until I was really thirsty. The
Singapore Bar proved to be long and narrow, a bar to the
right, some tables opposite. There was nothing interesting about it except that a jeweller had a little booth by
the doorway and that you could see through its windows
a beautifully dilapidated church on the other side of the
street. And—oh, yes—a hand-grenade was thrown in
there the other day. Here I soon got into conversation
with three Scottish soldiers. After a bit we went up the
road to the Washington and then to the Rendez-vous.
Neither of these places had any particular glamour: the
Washington was upstairs and empty, the Rendez-vous
labyrinthine and loud with a radio. Description is hardly
necessary; enough that I felt at home with my soldiers,
who told me (and subsequently I have heard this often)
that they resent civilians as a rule; enough that a great
deal of beer was drunk, the sky became purple, the air
relaxed its pressure and one began to notice that Bols
spelled backward is Slob, and Gin is Nig, and that above
the easy, corny, marshland of *Gemütlichkeit*, of Slob and
Nig, the glittering bottles achieved an aerial exactitude,
protested some aristocracy of wing and alp and sky.

I know how conservative I am once I get started; loyal
even to my bad habits and quite prepared, I think, to find
domesticity in a brothel, or tomorrow's breakfast as
exhilarating as tonight's champagne. I went back to these
pubs again and again, taking a taxi only as far as a dollar
would pay for and then walking about a mile so that I
could start off at the bottom end, as I had done the first
time. Once I met Tom Driberg, just back from Korea, in
the Rendez-vous. Probably the nicest time, though, was
when Allan accompanied me and succeeded in buying a
copy of Proust's *Les plaisirs et les jours* in the Singapore Bar.
Then one night I met a dark young soldier who

announced promisingly that he was a member of the
Anti-Vice Squad. After some drinks we walked down to
the Esplanade together. Beyond it we came to one of the
bridges across the small curving river which slips down
through Chinatown, meeting the sea discreetly at the back
of the big-business section. We stood talking for a long
time, it was already quite late, and I couldn't help thinking that the view from there was—was *really*—Venetian.
There was something gently theatrical, delicately emphasized about the place, with its sinewy bridge, and a lawn
in front of the Marine Police Station, and a tree, and the
dark water underneath reflecting ghostly arcades—
exciting too because I am still conscious of the fact that
there may be communist gunmen about, and surprised at
myself for not caring more, for turning my back positively
luxuriously upon half-open doorways and dark alleys,
conducting a conversation upon vice (well after midnight)
in such an exposed position, with nobody else in sight.
Not that vice was particularly rewarding. There were the
tarts in Lavender Street. There was a celebrated trans-
vestist rejoicing in the name of Peggy Lee. And—in the
ambience of vice though not itself necessarily vicious—
there was a bar called the Savoy whose presiding genius
was not a girl but a boy: a boy soprano, Terence.

So the next evening I left out the intervening pubs and
paid the Savoy a visit. I found that it was quite a big
place on Orchard Road, the ground floor of a stark
biscuit-coloured apartment building, shabbily modern,
with a tobacco-stand by the doorway, and a newspaper
seller, and a taxi parked (in the sultry way that taxis do
park themselves by peculiar places) and a tri-shaw
wheeling by with that special tigerish slowness of theirs
(tigerish because of the gleam of brass). Big windows on
the side street, curtained in pink. Children and youths
hanging on to the outside of the windows, peering. And,
above all other impressions, noise. Shrieks from the most
powerful of amplifiers, and then a wailing, wobbling,

abruptly rising, ultimately *fortissimo* and outrageous music. Terence singing. . . .

Inside it was—well, not like any other bar I have seen except, perhaps, for a wide-open town in the West of America. Large and irregular, with a primness of tables here and there, table cloths, artificial flowers—and a murky wrangle of booths growing ever more secret towards the back and the lavatory—and a part of the bar itself which was declaratory and public, and another part at right angles which was recessive and intimate—and a bottle-neck with a sofa and a table piled with newspapers —and a large peasant kitchen harbouring a rather charming Idiot Boy—and of course the piano and the microphone and the radiogram apparatus, endlessly instable, endlessly alluring, for a sailor at the bar could turn the dials up or down while hidden behind a pillar, and one soldier could be fighting over the microphone, and another attempting to play the piano, and a third choosing records for the automatic player—a drunken shout would seem loud until a giggle became catastrophically so, as the microphone picked it up. And, in the foreground to all this, a cleared space in which sailors were dancing with some attractive girls, or with each other, or alone. I noticed a splash of blood on the floor near the entrance.

I soon got to know Terence, a tall willowy youth I took to be Malay until he indignantly corrected me—he is Portuguese-Eurasian with, I suspect, much Indian and some Malay blood—and through Terence I met the girls: the dashing magnificient Sadie, an expert at *jogget modern*, the dance in which the partners move opposite each other without touching, fluttering their hands, wriggling their hips and sinking gracefully floorwards; Maria, who is very pretty and sedate, with the blooming sexuality of a Victorian heroine so that one associates her with the romantic symbol of the Rose—the red rose, the dewily blushing Rose, the Rose perilous and pubic—by the way Maria, like so many of these girls, has one child, if not

two; an Indian girl with a classic profile called Irma; and
Natalie, who is older and less pretty but nevertheless
the most practised hand amongst them, the most estab-
lished member of the group (she actually works at the
Savoy full time) and by far the wittiest. Also Sam, the
Tamil pianist.

Recently I have been at the Savoy a good deal, not only
in the Slob and Nig periods late at night, amongst the
ithyphallic and the sodden, with the noise of breaking
glass and the tussle and smack of a fight—and with
strange young men soundlessly manifesting themselves on
the sofa or in the end booth—young men with crew hair-
cuts and cadaverous faces and huge eyes who look as
though they had crawled out from under stones, or who
have the febrile ambiguous delicacy of creatures on stalks
which are about to become dragonflies—but, as I say,
during more domestic times of day as well—at noon, when
Natalie is busying herself with her sewing-machine and
Terence is wondering whether someone will give him a
gold crucifix for Christmas, or early in the evening when I
arrive with an armful of parcels and a mop or another
broom. Ellis, whom I took there, said it was the Infantile
Paradise itself, completely carefree and amoral. Allan
liked it, though he blushed at one or two of Terence's
remarks. And it has granted me a number of nebulous
adventures. Once a book of my poems was torn up before
my eyes by a complete stranger who 'dipped into it' (if
anyone so large could be described as dipping) and
uttered the single word 'shocking!'

For the rest, I have got to know the students rather
better, and I have become perhaps slightly disenchanted
with R. I go to the students' canteen fairly often, drink
sweet coffee (made with condensed milk and never
delivered to your table without plenty having spilled over
into the saucer) and wonder at the absence of nearly all
other members of the staff. The students say they want us
to come to the canteen, want to meet us and talk to us but

they are not without their suspicions—the bearded Indian in one of my tutorials told me the other day, 'You come here now because you are new to the country and still have your own ideas—we have seen this thing before with the newly-arrived lecturers—after a bit I'm afraid you will not feel the same.' There's a good deal of heavy irony and sarcasm to this kind of talk—especially noticeable in the undergraduates' newspaper—but the odd English used, and the odd sing song intonation, emphasize a certain childishness in their attitude. I got the impression that my Indian would be quite *disappointed* if things turned out differently. (On the other hand it does seem strange that not a single professor ever puts in an appearance.) I have also had a long conversation with the poet Wang Gung-wu about my idea of establishing a Creative Writing Group. I was very impressed. Instead of welcoming the idea, he very coolly and charmingly questioned it: would I be good for them, was I too Western an influence? And, also, the authorities wouldn't like my presiding over a very nationalist, left-wing affair? A good-looking young man, highly intelligent, with marvellous teeth.

Yesterday Allan and I felt depressed. I went over to see him, and we hung about being melancholy over the social life here, and the lack of prospects of better housing, and he produced the little mimeographed sheet which we both felt had rather misinformed us in London. It can be a lonely life. Even if you have two or three families you can call on say twice a week each (and they won't always be in) and if you take the average visit as lasting one hour, there is still a hell of a lot of time to oneself, and I wonder what he does with it. (I strew my place with gardenias and frangipani, insert exotic sprigs into the screen I have now hung across most of my archway, play Noël Coward, think of food, another evening of Snodrog Nig. . . .) Suddenly there was a whispering noise, a noise of rushing, muffled cracking, and looking out into the bright dull air ('the enormous *naïveté* of the unrefracted light,' says

Thomas Mann in *Mario*, which ultimately cannot satisfy 'the deeper, more complex needs of the northern soul') we saw that one of the big casuarinas had fallen. It was catastrophe in whispering lace, huge, almost voiceless, cruelly frivolous, and it appealed to our low spirits. Things happen, change occurs, people grow old and die, but the atmosphere of the place hides all this.

This morning I sent R. a note full of literary despair but his response to a phrase like 'haunted by the remote twittering of birds' was to say when he came around, and he did kindly come around, 'Yes, I suppose the birds *are* rather noisy here. . . .' On the other hand, he was very unhappy about the tree.

December 7th

It's odd to think that three days ago I came quite near to being killed. The Muslim riots broke out on Monday, with echoes on the following two days, so that even tonight with no incidents reported there is still a curfew and I am more or less imprisoned until daybreak with six bottles of Tiger beer, *Sons and Lovers* and a radiogram which I have just bought second-hand from one of the higher-ups in Radio Malaya.

All this was due to a young girl the Malays call Nadya, (alias Maria Hertogh) whose case came before the Supreme Court that morning; her Dutch parents were petitioning for her return after years spent as a foster-child of the Malays, during which she had not only become a Muslim but entered into a marriage with a Malay school-teacher. The authorities appear to have behaved with the most incredible stupidity over the whole affair: they placed the Muslim girl in a Catholic convent while her case was under consideration and they ignored all evidence of the Malay community's discontent, and especially of the doubtful attitude of the police force which is almost exclusively Malay. Vast crowds formed in front of the Supreme Court Building;

the Ghurka riot-squad was first introduced, then with-drawn; an Eurasian special constable let off a pistol. . . .

On Monday afternoon I was visited by Gung-wu who talked for a long time about the possibility of creating a Malayan poetry out of a fusion of English, the native languages and the local idiom. The result was that I didn't start on my almost daily shopping expedition until about five-thirty—by which time, if only I had known it, the riots had been out of hand for hours and some fifteen or sixteen Europeans had been killed. Gung-wu had said nothing of all this. Shortly after I had left, Ellis came round to warn me not to go down town and left me a note. I got a taxi without any trouble, drove along Orchard Road and stopped at my Chinese grocer (Sing Seng Hin). Here again there was no word of trouble. I then walked down to Government House, blithely hugging my gro-ceries with me and pausing from time to time on the way.

I went into the Savoy for a drink. It's almost empty at this time of day, except for a stray or two from the congre-gation of servicemen at the Singapore Bar; one can watch Terence and the girls preparing for the night and talk to them more freely than later when the crowds begin. Sadie comes swinging in through the Shanghai doors in one of her extraordinary costumes: red velvet bodice, orange sarong and a sort of cummerbund in green, pats her hair in front of the looking-glass behind the bottles, tilts her head, makes sure of an earring and then, with that char-acteristic mixture of pose and humour which is common to all of them, sweeps around, all magnificent haughti-ness, bursts into laughter and says something to Terence in unrepeatable Malay. They dance, fight, hiss curses at each other but always, in the midst of the teasing, assume those consciously theatrical gestures which fill me with exhaustion and wonder. Are they really children? Isn't there something arid about this continual display of passion—or perhaps it is a passionate pride which, doubt-ing the adequacy of any possible recipient, doubting even the adequacy of themselves, seeks to destroy itself in exaggeration and the grotesque? Whom do they consider to provide the limelight in which they move, and which they both woo and condemn—surely not the two soldiers at the bar, nor the elderly racing-man who recently fell into a monsoon drain and sprained his shoulder so badly that he cannot shave, nor me? And of course they will never enter the real world of the theatre to which they both aspire: they act too much to be ever successful as actors, they despise or at least guy their audience and themselves too much; Terence will never sing on a genuine radio programme, Sadie will never dance in a high-class show; it is doubtful if she will even succeed in marrying one of the serious sad-faced boy-friends who follow her, almost grimly attracted.

The bar is quiet enough for Terence to ask one of the soldiers if he would like to see his photographs. These he produces from the large drawer under the counter in which he seems to keep most of his belongings. Terence as a sailor-boy, delicately tinted. Terence as Carmen Miranda. Terence as a young man about town. Terence simpering. . . . He hands them over with a smile of extraordinary sweetness which quickly fades as he waits for the expected compliment, his eyes twitching nervously. Meanwhile the other soldier is trying to bargain with Mrs. Lee for one of the pink plaster nudes 'draped' in a swirl of silver paint which stand on the dusty top shelf. She isn't in the least surprised that he wants to have it, reaches it down and places it in front of him, naming a high price and never for one moment relaxing her firm grip on its ornamental base. There it stands in all its hideous insouciance: an odd rival to the various manifestations of Terence nearby. Both in a sense represent art but, while Terence's soldier treats the big photographs in their gold frames with a great deal of respect, his mate tries to grab the statuette, wheedling and jeering. If it were later at night he would obviously regard it as something to steal, not to buy, and I think he already feels conscious of this. After Terence has shown both the portrait studies and a great many snapshots (and some of the recent letters he has received from P. and O. liners on their way home), he announces rather primly that it is time for him 'to take his bath' and disappears, with a new set of clothes over his arm, to a mysterious cubbyhole beside the lavatory. I can't imagine what kind of bath is possible in so restricted a space and I have never heard the sound of a shower. However he certainly looks very fresh on his return. His trousers are spotlessly white and he wears a singlet of blue and white stripes which, although his chest is quite well developed, shows a rather too indolent line in front. His first job is to rectify this by much fussing with straps and buckles. He tightens himself into a wasp-waist and then, reassured about his figure, his arms come to life again and his hands flutter, as though he wished to gain security from the atmosphere around him, as though he wandered through petals and gossamer with admirers' glances made tangible, and flattery possessing the air like a south wind, and it is now that a great deal of hair-combing takes place, and an enormous bottle of eau-de-cologne is produced from the same drawer which contains the photographs. With this he perfumes his handkerchief and coquettishly dabs himself behind the ears.

This was the sort of atmosphere I expected and I can't remember having noticed very much difference except that there was a number of Eurasians in the place, as there had been at the time of the Nonis trial (Nonis had been accused of murdering a little girl and his acquittal was very popular). They seemed much less intense on this occasion. However I was not in the centre of things as I had discovered a European acquaintance called Jeremy Duff-Williams and we were sitting in one of the more remote booths, lazily ordering a second round of beer and pleasantly conscious of the fact that there was nothing particular to do, no conscience about returning home, and that what had started out as a casual visit might develop into an evening of serious drinking. Suddenly there was a new tension in the air, Mrs. Lee (who never rushes) walked rather quickly to the doorway, Natalie came up to us and said, 'There's a busload of Malays outside. You'd better leave at once. It's dangerous for Europeans here.' And hardly had she said this when Mrs. Lee and Sadie began to close the steel gates out in front. We were still confused, for Jeremy had little more inkling of the situation than I, but we decided at least to take half measures and so hid ourselves in the lavatory. We were both inclined to scoff at the idea that there was any real danger: I remember thinking how remarkable it was that there were hardly ever any dirty words or drawings in this particular lavatory because, I imagined, the place is so completely unrepressed. Thoughts of Germany and England versus the Mediterranean countries. Thoughts of Piccadilly Circus and Leicester Square. The beginnings of a sociological pattern, for why should not the same be true of the Singapore Bar or the Rendez-vous?—was it because they were mid-way in the course of a serviceman's evening, bright with yearning, loud with whipped-up cheer, and only here was childish fruition achieved? Terence began banging on the door very loudly. 'Get out, get out at once. You must leave. Mrs. Lee won't have you staying here!' So we came out, had a wild glimpse of a shuttered room and an even more shadowy kitchen, while Natalie whispered encouragement to us and unbolted the back door. 'Don't go back to the main road,' she said. 'Don't let anyone see you. Keep to the side.' We stumbled in the wasteland behind the house, saw it stretching away to our left, a low hairy gap under brown sky; for a moment it seemed that safety lay only here in some primitive hiding place, a sort of going to earth; but Jeremy, who was trembling, moved out of the shadows on to the road, telling me to walk fast but not too fast, and on no account to run. The road was quite empty. Looking back after a

few paces I saw blurred white figures massed at the inter-
section, only forty yards away, and two or three of these
figures detached themselves and seemed to hesitate as to
whether they should follow us. We walked fast uphill,
entering a district of which I knew nothing and in which I
was entirely dependent upon Jeremy and expecting at any
moment to run into another group of Malays, coming
down to meet their friends. Once the murky pattern of
leaves beside a gate post stirred, and a dark figure rose
towards us, but it was only a coolie or jagger who meant no
harm. Half-way up the hill, we looked back again. Our
pursuers seemed to have given up the chase. Jeremy
turned right and I had a moment of horror because I
thought he was leading me back to the main road. On
occasions like this one's mind is in a turmoil and at the
same time that one is very frightened one is also pre-
occupied with practical questions: How shall we get
home? and even: Where can we get another drink?
Finally Jeremy rushed up the drive of a strange house,
brushed past a Boy at the door, led me down a passage and
into a bright little room, surprisingly unlocked. A beige
rug. A brand new H.M.V. radiogram. A refrigerator in
which Jeremy began to rummage for beer.

This, I discovered, was a well-known boarding-house;
the room belonged to one of Jeremy's friends who did
part-time work in the Marine Police and who was naturally out on the job at the moment. Here we hid out from
8 p.m. until 5 the next morning. Jeremy kept telephoning
the police with whom he seemed to be on very good terms
and later contacted the actual owner of the room who gave
us his permission to stay. The situation was bad, the
military was being called in, things should quieten down
but they expected worse tomorrow. A man and a woman
had been found murdered within a couple of hundred
yards of the Savoy. In the interval we listened to the
radio, hearing various Muslim leaders calming the mob:
the chief Kathi of the big mosque in North Bridge Road

and the Malay politician, Date Onn bin J'affar, for
example. There were monotonous announcements from
Radio Malaya in Malay, Tamil and several Chinese
dialects—on and on and on. And suddenly there was a
new commotion, our hearts leapt into our mouths. For,
ignoring the twitterings of a Chinese Boy and a dazed
mutter from a European woman lodging in the house,
who happened to be in the passage, an enormous Asian
suddenly stood in the doorway. We looked again and saw
to our relief that he was Chinese. He was in fact a policeman friend of our host, who had come to warn him of the
danger, and he proceeded to cheer us up with a long
series of anecdotes and philosophical disquisitions on
politics, corruption, women, uttered in the deepest of bass
voices. From time to time he paused and I listened for the
sounds of approaching riot (how often one has read in
books that an angry mob has a voice all its own, which
is terrible to hear) but the night around seemed quiet.
When the beer ran out, this Chinese insisted on going
shopping for us and returned a few minutes later with six
bottles of Tiger and a great quantity of cooked food in
banana leaf wrappings. He had walked right through the
rioters, he said, and had amused himself by pretending to
be on their side and hearing their comments.

After this helpful man had left we got some sleep but
were woken up very early by the Marine policeman who
could hardly have been expected to be in the best of
moods. He had spent the night evacuating women and
children from the Swimming Club by launch, and he was
now tired and brusque. He told us that the city was
absolutely quiet, with armoured cars patrolling the roads
and soldiers everywhere. There were no taxis about but
we could almost certainly get a lift in one of the military
cars. And that was that. 'By the way,' he added 'we expect
it all to start up again tomorrow.' I didn't quite follow the
logic of this remark—it was already tomorrow to me—
and if the military were in control, why should there be

Below the closed flags of laundry hung on poles
from the upper windows. (p. 157)

3. ' Below the crossed flags of laundry hung on poles
from the upper windows ' (*p. 152*)

any recurrence of trouble?—but we obviously had to leave.

It was intensely dark outside and very quiet although there was a noticeable absence of the armoured cars our friend had referred to, and neither of us felt particularly happy. However we walked down to Orchard Road and turned south. Battered and burned-out cars appeared on both sides. There was much broken glass on the tarmac. We came to the Savoy, still tightly shuttered and without a light. Jeremy's idea was to get back to his own flat in Jacaranda Road (which he shares with the emotional Rex Kim Seng) and my idea was to break the journey at the gates of Government House where there are always policemen and sentries. But tonight the gates were completely deserted and we had to go on, without reassurance. Jeremy chose alleys and by-paths. But when we arrived at his flat, there was another twist to this extraordinary evening. Rex, who had heard nothing of the riots, or at least not enough to counterbalance his jealousy over Jeremy's activities, interviewed us through the shutters and, hearing Jeremy mention the dreadful name Savoy (of which Rex is equally an *habitué*), firmly and vituperatively locked us out. In the end we found shelter in the Cathay Building, first on the balcony of the American Club and then in the main room of Radio Malaya, where we heard the first news go out. One of the announcers questioned the script that someone I took to be a very high official handed him. 'Good God, you can't expect me to read this over the air. It's a hell of a note,' he said, with reference to a statement that Singapore had passed a quiet night. 'After all a lot of people have been killed.' So the script was changed and Singapore was told that it was reverting to normal.

When it grew light Jeremy and I went up in the lift to the very top of the building. We had a magnificent view of the sea, the islands and the jumbled tiled roofs of the city; spires and cupolas rose firmly into the clear air, and there was more green than one had expected; business was starting up, traffic moving, and a succession of military cars and trucks did in fact now patrol the roads. I decided on breakfast in the restaurant and there found a number of people I knew: Derek Cooper of Radio Malaya with his shirt all bloody—his car had been burned and he had narrowly escaped himself—also the oddly elegant and glamorous John Forbes-Sempill, Singapore's actor-manager, who had festooned one of his large cars with chicken wire and performed many acts of gallantry, like a character in Dornford Yates. It was with some trepidation that I telephoned R. I felt that he would consider himself inadequate to my night's adventure—would have to be polite and helpful about it while actually dismissing it as a nuisance. Since it was impossible to get a taxi, he picked me up in front of the Cathay Cinema. I lurked inside the nearly-closed steel doors until the last moment. We drove up Orchard Road behind an army car. He told me that examinations scheduled for the end of the term had already been cancelled since many of the students were stranded in distant parts: the rather fashionable district of Katong is next door to Geylang, where there is the heaviest concentration of Malays.

One or two university people seemed mildly interested at my escape; I was the only member of staff to be out all night but two professors, on their way back from a big party at the Commissioner General's in Johore Bahru, were stoned near the entrance to the university and one of them went about for several days with a large bandage on his head. Allan came over here to listen to various gobbets of news: there were stern pronouncements by the Colonial Secretary—a large area around the mosque barred to traffic, a twenty-four hour curfew imposed in Geylang, a general curfew during the hours of darkness; the radio devoted itself to dance-music in the long intervals between its multilingual messages. In the course of discussions with a number of excited Europeans I learned a good deal more about the cause of the riots and the strange story of the Maria Hertogh case. It does seem to have been almost exclusively a Muslim affair, partly religious, partly nationalist, although the communists did their best to make it otherwise. What was most frightening about it was that it tapped hidden reservoirs of hatred towards the Europeans. One heard stories of the most dependable syces, and servants who had been in the family for years, having joined in with the mob. And of course my conventionally romantic attitude towards the Malays has suffered quite a set back.

Margaret told me that our Muslim students were very unhappy and ashamed but, when I went over to the canteen, I found it impossible to play the role of a hero. My left-wing friend James Puthucheary (whom the authorities think is probably a communist—he fought against the British in Burma) quickly switched the conversation to student politics in India, telling me how the girls had found a way of suffocating tear-gas bombs with their saris. He was more interested in criticizing the conduct of the riots here than in sympathizing with me. Gungwu, too, was of little help: all poise and abstract speculation and as delicately remote as a mirror. I felt myself becoming irritated with him, which is a pity as he is to be my son in the performance of Sophocles' *Antigone* we are planning. We are to play a strong scene together.

Life has quietened down now and this damned curfew will be over soon. On the first two nights I slept at Midge's, taking with me a saucepan full of Chinese food from the canteen and a large hammer for defensive purposes. Nothing happened, of course, except that on the second night I had the courage to borrow a couple of beers from R. . . .

Christmas Day

. . . I have just been feeding fried egg to a praying mantis. A charming delicate elongated creature far too good for such bourgeois nourishment, with a head that turns from side to side gravely following one's movements, slender arms which it appears in cat-like fashion to lick (or does it neurotically bite its nails?) and a tiny mouth whose intricate mechanism is coloured deep red. It was Ah Ting who, following some perverse fantasy of his own, decided to place this beautiful insect on the scarlet paper tongue of a Javanese mask I have bought where it now sits, poised above its folded hands, in which it is as interested as Firbank or Cocteau.

Despite this I am spending a tepid and vacuous Christmas day, full of self-pity, with a great urge to do something catastrophic like breaking plates or finally fulminatingly losing my temper with Ah Ting, yet at the same time so much vague distrust and disbelief in the purity of my motives, or their very definition. I have always been fond of Christmas and I don't think I am really caring enough.

My depression started off with an invitation to Christmas dinner. At the last moment Allan invited me to share a Christmas Eve turkey with Brian Harrison and himself. Harrison has the top part of his house and is nice but military and old Malayan. It was odd sitting down to such a meal in the blaze of noon, with the Boy who served us uninterested and off-hand and Harrison, who was in a hurry to get off to some police duty, fairly marching the courses along and giving crisp commands about brussels sprouts and mincepies. He gulped his coffee, rushed upstairs and re-appeared a few moments later, strapping on his revolver. Allan took it all very quietly, not speaking for long intervals, and I felt, as so often here, the conversation bulking up inside me without any hope of outlet beyond grunts and sudden feverish changes of subject.

Yesterday evening I went out again, this time to a large party which the W.'s gave, principally in the open air: a nice even revolutionary idea, what with a nearly new moon, masses of flowers and excellent Chinese food, cooked by

an imported chef. Since Ah Ting and most of my furniture had been borrowed, and there was an alien Boy in my
own kitchen, I was aware of the party from its start and
soon joined it. I found a small circle of chairs on the lawn
near the light of a standard lamp. There was an old
Eurasian lady who had had an adventure in the riots—
for some reason a group of Javanese toughs took her
under their wing, escorting her to Kallang Airport—and
for a moment we were courtly together, which is often
quite easy with the richer type of Eurasian who may be
more English than the English, and lord of some little
manor in Katong or Paya Lebar complete with ponies,
paddock, tennis-court and any number of Austral-
Alsatian dogs. A young and really very pretty Eurasian
girl was sitting next to me and after a bit I turned my
attention to her, complimented her (gaily? daringly?) on
her dress and did my best to keep the conversation going.
My first compliment was well and complacently received
but she soon became restless, perhaps out of her depth,
and I was horribly aware that my attempt had been a
failure. I think the moral is that you can be too polite with
people who are socially unpractised, I don't mean only
the natives but also the many representatives of the New
Britain on the campus. What you take to be a delicious
decorum, familiar enough to be handled amusingly and
with a certain amount of sexual pressure behind, is inter-
preted by them as being a kind of old world joke whose
amusement lies in the fact that one can soon relax from it
into, not a liaison, but a pally democracy.

Allan soon appeared and I realized that we would
inevitably drift together and become frivolously marginal.
No doubt his respectable appearance, the charm inherent
in his youth, would rescue him from time to time and, as I
glided morosely about, more and more frank about my
desire for another drink, I would catch snatches of his
small talk, observe the thickness of his hips and remind
myself that he possesses a motor-bicycle. Finally I took

him into my room for a secret drink. He is a queer chap, seems half-asleep most of the time—a be-spectacled curate with wavy hair who's been up all night decorating the church for the Harvest Festival—and then suddenly he will make a reference to *Alice in Wonderland* or Lautréament, leap up and do a few ballet steps or take a flying leap over a chair.

Nearly always at parties I end up by wanting to go somewhere else, taking the party manners and elegance into more brutal surroundings, and incidentally pleased that I have already had almost enough to drink, but yesterday there was a special reason, for Terence was due to put on his Carmen Miranda act in full costume. He had already presented me with some of the glass balls he is using as fruit for the head-dress.

I got down to the Savoy just before ten-thirty. There was a police van outside and policemen with rifles stood at the entrance. As usual, rows of children peered in through the windows. I entered by the back way (the same I used for my escape) and slipped into a booth already occupied by Sadie, Conrad and a battered looking soldier from the Federation. The place was packed and someone had already broken the glass Shanghai doors. Someone else had stolen all the fish from the aquarium. There was much whispering and giggling from behind the scenes: Terence was evidently wavering between the lavatory and the kitchen where he no doubt displayed his costume to the Idiot Child; soldiers, catching a glimpse of him, screamed; Sam hurtled through Chatanooga Shoeshine Boy; decorations glittered, coloured lights glowed. But when poor Terence came out, smiling and blushing, catastrophe occurred. A drunk was fooling with the microphone, Mrs. Lee had switched the loudspeaker off and, before order could be restored, someone had started tugging at Terence's sarong and someone else was making a dive for his head-dress. I expected him to fall into a rage but his vanity must have been really hurt—he retired quite meekly.

Today I have seen nobody but the praying mantis with whom I shared my lunch-time egg. Neither R. nor Midge and Ellis have included me in their Christmas. I don't feel in the mood for the roast chicken I have ordered for this evening, largely to impress Ah Ting who considers it important enough to justify calling in the aid of his father. I imagine that the Chinese must have some sympathy for us at this time of the year since this is the only Christian festival which approximates to theirs in its prodigal use of brightly coloured paper, tinsel and symbolic figures.

An hour or so ago I asked Ah Ting to put one of the blue-green rotan chairs, which I have substituted for the heavy furniture, on the little terrace at the back, near the bougainvillea and facing the cachou tree. I suppose I should have really sat under the fig, which I have tried to appropriate by fitting up a flex and a Chinese lantern (all efforts of this kind take up a disproportionate amount of time and ingenuity, make me thoroughly hot, and don't achieve much difference) but the fig is near to the house and the back door and the earth is damp and bare below it. So I sat farther away. I read, smoked and tried to imagine myself fully in possession. All this part of the garden was mine. And yet it felt slightly eccentric to be sitting there, since nobody else ever does it, so that what was perfectly normal could in a moment balloon into a sort of absurd moralism of 'taking a stand', 'showing the others what they were missing' and so on.

After a little I became aware of a rustling in the cachou tree. It was different from the wind in the leaves or in the tall grass on the bank above the garages; it was inter-mittent, suddenly quite loud, with now and then the crack of a breaking twig, and yet it was like a kind of language which one wasn't supposed to hear, and which nevertheless secretly pleaded with one to listen to it. Even the hens over-running *my* lawn didn't succeed in drowning it, for their squawks belonged to a separate order of sound altogether; they were far louder, of course, and so were the tuneless melancholy birds, but my ear was trained to a largeness not of sound but of silence or, at least, softness; and when it came again, when a twig broke and then another and still it did not cease, it seemed that its shyness was really a form of coquetry, a disguised insolence. Furthermore it was happening in *my* tree, my nicest tree but the one farthest from my house and hence most capable of owing another allegiance to the wilder country beyond the gardens. I began to study the leaves. I soon made out the brown body of a boy amongst them. He was crouched high up, on one of the golden-green branches, and he was reaching out very stealthily but expertly to pick the nuts. One leg was drawn up; the other lay almost flat on the bough, as smooth as silk; his slim gleaming shoulders were turned at an angle; for all the nimbleness of his fingers the line of his arm retained its fluidity, the curve to the arm-pit was softly, delicately drawn, and it was as though the flesh had a confidence in itself, an innerness and passivity, which had nothing to do with the act of stealing. Then he saw me. He drew back, one hand pressed to his mouth, but this movement, which turned his top into angles and showed the extreme thinness of his wrist, was still counterbalanced by the suavity (you could almost say the self-satisfaction) with which the line from chest to belly filled out. When he realized I wasn't angry he gave a brilliantly ingratiating smile. It was more like a smile of complicity. And, as I smiled back, I felt more eccentric and bewildered than ever. For one thing, there wasn't a person in sight and the grass, the road, the marshy valley beyond were all completely empty. How had he got there? And in what did the complicity consist? One thing he did seem to have done—he had subtly devalued my sense of ownership, my pride in my tree. For I suppose I wanted to join him and plunder my European self.

PART TWO

QUEER CAMPUS

January–June 1951

CHAPTER 1
The Keys of Ah Ting

AH TING was the boy châtelaine of my flat at the university. During the first few months, when I was settling down, I saw more of him than of anyone else; he became involved in all my fantasies about the East. Other people might be met in the staff room, where we sat in bare-kneed rows on our cane chairs and were guardedly hearty with each other, or at cocktail parties, or in the disturbing highly-coloured night world down Orchard Road, but Ah Ting remained at base, mended and washed my underwear, presided wonderingly over my hangovers, got under my skin and into my hair, and yet surprisingly turned out to be an adventurous accomplice when it was a question of plundering the gardenia tree, capturing Atlas moths or sticking frangipani into the matting I had nailed up to screen my bed.

His sandals slapped, his bare feet shuffled, up and down the oblong box of my one big room, whose decoration he had helped me accomplish. I had desperately wanted to impose some personality, a word I found I was using more and more as I faced the surburbanism of the campus and the curious refusal to cohere of the world beyond it and, although there were times I would have called Ah Ting anything rather than imaginative, he had not opposed my purchase of cheap low-slung arm-chairs in blue-green *rotan* to supplant the conventional heavy furniture, or the Chinese sleeping-mats I strewed on the mushroom-coloured tiles, and he had assisted in the hanging of a couple of sarongs on the wall together with two Javanese masks, said to be of a God who dieted on virgins. Changing the disposition of the furniture from day to day, I would command him to carry my potted plants from one place to another in an attempt to create some theatrical effect behind which I could be gently paranoiac. His own contribution might be a dozen huge canna lilies, bright scarlet, which he stuffed into any orifice he could find. Only one of my decorative ideas completely baffled him. In Montreal I had become familiar with a discreetly deft use of goosenecked lamps, which were turned to the wall in order that they might embarrass none of those nuances which glimmered from one colonial poet to another as they sprawled on their studio couches, drinking rye and listening to Mozart. But Ah Ting could never understand why I wanted to light my matting screen from below. The gooseneck, he firmly insisted, should be placed by my bed.

In the end, however, it is not Ah Ting's virtues that I think of, any more than his vices. It isn't the rare moments when he would rush in, genuinely childish at last, to announce a swarm of bees on the fig tree, a rat in the kitchen, or a helicopter returning from the jungle bandits, nor is it the dinner-party he spoiled, out of an obsession with economy, by serving a morass of onions in which lay concealed the small supernumerary piece of steak I had bought at the last moment to eke out the other meat. In the distorting glass of those days, where personal vision was both intensified and warped by solitude and heat, he seemed a sort of diminutive Swiss governess-cum-boy scout, who rattled his keys as he persisted in locking me in or locking me out. His appearance was as clinically neat as the high green walls punctuated by their massive glossy shutters, whose functionalism dominated any possible aesthetic effect; his tidiness imprisoned me even more successfully than the wire netting attached to the windows as a further precaution against a nearby Javanese *kampong*, wire-netting against which I used to hang, a spiritual prisoner, staring out across the blazing gravel to where the *amahs* pushed prams down the private road on their way to the Botanical Gardens, or at the figure of one of the university officials, almost bursting from his intensely white shirt and shorts, as he descended the steps of the students' hostel, his face flushed with some triumph at a meeting of the Senate, or with the anger consequent upon a too lengthy sub-committee to consider air-conditioning the lavatories in the Arts Building. 'I'm damned if they can keep me cooped up here. The Housing Committee have *got* to see reason!' I was likely to mutter to the silent figure of Ah Ting beside me. But such matters were outside his ken. He smiled only at my vehemence, not without a hint of that superiority of his, and, since luncheon was over and it was time for him to go off duty, proceeded to lock every door within reach and close every shutter with a tremendous series of bangs. Enclosed now by both wire and wood, I would have been grateful if some native had indeed thrown opium through the cracks, as they were said to do, and then inserted a crooked stick to explore the massed gardenias on my dressing-table in search of my wrist-watch. Although I was anxious to get some writing done, it was not easy to concentrate during the siesta. It was even harder to sleep. At precisely two-thirty the Tamil *kebuns* began to mow the grass outside and then to sweep the gutters with their stiff brooms. So I would doze in a cloud of prickly heat powder until once more I heard the sound of Ah Ting's keys.

These were his badge of office. He wore them in a ring attached to his belt and the first thing I saw in the morning, as he bent down to place the pot of tea by the bed, was the rust they had made on his brief shorts, into which his smooth pale thigh disappeared only a few inches from my face, flesh at once taut, plump and reticent, so that it possessed its own locked-up look, for it neither varied in surface tone like a white man's skin nor did it secrete, as do the gleaming skins of Tamils and Malays, a deeper intensity of purple or a series of shifting yellows and mauves. His keys jingled when he arrived and again when he left; he evidently removed the ring and swung it on his finger as he skirted the house; I liked to imagine that this music expressed in some way what he was really feeling, that it was freest in the evening when he was going back to his father and that in the morning it was not merely brusque but eager, slapdash, irritated, perhaps even angry, for if I badly wanted him to like me I also wanted to have somebody whom I could respect as an individual. Yet more and more the keys became symbolic of a routine. Against this routine the few interesting things Ah Ting did took on an appearance of eccentricity, of something abnormal. When he was dusting my books, for instance, shaking them to dislodge the gekkos which hid at their backs or squashing an occasional cockroach whose presence was betrayed by its long antennae, he developed the practice of reading out their titles in a sepulchral murmur. Until I stopped him he would do his cleaning in the early morning, when I was still in bed, and there was something intensely irritating about those furtive movements of his, like a series of delicate burglaries, especially when they were punctuated by an almost indefinable monotone of 'Chlistopha Ishawood . . . Chlistopha Ishawood . . .'. This habit extended itself to the conversations he overheard during the day, racy conversations with Midge about attempts to re-organize the Repertory Theatre or with Allan on the sexual possibilities offered by the Happy World amusement park. Arriving all self-confidence with drinks or tea, saluting everyone in turn with a painfully enunciated 'Hallo, Mem Midge. . . . Good evening, Sir', no matter how deep our conversation might be, he would retire a little later through the bathroom and into the courtyard (for that was the only way out) repeating in his Oxford accent a dreamy diminuendo of 'Bloody shame— bloody shame'.

One day, after he'd been with me for about a month, he cut his finger rather badly while opening a tin of mushroom soup in the kitchen. He came to show it to me, grinning broadly in derision of the blood but with his

round monkey-eyes open wide as though in recognition of
something with which he could not himself cope. It
seemed an excellent opportunity to be fatherly. He had
wrapped some tissue paper round his finger but large
drops of blood flecked the tiles as I led him into the bathroom. I ran the tap hard, held his hand under it and told
him to be brave. He looked down at the rosy swirl of
water, snorting with amusement in his best stoical manner, as though he was determined to show that this wasn't
really happening to him, but I couldn't help noticing how
frail he suddenly became, how small he was and how
flimsy his shirt looked as his neck became more and more
exposed, the collar falling away to reveal an amber cavern
through which his spine rose, austerely innocent and
defenceless. Then I got the iodine and a Band-Aid from
the drawer. I gripped his wrist, poured the iodine over his
finger and only just dared to look at his face, because I felt
that if he winced he might think it an affront to his pride,
even if he didn't resent my causing him pain. His body
jerked back at the impact, a movement that became coarse
because his laugh accompanied it, and as I attached the
bandage he had already escaped me, by being polite, by
smiling what looked more and more like a lack of confidence in my ministrations. 'Thank you, Sir. Don't wolly,
I fix.' Did ever a child have a more Italia Conti diction?
And, foolishly sensitive as I was, my feeling turned out to
be right for two hours later, when he came back from his
rest, my bandage had gone and my iodine had been scrupu-
lously washed away. He wore the traditional Chinese
remedy: the striking part of a matchbox affixed to the cut.

Then again this routine of his, emphasizing only the
boredom or frustration of day after day which seemed to
present me with nothing more exciting than a glass of
lukewarm lemonade into which I tried as monotonously
to introduce a stick of glamour and excitement, was never
directed at what I really wanted done. Ah Ting never did
my shopping, never took the initiative over the planning

of a single meal. I might be still twenty yards from the house, dripping with sweat, my arms filled with parcels, when he approached me with 'What for dinner, Sir?', his face all nagging blankness. And often I would come home to find he was out at his *makan*, that I had forgotten my own keys and that every door was locked. Even if I climbed over the courtyard wall I still would not be able to get into my room. Then it was that I cursed the jingling of those self-righteous boyish keys. The apparent conceit in his unimaginativeness was what I resented most.

I remember the first time I asked him to make me an omelette. It looked like a volume of Elizabeth Barrett Browning's poems bound in brown vellum. The second omelette I decided to supervise personally. When I went into the kitchen Ah Ting was well on with the beating of the eggs, so much so that a yellow fluid already congealed in the bowl. I had a vision of Edwardian editions of the *Rubaiyat* or the *Indian Love Lyrics*, the *Aphorisms of Marcus Aurelius, Saint Thomas à Kempis* . . . something really liturgical and limp. So I threw away the mess as dramatically as I could and proceeded to make the omelette myself. Ah Ting managed to look both contemptuous and attentive; he gave his little snort, he brightly and smilingly watched. I felt heavy with responsibility, although I knew I must toss off the omelette as lightly as though it were an epigram. A mere whisk of the eggs, a moment of gaiety in the pan, a deft and debonair gesture with the spatula. And for once I was lucky. My cooking was a success. Perhaps this gave me the confidence that I needed for our first serious quarrel, which occurred when Ah Ting had been with me for just under three months. It all began with his trying to bully me over the time I intended to have dinner, prompted I couldn't help thinking by his desire to get home as soon as possible.

'What for dinner, Sir?' he began, and I should so like to be called *tuan*.

'Oh, I don't know. There's that ham isn't there?—the

Australian ham in the big round tin. We might as well
have that.' Even as I answered I knew that I was introducing the wrong sort of thing, for Ah Ting was quite
incapable of understanding any mumbling, uncertainty or
tentativeness while my continual, usually unconscious, use
of the word *we* did not absorb him into mutual domesticity.

'All or half, Sir? And how many potatoes? And . . .'
his voice slowed down, as though he realized how much I
hated this kind of questioning but was nevertheless powerless in its grip, 'do you want some marrow?'

'By all means let's have some marrow,' I replied with
false heartiness. 'As for the potatoes, why not cook about
six?' But no sooner had I said this than the ghost of a smile
lit up his face.

'Please, Sir, there are no potatoes.'

'Damn it, you've just asked me how many I wanted—
you can't tell me there are none now!'

'I just remember. I go fetch chips from canteen. . . .'

'Alright, but later. It's too early yet.' This seemed to
baffle him. He paused, drew a deep breath and then asked
me in his chilliest tones and with each syllable carefully
separated from the next—

'What time you want dinner, Sir? Seven?'

'No, not seven. Seven's far too early.' To which, as I
always ultimately do, I found myself appending a justifi-
catory explanation. 'I am going out first. Get it ready for
eight.' I felt that my tone declared the matter to be
decisively closed. The chair creaked with my tiredness. I
stretched out my legs (in their ridiculous shorts) and was
wondering whether to shut my eyes, or sigh, when something in my lumbering sprawling posture caricatured
itself so much, became so lost and bleak, that it pulled me
up again. I was 'dressed for games'. So was he. We should
go off to the locker room and change. Or run off somewhere, and shout at each other, and kick a ball. At least I
should be managerial and authoritative like a prefect with
his fag. So I looked up and said as tauntingly as I could,

'After all you're lucky. Mrs. ——— tells me that nobody around here eats before eight-thirty or even nine.' At that the brightness in his eyes sharpened, the slick curve of his hair almost gave a snap, and I expected to see an electric spark crackle from the metal fastener of his belt. But he said nothing.

Instead, as I sank back again, he walked across to the switch and turned off the fan. It moved slower and slower through the twenty-three circles it takes to stop when running at normal speed. Boredom had often counted them, as it had counted the forty-six books in the top shelf and the eighteen most un-Tudor beams. But why did Ah Ting do this? Was it simply one of his practicalities, like the business with the shutters and the keys? Or could it be that he wanted to force me to get up from my chair and go wherever I intended as quickly as possible? I even suspected him of some secret perversity, for he walked out with an additional alertness, and glanced back once in a mocking way. He didn't trail, as he usually did, especially when disappointed and bored. Nor did he march. And I remembered how, at a time when Allan was buying clockwork peacocks and grasshoppers, I had myself brought back in quick succession a toy rather like a merry-go-round in which pink celluloid ladies rotated, dancing, and a pair of magnetic dogs. Ah Ting had placed one of these dogs on the metal wire supporting the lady so that, as the wire jumped up and down, the dog pushed rhythmically under the dancer's skirt. He had been much amused by this obscene gesture.

Now I sat exhausted, conscious of the absence of gin and vermouth for it was the end of the month and the pile of red Malayan ten-dollar bills which I kept hidden at the back of the radio had dwindled almost to nothing, watching the pattern of the blue and white sarong on the wall. Through the shutters the jacaranda trees seemed made of paper for a window in Selfridges or Harrods. The evening air was empty, unpossessed by its birds. A large car was

suddenly brisk on the gravel: the sound could have been
far away, a distant explosion or disaster, or very close, very
dry, the cracking of a biscuit. It didn't matter. Vaguely I
knew that a prominent dentist had come home next door.

'You said you were going out. You not going out. Why
you say dinner not at seven?'

Ah Ting again.

'For the simple reason that I don't wish to eat until
eight.'

A pause. Ah Ting drifted across the room, moved a
volume of Herbert's poetry on top of the Grierson antho-
logy, stood at the window, came over to the coffee table
and picked up an empty packet of cigarettes. I closed my
eyes once more.

'Please, Sir. Will you give me an English lesson, Sir?'

It was this, of course, which was particularly exasperating. In the midst of all one's irritation, the sudden
suggested intimacy over the *Malayan Reader*, Book II:
positively 'clustered heads in the lamplight' as a more
reasonable father and son relationship was momentarily
introduced only to be destroyed at once by Ah Ting's
refusal to be taught.

'No, Ah Ting. I'm not going to give you a lesson tonight. I told you I'm going out.'

'But you haven't changed.'

'I'm going out unchanged.'

It seemed necessary to make a move immediately. I
went first into the garden but turned towards the back
because the bearded dentist was now dandling his baby
amongst the frangipani trees to the accompaniment of a
series of uninhibited guffaws and chuckles and he and
I were supposed not to be on speaking terms. Knowing
the local habit of addressing sarcastic memoranda to one's
colleagues, I had recently sent him quite an innocent
letter about his hens. He had not replied. I was also
anxious to show Ah Ting that I had no intention of being
hurried. I noticed how enormously the purple bougain-

villea had grown and blossomed. The sky was just dark
enough to make the thin dull flowers luminous. I walked
to the edge of the terrace and looked at the sweep of the
small valley, letting the bougainvillea brush me with its
damp clear petals, arching itself into a bower where only
a few weeks ago the *amah's* henhouse stood—for here,
where my co-tenants were concerned, I *had* scored a
victory. Feeling its sharp thorns, I followed the nearest
dangling and lounging branch up until it edged the sky,
casuarinas intervened, and the new moon lay tilted:
metallic, beautiful, portentous. Shouldn't Ah Ting be
made to realize that his own people had once been prepared to postpone dinner while they wandered through
the almond blossom, with poems on their lips? When I
looked back, I thought I could catch a glimmer of white
behind the stone trellis beyond the fig tree.

I found Allan in his house next door. He listened sym-
pathetically as I gave him a detailed analysis of Ah Ting's
shortcomings. His own tussle with the East was far more
relaxed and delicate than mine; although he also seemed
to be playing a role, it was a comedy one which he seemed
to perform exclusively for his own amusement. He was
the whimsical bachelor who did most of the conventional
things but with an inward titter which gently devalued
them, a private lyricism which now and then placed them
in a new light. Thus as I envied his display of drinks,
including both the expected Benedictine and a flask of
Japanese brandy, the evening wind began to tinkle in an
enormous mobile he had hung from the ceiling. Nor was
this silvery music the only sound. One of my own records
began to fill the air and he turned to me with a wry smile:
'I see what you mean. Ah Ting is singularly unrepentant.
Or perhaps he has a passion for Lena Horne.' But this
wasn't all. When I got back I saw, to my astonishment,
that Ah Ting had placed the alarm clock on the table to
remind me of my lateness. Even I could not avoid a show-
down after this. Although intensely nervous, I called Ah

Ting in, made him sit down in a chair facing me and gave him a real lecture. Threatened with instant dismissal, he burst into tears. This, of course, was the last thing that I had expected. He wasn't a monster after all, he was still a child. He couldn't have done a more psychologically appropriate thing.

In the weeks that followed Ah Ting was somewhat more subdued, so that even the sound of his keys seemed less obtrusive, but there was still one thing which showed up the inadequacy of our relationship, and that was the evening English lesson. How often did I list my griev-ances! No sooner had I begun to explain the meaning, context or history of a word than Ah Ting firmly lost interest. He wanted words in his vocabulary book and that was all. If I stated that *chalk*, for instance, was a kind of rock, and a colour, as well as something used in the class-room, he would direct his smiling button eyes upon me, utter his peculiar little snort, and say 'Please put down in my book, Sir.'

'But don't you think you ought to know what the word means?'

'You put in my book, Sir. I learn.'

'That's just the point. You don't learn. What do you know about any of these?' And I restlessly thumbed through his book, disconcerted at some of the definitions I had myself put there on previous, maybe slightly tipsy, occasions. *Angel*, I read, was 'a sort of holy bird which helps people', finally crossed out in favour of the weak substitution, *spirit*. Or *foxhunting* which I found I had described as 'game on horses chasing small animal with pointed face (very sad because finally killed)', although here too the parenthesis had been deleted in favour of 'men helped by dogs (hounds)'. For Ah Ting had the gift of strangling my imagination. Little blurts towards tenderness or humour lay abandoned, and half obliterated, on the page. 'Please, Sir, we go on now, Sir,' Ah Ting broke in, with a whiff of onion breath, as I watched both white cliffs and clowns' faces dwindle away behind the hard fact that *chalk* is 'a white stick you write with'.

Furthermore we frequently found ourselves at cross-purposes over Malay words and place-names which I couldn't reasonably be expected to know. Where is *Tinggi-Tinggi-Palat*? I was asked: what is the meaning of *sungei* or *kramat*?

'But these are Malay words—and you speak good Malay. Surely you know them already?'

'I not know.'

'I've heard you speaking Malay to lots of people.'

'I speak a little Malay, Sir, but not *sungei* or *kramat* or *Tinggi-Tinggi*' Ah Ting replied with slow distinctness, half-humorous, half-wooden. *Tinggi-Tinggi* sounded funny and he smiled when I did.

'You certainly laughed hard enough when the Eurasian boy was here, teaching me the funny words.' For some time ago I had had a brief lesson in the naughtier aspects of a naughty language.

'I not remember' was the answer, quite wooden now, and with that additional splutter Ah Ting used when he was determined to be stupid, or righteous, or both.

'Well, you can ask Mr. Webb.' For I was, I fear, only the third, and perhaps the least important, of Ah Ting's father-images. The Registrar gave him his first job and he now lived with his father in Mr. Webb's house. His father was Mr. Webb's Boy.

And then, again, the book itself had a rather prim liberalism which couldn't be farther from Ah Ting's Hailam mentality. Most people described the products of that out of the way island as boorish and stupid (they have also a mild reputation for homosexuality). I don't think Ah Ting was fundamentally dense but he had little affinity with the *Reader's* Malayanism: mutual adventures of a Chinese (Beng), a Malay (Ahmad) and sometimes an Indian (Chandra) had no appeal for him and he gained nothing so far as I could see from the respectfully modern handling of religion. He knew nothing of religion (hence my attempts to explain what an angel was) and he had no interest in Malays, except to look down on them. My Indian students, constant visitors to the house like Shakuntala and Ramachandran, were clearly objects of amused contempt. Rama was never acceded a Mister; he was 'the Indian' or just 'Rama'.

I had frequently tried to get him away from the book altogether. One or two pages of his vocabulary were given up to a series of words associated with his job; they led, in fact, to a detailed and wildly ambitious schedule of instructions as to how to valet me when I was asked out to dinner. There was even (from very long ago) a paragraph or two on wines and liquors, which was designed as a sort of butler's guide. . . . But he always dragged me back to the lesson as he saw it: his reading two or three paragraphs of the story aloud, in his queer precise diction, with that extraordinary Oxford accent of his, followed by words and vocabulary. Chairs were drawn up to the slickly varnished table with a squeak, the toc-toc bird popped its bottles of mirthless champagne in the darkness, a gekko chirped overhead, and Ah Ting began:

'Whan the rivah wors flooded, Beng and Ahmad luved to pley neah the . . .? . . . whoof? . . . Please, Sir, what is woof, Sir?'

'Wharf. A piece of wood going out into the water for boats to tie up against. No, not a piece of wood. A wooden platform.'

'What means pletfarm, Sir?'

So it went on, a thread of monotony across the days, more intense than the slap of sandals, the rattle of keys, the bare leg projected to open a door already ajar, the bare foot nuzzling a mat into alignment; at once more and less personal than the long silences at the windows when we both seemed to be waiting for something, life to begin, my diary to form itself into a book, my book not so to lose touch with reality that it became entirely private and byzantine, a sort of prose furniture to emptiness, a labyrinth in a vacuum. He locked me in and I wrote; he locked me out and I fumbled at bars and people. Sometimes I caught him reading a page that I had left in the typewriter. Inevitably, he snorted.

One morning I couldn't find him anywhere. He wasn't in the kitchen. His vocabulary exercise book lay spread on the table, though, and he had evidently just cut a photograph of his late employer from the *Straits Times*, for the Registrar stared up at me, with a sort of bonny scowl, from the frame Ah Ting's pencil had drawn for him. The room was bare and neat, with the legs of everything immersed in cigarette tins filled with cooking oil, because of the ants. Had he not also tied bandages soaked in oil round the legs of the dining-table? Bills were draped on nails, paper-bags carefully piled together, and my underwear, scrubbed and darned, hung up to dry. Some of my old manifestos still taunted me from the walls, where I had hammered them late at night, (Brush this, clean that, hang the heavy European clothes in the sun twice a week) but the days of real optimism (alternations in Malay, Indian and Chinese food) were long past. Where could he be?

It was then that I heard a faint sound, familiar and reassuring although I could not place it at first; a sound of sleepiness and complacency, as capable, it would appear, of threading memories together as is the drone of a bee, which will dissolve the whole of Time into one eternal summer's day. What was it and where did it come from? I gently opened the window an inch or two and there sat Ah Ting upon a kitchen chair by the dustbins while an elderly Chinese barber, whose bicycle rested against the wall, snipped his glossy cocksure cap. But that wasn't all. Thinking it might be friendly to join them, if only for a moment, I went to the courtyard door. I couldn't open it. So scrupulous was Ah Ting's routine, so deep-seated his desire to protect me and my belongings, that he had locked himself out.

CHAPTER 2

Down Orchard Road

WHEN Ah Ting presented me with one of his enormous shopping lists, written laboriously in his big round hand, it was to Orchard Road that I had to go, walking a mile to the nearest bus stop through the mid-morning heat. And when at night he saw me put on a clean shirt, much too starched, and a pair of thick but comparatively civilized black trousers, and asked me in quick succession, 'Have you got your keys, Sir?' and, 'Have you put your identity-card in your pocket?' it was still Orchard Road which funnelled me into the city, whether I took a taxi or not. The great Bukit-Timah Road was actually nearer, to be reached by duckboard across our marshy playing-fields and over the monsoon drain, but this broad highway, with a canal running down its centre, was somehow too exposed, speedy and indiscreet; it was all right late at night, in a taxi whose price you had bargained about, but at the beginning of anything it put too much perspective about your way of life, seemingly involving you in the whole geography of Malaya to which it led across the Straits of Johore, and anyway it plunged you in a part of town you needed to reach indirectly, after a few drinks, for it entered the Arab quarter by the Rex Cinema and the stench of the Rochore Canal lay all about it.

To go down-town by Bukit-Timah was to see the statistical pattern instead of the bright particular, to find experience already exhausted and anatomized. But Orchard Road starts by being desultory amongst nursery-gardens, ends in the green beginnings of the ceremoniously governmental part of town, and is itself approached obliquely through two sorts of steaming foliage. It is a

hybrid street, half European and half Chinese. Its shops
are arcaded and their yellow or blue stucco throbs with
light. Heat polishes the new buildings and depresses the
old, whose faces sag behind skimpy shrubs until they
resemble old whores, dabbing their wrinkles with tissue
paper stained oleander-pink and bougainvillea-mauve. At
its end is Singapore's one skyscraper, the Cathay Building,
which is also a cinema and advertises the current film in
electric lights on its roof, with an advertisement for brandy
on the reverse side. But to get to Orchard Road in those
days before I acquired car or motor-bicycle, I had either
to call up a taxi, and the best ones came curiously enough
from G.H.Q., or to walk through the Botanical Gardens
or down the suburban decorum of Nassim Road. Having
lectured at eight and given a tutorial at nine, the 'Botanics'
seemed too lush. It was hardly decent to plod through
them, ignoring the monkeys. Besides, Communist hooli-
gans were said to hang out there and nothing, certainly,
could have been more appropriate to the ambiguous atmosphere of Singapore than the embarrassment of meeting some impeccably clad but fanatic schoolboy, with
quite possibly a bottle of acid in his carefully manicured
hand, amongst the orchids and cannon-ball trees.

Usually I walked down Nassim Road, from one patch
of shadow to the next, with the clotted but vacant foliage
of the business-executives' estates hanging motionless
above, conscious of the patches because one night I had
just missed stepping on a black cobra in the middle of one.
It was a road for big American cars, which never offered
you a lift. To walk on it felt ghostly and when you passed
a native, as you occasionally did, you noticed that he
looked even more irrelevant. It was difficult to believe
that this was his country. You knew you were getting near
the bus stop when you came on the villa of Aw Boon Haw,
the Tiger Balm king. Now old and benignly philan-
thropic, Aw Boon Haw represented the cream of those
towkays who had risen in legendary ways from the poorest

of beginnings. His Tiger Balm came in small round tins and was reputably specific for a vast range of maladies. It was only natural that the tiger should form one of the decorative motifs of his villa, woven into the wrought iron of its exclamatory fence, reappearing in plaques let into the façade, and climactically reproduced in painted concrete upon the lawn, where it tyrannized over a variety of other animals. Relief at arriving at the end of one's walk was tempered by visual unease. It was surely the sharpest, hottest, scratchiest of villas; it possessed no shade trees and far too much gravel. It barked at you like a side-show at a circus. It wanted you to go in. When I did so I found a splendid but far too cluttered collection of jade, some of the usual oleographs, not I think of the grand parents of Aw Boon Haw but of the tycoon himself and of his brother, for they formed their own mythology, a good deal of gloomy interior decoration and in lonely (and hence all the more brilliant) isolation on a central table a copy of an American comic called *Pep*.

Comparatively few Europeans trusted themselves to a bus, although it was the only economic means of transport for a service-man and his wife (except late at night when the soldier could knock his taxi-driver out and escape into camp before the man recovered), and you couldn't help feeling that merely to step into one was socially daring, the first faint step towards going native. I never saw a senior official in one during the whole period of my stay. Snobbery had, I am sure, more to do with this than the element of danger although it is quite true that the Communists burned a bus from time to time, first ushering the passengers out and then pouring petrol over the seats, and during the riots a number of people had been trapped in some crowded interior. One acquaintance of mine had been separated from his wife and child, jostled to the edge of the Rochore Canal and beaten until he fell across the parapet. Lying there he was still conscious enough to hear the thud of the *chungkol* handle as it narrowly missed his head. Luckily the wood broke before the *coup de grâce* was delivered and something drew the crowd away—a final kick just not succeeding in tipping him into the water. But the Communists were not trying to murder us yet. After the first few rides I no longer looked for a hand-grenade in somebody's pocket, if such indeed would be the place for concealing one, and a peculiarly shaped parcel or basket no longer had me edging away. For a bus was, in fact, the liveliest and friendliest of places, with a picnic-party-going atmosphere all its own, where bright clothes and bare arms yielded gratefully to the coolness of move-ment and a sudden lurch sent everyone swaying and joking; nothing could have been a better introduction to popular life. In the bus, you learned that special combina-tion of light-heartedness, dignity and *laisser-aller* which characterizes the people of Singapore, and which is per-haps due to the variety of checks and balances provided by its different races, for a grave Chinese schoolboy might be sitting next to two willowy Tamil clerks, the reasonable-ness and trustworthiness of his unwavering gaze con-trasting with their bright-eyed more spiritual effervescence, while farther down the aisle a Malay girl concentrated, for all the brilliance of her costume, an earthier and more secretive light. And, even though you knew that the gay young conductor was busy fiddling his fares, how beauti-fully he smiled at the *orang-puteh* who had joined his musical comedy crew!

The Cold Storage, where I did much of my shopping, although I should have liked to be more adventurous, stood white and antiseptic beside the huge market, where one could at least go for vegetables and fruit. Two police-men patrolled in front of it, stocky apathetic little Malays who always cupped the muzzles of their rifles in their small brown hands, perhaps realizing how ineffective such weapons would be in a crowd and yet how necessary it was to clutch them and so prevent some Communist bearing them away into the jungle. These police, who could also

be found in great numbers at the Hongkong-Shanghai
Bank a little further down the street, emphasized the
importance, if not indeed the positive sanctity, of the Cold
Storage; it was more than a shop, more than the smart
little businesses which occupied its arcade upstairs, more
than the restaurant and the lounge—it was Europe itself
(plentifully supplied by air from Australia) and yet it had
a pinched, discreet, suburban look which suggested to me
that, unlike the big stores and gloomy cafés of Raffles
Place, it was specially designed for the post-war colonials,
the newly genteel. I used often to compare the more
generous and yet shabby air of the G.H. Café downtown,
where cosmopolitan businessmen talked about racing and
the price of rubber, with the nervous brightness of morning coffee in the Cold Storage.

At her desk a lady manageress would wait for her
gossips to arrive, staring down at the magenta varnish on
her nails and patting occasionally a frizzy permanent. As
soon as a likely-looking group of ladies appeared at one of
the tables near her, she leant across.

'Rather hotter today, isn't it? A nice bit of breeze
earlier this morning though.'

In a few moments she would be invited to join them.
She gestured to a smart Chinese assistant to take her place
and permitted herself a cigarette. Across the chink of ice
in glasses, the death-rattle of lemonade sucked up straws
into the mouths of violently blonde children, the muted
faintly ironic tones of the Chinese waiters, I used to catch
snatches of the ensuing conversation—a conversation
without a single Eastern note.

But there were plenty of these if I continued in the bus
as it swept alternately by shops and garages. The shops
were so liberally decorated with good luck *chops* that you
seemed to wander in and out of a giant alphabet; you
approached them carefully over bridges which covered the
monsoon drain, up and down steps, skirting things drying
on sheets and things laid out in baskets, pushing through

bevies of half-naked children and bicycles and trailing bits of sacking, until you faced some complicated cavern of sight and smell, hung with galleries of dried and twisted fish in grey-browns and ashy purples or heavy with sacks brimming with melon seeds or runtish bits of ginger. A whole family in pyjamas might preside over some recess full of abacus frames or weighing rods exquisitely marked in brass, surrounding these precision instruments with an air of family cosiness and sweetness, emphasized by the almost too intimate appearance of a smile when it is full of gold teeth, and by soft blurred clothes which looked as though they had just got out of bed; a single fat Chinese, wearing only a pair of floppy sleeping pants, stood ready to offer you a cigarette and a bottle of orangeade when you made your order at his grocery, while retaining his aid of expert and slightly naughty bachelorhood; but what was most striking, perhaps, was the great number of youths who were not so much attendants of their stalls as arrogant and gracefully self-sufficient emanations of them, some lying asleep on sacks, some combing their long black hair over a pile of gasping light blue fish, others staring dreamily ahead as they performed those gestures which were a kind of routine, kicking their sandals off, rubbing one foot against the other, pulling their singlets up and rolling them to cool stomach and diaphragm. Catching sight of them only briefly from the bus, I could contrast their ubiquitous but undemonstrative nudity, in which sex seemed to take on a new chiller more fish-like existence, all floating hair and slippery skin, with the even more uniform costumes of the boys and young men around me —each white shirt had a fountain pen clamped between its buttons, each wrist wore a stainless steel watchband, each pair of trousers was of the same grey or blue cotton, with accentuated waist and widely ballooned hips.

At the end of the journey it was always with a gratefulness for the sea, and for the big buildings and wide spaces facing it, that I got off. Standing on Collyer Quay, before going off to shop in Change Alley or to wander through Chinatown, I watched the water flapping against the stone embankment. Farther out a sampan bounced, a gold wavy line of reflection stroking its side. In the distance there was the blue shape of somewhere in Indonesia. Often I would end whatever I had to do by paying a visit to the Maxwell Road market. Here the solitary adventures of my morning, extended into all the variegated confusions of China Street, the platters of purple rice, the ceremonial fish and lanterns, the boy suddenly come upon gently but inexplicably rocking two live ducks in a bath of water, finally came to rest on a number of large bowls in which sea-horses were kept. Speckled orange and black, these strange creatures could make anyone feel cool and relaxed. By scarcely perceptible gradations they interlocked their tails, rising and falling together in a twilight of the profoundest sympathy.

Sympathy was, I suppose, one of the things I was after and now that Ah Ting had lost his first promise, and the European side of campus life looked like dwindling in my distorting-glass, I was anxious for new contacts.

It so happened that the first of these occurred when I had been on one of my expeditions down Orchard Road and was taking a rest in a most un-European way by sitting on the grass outside the British Council Building and hence, I suppose, letting down the team quite considerably. A sports car careered by with two tilted profiles, two scarves fluttering; a good-looking woman turned round; the car swerved into the curb and stopped; a tall thickly-built man with a mop of dark hair and an engagingly clumsy manner jumped out and came towards me. Immediately I put him down as someone pretty important. If you behaved as though Singapore were the South of France, you were bound to be high in the official scale, and this probably meant that you had other qualities. I imagined that he was attached to the Commissioner General's office.

He told me he had guessed who I was, said he had long
wanted to meet me and introduced himself as Rudolph
Greene. His wife joined us. She was even prettier than I
had imagined but had perhaps lost something by being no
longer a profile in motion. Her copper hair was drawn
back smoothly from an oval face, whose skin had a quite
remarkable pallor; her eyes were grey-green and set rather
far apart. She was small, though, and she held herself with
a good deal of tensed energy, which gave her a little girl
sexiness, a bit gamine.

It soon transpired that we had mutual friends in
London and that the Greenes were familiar with all my
Bloomsbury pubs. We drove off to Princes for drinks.
This was one of the better places, at the upper end of
Orchard Road. At night it emitted a very genteel blonde
glow (candle-light and fair hair, very discreetly shaded,
very softly and expertly waved) from its wide expanse
along the road. It had highly coloured steins with pewter
lids in a panelled and red leather bar; spider orchids
dotted the entrance to the dance floor; beyond lay a prosperously enervated twilight suggestive of stockbrokers'
bedrooms—'Let's just have the one lamp on, darling, so
that we can see each other a weeny bit:' very pink feet
kicking away feathery mules, bodies smelling of bath-
salts. At noon, though, the bar was manly; people in
navy-blue blazers laughed too loud; the air-conditioning
was as dense as a cold shower.

As we talked over our long drinks I found that my first
guess had been wrong. Greene *was* attached to the Singapore Government but in some vague advisory way; he was
an agricultural expert, with literary interests, and didn't
seem too clear about what he was expected to do, except
that it was 'frightfully dull and worthy'. Dullness seemed,
in fact, the principal worry of both of them and yet, as their
argument continued in its vivid slangy way, I got the
impression that they were refugees from bohemianism
who really wanted respectability, provided it were suffi-

ciently lucrative and highbrow. They were very highbrow indeed. Although they brightly made fun of things, this didn't mask an underlying desire to get on and make the right connections. I had a sinking feeling when I wondered if they thought I filled the bill. And it wasn't exactly flattering to be included so soon in their personal strategy. Of course, they admitted, ambition was a bore, only to be persisted in as a means of exploring the East in which they both professed a 'passionate' interest: 'a search for values' was the way Rudolph put it. Mrs. Greene was still beautiful in repose but she did everything to hide this. She narrowed her eyes and made calculations with a predatory air; she pouted and sulked when I disagreed with her, she looked up into her husband's face with a Pollyanna-ish smile. (She was called Polly.) She suddenly took out a long black cigarette holder, lit a cigarette, puffed it voluptuously, and said in that mixture of defiance, sentimentality and inner unease I was to hear so often in Singapore:

'Of course, I'm an engine-driver's daughter. Grew up in the Yards. Really and truly. The family's been Labour for generations.'

'Polly and I met at Oxford. She has a strong Trades' Union background.'

'And Rudi's the son of a Bish! All roly-poly and Liberal, but a darn good poet and I love him.'

It is difficult to explain why Polly's remark jolted me into a realization that I was beginning to be disappointed with the Greenes. There was something about their marriage which seemed wrong; at times I felt I was expected to flirt with both of them independently. But, beyond this, I suppose that romantics are likely to be snobs—not snobbish about being of working-class origin but snobbish when this is used for furthering some quite different aim. In any case, I had lived in England so briefly since before the war that I was continually surprised by social facts and manoeuvres of this kind. Yet, although our meeting had lost some of its initial glamour, I certainly wanted to know more about the Greenes. This was easily accomplished. As I told Ah Ting with some pride on my return, I was invited to dine with them two days later. It was my first dinner party outside the university circle.

They drove me out to the Gap where they had half of a house on a hill overlooking industrial developments, coconut palms, red earth, all the tumbled scruffiness of the West coast where much jungle has been cleared, often only to result in erosion. It was a house on pillars, with vast open spaces underneath it, and a tired air of space not used and architectural domination: yards of galleries, rows of Shanghai doors, but everything somehow shabby and a yawn.

'I say, yes, you could do something with this space underneath, couldn't you? Hang Chinese lanterns or something?' Polly was enthusiastic without conviction.

'It's certainly got immense possibilities' I said when we arrived upstairs (my romanticism appreciating the shadowy setting: dark figures gliding along galleries, a place for monkeys, another that could be dense with plants) but what I really saw was yellowing walls, an obvious Javanese batik of long-nosed figures, one of those slick over-polished Balinese sculptures in wood and, under the windows, a little menagerie of real cosinesses in china and pottery.

'I'm fond of these,' she said and then, with a theatrical brightness (like putting on a dirndl or gipsy earrings), 'Shall I play some of the Britten settings to Donne? I do so like it when people want to hear them.'

There was a gramophone camping out in the corner but I first asked rather wickedly, with my eyes on the pottery, 'Do you find that you both have the same tastes?'

'Oh Rudi and I usually like the same things . . . very much so really.'

He agreed as though this were a mathematical proposition, with an intensity that forced its way past his soft almost feminine face, and I noticed how frequently this happened, how frequently he dealt with things his wife said as though they were problems that must be fiercely grasped, while another part of him remained easy going and passive. It was this that shook his head with un-natural vehemence, twisted his body into strange un-relaxed shapes and pummelled his public schoolboy's vocabulary, which was full of *chaps* and *damn-its* until it elongated itself into dry genteel vowels. 'He's quite a nice *guy* but as for his politics I couldn't really s-a-a-ay. . . .'

Dinner was, I gathered, an adventure in which I was expected rather breathlessly to share, not quite as a prin-cipal because it obviously reflected their marriage with its ambitions (a damn good dinner, *what?*) and its guilts (but interesting, out of the way, not pompous re-a-lly . . .?). I thought of Greenwich Village, with its flasks of chianti and 'spaghetti done in a new way'. Or Soho.

The soup was borscht and they declared it a failure the moment it arrived. It was red and hot. Although I liked it, I felt I had to commiserate with them. Then I said:

'Funnily enough, the last time I had borscht was years ago in New York. There's a place near Carnegie Hall called the Russian Tearoom. . . .'

'I should love to go to America,' cut in Polly Greene, 'but not for more than a visit. I imagine it's pretty stifling culturally. All the artists in California are crazy and the ones in New York are mostly Jews. Not that I'm in the least anti-Jewish but it would be a limitation. Of course the pace must be exciting and I should adore the negroes—only I suppose they would fill me with the most ghastly guilt.'

I said something about New York and Greene chipped in with the statement that it wasn't America. He began to develop a theory of social tensions, putting his elbows on the table and cupping his chin in his fists.

'Your American', he said 'is a chap with a split mind, re-e-ally. He wants to have his cake and eat it. His social dynamic drives him towards ever increasing collectivization but he retains the myth of the free individual. Americanism is an attempt to resolve the tension between the individual and society by . . . er . . . creating a society of individuals. The true individuals have to be regarded as rebels and purged. America is a country where economics are called ·n to do the job of ethics and hence the society of individuals is never more than a re-assuring fiction.'

'Stomach ulcers', I said heavily, 'as the agenbite of inwit.'

At which Greene took his elbows off the table and made a noise with his spoon in the empty plate of soup.

'I do love an epigram,' Polly said jauntily. 'It's such a shame that the art of conversation. . . .'

Greene, who had evidently been thinking, broke in before she could finish, 'As a matter of fact, Polly, it might be just the place for you. You have a kind of flair for the fleshpots, you know you do. I suppose it's the puritan in me that can't quite stomach all that materialism.'

'Don't be a beast,' Polly answered him, halfway between flirt and fairy-child, 'What would I do with a lot of dyspeptic old men and callow Adonises?'

'I'm not so sure about the Adonises,' he mumbled in sudden gloom.

I was staring at a dish in the centre of the table with some embarrassment. Noticing my interest she turned to me. 'Yes, we're especially fond of that bowl. It has a lovely rhythm, don't you think?'

'As a matter of fact, I rather prefer the soup plates,' I said.

'Oh but they're so dull. Rudi gave me the bowl for my birthday.'

After all this one could hardly be expected to greet the meat course with equanimity. I felt I had to help it on, give it a moral push.

'I don't know whether you'll like it,' said Mrs. Greene, 'but it isn't, actually, a complete step in the dark—I mean we've tried it before.'

'We're not exactly inflicting it on you. You're not our

guinea-pig,' her husband added, looking boyishly at a large brown casserole.

'The borscht was . . .'

'Yes, I must confess the borscht wasn't quite fair. . . .'

'But I thought it very nice,' I replied.

Each new emphasis on culinary experiment only established more firmly our status as amateurs pleasantly excited by the prospect of disaster. The dish came from a beautifully produced little book on Mediterranean cooking published by Lehmann with illustrations by John Minton. It consisted of a powerful number of ingredients: one kind of meat enfolding another and spices galore. I thought it delicious. Lichees and ginger followed.

And afterwards we drank chrysanthemum tea and they showed me how they made Chinese characters (they were learning Mandarin) with ink and brush. We talked of secret societies, death houses, wayangs, and I soon realized that Polly Greene was a keen amateur anthropologist. Her enthusiasms were a trifle angry and had the effect of increasing the emptiness of their barn-like sitting room. 'You must see it, it's a typical *kampong* . . .' she would say, and I felt myself turning uncomfortably away, partly no doubt because I dislike knowing less than anybody else. I wondered if she shared with me a contradictory attitude to being in the know, if she was glad of it and at the same time felt it to be embarrassing, because it separated her from other people. Or perhaps she wasn't in the know at all?

They talked a good deal about a Jewish sociologist and his wife who had recently left the colony. I gathered that there had been something the matter with them and asked what it was.

'Nothing really,' Polly exclaimed, 'except that they didn't keep in well with Government. Rather independent and eccentric, you know. Didn't write their names in the book at Government House or Bukit Serene and spent a lot of time living in the local kampongs. Not that I blame them. We'd probably do the same if we were on our own.'

'Do you mean to say people resent one's living with the natives?'

'It's the colonial mi-n-d,' drawled Greene in return. 'I don't think they'd bother in the least if you were living in kampongs up-country but close to Singapore might seem a bit like mixing business with pleasure.'

'As though you actually enjoyed it?'

'Stupidly snobby of them, of course,' Polly broke in. 'Still it's all part of the pattern here.'

'Oddly enough,' Greene continued, sipping chrysanthemum tea reflectively 'you could get away with a . . . with a purely sexual interest, damn it, easier than you could a cultural one. Paternalism involved Malay mistresses, if only to learn the language. You know, the sleeping dictionary idea. Now that we're more progressive, we tend to marry, if anything, and that restricts us to the better class Chinese.'

'M. has a Malay. . . .,' Polly began excitedly but her husband looked aggrieved and cut her short.

'Dash it, darling, that was told us in strict confidence and anyway it's probably untrue.'

'I know it was told us in confidence but I saw it with my own eyes. That night we went back with him for drinks, his *amah* opened the door for us in a sort of nightdress—ever so cosy and domestic. Not that I blame him. They're sort of savage and sophisticated both at once, madly beddable. Much more so than the Chinese though I do say it myself.'

'I agree,' I said. 'I'm not going to marry a skeleton in a cheongsam.'

But this wasn't an occasion from which I had to tear myself away. I felt that it was suddenly, even overpoweringly, time to go. Rudolph drove me back through a mixture of jungle and suburb, mumbling enigmatically, as though he stood on the brink of a great confession. I welcomed the cool night air and experimented with a number of silences, which I tried to make complacently normal, puffing my cigarette to myself, because I felt a great need for apartness. I thought of them together in that great galleried house, hounding each other, clashing their ragged edges. And the confession never came.

I didn't see them for some weeks, as they were both called away to Malacca which prevented my asking them back, but there were later occasions when they were friendly, at parties or in the Cold Storage. I think they vaguely respected me as someone who did not share their social ambitions and to whom they could reveal their conspiratorial plans. Once when Polly was being particularly uninhibited on a divan-bed at a party, while Rudi read Auden in a corner, trying his best to be modern but looking intensely miserable, she gave me a sudden wink. Later I heard a rumour that they were thinking of adopting a Cantonese baby. Once, when the new Governor had just arrived, I met Polly coming out of the Marie-Rose dress shop. She told me, when I asked her, that she had been buying 'something to stun the Guv' with', and added inevitably, in view of that parallelism of hers, that it was 'a sort of modified cheongsam, with the T'ai pattern in silver-blue brocade.'

Forced back on my pub round, I found that I was visiting other places as much as the Savoy, which went through a slack period when the military authorities imposed a temporary ban. At the nearby Bright World Cabaret I used to sit, bathed in a sentimental blue light, watching the bedraggled row of dance hostesses opposite, with their frizzy hair, scrawny figures and mauve skins. To dance with them you had to buy a book of tickets, one of which you must deposit by the side of the shabby hand-bag that marked their proprietorship of a table. They were tarts, I suppose, but motherly ones, who liked nothing better than to tell you of the children they had left at home. But often I ranged quite far afield, as far as Lavender Street which had such an unsavoury reputation that it was out of bounds to troops, or the equally proscribed Syed Alwey Road off which there were two alleys, one specializing in Chinese girls, the other in Malays. The Chinese alley was the more popular and it was a really sinister experience to walk down it, for it was long, narrow and quite dark and you brushed past a continuous phosphorescence of white clothed men, crumbling and reforming against walls full of whispers, while now and then the sharp bird-like cry of a hawker suggested that your presence was known and that a secret message was being passed up the alley ahead of you. On the other hand, the Hollywood Hotel in Lavender Street seemed perfectly respectable and was usually so empty that I got to know its Chinese waitress, Molly, rather better than I wanted. She used to flirt with me in a bony angular way, showing her brazen gold teeth, slapping and pinching me until I promised to write to her ex boy-friend's commanding officer about a wrist-watch she had lost, or agreed that I would take her sometime soon to dance at the Happy World. Above us as we talked a group of students from the Teachers' Training College, unable to find other accommodation, sat solemnly over their notebooks, occasionally brewing each other a cup of Ovaltine.

Never have I listened to so many conversations, found casual contacts flowering so quickly into intimacy, been hammered so hard with the points of so many anecdotes. At the Rendez-vous it was Major Tennyson, ex-Indian army, a bit down on his luck at the moment, waiting for the fellow who promised an opening on a rubber estate and signing chits for his stengahs under the quietly despairing eye of the manager—he had a bit of a place in Hampshire, not more than a bungalow really, but you got some damn good ratting; at Bugis Street it was the young stockbroker, Norman, whose mysterious disappearance from the coffee-shop table for an hour at a time I couldn't account for, until I found that there was an opium den less than a hundred yards away—eventually his boss found out, commandeered his passport, and had him sent home to Kensington; at the Ai Hoo Kee it was the tough-looking sergeant with a passion for Sibelius, at the Washington the man who had been dismissed from his estate because he and a fellow assistant-manager had tried to relieve the boredom by playing Russian roulette—he had shot himself 'right under the left tit', as he told me a dozen times, 'right under the left tit, a shocking affair, and the medico tells me I'm lucky to be alive'.

But there were nameless places too, mere holes in the wall or stools set out on the street, and at one of these I met a young Chinese business man who spent no less than two and a half hours telling me about his wife, with the red drink-flush growing brighter and brighter on his high cheek bones: 'I went to see her parents because of my friend. My friend wanted to know a nice girl with idea of eventual matrimony and he asked me if I ever had any nice girls in my class at school and I told him there were some nice girls that were not so bad. I was being a decoy, see? I was not worrying for myself. But her father was my old school-teacher, *in't it*? and he knew I was a nice boy, so the old people got the idea that it was I should be married. Well, O.K., I was not worrying now either. She was a good class girl of simple taste, very quiet but intelligent. When I told my friend, he thought I was pulling his legs. No, I said, I'm not pulling your legs, I like quite well to be married to this young lady. But every time I said well, all right, it's time for us to be getting married now, the old woman said how many tables would I give at the wedding —she wanted fifty tables! I was a boy just beginning in business. It was impossible from every point of view. She insisted then that I was a mediocre fellow, that I was mean, see? Very much argument was the result. Plenty of comings and goings la! It was too bad, because just when we were all fixed up and getting married my girl friend came back from Hongkong. My girl friend is a film star. . . . I met her again by accident, the night before I was married.

I had much longing for her. I had sexual intercourses with her when I was being married and then my wife got mad and in the end she went away. She went back to her people. Now I hear she has T.B.—she is dangerously ill. I don't know, I can't go into their house. I hope to see my girl-friend when I go up to K.L. to take part in the Eastern Area contest. I am a Gold Medallist in ballroom dancing, tango, fox-trot, rumba, samba—I like samba best. I participated in the contest in Australia. I like my wife but my girl-friend is very attractive too. She is a film star. . . .'

It was revelations like these, acquired long past midnight in the patchwork of alleys and coffee-shops and bars to be reached down Orchard Road, with the cockroaches in the broken lattice work, the rats popping up and down along the edges of the monsoon drains, the overflow from the lavatory slowly spreading across the stamped earth floor, that began to take up more and more of my imaginative life. I knew that, for the most part, I was collecting a series of marginalia, of odd remarks, lonely confessions, gestures exotic and rootless, although I had often enough, as an English Lecturer, criticized modern writers for their addiction to aberrant types. The most I could do, however, was to plunge in deeper, not merely to observe but to become personally involved. Soon I found that I was spending much of my time in places frequented almost entirely by Asians and here, although I could hope for little real communication, I did have the sense of being absorbed. Satire, so to speak, became a pervasive, perhaps too relaxed and flowery, lyricism. Now I wanted to bring some of the things I had found down Orchard Road up again, to a closer relation with my other more orthodox life, but my first attempt to do this was extraordinarily unsuccessful. . . .

This was the dinner party I gave for a European and a Chinese, neither of whom would have been approved by the colony. It interested me to recognize, with whatever formality Ah Ting and I could muster, anyone whose eccentricity was complete enough to have a sort of moral force, anyone who could be assumed by his very remoteness to have a different way of life, which my sentimentality could believe to be imaginative. So I chose Jeremy Duff-Williams and Rex Kim Seng. As a matter of fact, neither of them was a particular friend of mine. They were an oddly assorted couple. Jeremy was very large and fair, with baby-blue eyes and a pink complexion. He affected from time to time a small wistful moustache. His manner had that kind of heartiness which easily degenerates into sentimentality, so that 'Old boy', had a tendency to recur as 'my dear' or even 'my sweet'. He spoke mysteriously of 'taking runs' in the countryside in the early morning and was also 'very keen to get Rex interested in badminton'. Rex, however, was a slim tubercular youth who resembled some Chinese version of a mad poet of the Romantic Period. He had a dangling lock of hair and a passion for dark glasses, behind which his eyes were narrow and feverish. The two of them had shared flats and rooms boisterously for the past three years, and Rex had brandished anonymous letters to Jeremy's employers throughout that period. No doubt Jeremy shared in the blame; perhaps he wouldn't have kept the jobs anyway; a sort of moral and emotional uncertainty by now possessed him, so that his youngish face and body seemed to exude helplessness like a dew, his eyes and voice were just frank enough, and cultured enough, to suggest the character they proceeded to undermine, and as soon as one had detected the essential vacillation one noticed a beeriness in the nose, a wideness in the hips, and a contrivance to the accent. But Rex had been much friendlier of late, when I saw him at the Savoy, and Jeremy had succeeded in impressing me with his poetic friend's virtues: he was assiduous over the housework and he made Jeremy excellent shirts. I suspect that a minor factor in my decision was that I secretly hoped Rex would make me some shirts too.

I did my best to see that the dinner was a success. I bought an enormous tree-chrysanthemum, crowded with small white blossoms, and I borrowed a radiogram on which a carefully selected series of records was to be played. When everything was ready, and I was quite satisfied with the air of slight exaggeration I had imparted to the room, I went through agonies wondering if they would forget to come. As the minutes passed I went out to the terrace at the back of the house and watched, through the clammy darkness, the headlights of car after car sweeping up the small valley. Anxious as I was I enjoyed the fact that the flat behind me was prepared so meticulously that I myself no longer seemed to own it; it was an alternative me, about which I could do no more than creep like a *maître d'hôtel*; only my guests would fuse myself and my projection together again. At last they arrived in Jeremy's shabby little van, more than half an hour late, and I felt them blundering in, entirely insensitive and informal, as though this were just a picnic or a snack. But this didn't worry me. They had come, and I would translate my need of them in any way they wanted: I would light candles on the table, which I felt to be a bit of a vulgarity, and then be utilitarian and practical and switch on the fan until it sent the candles guttering. The service could be held up while Jeremy went into the lavatory, which was my only exit into the courtyard and the kitchen. But I wouldn't suddenly joke with Ah Ting. He was my ghostly servant, even if he was smiling in wonderment and dying to talk Malay to Jeremy; he was part of the décor with which I hoped gradually to quell my guests.

The dinner, which I thus took far too seriously, went off quite well, although the drinks tended to edge out the meal. Rex crooned at me graciously and Jeremy, tired after his day's work at the ice factory, looked as though he might contentedly fall asleep, with his pipe in the corner of his mouth. About ten o'clock we decided to drive down-town. It was then that things started happening. I sug-

gested a brief visit to the Savoy, Jeremy parked his van
on the hill at its side, I got out and immediately fell six
feet into the monsoon drain. Everyone had told me that
one must fall into a drain at least once during a tropical
visit but it wasn't pleasant; the concrete was sharp, I cut
my arm quite badly, and worst of all I didn't dare to think
what filth was lying at the bottom. We entered the Savoy
in a rather panicky state, Jeremy anxious to examine and
wash my cut, and I remember nothing of it except that
it was naval pay-night and that, as we came in by the back
entrance which I always considered the privileged way,
past the idiot boy on the right and the lavatory, a young
sailor was standing by the bar, with a sleepy grin on his
face, completely naked. Terence, whom I had not seen for
some time, became suddenly interested in the prospect of
a bandage. With one of those characteristic gestures of his
he offered me his handkerchief, drenched in cologne. He
wrinkled his nose at the blood.

Soon afterwards we drove to Albert Street where
Jeremy introduced me to a drinking place I had not
noticed before, although I was so often in the district:
a tiny hole hidden behind the refrigerator of a green-
grocer's shop. There were two trestle tables and five or six
greasy stools. We sat down with our Anchors and in a
minute or two Jeremy was off again, to get me iodine.
Meanwhile Rex got into conversation with a European
who had just come in. He was a wispy nervous little chap,
but I always called him the Hangman because he used to
drink at the Savoy on the night before he had to execute
someone at one of the jails, supposing his story to have
been true. He tried to evoke sympathy for the role he had
to play. 'I don't like to do it, mind you,' he would say,
'but somebody has to and I'm as good a choice as any.
I've nerves of iron.' Nevertheless his hand always seemed
to be shaking when he lifted his glass. 'Funny thing,' he
might add, 'I went to look at the poor bloke this evening,
to get the measure of him like, and there he was sitting

cross-legged on the floor, fairly gobbling up his fried rice! A little Tamil he is, and Tamils come so skinny that it's quite a job getting the drop right.' He grew more talkative at each drink and used to try to get others to join him, but even the toughest characters sheered off pretty soon.

Since Rex was talking to this depressing individual in Japanese, an accomplishment of which marginal people like Rex are immensely proud, I did my best to make friends with the only other customer, who was in his way equally odd, for he seemed no older than a schoolboy, was neatly dressed, and smiled with Indian brilliancy into a glass of orangeade. He wasn't at all the sort of person you normally met in a dive. I hadn't made much headway however, when Jeremy came back, only to point out to me that Rex and the Hangman had disappeared. 'Rex's in a funny mood,' he said, raising his eyebrows. 'You should-n't have let him drink so much gin.' I didn't take this seriously at the time.

A few moments later the three of us were heading for Jacaranda Road. This had presented a problem because the Indian had a bicycle, to which he was much attached. It was a beautiful bicycle, with multicoloured brake cables and an embroidered saddle and on its rear hub a chromium-frame disc to contain a photograph—this, however, was empty. The Indian held the bicycle close to him as Jeremy invited him to come, so that it seemed an extension of his shy, nervous but potentially gay personality; when he moved in the throes of hesitation and slow acceptance it gave a low pitched vibrant purr. Finally he allowed Jeremy to put it in the back of the van, where he could crouch by its side.

We stopped by the same gap in the hedge through which we had both stumbled during the riots. It was dark and could have been miles in the country, Jeremy rattled the shutters until one of them gave, felt for the switch. The single room was large, yellow and decayed, full of odd pieces of cane furniture covered here and there with

bright bits of cotton in blue and white checks or arrangements of pink roses. The brass beds were partly concealed
by a bamboo screen. Rex had embroidered the pillows
with two large initials, one in pink, one in blue, but the
covers were grey with dirt. Jeremy showed me his books
on a shelf of his own making, four big ones on personality
and salesmanship and a dozen Penguins. He pointed out
Rex's sewing machine and work-box and then, with a
wink that contained a trace of pride, drew my attention to
a rusty *parang* hanging from a nail above the toothbrushes
and Brylcreem. 'I usually keep that hidden,' he said. 'Rex
brought it from Sumatra but it isn't really wise to have it
around.' Then he left to get beer. He was to park his van
in the firm's yard and come back by taxi.

The Indian youth and I stood facing each other under
the electric light. He was delicately motionless, as though
all this was not in the least extraordinary, and smiled
without ceasing. I tried to draw him into some kind of
complicity by indicating that I found Jeremy's domestic
pride in Rex amusing and rather touching as well as silly,
pointing to the sewing-machine and *parang*; the room
hummed with silence, hot colours and tatty cosiness; I
noticed some Christmas cards pinned to the wall, snow
scenes sprinkled with tinsel but already yellowing, and
also a coloured photograph of a Chinese beauty peeping
out from a deluge of blossom, thinking that it was particularly irritating when Asians accepted our own sentimentality about their way of life, and even out-did us. He
did not join me on the sofa but went over to a basket chair
on whose edge he perched, very upright and composed,
as though the room were quite incapable of absorbing
him. His shorts were very white, his anklet socks palest
blue, and his thin brown legs prickled with spiny hairs.
After a long but brilliant pause he broke the silence:

'Did you by any chance see the picture of the Tales of
Hoffman?'

'Yes. I'm afraid I hated it.'

'Really? I think you must be very hard in your opinions. I think it was so colourful. And nice.'

'You're pretty colourful yourself,' I said.

Then Jeremy came back, remarked on the continued absence of Rex, opened beer and succeeded after a struggle in getting an Australian station on the radio. He talked to the Indian in Malay but even this did not produce much conversation. 'I think he's frightened of you,' he whispered to me when I told him I felt rather out of things. 'After all, you're at the *Skula Besar*'—the big school, in bazaar Malay—'and he's never met anyone of that rank before.' Before I could investigate any further, I found myself out of things no longer. Footsteps sounded on the verandah, a shutter banged open, and Rex had returned. He cut short Jeremy's accusation of having deserted the party by taking the offensive in a series of silky innuendoes, delivered half-smilingly as he glided about the room, touching things in order to establish his position there, and alternately putting on and taking off his dark glasses with their white celluloid rims.

'So you are having a nice party, I see, and you have brought back a very nice friend, and you have not worried at all that I was unavoidably absent . . .,' was the way it went, each new remark rising with a kind of lilt, as though he were pleased to have thought of it, from the repetitive whine into which the last remark had sunk.

'Rex, don't be silly. Of course we were worried,' Jeremy replied. 'We've got some beer for you too.'

Slowly Rex's eyes swung over to the beer, caressed it, extracted all its possibilities of excluding him and fostering extravagance, luxury, disorder, debauch, until his large foetus head tilted and his thin body swayed forward.

'Did you spend that money I lent you, Jeremy, on buying beer? You know, Jeremy, that wasn't very kind of you, was it, when I have to work so hard because I do not get European wages like you. . . .'

'I was only returning Patrick's hospitality.'

'Besides, Jeremy,' Rex continued, paying no attention to this remark but straightening the tablecloth and stroking its fringe, 'you know how I hate your continual drinking. Are you sure you really wanted me to enjoy the beer? Or did you just want to make a nice mess in my room and entertain your new friend with your drunken ways?'

In the midst of all this there emerged the story that Rex had been kidnapped. Jeremy obviously disbelieved this. He managed to slip across to me his opinion that Rex felt that he had lost face by his rudeness in leaving the party and that aggressiveness was his way of overcoming his guilt. He would calm down soon. But he didn't calm down and I felt that Jeremy was altogether too defeatist about his capacity for temperament; I felt that perhaps both of them needed a scene.

Anyway, the scene came. Rex began to throw knives and forks indiscriminately, without taking aim. Jeremy struggled with him. Rex broke free, threw an ashtray which cut Jeremy on the cheek, and leapt in passion for the *parang*. At this point the Indian and I fled into the garden, the Indian rushing immediately to his beloved bicycle. For a few moments the shuttered room seemed to rock with various kinds of noise. Then Jeremy appeared, almost as hysterical as Rex, with the cry 'He is chopping up the radio! Take care, he'll be after you next.' At which I went into the road, hailed a taxi which was (quite miraculously) passing by, and told the taximan to wait in the shadows. Rex next locked Jeremy out. Jeremy tried to parley, failed, and sought another entrance at the back where Rex's sister lived. Then two figures flashed by, chasing each other round the house, with Jeremy screaming. Windows opened, Asians appeared with the yellow light leaking around them, women's voices volleyed down the air. The Indian followed me wherever I went, wheeling his crisply whirring bicycle. 'Your friends have very much disagreement, I think.'

Finally, after a long period of silence, Jeremy joined

me, his shirt torn, blood dripping from several cuts. 'We'd better make a bolt,' he panted. 'Can I stay the night with you?' As I agreed, Rex came down the verandah steps, seemingly a good deal less excited, and I went over to him and gave him a reasonable little homily about the duties of guests and hosts and the importance of social decorum. Although I scarcely realized this at the time, he punctuated my gentle advice by hitting me repeatedly with the Malacca stick he had substituted for the *parang*. As often as I spoke, he hit. Suddenly I began to lose my temper. Jeremy dragged me away. The Indian disappeared on his bicycle with a last graceful wave. After a nasty minute, when the taxi's engine wouldn't start, we drove away.

The next morning Ah Ting made it plain that there was something the matter with me. Following his astonished glance, I saw that my legs and thighs were one almost continuous bruise. I shouldn't be able to wear shorts for a week. And for a week at least I shouldn't feel particularly anxious to go down Orchard Road. As so often before, I resolved to let myself be locked in so that I could get down to some serious writing: something objective, something firm. Jeremy was, of course, in far better shape than I. He borrowed one of my best shirts, spruced himself up with the oddments on my dressing-table, and made a joke or two for the benefit of Ah Ting.

'I'll probably get Rex deported one day. He's really here illegally, you know. But I must go back. He's *such* a child.'

'He's a dangerous madman.'

'Yes, I suppose so.' And Jeremy's smile had all the fatigue and fatuity and indulgence in martyrdom of his type, living that most marginal of existences, the life of a white man in the tropics when he is neither a *pukka sahib* nor able to be really interested in the country. 'But he's fond of me, you know. And anyway,' he straightened his tie in the mirror, 'where else could I find a place to live?'

CHAPTER 3

The Cannas on the Campus

SOMETIMES the students troop down to meet me here in my house. Often they invite me to coffee in the canteen. Or they come to a creative writing group I have organized. 'Why can't we write about native trees?' somebody asks. 'I try to write about a *tembusu* but it always ends up as a pine or some other European tree. We all put snowdrops and honeysuckles into our poems and stories.' They smile helplessly. They seem quite pleased with themselves. When I try to sound them out on their childhoods and families as we sit late at night on the lawn in front of the arcades, they become feather-brained, unable to remember. About customs they disagree among themselves.

We talk of university personalities without quite understanding each other. Mr. So-and-so, I am told, is very good-looking and a typical Englishman. When I met him I find the sort of person who might be a female impersonator in a music hall in Islington or the Edgeware Road. Mrs. Blank is said to have great taste. I ask the student who tells me this to give me a description of her living room—this student, by the way, is nearly thirty and has an excellent reproduction of a Picasso in his cubicle—but all he can say is that the lady has a carved cocktail cabinet and manifests the utmost ingenuity by hanging her Christmas cards on scotch tape.

Nearly all the students declare that they are rootless and frustrated, the latter word being especially popular. Most think of themselves as puritanical. Inquiring more deeply into this, I find two principal facts: one is the dominance of the family and the parents in Asian life, the other the fear of offending the authorities by a too open or forceful discussion of politics. A student feels that if he drinks, smokes and amuses himself at night, word will get back to his parents. The women students represent this conservatism close at hand; they are 'Matthew and Waldo, guardians of the faith. . . .' And the boys, who learn about dates and campus affairs from the movies, resent the fact that few university girls are kissable. 'We spend ten or fifteen dollars taking a girl to a social—taxis both ways, refreshment, perhaps *makan* after—and then when we get her back to the hostel all she says is "Thank you"—no romance at all. It's a waste of time. I tell you honestly Mr. Anderson we are quite disgusted with this sort of treatment!' And the benevolent beetle-face of the speaker gleams disapproval. But charming cadaverous Walter Ayerthuray snorts, wriggles, bites his nails and then shoots out with a strangled oblique, 'Why bother, man? Treat them like slaves. Treat them like dirt. Ignore them altogether. Cave-man stuff.' And everyone laughs hopelessly over the orangeade, the coffee slopped into the saucers and someone's pink immoderate plateful of iced *kachang*.

Since James Puthucheary and the others were arrested last December (they are detained on St. John's Island) there has been a lessening of political activity, except for various inside bits of sarcasm and cynicism in the university newspaper. The odd thing is that the students' suspicion extends far beyond the Government and the police. They actually think that their Professors and Lecturers will discriminate against them if they take too open a part in even their own student politics. I have heard this feeling expressed by a solid non-political Honours student and also by a highly intelligent schoolboy, who will not enter the university for at least another year. 'Gung-wu should not have written a letter like that,' he said of a mildly critical piece in the paper. 'Not until he has passed his exams. . . .' Since passing exams (dogged 'mugging' to achieve a triumphant forty per cent) is everybody's principal worry, it is not surprising that there is a good deal of tension about.

At night the long rows of hostels, only fifty yards from my window through the faint mist of the casuarina trees, grow dense and throbbing with suppressed life: the anti-septic arcades, the ping-pong rooms, the lounges, bare and casual as those in an American summer hotel, the virginal little cubicles, the huge empty lawns, the tricky arrange-ments of potted plants on steps and terrace, and recently the mysterious invasion—surely due to R.?—of the walls by a silent array of modern reproductions so that beyond the black hair, sing-song voice and incredibly pink tongue of the man talking about prospects in the Harbour Board Police, one is aware that the swathed and mottled sleepers of Henry Moore have taken up their position, as in-different to us as we are to them, or emerging from the lavatory, pre-occupied with the heat, the avoidance of an official in the distance, a rumoured increase in the Cost of Living Allowance, one finds oneself under the melancholy gaze of a Roualt clown—all this is suddenly enlivened by a burst of jazz followed by cat-calls, stamping of feet, the sob of a harmonica.

It is now that I can imagine the anguish with which Margaret, a stout opponent of the prohibited but weakly controlled Freshman ragging, has listened to 'strange sounds' from the hostel blocks, has been granted 'un-mistakable signs', has conferred with ragging-resistant Catholic students and has then, with her courage and her nervous vehemence, protested 'on the highest level'.

Students have defended ragging to me as a necessary break with the provincial school and home; the usual line is that it is no more than 'good clean fun' and that it is the authorities who, by making it illegal, encourage ragging to excess; a boy, I have been told, needs to learn to undress before other boys, to discuss the facts of life and so on. But there have been occasions when stranger things have happened. Strangest of all to me is that such things should not recur beyond the ragging period and that the moral tone (as one's Housemaster used to say) should be so high.

Despite this conventionality the students manage to keep their position distinct from, and perhaps very gently hostile to, the workings of the university itself and there are times when one actually wonders whether they are indispensable to it, whether the whole elaborate organization might not continue in full protocol without a single person being taught. There is a Kafkaesque-feeling that one's colleagues would have enough to do keeping up their positions, telephoning each other defensively from the hot seclusion of their offices, composing acid memoranda on the noise of the radio next door or defects in the parking arrangements outside the main entrance, worrying about housing and money, and doing a little research before disappearing on leave. As living human beings the students often seem remote from what is discussed at Faculty Meetings or during the big cocktail parties the Heads of Departments give. This may be partly due to old-fashioned ideas about natives which are still prevalent in some circles, while another reason is that we cannot help realizing that our stay in the country is limited: we are, in fact, training those who will ultimately supplant us. But, quite beyond these rational explanations, the university has its peculiar range of ambiguities which help to give it its brightly nervous air.

First among these is the fact that it isn't Government, isn't part of the Colonial Service, and yet it is permeated with attitudes which one imagines must be derived from that hierarchic organization; it hasn't yet succeeded in becoming *Malayan* and the suggested establishment of Professorships in Chinese, Malay and Tamil Studies is taking a suspiciously long time to bear fruit; the result is that, more than other universities, it is engaged in producing a bourgeois *élite* of students who are either secretly unhappy about it or who remain childishly ignorant of what is really happening in their country. One feels the existence, somewhere, of a hard core, symbolized by an elusive *They* who finally control its aggregate of loneli nesses and frustrations. The most obvious sign of this colonialism is the behaviour of the Professors. Quite unlike the democratic free and easy atmosphere of McGill, where I used to teach, a Professor is a superior being who carries on a sort of foreign policy with other Professors, forming and re-forming cautious alliances and occasionally entering, with envious enjoyment, upon a state of war. A Lecturer is approached by a foreign power through his own head of government, casual contacts being discouraged; representatives of a department will plan the strategy to be used at the next Faculty Meeting. Thus the cosiness within a department is likely to be won at the expense of good relations outside it although, on a higher level (to use the favourite phrase), one's own Professor may, at a meeting of the Senate or even the Council, form temporarily part of the mysterious body known as *They*, support new decisions, and return to his fold with the exalted half-shamefaced look of a betrayer. *They* are that element of real power which flickers from group to group, now the Housing Committee, now the vice-chancellor, but since it is difficult to believe that responsibility is an evanescent thing, residing temporarily amongst people one may know quite well, one tends to see it as Government policy—or to doubt whether it exists at all. Sometimes it seems no more than a negative tact: not to offend the students or, even more important, not to cause any fuss with the supposedly critical *Singapore Standard*, owned by none other than the Tiger Balm king.

Another disturbing factor is provided by the degree of uncertainty, entertained at least by the more imaginative amongst us, as to *where the university is*. Highly organized, expanding rapidly, very rich, it still has no precise location. Being so new, it has not fused the two colleges which gave it birth and which are situated in different parts of the city. Hostility between Departments (or, at

Lecturer level, isolation and apathy) is thus extended to rivalry between places and institutions and it is a commonplace on our campus, devoted to Arts and Sciences, that the Medical School has a cruder, tougher, more adventurous spirit, and that the bickering there is far more serious than it is with us. But when we look down our noses at the raucous doctors and dentists, we have to remember that every art student is a doctor *manqué*, for the Asian wants to be a doctor, and have the inflated medical salary, more than anything. I recently had the chance of discussing this with a very lovely Tamil girl who happens to be a Methodist. Her ideal husband, she told me, would be a Christian who belonged to the same caste as she did, or possibly one caste higher (she was of the tailor caste herself), and who practised medicine. In fact her father would be prepared to send a boy with these qualifications and aspirations to Cambridge for training, paying all expenses. As for the internal dissensions within the Medical College, I can only quote an important member of the hospital staff who is both a friend of mine and a notorious gossip; apart from the usual stories of surgeons who have left swabs in the body after an operation or wrongly diagnosed complaints, he often regales his guests after dinner with his anecdote of how a most eminent doctor (of course his *bête noire*) insisted on castrating a Chinese youth who had quite a mild case of hermaphroditism. 'Better without them!' he is said to have grunted, leaving the rest to a scared assistant.

Nor is it just that we exist in two places, because we are supposed to be moving to a third. I have visited this supposed site on the outskirts of Johore Bahru: seven hundred acres between the Leper Colony, the Mental Hospital and the T.B. Sanatorium, and all rough bush country, and within range of the bandits' rifles. This 'move to Johore' is unsettling, not least because it brings a little closer that dream of a fuller tropical life which nags us from the banana clumps at the end of our gardens, where the servants live. People feel that the university ought to be actually in Malaya. But of late the proposal, which seemed at one time to be in the highest and fullest sense a decision *They* had made, has become associated with one particular Professor whose go-ahead policy and hearty executive manner are slowly becoming isolated, so that what three or four months ago was the pomp of power now appears as a somewhat petulant idiosyncracy. It is awful to see a man *They* have deserted, as the God abandoned Anthony. Yet no one can be sure as yet. Chinese business men have bought up lots on the edge of the new site, and Chinese business men are not fools.

All this, of course, is a Lecturer's point of view, the prejudiced point of view of someone who is not likely to become a *They*. The important thing is that people *are* prejudiced, whether rightly or wrongly. This does not mean that the university is making an ineffective beginning; it does suggest that it has a rather large number of growing pains. The nearest I have myself got to wielding power was my recent membership of a sub-committee to consider the wearing of gowns by members of Staff while lecturing. I was pleased when they asked me to join this body because I had spent hours and hours at Faculty Meetings (although I cut several), during which there was never the slightest attempt to draw the younger people into the discussion. We sat in our two rows, with our round cigarette tins on the table in front of us and the usual dark-blue thunderstorm growling over the tufted hills to the north, while the Professors 'needled' each other, droned on towards some 'gracious compromise' and occasionally admitted that a point had been perhaps 'unduly stressed' and that an apology deserved to be 'handsome'. Now I had to discuss whether it wouldn't add dignity and increase community spirit if both students and staff wore gowns during lectures. Since most of us give only four or five lectures a week (my whole schedule of organized work falls on no more than three days), and since it seemed quite feasible to wear a gown over a long-sleeved shirt, I concentrated on ensuring that the gowns worn should be those of our old universities and not the theatrical affairs, in brilliant blue, which are given to the students on graduation. Others spoke of the possibility of getting a light-weight material, or went into details about places for robing and disrobing. It all seemed easy enough.

But later that afternoon I went round to R.'s for tea, taking my monkey with me because R. had promised him part of a durian he had acquired, and I happened to let slip that the sub-committee had been in agreement. I knew that R. was a staunch memorandum writer, although in his case there is a half-joking atmosphere to the extremely elegant English he composes—he grimaces himself at the more insulting passages, regarding them as opportunities to let off steam and as aesthetic rather than practical in nature—while most of his productions are intensely conscientious analyses of the part English can play in the development of the university. He seemed absolutely thunderstruck by the news. The botanizing side of his nature, and his own success at athletics, have evidently made him fond of informal dress, although it is difficult to remember, in view of his sensitive and even melancholy appearance, that he probably grew up in a world of hiking parties and nature-worship, and that he takes good health so seriously. 'What infernal cheek!' was the way he saw it, although I don't remember his actual words: 'What unwarrantable interference with the liberty of the individual! Sheer pomposity and pretension. . . .' Long into the night, wearing I suspect his shirt unbuttoned to its farthest extremity, he hammered his typewriter on his great austere balcony, with his beloved moths circling about him. At the next Faculty Meeting our report was found unacceptable and we disbanded in shame. R.'s counter proposal was adopted: namely, a detailed physiological examination to be carried out by the Medical College over an extended period, of the precise effects of temperature, the muscular actions involved in the act of lecturing, the weight and porousness of various types of cloth in conjunction with various types of shirt, upon the European system, physical and mental. This was the nearest to shelving the proposal that even R. could get.

The students would have been delighted with this story, if there had been any chance of their hearing it, for they have a genuine feeling for expressions of independence and personal fantasy provided they do not have to make them themselves. But there are few bridges between their world and 'ours'—not mine really, because I see more of them than almost anyone else. Going to my little hut of an office at five minutes to eight of yet another miraculously perfect morning, whose air shines as glossily as the paper of a very smart magazine, reminding me of the four or five perfect mornings of childhood, with the gardeners swinging their knives through the strong wet grass and a group of Malays from one of the kampongs already stooped on the steep bank, which they search indefatigably for some medicinal herb, I pass colourful dresses and gleaming whiteness as I walk down the bare cloister: Gung-wu, perhaps, with his air of immense confidence and charm and his slightly more adventurous clothes, striding to the office of the *Malayan Undergrad* with typed comment on last night's meeting of the Students' Council. Or his friend Beda Lim, browner, shaggier, as befits the humanist of a more generous less-poised tradition, who tells me, on the basis of a film he saw the previous night, that he has now decided not to be a musician or a journalist or a painter or the impresario of a ballet, that it is the job of a film-director which really excites him and where, please, is Wardour Street and can I give him a letter of introduction to John Grierson?

Entering my office I switch on the fan and, having asked the four tutorial students to come in, partly close the shuttered doors. A cockroach or two scuttle into hiding, a long white smear revealing where they have feasted all night on my *Oxford Book of English Verse*. I light an absurdly frivolous cigarette (Balkan Sobranie, black, with a gold tip), give my too heavily complacent academic smile, and ask Miss Shakuntala Gune (who is privately my friend and almost my romance) to read her comparison of Donne's *Apparition* and Wyatt's *Awake My Lute*.

About two months ago Shaku came up to me after a lecture where I had scored a success by referring to the canna lilies planted round the university as the scarlet ladies of the campus. She announced herself as a First Year student passionately addicted to literature and life, especially life. (It is only recently that she has attached herself to the tutorial group.) What I saw was a brown-skinned seventeen-year old, very small, rather badly dressed, and capable in moments of dejection, of which there were many, of a certain dumpiness, as though the world had thrown her aside and she had landed just anyhow. Sometimes, to do her justice, the Dickensian waif or the exotic slave-girl emerged from this air of collapse. Once encouraged, however, once told that she can pass in economics if she keeps her nerve or that her latest boyfriend, claimed to be the very replica of Richard Widmark, will be more attentive if she herself manages to be more reserved, a smile of extraordinary beauty and liveliness begins to break through the tears gathering under the long lashes, she looks up wonderingly and then enthusiastically into my face, and I can enjoy the olive smoothness of her skin, the tilt of her nose balanced by the passionate fullness of her lips, and the intelligence that adds to the softness of her large eyes. That first meeting was continued for two solid hours of literary generalization in my flat, interspersed with anecdotes of her stormy adolescence and long passages of advice from me, of which I should hardly have thought myself capable, and at its end she left with my copy of Baudelaire firmly tucked beneath her arm and her curly head held high.

Nowadays she often comes to visit me and we sit on

the terrace at the back, discussing the boy-friend who takes her to a moonlit mangrove swamp on his 500 c.c. Norton or the rival who prefers a genteel walk along the McKitchie Reservoir, wondering whether the other girls in the Mount Rosie Hostel are right in criticizing her for being too emancipated, or mutually appreciating her latest short story with its permanently Victorian setting: alternate shots of an English Rectory, complete with red Turkey carpet in the study, mullioned windows through which the sunlight falls on the stone flags of the hall, and an almost year-round display of nightingales and daffodils, and a 'bare Yorkshire moor, terriblee lonelee and desolate, with black *frowning* precipices and crags absolutelee *bitten* by the wind'. For her romanticism is endless, beautifully articulate and by no means always expressed in clichés. Admittedly at dances in the Oei Tiong Ham Hall she has a tendency to faint, if the Richard Widmark boy-friend happens to be escorting someone else, but on one occasion, having fainted and been wafted out onto the starlit balcony by attendant Mount Rosieites, she soon returned with an uplifted expression of renunciation on her face and spent the rest of the evening dancing with me. 'Your eyes are *intensely* bright,' she said. 'They remind me of my mummy's.' During picnics organized by the Geographical Society she is discovered at some comparatively deserted place communing with Nature or defying the afternoon thunderstorm from a red laterite hillock, Singapore being disappointingly flat. She rarely seems to walk through a public park, either here or in her native Muar, without being approached by distinguished Europeans with 'fixed gleaming eyes', who are accompanied by outsize dogs. Nevertheless I don't find all this irritatingly affected because it never occurs to me that she is not sincere. Truth blazes in her face, misery shatters it, innocence remains, firm and clear, and I am relieved to find nothing clammy or selfish about Shaku's adolescence; she throws everything into her too melodramatic metaphors so that there are no secrets left to curdle and twist behind her face, no *arrière-pensées*, no oblique shifts between different kinds of embarrassment, no self-consciousness. I think I like her because she lives, as I often want to do, through a series of artistic gestures: poses, if you insist, but poses which absorb so much more of one's personality than all the explanations and hesitancies normal amongst intellectuals.

The other night I took her to one of the very best hotels. Her entrance was unimpressive; small and a trifle clumsy, she dropped like a pebble into the insulated aquarium-dim atmosphere of the cocktail bar; a few people looked up as though I had committed an indiscretion in presenting them with a mere child; but a moment later, no longer dumpy and dispossessed, she sat poised over her gin and Italian, as though she had been dining out all her life, and I could see the ripples her entrance had caused spreading across the room. Then she saw the cat. It was one of those beautifully monstrous creatures which suggest years of luxury. Shaku seized it without hesitation or embarrassment. Its response was instant. Their mutual admiration was passionate and beautiful. Shaku escaped me by retreating into childhood —no, she ran away from me into the forests of youth, she ran ahead of me into instinctual places I had never quite achieved. And I was left with an epiphany and a picture.

And now, in the small shuttered room, inclining her long graceful neck above the essay, her mouth trembling with anxiety, she soon rushes into an excited description of what she understands by Sir Thomas Wyatt's fearful threat to the mistress who has discarded him: *Maychance thee lie withered and old*. . . . Feminine to her fingertips, she spares us nothing. The woman will be old and lonely and frustrated yes, but she will also have an 'ashen-grey rough and horriblee scalee skin', her fingernails will be dry and cracked and bitten, her hair thinning and falling out, her teeth decay, her breasts. . . . There is a sharp in-

take of breath from the exquisitely neutral Miss Swee
Kok but the two boys listen admiringly, their spectacles
glittering. Her breath . . .

'Miss Gune, you make this sound like an advertisement for Before and After. Try to be a little more controlled, a little more intellectual. . . .'

The real intellectuals, however, are Gung-wu, Beda Lim
and their followers. They discuss montage and atonal
music, Philippine politics, university life in China, the
poetry of Auden and Thomas. They do not discuss Sartre
or Cocteau or Gide or Kafka as yet—and what they do
say often seems to spring at one from odd angles, in quick
spasmodic gusts, for they cannot be expected to know a
great deal about their subjects and their outlook is queerly
different from ours, lacking the concept of personality
and individualism, lacking the complicated romanticism
and anxieties towards sex, and presented in an honest
practical often *naive* way without flourish, wit or epigram
—and without the private jokes and understandings of a
Western university clique.

Western culture is a dish from which Beda Lim picks
up a bit here and a bit there with a kind of admiring
clumsiness: does a play have to have a climax? What is the
actual meaning of *dénouement* (or *entrechat*, or *weltan-
schauung*, or—for his questions leap from place to place—
fanny?), is there likely to be an entirely new art form?
Is a Rolleiflex better than a Leica? Gung-wu, poised and
with a sort of ruthless charm, attacks this same dish in his
more brittle way; he slices and chips; below the sound of
eating you are always aware of the apparatus, the clink of
knife and fork upon plate and then suddenly (as happens
outside the metaphor, in real life), you see that he is
actually eating the peas with his knife! 'Eliot's myth and
his notes and Miss Jessie Weston and all that . . . a very
clever gentleman of course but in Malaya we perhaps
require something . . . a little more direct . . . and explicit.'
Always the pauses for irony, the smiles and tilts of the

immaculate head as the deliberate reticences and under-statements are slid in.

Opposed to the intellectuals is a little group of First Year Tamil students which I am beginning to get to know: this is important to me as so far Shaku is my only First Year catch. 'We are generally thought to be crazy good-for-nothings,' Walter Ayerthuray explains in his nervous passionate way, very different from the dreamy cynicism of my older friend, and first stand-by, Rama. 'Some people consider us an absolute disgrace but I shouldn't be surprised if we astonished everyone in the Inter exams!' A confessed rebel, he nonetheless reveals in these remarks both the austerity of his upbringing in Malacca and his own personal desire to belong, just as when he talks of girls—'Girls are an absolute nuisance and a waste of time'—one sees trousseau saris and gold bracelets at the end of the vista.

Here is Narayan, an eager youth with crinkly hair, big eyes and an amusing face which looks as though it has been specially made to poke its way wherever it wants to go. He brings me a poem addressed 'To Sunny' and con-taining several lines of the 'Dear Sunny, how I love him' sort.

'You mean this isn't written to a girl?'

'No. One of my friends whom we call Sunny. Some-times, I don't know how to express it, I feel inspired by him and experience very strong emotions. Is it any good?'

Some days later he speaks of his poem again.

'You know that poem I showed you—not very good I think—well now there are people who say I must be a *homosexualist* because I wrote it. Do you think I have tendencies of a homosexualist nature?'

And he looks pleased as Punch. I feel some of this insensitivity of his in his description of the Japanese Occupation. Like most students he has obviously no deep hatred of the Japanese although he doesn't go so far as

James Puthucheary who declared them the unconscious
liberators of Malaya. To some extent he may feel proud
at having had to learn Japanese; also at his ability to
survive. 'There has been a good deal of exaggeration,' he
tells me. 'The Japanese officers were often very pleasant,
real gentlemen. Individually they could be quite helpful.'
As he says this one wonders whether some racial kinship,
a deep distrust of Europeans, is not more gripping than
any political theory. Students never talk of the *politics* of
the Japanese, their Fascist organization, their imperialism;
they describe face-slappings with the sort of glee they use
for memories of ragging, turn to a couple of tortures and
atrocities which they recount with what sounds like complacency, and conclude by playing down most of the
horrors. Is this because the East is more stoical? Death
certainly doesn't seem to mean as much to them as it does
to us. But then, as I said, personality is far less nervously
fortified. . . .

One day walking with Jack de Silva, whose first remark
to me months ago was 'Well, what do you think of us
half-breeds?', I find myself greeted by children who call,
'Tuan, tuan!' Jack disapproves.

'They still look on you as a superior being! They would
never call to me like that.'

'Oh well. I am called Red-Headed-Devil much more
frequently. And I've seen Malay children carefully cross
their fingers before they passed me by.'

But subsequently I discover that I have made the same
mistake as many Europeans over the Red-Headed-Devil
business. The Cantonese do indeed call us a phrase that
might be represented phonetically as *hoong mo kwai* but
this really means light-skinned hairy devils, the 'redness'
describing colour not hair, and the hair being that of the
body rather than the head. Nor do the Cantonese treat the
other cultures better. The Indians are *kee ling kwai*, which
is considered very insulting, although the authorities
differ as to how the Malay epithet *kling*, from which *kee*

I

ling derives, originated. Some say it is onomatopoeic, referring to the clanking of chains on Indian prisoners, the Indians are clanking devils, the sons of convicts. Others claim that *kling* was the name of a great king. As to the Eurasians, they are *chup choong kwai* (the same *chup* as in chup suey), plenty mixed-up devils. But in other dialects, Hokkien for example, the devil is omitted—we are not in quite so bad a position as most of us think.

I must not give the impression that Narayan's breeziness towards the Occupation means more than it does; he can show the same impersonal (insensitive) excitement over a relative's death or an emotional adventure. It is just that his attitude contrasts oddly with the stories the Europeans tell of the horrors of internment when they were, to use their phrase, 'in the bag'.

A different form of this stoicism was revealed by Gung-wu whom I met the other day in the Y.M.C.A. Its dining room is about the only one open to the light and neither elaborate nor cluttered: the view from the windows is pleasant; Asians and Europeans meet here on completely equal terms, over white tablecloths and bottles of iced water. This atmosphere suited Gung-wu. Rather to my surprise, he joined me. He has gone in for ties recently and wore a sober blue one.

'I have just had a long talk with a young girl who is dying of cancer of the breast,' he began. 'She has less than a year to live. I don't know why it is but I seem to be attracted to the sick. There seems to be some sympathy . . . some bond. Perhaps', and a brusque student tone succeeded his pensive one 'I'm also destined to have a short merry life. Who knows? It is in the lap of the gods.'

'Too much romanticism . . .,' I ventured.

'We were at the Cathay—quite a stirring film with Alan Ladd as a pirate,' he explained, introducing the important words with that special heightened emphasis of his, as though he had discovered them for himself, tasted them with relish, and then imparted to their pronunciation a hint of humour, or perhaps just of that inner vitality of his which no language or role in society can yet express. 'And we then talked in the Cathay bar. Oh yes, she had a drink. She is reasonably free and easy for a Chinese. Very nice and intelligent.' He smacked his lips, paused and ran his eyes a trifle self-consciously over the menu. I imagined all the words twisting themselves into arabesques of steel and glass as they met his glance.

'Would you recommend the shepherd's plate?' At that moment I could have sworn that I heard an oaten flute.

'You make it sound like a poem,' I said. 'But it's pie, not plate.'

He gave his order to the waiter. 'Some of this shepherd's pie and a fried egg on top.' Then, turning to me, 'I am a great believer in eggs. The albumen is very strengthening. When I intend to take a girl dancing I always eat several eggs.'

I knew this to be true but still thought that Gung-wu must be the only student in the world who fortified himself before dancing—surely little more was permitted by even the emancipated Miss Fu or Miss Lok?

Between mouthfuls Gung-wu read me a Chinese poem he had just written, with the waiter as audience as well. Its English title was *Death and the Maiden* and it had taken ten minutes to compose. As I listened to it, and the explanatory notes which Gung-wu provided, I saw the first bands of soldiers strolling down to the Capitol, several abreast. They wore civvies as they swung through the moist blue air: sharkskin shirts, cotton trousers in lurid stripes, occasionally a smart gaberdine suit from the Tottenham Court Road. They were foolish, gay, frustrated, lonely—all their knowledge no more than the bleak army common-sense and routine, which at once caged their youth and gave it tolerance. They were innocent because they had never had time to think, never had responsibility, never been other than the passive recipients of life. For all his mannered self-conscious vitality, Gung-wu was far more civilized than they. He was, in fact, one of the most interesting young men in South-East Asia. I felt angry with myself that I did not yet appreciate him more, that my eyes were drawn away to those crude little groups swinging down to the Capitol and the souvenir-shops and the Padang, and then to where, on the other side of the street, two Indonesian youths stood talking against the soft blue-green of grass and foliage: two youths whose jet-black hair was wildly contorted with grease, whose flowered shirts flapped outside their trousers, and whose faces, bolder than even the immodest cannas on the campus, seemed moulded by centuries of sunlight, the noses squashed and tilted, the lips very full above rounded chins, and the eyes smiling yet sleepy, for they needed to provide no more than a cynical or frivolous commentary upon features so absolutely, and abstractly, committed to the sun.

CHAPTER 4

Matins with the Monkey God

A FEW SUNDAYS ago I had the curious experience of visiting a church where the service was personally conducted by the deity. Or so, without risking myself on theological profundities, I gathered.

An anthropologist friend of mine suggested taking me to one of Singapore's many spirit-medium cults. I was flattered by his offer for he has the reputation of being single-minded and cagey about his work, and of loping off into the scrub jungle, or the waste of attap huts in the suburbs, in a particularly lone lean passionate way, at once emotionally boyish and intellectually formidable. We were to see, he promised me, a manifestation of the Monkey God, who would enter the body of a medium and give advice on health, finance and marriage to those who wished it. I told him the little I knew of this particular God. I had read in Arthur Waley that he was one of the most ingenious and amusing figures in the spread of Chinese Buddhism—in fact, the *enfant terrible* of the movement. I had also been shown episodes of his life in the tortured concrete which Chinese millionaires like to put in their back gardens, disguised as grottoes, alps and pieces of sculpture. He had been abrasively present among the scarlet canna lilies under the frangipani trees, peering from an orifice or scaling some oven-hot stretch of imaginary ice. My friend remarked that the Buddhist Monkey God was a comparatively remote ancestor of the creature we were about to see.

We had parked our car by the Church of St. Theresa and now walked up a dusty lane, between hedges of hibiscus and bougainvillea, with the sun beating down on our bare heads. My companion had the shyly pleased air of a man who is about to reveal his dearest secret.

'I'm afraid it may strike you as a bit grotesque,' he said finally, as though determined to be modest. 'I mean, perhaps there isn't a great deal of religion to it. The Chinese are apt to be materialistic, you know, and they go to a medium with the idea that maybe there's something in what he says. Might as well try it. Like buying a ticket in a sweep.'

We passed a couple of houses, a temple, several fierce-smelling pig-sties and a small rubber factory. A black butterfly zig-zagged out in front of us. The air was full of the bells from St. Theresa.

'Have you. . . .?' I decided to ask, with an odd feeling that I might be considered indiscreet so that I didn't like to finish the question.

'No—not this one.' He gave his boyish smile. 'There was an Indian diplomat over here who did, though—in English—and I must say he got some quite cogent answers. The Monkey God *can* be exceedingly equivocal.'

The butterfly wandered off to the right, disappearing in a clump of tapioca. A naked child sat on the ground, pouring the red laterite dust slowly over its belly and looking up at us with enormous liquid flirtatious eyes.

'My own theory', my friend began, looking leaner and more professional every moment, 'is that . . .,' but he caught sight of the child, remarked that it was a jolly little beggar, waved, and then rooted out a bit of wood with the toe of his shoe and kicked it in the child's direction. He kicked much too hard. The child turned round and crawled away, its shining rump high in the air.

'You were saying?'

'My own pet theory is that, although quite respectable people join the cults, their main appeal is to what I term the *liu min*. Have you come across the phrase?'

'No. I'm afraid I don't know any Chinese. Except for something that sounds like wa eye boy see kwye bitchu and means Can I have six bottles of beer? in Teochiu.'

'Well, the *liu min* are the Flowing People: the most volatile social element, so to speak, who have', and he frowned, 'no integration with the community. Spivs, black marketeers, floating proletarians of all kinds. We have a lot of them here, of course, because so few of our folk are indigenous.' He frowned again, bending his head over me, and I felt the force of his knowledge and enthusiasm bearing down. I waited for his embarrassed smile. 'Sorry to be so technical but you see what I mean? If you keep in mind the concept of the *liu min* together with what I said about luck, you'll be close to the . . . er . . . *raison d'être* of the cults.'

He grunted and I realized that we had arrived. A series of very beautiful bicycles rested against the fence. They were festooned with red and blue cables and some of them had velvet saddle-covers with long fringes. Inside was a small garden, a verandah and an ornate shed.

'The Temple,' he explained as he strode forward, to be greeted with smiles and bows. 'They used to meet in a private house but they've done very well financially in the last two years. Old Kok's an excellent organizer and businessman, a very decent chap too, you might call him the Dean and Chapter rolled into one—ah, here he is.' He started pumping the hand of a large immaculately dressed Chinese who rose from a table on the verandah, where he had been drawing up some sort of a list. I was introduced. Mr. Kok called for orange-pop, of which there were great quantities in evidence: bottles in rows on a side table and others already grasped by the dense crowd that billowed in and out of the Temple doorway. Women and children comprised most of the congregation, I noticed, but these seemed to come from both poor and middle-class homes; some wore the loose gaily-flowered pyjamas which give them in public a look of rather hysterical domesticity, others seemed poured into the trimmest brocaded choongsams and observed us through the latest horn-rimmed glasses. One very pretty girl was

wearing a two-piece she had obviously copied from Elizabeth Taylor's last appearance at the Cathay Cinema.

The God himself was about to be absorbed into the
skinny body of a Mr. Lim, whom we sought out behind
the altar where he was busily making himself up. Mr.
Lim was a small competent-looking man who seemed
genuinely pleased to see my friend again, and would have
liked to discuss technicalities if he hadn't been so occupied
smearing streaks of white, vermilion and ochre on his
face, and immersing his neat loins (he wore what looked
like a pair of navy-blue bathing trunks) in a pair of yellow
sateen breeches over which he then slung a sort of fur
sporran. He was a clerk all the week, I was told, but
managed to get down for a daily even-song as well as
putting in two grand appearances on Sunday, which
meant that he must cut his tongue (he is a tongue-cutter)
about thirty times a week. The Dean was also a clerk, but
a more important one, in the Government Service.

The Temple was small and excessively hot. There were
boys who clapped gongs and were possibly neophytes.
Their expressions were remote, like those of jitterbugs.
They would play for a little and then stop, scratching one
leg with the foot of the other or looking vaguely over their
shoulders in the direction of their bicycles. An inner circle
of women stood packed against the walls, wearing the
familiar blue tunics and black sateen trousers of the *amah*;
their faces were blank with dignity and patience, and they
suppressed wriggling children with hands so effortless
that they might have been patting a dress or stifling a
yawn. The air was murky with incense. This made it
difficult to appreciate the confusion of the altar or altars,
for there were niches containing figures at the far back
and then there was a great array of punitive instruments
(swords, daggers, a spiny prick-ball) and in front strips of
coloured paper were being spread out in symmetrical
rows. Charm papers, explained my friend.

'Good Lord!' he added excitedly, 'There's a holy pic-

ture, too. In all my experience of this cult I've never seen
Lim do a picture.'

I wondered what *do* signified.

'Oh, smear it with cockerel's blood in certain ritual
places—the four corners and the brow, chest and loins of
the deity. Possibly his own blood too. Then the family
will take it home and hang it up. I wonder what they'll
be expected to pay?'

Gongs alternated with silence. Lim fluttered in the
background, looking tatty and nervous, like someone who
has dressed up for a shipboard party and doesn't want to
risk facing the judges and the crowd without the support
of his wife. My friend pointed to the money-plate.
'Waiting for it to fill up,' he whispered, drawing me
aside. 'Let's get a breather.'

On the verandah we declined a second bottle of
refreshment: cherryade, this time, for the orange-pop had
given out. My friend gripped my arm.

'By the way,' he said in a low tense voice 'you'll forgive
me if I ask you not to tell Mrs. Greene that I brought you
here. You know Mrs. Greene, don't you?'

'Slightly. I've met her at a few parties.' I didn't tell
him about the dinner-party and the disillusion which
accompanied it.

'Well, Mrs. Greene is supposed to be doing research
on charm papers, a field which approaches my own of
course but is by no means the same thing, and I thought
she might enjoy a visit here. I regret to say she proved
untrustworthy. . . .'

'How irritating!'

'She not only came here the very next Sunday on her
own and created quite a commotion, but she started
telling other people her theories as to the precise nature of
my work.' He grimaced mirthlessly. 'After all, there is
such a thing as ethics. Besides, it's so damn silly of her.
I told her if she wanted to extend her field she ought to
look into Chinese sororities—some interesting Lesbian

stuff there, I suspect, which a mere man can't hope to penetrate. Romantic friendships, suicide unions and so on. I though she had taken the hint.'

But the performance was about to begin. Mr. Lim now appeared and went into a very efficient and punctual trance. He sat on a chair, bent down and inhaled the smoke from whole bundles of joss-sticks arranged on the floor in front of him. He no longer looked nervous, or competently humble. Something undoubtedly simian flickered through him, a new agility twitched his muscles, a bright cunning came into his face. He inhaled again. He began to show the signs of possession. He rose, bent at the waist, head cocked to one side, eyes darting here and there in the crowd. He fingered the lobe of his ear, licked first one burning joss-stock and then a mass of them together, and was offered a banana which he nibbled with careful relish. Then, with an intense rhythm beating in his left leg and a flutter of satin and fur and a whirl of the money-tail whisk he now held in his hand, he was off into the garden, with the crowd following him. Here the women lined up to give him their names. These names were written on thin oblongs of cardboard and as soon as he had noted them, without looking any the less monkey-like as he did so, they were placed in baskets of brightly coloured paper and set alight.

'The women who intend asking him questions. . . .' whispered my friend. 'The baskets are known as "golden pecks".'

There wasn't time for him to give any further explanation for the Monkey God now jigged his way back to the Temple where he was immediately offered a long gleaming sword. He brandished this, whirling it round his head and lunging in the direction of the apathetic gong-boys, who made way for him stolidly. All the skinny energy of his movements only accentuated his mask-like face with its impersonal monkey cuteness. He looked enormously professional now, a wild, saucy but essentially astute figure, and I couldn't help feeling slightly sick. It was all so prompt and pat. And yet, even as I told myself that I was being hoaxed, the heat began to have its effect—or was it that there was something really evil in the air? I found myself thinking that the Monkey God listened and waited like this, grinned, whirled, listened and waited, until all the big dreams and religions and philosophies fell to pieces, and he was left alone in the rubbish to nibble and lick.

'Surely one of Eliot's Waste Land Gods?' I said to my companion, more or less to re-assure myself that we were still onlookers. 'God of the broken spring, the nervous tic?'

But the anthropologist was not impressed by this sudden morality of phrase.

'One of the reasons I consider this to be the most sophisticated of the Monkey God cults is that these people believe there are no less than five Monkey Brothers of increasing ferocity. Lim is possessed by the second Brother. So you are fortunate. It could be much worse.'

And he turned back to the show: the tongue-cutting now (how naughtily Mr. Lim performed this more abandoned gesture) and the sacrifice of the white cock, which looked half-dead already (Mr. Lim couldn't have been more neat) and then the sprinkling of blood, and the licking, and the stamping of bloody stencils upon almost everything within sight: the backs of children's necks, piles of shirts and underwear, somebody's bicycle, the picture.

During the consultations my friend showed me two annexes on each side of the Temple: in one was the processional chariot of red lacquered wood lined with spikes; in the other, which I took for the vestry, we found a melancholy old man with a long dangling moustache. 'The previous incumbent,' my friend explained. 'Rather a tragic figure. Last festival day he was determined to perform, too, although he is not possessed by the Monkey

God but by another deity who is no longer so fashionable.
The authorities tried to dissuade him, telling him that he
was too old and sick. But he persisted and there was nearly
a *fracas*. Hardly anybody joined his procession although
he flagellated himself unmercifully. They were all following Lim who was out-doing himself with the prick-ball.
Lim was. . . .' He broke off with a gasp, staring out
through the small side-door. I wondered what was the
matter. 'Good Lord, what infernal cheek! It's that woman
again.' After this outburst of astonishment, his face turned
grey and cold. I had seen that look before, in the jungle,
when one botanist caught another horning in on his
territory. Polly Greene was mounting the verandah. Her
fair hair shone, her dark glasses gave her the appearance
of a film star, predatory but aloof. She passed two youths
by the balustrade with what must have been a hard sexy
stare and then fluttered at Kok. 'Well, anyway, it's over.
There's nothing for her to see now.'

We slipped outside, to avoid embarrassment, and for
some time paced up and down in the rear of the Temple
where there was a tulip tree ablaze with scarlet flowers.
Finally Lim joined us there. He was once more the neat
white-clad clerk, poised but deferential.

'You like? You find satisfactory?' Lim asked me.

'I thought it went off awfully well,' I answered, hoping
that this wouldn't sound too much like the remark one
makes to someone who has been putting on amateur
theatricals. But Lim's interest in me was only perfunctory.
He turned to my friend, eager to refer to a matter they
had obviously discussed before.

'You hear anything yet about new flat for me? I know
very difficult but please Sir I need, I need very much.'

Just for a moment, as he looked brightly up, I thought
I saw a faint hint of the Monkey God. But no. That evil
creature existed no more. He was a Chinese clerk asking a
favour of a Government servant.

CHAPTER 5

Buying a Monkey

IT'S odd enough to buy Christmas presents in a blaze
of tropical sunlight, as I had to do a few months ago,
with the shops full of crackers (unlikely to explode satis-
factorily in this climate) and tins of biscuits (almost
certainly damp) and little casuarinas pretending to be
Christmas trees, but what makes it exasperating is that it
is so difficult to find anything one really wants to buy, and
yet the more one droops and wilts, the louder grow the
touts' voices. In Stamford Road, Hill Street, High
Street, there is an Indian outside every shop, and if he
isn't there when you arrive he pops out immediately with,
'Yes, Sir,' 'Hallo John,' 'Tuan, Tuan!' in greasy, over-
confident excitement, and nothing you can do in the
sauntering, languid, fastidious, ironic or cynical way can
have any effect on him. A cold stare, an amused mocking
smile mean nothing; a shrug of the shoulders draws him
closer, a gesture of dismissal incites him to more elaborate speech. You move away. He follows you. You move
faster—and enter the ambience of the tout next door. And
then, gliding from his position by one of the pillars of the
arcade, the money-changer is at your side. Brush past him
onto the street. An old, incredibly battered and wrinkled
trisha-driver in a grey crew-cut slows down, turns his
melancholy gaze in your direction, and chants sepul-
chrally, 'Singapore Bar! Singapore Bar!'

Maybe it's a matter of personality. To the tout you
have only one quality; the comparative whiteness of your
skin. You may be an American or Dutch business-man, a
tourist, a stoker off a ship, one of the innumerable servicemen, a long-term resident with a string of race-horses, an
anthropologist, a poet—the tout does not discriminate

amongst nationalities and classes, and can therefore hardly be expected to understand faces and moods. The money-changer, or for that matter the man with the cellophane packets of stamps, does not discriminate either. And the trisha-man invites you, because he has been paid to do so, to the doubtful amenities of Bras Basah Road and the dreary little bar at its lower end. The trouble is that the tout doesn't understand window-shopping, especially its negative delights; he doesn't see why you should want to torture yourself before the carapaced horror of an enormous dressing-garment embroidered in golden dragons, or a troupe of ebony tuskers, or a tea-set encrusted with what appear to be centipedes; he finds no incongruity in the American ties juxtaposed with (Edwardian?) negligees, and the shirts patterned in newsprint dangling in front of a slick Balinese sculpture. And, suppose you speak to him, your civilized annoyance is altogether too clipped and muted and fast. Even your wit has no effect. So, afraid of your own potential aggressiveness you become flustered and slip away. 'Hey, John. Come inside. Plenty to see inside, John!' follows you.

Christmas, though, is the season in which one is supposed actually to buy things and somehow or other one must get into a couple of shops. The big stores in Raffles Place are easier of access, admittedly—one has only to escape a couple of newspaper boys, trample on the pride of a spiv selling sunglasses and flatten two or three money-changers in sarongs and tarbooshes, and the doorways are gained, the cool interior opens before you, and there may even be a tang of air-conditioning in the atmosphere. But there will also be the extra Christmas help and, fond as I am of Asians, I don't like their genteel shop-assistant class: a pious hermaphrodite amongst the men's ties, Eurasian virgins in pince-nez tramping happily through aisles of Chanel and Morny and Yardley's and French Fern, a Brylcreemed Indian nattily surveying the golf clubs. And it is all, somehow, so sad. Saddest of all are the men's suits and the bolts of worsteds and tweeds outside the tailoring department: winter-weights for an England eight thousand miles away and deep in another financial crisis. Even if the materials aren't particularly good (one is too hot to feel them, anyway), they bring back memories of the Vicar and the Squire and the galloping Major . . . until, alas, a real Major approaches, enormous in white shirt and shorts, to ask in the accents of Manchester for a nice thing in cummerbunds, and one realizes that the old world has gone.

Still, something must be bought for Christmas—one present at least must be given—and so I take a taxi to Thieves Market, which is a shambling colony of huts in the Arab Quarter. Rochore Canal is flooded and each tiny shop must be entered warily over a wobbling or sagging plank. Friends keep on telling me of the bargains they have purchased here; entire Chinese bedsteads in gold and red lacquer, made up of some ten different component parts; posts, canopies, shelves, inner and outer layers; ancient pieces of brocade; small pagoda-like boxes; buddhas in ivory and faded wood. But now, anyway, only two or three shops deal in 'antiques', the rest devote themselves to surplus army blankets, tools and crockery, and there is little to do except unwrap parcels, plunge deep into bundles, pull bits and pieces out while a surprisingly indifferent boy continues gilding a Victorian lamp. If anything pleasant appears—a panel of intricate lacquer work, for instance—it is almost certain to fall to pieces in your hands. As a matter of fact, this decrepitude is quite a temptation, for, when the boy-guardian offers you a certain object for three dollars more than it is worth, you have only to give it a vague pressure and a flower or bird disappears in dust. Enough of these explosions, and the price might drop. But the real aim is vengeance. Vengeance, or at least a sense of justice, has formed a part of my shopping ever since I discovered that, in bookshops, it is possible to play upon a shelf of books, and especially a row of books crowded upon a table, in somewhat the same fashion as one plays the piano, discarding the authors one doesn't like until, in some cases, they altogether disappear, while encouraging others with a deft staccato movement. Thus, to the accompaniment of faint sighs, mild diminuendos and muted but decisive plops, I have 'brought' W. H. Auden 'out', dismissed Alfred Noyes and subtly altered the relative prominence of Truman Capote and Dos Passos.

And now it is already Christmas Eve and not one present has been bought for, even when I have succeeded in getting into a shop, there has always been eventual disappointment. Fantasies have ballooned as realities seemed more and more inadequate. Why not a waistcoat of crocodile skin? A tie in black cobra or hamadryad? With such thoughts in mind—at least with the desperation implied by such thoughts—I walk down Rochore Road on the last morning. Rochore Road is a crowded Chinese street, dense with modest little shops selling provisions, lanterns and red candles, medicinal objects such as dried antelope horn, cheap metal toys, while along its five-foot ways are the barrows of hawkers, and between the hawkers and the shops you can scarcely walk for the children and the bicycles. This street has two advantages: first, as the quality of the light indicates, striking the buildings and stiffening them into a kind of crouched expectancy, it leads to the sea; second, about two-thirds of the way down on the left there are three or four animal and bird shops. Blue macaws, green and yellow parrots, white cockatoos swing outside. Within is a corridor where, from time to time, one may come upon a *musang*, a pair of mouse-deer, a coiled snake—in addition to the smaller birds and the poultry and the rabbits crowded noisily (and cruelly) together.

It is now, suddenly, that it happens. The idea that one should purchase something in a sense useless, not even a present that one dared to give anyone but oneself, has a

special kind of charm. It has the charm of madness. No, of
course not. Absolutely impossible. Far too expensive. In
any case one has only ten dollars in hand and the bank is a
long way off and will be shut in less than an hour. And, of
course, as all these commonsense responses occur, as
Propriety, Responsibility and Economy have their stern
dignified say, and employ their immutable arguments, a
dozen little wishes and half-hopes and imaginings from
the Past cluster together, an amoral subversive crew, and
in their midst there is an extraordinary figure, haggard,
boyish, whimsical—with an excited aggressive glitter to
his eye and yet an abandon amounting to weakness in his
posture—who must be some quite important Inner Self or
Id for he keeps on shouting in one's own accents 'Buy—
this purchase will take me out of myself and confirm me,
this will be something tangible, an avenue into Life. Buy,
Buy! I shall be transported with excitement.'

So it is that I buy the monkey which is not a monkey
at all but an anthropoid ape, a little gibbon or *wa-wa*
hanging tightly on to the stomach of a Chinese boy,
dragging at his singlet with long thin black fingers, burying against him his black wrinkled face with large opaque
circular eyes—a pear-shaped thing of silvery grey fluff,
round-headed, white-ruffed, with enormous arms which it
waves above it as it dashes across the floor. It does not
wail when I take it but chatters in shrill staccato. I am
terrified that it will catch cold. I have been told that *wa-
was* have weak lungs and often get T.B. And, once home,
there is so much to do for the *wa-wa* is probably a great
deal younger than one had imagined (what size do they
grow to, anyway?—one has only dim memories of adult
gibbons at the zoo) and possibly neurotic as well, if it has
indeed been untimely ripped from its mother's care, as
someone suggests. I have to go out again for food:
bananas, star-fruit, two mangosteens and a papaya, and
then it will eat nothing but the papaya, and has to be fed
that. I have to search for a cage, which is expensive and

too small (a senile cockatoo is dislodged from it) and later must start complicated negotiations with the local carpenter for a healthier cage which, after much delay, turns out to be far more expensive, and cumbersome and incorrectly made beside. Christmas is thus permeated with the cries of infancy. The *wa-wa* chatters and chirps no more. Its lips protrude like the opening in a pillar-box and it wails. You move a foot from it, reach out for your cup of tea even, and it wails. You fold it up into a packet and pop it into its cage, and its screams fill the air. If it catches another glimpse of you, a sort of whooping hysteria accompanies the wailing; it falls over backwards and bangs its head against the wire floor. And then, most dreadful of all, it sneezes. Suddenly, in the dead of night, I hear a sneeze. 'It only sneezed once yesterday—it has sneezed three times today,' I tell myself, aghast. They are said to be terribly delicate. But in the morning it is still alive.

Coming back from a Christmas Eve party, I cannot fall asleep with my clothes on, reflecting muzzily on my hostess's rather obvious rhinestone and white satin gown, or her barbecued steak; nor can I cry out against fate and loneliness and the monodrama of sex. I must feed the *wa-wa*. I must let the *wa-wa* drop bits of slimy pink papaya all over me. I must accept the fact that the *wa-wa* is by no means house-trained or human-being-trained. In return, I get perhaps a chirrup instead of a scream; the feel of the fluff over its hard flat back; the aureole that light makes of the fur on the arms and legs, with the thin long bones showing through as in an X-ray; the way it runs with mad purpose, trips over, sadly surveys itself and, lying on its back, shakes its head from side to side. And I notice how, as I lie awake quite sober, praying against another sneeze, the visual and tactile images remain to the degree called I believe empathy; I can still see and feel the monkey more than a dog, or my beloved childhood ferret (which came to me in a paper bag and whose breathing I listened to all night). Evidently I have always wanted a *wa-wa*.

Rather as a frustrated mother is told she would do better to have a child, my friends spend the next few days telling me that the monkey is good for me; the anthropologists say that it will put me in touch with the East, and the psychologists suggest that I may turn it into a son image. Personally I think it is more likely that I shall have to psycho-analyse the monkey. It has all the complexes: it has a soldier complex and a tall-man complex and a complex about university wives (it has just bitten Mrs. Y. on the chest)—it doesn't like mechanical toys, brooms, music, poetry (it chatters furiously when Wang Gung-wu, the young Chinese romantic, comes to discuss the possibilities of a Malayan idiom) while my singing makes it apoplectic with rage. It isn't interested in sex. It *does* like cigarettes, beer, stilton cheese, eating the mosquito net and climbing up the plumbing in the lavatory. It does, to a frightful extent, like me.

'Be independent. Go and play,' I tell it in the lowest voice I can command, as I throw it from my chair to a cushion on the sofa. For a moment it lies spread-eagled in miserable abandon. Then, recovering its poise, it pretends to have taken my advice to heart, rushes solemnly to the window, climbs the wires and looks out intently, swinging on one arm. In a moment the soft *wa-wa* sound begins. It has seen the postman or the celebrated dentist who lives next door; it is afraid. Croons give way to whoops, for the intruder is evidently approaching, and a mad scramble down begins. Half way across the floor to me, it looks back over its shoulder, absurdly projecting its black rump like some scandalized but saucy cocotte. I wave it away. It circles my chair, performing masterpieces of obliquity. I motion it off more fiercely. It folds its arms across its chest, making a parcel, and posts itself to oblivion. But as soon as I start reading again it proceeds to creep towards my chair, to insinuate itself up the side of openwork cane, and when I next look it is stretched out towards me, its head and rigid extended arm over but *not quite touching* my chest, and its gaze fixed in impossible melancholy upon some distant point in space, all the more pathetic because of the contrast between those violet-grey eyes and the disgruntled little face.

All this has not prevented it from being called 'engaging' by Margaret and 'elegant' by R., who muttered something further about Eighteenth Century blackamoors. It must have been this elegance which prompted Allan and me to name it Chi-chi, although personally I think this is going a bit far, so that I do my best to transpose the sound into something more animal-like, *Tchee-tchee*, when the heartier people ask what it is called. Certainly it looks graceful enough when it can be persuaded to play in the screen of tapioca behind the house or in the nest of bougainvillea nearby. Suspended in the shallow splash of leaves it resembles some delicate creature in water-colour, a condensed shadow amongst the brighter foliage, and there may be a moment or two before I notice where it is but when I do it is always with the same sense of expanded sympathy and delight, as though back in childhood one were to receive the perfect gift. I have almost to rub my eyes in order to convince myself that I own a monkey. This elegance of Chi-chi's is, in a way, curiously stationary: an abstraction of all his movements and miseries; the projection of something important but elusive in oneself, like a mood. For of course he is in fact enormously busy even when he is not also prodigiously anxious. He swings from one pale tapioca stem to the next with such vigour that he might be some mad athlete determined on reaching the end of the world, or he picks and tears some object near at hand like mischief personified. One moment he hangs there, against the intensely blue sky, like something permanently appropriated by a picture of great charm and tranquility, and all the more permanent, somehow, for being fragile and delicately grey, so that he seems positively to need the artist's vision; the next, he changes into homunculus and grotesque, not the centre and fruit of anything but its sardonic, piteous shadow. Then, noticing my interest, he flops down on the grass, recovers himself and sways towards me. His fur ruffles to my breath. It is lighter still underneath, beautifully warm, and it smells of sunshine.

Nowadays I hear his whoops early in the morning, when I am only just awake. It is the gayest time of day, before the heat has been able to concentrate. The shutters are open, the tiled floors invite one to walk on them in one's bare feet, and Ah Ting is running cold water into my bath. Yesterday's gardenias, crammed into bowls on the table by my bed, the dressing-table and in several other places throughout the two rooms, are beginning to come into full flower. Bulbuls are nesting in the tree by the side of the house. Lying in bed I can just see, through the half-open shutter, a lizard pinned to the fig tree like a monstrous brooch. Ah Ting is barefooted as he comes to announce, 'Please Sir, your bath is *rrready*!', and behind him is Chi-chi, just released from his cage and terrified lest Ah Ting shall prevent him from reaching me. In a moment he will have flung himself on my bare chest, in another he will reach under the pillow for the cigarettes I have hidden there.

Chi-chi's idea is to begin breakfast with cobwebs and tap-water, climbing pipes or window-netting for the first, which trail from his long fingers as he rather bemusedly observes them, rather tentatively puts them into his mouth, but scooping the latter eagerly as he crouches on the edge of the bath. To tight-rope round the bath is a speciality of his and only once has he fallen in. I lie submerged in a sheath of apple-green coldness, preoccupied with all the delights of beginning although I know that this Peter-and-the-Wolf of a morning will soon grow sweaty and irritating and fatigued, but that new flash I detect in all the glittering reverberations of light is not a golden oriole outside the window but one of my razor-blades in the corner of Chi-chi's mouth, protruding at a jaunty angle. . . . 'Chi-chi, for God's sake!' And Ah Ting has to catch the indignant monkey, recover the razor-blade, and then chase him into the sitting-room. (Ah Ting is rather good with Chi-chi, as though European eccentricities can be dealt with firmly when they come Chi-chi's size. I often see Chi-chi borne away swinging from Ah Ting's hand, looking glum but resigned. He never bites Ah Ting.)

In the living-room, though, is the breakfast table and on the breakfast table is the butter in its usual half-melted state. It doesn't take long for Chi-chi to climb the table leg. To prevent this we have taken to an unorthodox method of defence. Someone left here the other day one of those ingenious mechanical toys which are made in Japan. This toy is called the Great Roaring Bear and when you wind it up it pads slowly forward, weaving its shaggy head from side to side and grinding out a horrible noise, between a growl and a whirr. Chi-chi loathes it, whether it's wound up or not. It's pathetic to watch him scramble up the table, pulling one of the mats as he does so, peer eagerly over the top, catch sight of the Great Roaring Bear and remain for a moment quite transfixed with terror before letting out a shriek and dropping in a heap to the floor. Not that he will remain subdued for long.

What *am* I to do with him? Bury him under a cushion? He will emerge in ten seconds. Put him in my bed? Sometimes this works, for it allows him to display a penchant for odalisque languors *à la* Matisse, varied with the flat-on-the-back gestures of a shameless dwarf. No, I shall throw him up a tree. However much he shrieks, he is too young to get down the thick trunk by himself. And then, of course, I shall feel bound to watch him as, forgetting about me, he climbs higher and higher, swings sickeningly from twig to twig, crashes down six, eight, ten feet at a time to recover himself at what seems like the last moment.

CHAPTER 6

Profile of a City

ONE day I stood with the others, shouting *Majullah Singapura*, Let Singapore Prosper! It was the day we celebrated our having been turned into a city (our first *British* City Day, that is, for the Japanese had metropolized us some years before) and we were all happy, in our rather passive way, to watch the big boyish-looking Governor in his cocked hat, and the shrewd Colonial Secretary, and poor Sir Henry Gurney, the High Commissioner, who was to be ambushed and killed within a week. The great crowds were extraordinarily patient and disciplined. That evening, during intervals in the long colourful procession, they wandered over the roads with practically no police to control them, but they always reformed their ranks before the next illuminated float arrived in a burst of fire-crackers. All day there was only one incident and that from a home-made bomb, which seemed to share the effervescence of the occasion by going off in a flash and a cloud of vapour, without hurting anyone, just as the dragon-dance began in North Bridge Road. There were far too many fireworks to worry about a bomb.

How handsome the city looked in its characteristically limpid fashion!—butter-yellow churches and cupolas, a Cathedral of icing-sugar, the broad meadow called the *padang*, with the Cricket Club arm in arm with the Supreme Court Building, and an oleander reaching up towards Sir Stamford Raffles' bronze buttonhole. You felt that our civic and commercial solemnities might at any moment float away like the balloons released by Miss Malaya to advertise a sneak-preview at the Capitol Cinema, and disappear (without causing much worry) over the shining sea and the tufted islands and the

Equator itself, a hundred miles away, a line seemingly no more imaginary than the line of these buildings, or than the political and social frontier presumed to throb here amongst the tri-shaws and the bicycles. For although the Colony, despite its hideous overcrowding, has a fine health record and appears to be reasonably well governed, no one could claim that it has much political vitality, either Communist or democratic. Few bother to vote in the elections. Terrorists burn a bus, murder a Chinese rubber or pineapple millionaire: memories are short, spirits resilient. The geographic metaphor is only too exact. Like a purse slung from the girdle of Malaya, we glitteringly bulge and frivolously swing.

After a little you take it all for granted: walking in Chinatown below the crossed flags of laundry hung on poles from the upper windows, but the pastel blurred colours of the buildings themselves and the damp heat suggest that you are wading through the washing itself; passing, in the yellow and green suburban dignity of Nassim Road, the younger schoolboys in their uniform of white short-sleeved shirts and royal blue shorts, or Malay schoolgirls in long white tunics over green skirts; finding, where a stretch of savage bristly open land suddenly appears in the middle of housing developments, a herds-man and his thirty or forty cows attended by a flock of delicately white egrets; watching the passage of a Chinese funeral, its brutal-looking lorries loud with gongs or strident with great wheels of frangipani and spider orchids and over the catafalque a paper stork or tiger; finally, grateful for the fresher light of evening, walking under the rengas trees on the university campus and reading once again, in the deep green air, the little notice which says: '*These handsome trees are Rengas. They produce a poisonous secretion and it is dangerous to handle their leaves or stand under them during rain*' to the accompaniment of the squishy sound of a football being kicked by the naked feet of the young *kebuns* on their water-logged field.

Handsome, insidiously poisonous? or glossily unknow-able? or, in the end, just boring? Perhaps it is the light that is wrong, the light that eats up and absorbs every-thing, destroying the shade of trees and awnings, thrust-ing through the heaviest shutters, and yet never seeming to lose its quality of indolence and even of impromptu: a moist light, almost lyrical, making you feel like an intruder upon some ghostly *fête-champêtre* of long ago. For, just as the reality of Asian life escapes you (all those bicycles and credits in the Cambridge, all that poverty and overcrowding and noise!—with the sing-song English speech reminiscent of Welsh, and the high precise notes of Chinese like the sound of a business-school of birds, and the tumbling rocky water-course of Tamil) so too, beyond the Cost of Living Allowance and the Grade B government house and the Ford Prefect on order, there seems to lurk some deeper, more imaginative life. Once this is glimpsed, the gobbling and clanking of tropical birds become both invitation and betrayal; the landscape grows emptier and emptier as life drains away somewhere else; the dozens of fair-haired European children in the Botanical Gardens seem a vulgar anomaly; you cannot fin-ally believe in the existence of the casuarinas and jaca-randas in your own garden. You know their names, yes, but the light has stolen them. You want to call them back. People will fill bowl after bowl with gardenias from their private gardenia tree, the dog will play with gardenia and frangipani sprigs on the terrazzo paving, and yet this plenitude of fleshy petals, this heavy mellifluous scent, is no more than the faintest of messages.

You always seem to come up against the same things: beauty and unreality. Beauty is constantly jolting you into delighted surprise, but it is never confident and complete, it is always a piecemeal affair of hints, contrasts, sparks struck out as the wheels of commerce and vulgarity grind together. Singapore is a city where nobody really belongs, where no culture is indigenous, no memory authoritative, no attitude other than immature. The man who tries to find out what 'native customs' are is faced by the co-existence of four distinct cultures amongst the Chinese, Malays, Indians and Eurasians, and many of these require further subdivisions—a Hokkien is not the same as a Cantonese, a boy from Hailam will not think the same way as a boy from Swatow. All speak different dialects. The mauve and white garlands of squid festooned across the front of a wayside eating-place; the fresh wet banana leaf plates at a Brahmin restaurant, dotted with the yellow and ochre vegetable curries you must eat with your fingers; the excitingly garish costumes of the Malay girls, with their marmalade-coloured batik sarongs, red or electric blue chenille scarves, plastic hair ornaments, high-heeled gold shoes, thick chalk-white rice powder—all these do not fit together to form a picture. The result of friendly inquiries will be not a sense of the bewildering richness of native life but an exasperating lack of information, coupled with considerable apathy on the part of those appealed to. For the old cultures are not very important any more—it's as easy as that. And the new unified culture is still to come—no doubt the forces of nationalism and Communism, the influences of the United States and Britain, the sub-influences of Hollywood and the U.S.I.S., or of the old-style planter and the Colonial Servant from the Welfare State, are all contending in various and subtle ways for dominance. Nevertheless how the Tropics cry out for the integration, if only preliminary, that an artist could give them! There's so much that a painter could use: such visual excitement, such vitality of form and colour (though not necessarily of mind), in a setting already strongly reminiscent of Raoul Dufy, not to mention Rousseau and Gauguin, and associated with just those off-notes of stridency and awkwardness that artists seem to profit by. But the creative life is the hardest of all to live in a colony. No one has fused the brilliant fragments into a compelling whole.

Against this background the whites seem no more than photographs, acutely defined in terms of surface personality, but isolated and ephemeral; the camera gives to the delineation of their features its bright but ultimately indifferent stare; they belong to nothing but their shadows. At their worst they are caricatures sketched in a few lines, whose malice encircles emptiness. They believe in themselves because they have been taught to do so, as a matter of routine, or because there is nothing else in which they can believe. Thus the snapshots that flicker from one to another are the hot little symbols of self-hood, proving their existence against the smudged clump of palms at the edge of the beach, with wife and children grouped at their sides: a present tense which slips back incorrigibly into the past, they are blurred snatches at some facet of that mirror in which western individuality admires its own image. Yet one can imagine how impressively R. might be portrayed, with his deep-set dark eyes and lean finely-cut face, posed in ascetic contemplation of his botanical specimens, drawing his gentle but impenetrable solitude around him. Half of one, after all, is so in love with personality that one is continually irritated by the lack of sharp edges amongst the Asians, a concomitant of which is the lack of solitude—the group-consciousness, the fluidity. When one does come upon some extraordinarily refined and Christlike face, such as is often to be found amongst the Indians, one's annoyance is increased when it yields nothing but deferential politeness, evades one's recognition, dissolves in giggles. Nevertheless R. remains in black and white and the meanest Asian is a painting. If he is less than our complicated bundle of attitudes and mannerisms, he is also incomparably more, because he has the formal qualities of a figure in a landscape. He doesn't comment upon his life, he lives it. One of the problems of getting to know Asians is precisely the difficult relation between art and life, because one loves and understands them intuitively, since they are beautiful, without necessarily being able to 'like' them or to appreciate their 'problems' intellectually. At least I know that I am never introduced to a left wing reformer without feeling that he and I will have little in common where the natives are concerned.

Before I came to South-East Asia I was given some very poetic advice by a friend of mine who had been an officer on Lord Mountbatten's staff. He told me that I had always lived in the North, in Europe and Canada, and that I suffered from the usual ingrained Puritan Romanticism, whose symbols were lonely questing things like towers and swords. 'In the East', he said, 'you will find not swords but lotus-flowers, not anxiety and ambition but acceptance and rest. You will be able to relax.' I can't say that I found this to be true: Puritanism occurs in much Eastern religion, and intense conventionality is certainly one of the most noticeable features of Singapore's Asian life. In any case, the unreality associated with so much unfulfilled and elusive beauty would have itself disproved him. The colonial system is no doubt responsible for a good deal of this local atmosphere. It tends to reduce its exponents to a dull, uniformity while falsifying any relation they care to have with the native races. It is very difficult in a colony to be just an individual—you are always an individual-minus, a representative of something no longer very clear or very confident, so that when you are in the company of other white people you have an odd sense of 'all being in the same boat', of some rather brutal minimum of responsibility and loyalty, while when you are out on your own, and probably disclaiming your privileges as a European, you still move under the glamorous spotlight given you by your colour. Life with your fellow white men is dull; life with the natives too mysterious and flattering to be quite secure. Nobody likes the British as a ruling class any more, except perhaps for some hero-worshipping Malays—least of all the British themselves. Your Asian friends will tell you, 'You looked like Gods before the War—now you seem to have shrunk in size, so that we can consider you as human beings and see all your faults.' The result is that your more imaginative colleagues are guilty and slightly hysterical while the others, well-intentioned and hard-working as most of them undoubtedly are, seem to cope with colonialism as they might cope with a disease. Their monotonous white clothes look clinical, like bandages. Red faces and running to fat are symptoms of a nobly-borne but fatiguing malady.

People take to social patterns in an attempt to fill this uncomfortable vacuum but it is official status that matters, or financial success, not class with its suggestion of an organic relationship, certainly not your value as an individual; you are sternly pigeon-holed by people you cannot help regarding as your inferiors and, once docketed you may be left to rot; there is always the feeling that each social vista is drawn with a cruel, and really somewhat tense and despairing accuracy, by people who must convince themselves that they are not left outside; if this is true, then all the drinking and promiscuity represent a privileged rebellion of the soul against rules, not as the free activities of civilized beings but as a kind of spasm. This may explain the enormous popularity of amateur theatricals, often of quite a high standard. The various groups will flock down upon the Victoria Theatre, significantly placed amongst the great white public buildings in the centre of the city, otherwise deserted at night, to watch a hardworking army wife clamber on to peaks of passion whence she throws herself at some innocuous young business man, disguised as a French count, with a velvet smoking jacket run up by a Chinese tailor in Selegie Road. It none of it leads anywhere, in the sense that she might become a professional or be better understood by her audience; it's a sort of officially recognized orgasm. And, since the category in the official files is 'artistic', it enables a greater democracy than is possible at other times.

You can, in fact, make love to your boss's wife on the stage.

Such patterns are curious things. People who have never lived anywhere more glamorous than Surbiton, never been abroad, certainly never embraced the cosmopolitanism of an Arnold or T. S. Eliot, suddenly find themselves regarded as *Europeans*, for this is the official recognition of anyone with a white skin; your Identity Card declares it to be your 'race'. Even Empire Builders prefer not to call themselves British; they are Europeans; and one odd result of this is that Asians, including my students, look quite incredulous when I tell them that Spaniards and Italians often have comparatively dark skins. Furthermore, most Europeans are also *bachelors*, since there are always far more men than women, and this quaintly Victorian word, with its gentle hint of naughtiness, once more delimits, without explaining or reassuring, the status of those who bear it. How many young men must return, after a day of handling papers which stick to their clammy hands at the office, to the lonely heartiness of some reconditioned Chinese villa, there to eat Tuesday's menu of Australian tinned soup followed by fried rice and some slimy segments of papaya, after which they may brood over a bottle of beer on the verandah, which is all they can afford if they are to pay back the money lent them for a car: 'Although I have never been on the Continent and have never had the slightest interest in foreigners, I am a *European* and, despite my long frustrating engagement to a girl in England, a *bachelor* as well; I am out here on my first *tour*, not that the stagnant office routine has any relation to the mobile and pleasure-seeking sound of the word, and I live in the company's *mess*, which is a good deal more monastic than militaristic; I am a provisional *Deputy Export Manager* and if I am lucky I might wangle a transfer in three years time to Penang, which looks like a picture-postcard and is said to be more English, or to Hongkong where the climate can be cool; it is months since I saved up enough money to buy my *camphor-wood* chest, which all the chaps regard as an essential symbol of having lived in the tropics—it's a modern design in varnished light wood but it does have a Malayan scene engraved upon it—and there doesn't seem much more I really want to buy, although I must send home a fan or two, and perhaps a couple of pairs of embroidered slippers, or one of those little bridges carved out of a single tusk of ivory. . . .' He sighs, watching the *chichaks* at their interminable play on the vast bare walls, and mutters '*Tida apah*', which is the Malayan equivalent of '*nitchevo*' and the last of that succession of new words which pin him down on the blank page of his loneliness.

Perhaps the most significant pattern of all is that accumulation of small annoyances and bitternesses which the steady damp heat accentuates. It isn't dreadfully hot but it is always, night and day, every month of the year, around 85 degrees. The voluptuous *pukka sahib* life has gone, and the patterns may now include Boys' Clubs and Study Groups. Nevertheless there is a certain sameness to them: morning coffee in the Cold Storage or the G.H. Café in Raffles Place, archery or swimming or badminton when the air begins to cool very slightly, followed by the cinema, bridge or amateur theatricals at night, with now and then dancing at Prince's or the Capitol Blue Room or Raffles Hotel as a treat. Meanwhile irritations mount: the *amah* sends back your shirts over-starched and buttonless; your Boy wants reassurance as to the exact mathematics and geometry of the pieces of toast to be served at breakfast; your Driver starts taking joy-rides in the car; tempers grow short at the office. My own special annoyance is the lack of enterprise shown by those who have enough money to make a really determined effort to lead a tropical life, not that it's money that's needed as much as a sense of the potential luxury of the place. Why don't they buy the masses of flowering plants available everywhere, and far from expensive too, until their verandahs are positively buried in them? Shade is worth a dozen arty-crafty tin silhouettes of palms and huts, sampans and hills and moons: shade and mystery and the kind of untidiness that suggests a house is lived in. However slippery the light, they should have creepers to filter it and make moving patterns on the floor. And banks of flowers might force their huge clinical rooms to yield some softness and obliquity.

If you let the grass grow on your lawn or anywhere near your house you will suffer from mosquitoes; if you bring in plants indiscriminately you may encourage ants. I suppose practical arguments like these have their value. And much of your money will be spent on trips by air to England or Australia for yourself and your children. But the fact remains that almost everywhere I like to go I am the only European. There are five or six companies of Chinese actors constantly touring the island but it is rare indeed to see another white face at one of their *wayangs*, and yet a *wayang* is a most stimulating experience, not only for the performance itself but for its fair-ground surroundings, its open-air cafés and crowds. Some take place at the side of the road with such a blare of music and pulsation of garish light that it must be hard indeed to drive past them but others you have to look for deep in the coconut groves and these are like drowned cities to which you must swim down. It is extraordinary how dark and still the groves can be when only half a mile away is a crowd of at least a thousand people, densely packed together; the sand is soft and directionless beneath your feet or the tyres of your car; just once, perhaps, you pass fairly near an attap hut with a light glowing through its lattices, yellow as some fragile grub. Then suddenly pressure lanterns sizzle and spit in the trees, the air is vibrant with loudspeakers, and you are threading through a labyrinth of booths piled with all the shining pastel colours of Chinese food. Girls in baggy flowered pyjamas squelch through the mud— the atmosphere is one of a midnight picnic or the night of

4.
Tamils also lived in the village
(*p. 190*)

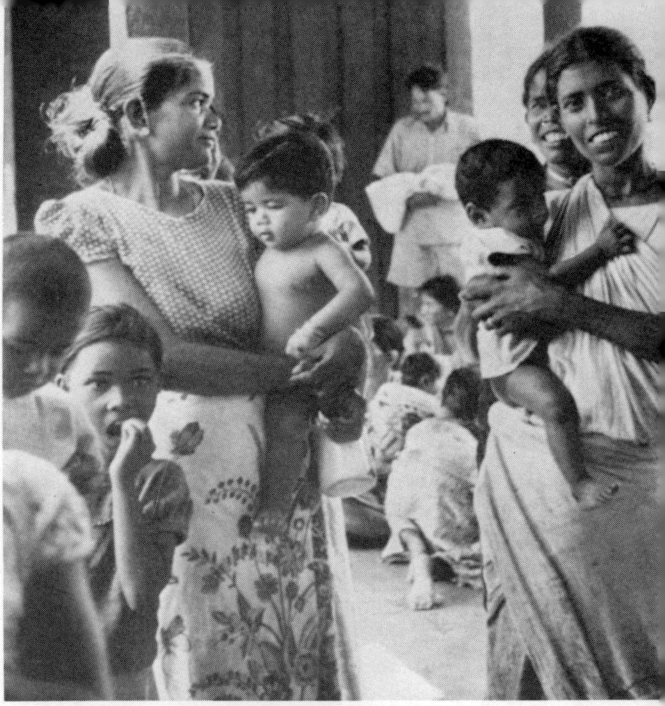

Crown copyright

Crown copyright

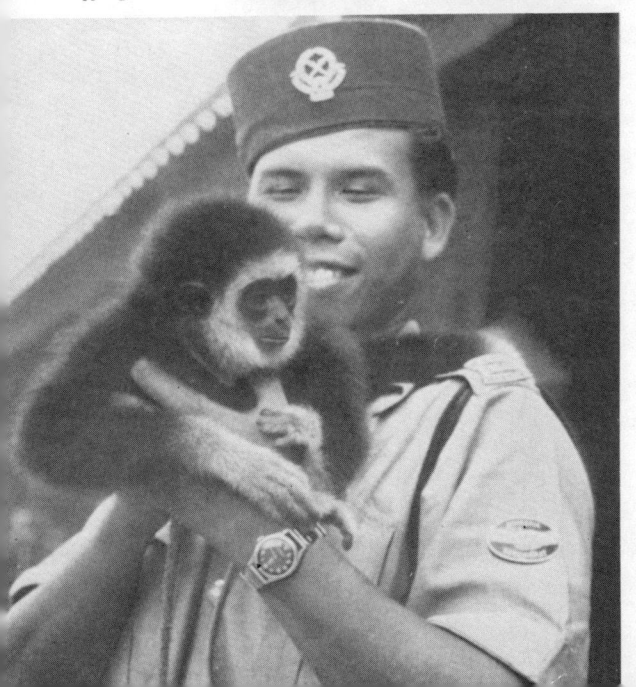

A gibbon's black disgruntled face, a Malay's broad pleasant one
(*p. 145*)

a great fire. Drunk with the bodies around you and with the sense of your own accepted foreignness, you are drawn towards the flames, which resolve themselves into sheets of rippling tinsel at the back of the rough stage, together with two-pence coloured scenery and the fantastic costumes of the singers, rigid as puppets beneath their finery, while behind you (for the *wayang* combines the Elizabethan and the Greek) there rises a great makeshift altar bearing the bodies of animals. It seems appropriate then, your personality surrendered to the crowd which restores it to you changed into both happy animalism and the liveliest visual sensitivity, that above the heads of the Chinese and the fewer, but very noticeable, Indonesians and Malays, the actors should use stylized gestures and have faces like masks, in which their eyes are pinned struggling, for what they are expressing through their clumsiness, through the usually rather hideous opulence of the colours around them, and in a ritual language scarcely anyone can understand, is surely some very primitive message about existence itself. But you must go again in the afternoon if you wish to get closer to the stage and appreciate its casualness, with small boys gambling beneath it, women suckling babies in the wings, and a coolie with a cigarette dangling from his lips slouching on to place a cushion behind the head of the fainting heroine.

When I say, though, that my colleagues seem to enjoy little or nothing of all this, preferring some 'daring' Anouilh play at the Victoria Theatre to a *wayang* at Tampenis or Nee Soon, just as they bathe at the Swimming Club while I clamber down the rocks of Point Labrador with my brandy and smoked salmon sandwiches (this luxury was only once) to lie naked amongst the hermit crabs in front of the bouncing blue water, smelling of oil, I mustn't go back on what I have said before and suggest that I have found the secret of tropical life. Burning joss-sticks, attempting to scent one's rooms with little

L

balls of yellow sandalwood, going off solemnly to dine off
dog and monkey stews—I pounce often enough but the
real thing mostly eludes me. There was, for example, a
recent Wine-Tasting Expedition. How wonderful it
would be if one could be satisfied with Chinese *samsoo* at
three or four dollars a bottle instead of Hennessey at
twelve! and how amusing in a Firbank way to say at one's
next party, 'My dear Professor, do have a glass of this
Snake Wine. It owes no little of its bouquet to an infusion
of lizards—dragons on the label, as you see—caught
flagrante delicto during the spring mating.' As for his wife,
there is another bottle for her, reputed by the Chinese to
be particularly feminine: Hen Wine, wine of the essence
of hens. But, to tell the truth, although some of these
wines are extremely strong and one or two of them faintly
palatable—*Ng Kah Pee*, for instance, which tastes gently
of shoepolish—my wine-tasting adventures have not
been notably successful. However, there's still toddy to
try.

I find that I myself long for darkness, not only because
there will be an hour or so during which the light-drugged
heat-drenched landscape, knocked out all day, will rise to
its knees in a vivid close-up, but also because night presents
a more familiar chaos, and the rather heavy drinking to be
expected in the Tropics will dissipate uncertainty and
guilt. Nevertheless I realize that my own interest in dives
will not be shared by many others, even amongst the most
adventurous, and that there are really very few satisfactory
places to go to. There are the clubs, whose colour-bar and
reputation for snobbishness no longer protect an aristocratic or even middle-class clientele; there are a few very
expensive hotels; and there are the Chinese bars catering
largely for servicemen, whose vast frustrated tousled wave
washes over the city at night, anti-civilian in principle but
very friendly if treated as human beings. Perhaps the
Esplanade will be better.

A canal, very smooth and solemn, moves through stone

walls into the sea, and then there is a big expanse of rough grass covered with eating stalls, and between the big stalls the Malays crouch over their portable stoves, fanning the embers below sticks of spicy broiled goat known as *satay*, and there are places where merchants have spread out their wares on the ground (women's sarongs in brown, orange, yellow; men's in checked patterns of black, white, grey and very dark green or purple), and there is a young Chinese doing embroidery, *Good Night and Sweet Dreams* in red wool between yellow flowers. Bottles of orange and cherry pop decorate the tables; here and there an Asian drinks stout; some people sit on chairs, some on little wooden stools only a few inches from the ground; smoke blows in their faces and they don't mind; a European doesn't want ice in his glass of beer and chucks out the cubes, a small boy promptly collects them from the grass and takes them back to his stall; there is the buzz of the pressure-lanterns, the sickly smell of carbide from the canisters used by the smaller stalls, and constantly the hiss of the cone-shaped frying pans into which a Chinese cook tosses a handful of bean-sprouts, a bundle of pale yellow *mee*, six or seven prawns with the shells still on their tails, a sprig or two of green vegetable, a few frond-like pieces of squid—dashes his spatula into water, into oil—juggles the steaming mass—claps a wooden cover over it—and is busy chopping another squid as it cooks.

Or you can drive out a number of miles to similar eating-stalls by the Rest House at Bedok where palms with metallic fronds are outlined against the sky and smart little waves rush up almost to your feet, each bearing on its back a viscous dab of moonlight. Your first Tiger Beer makes you observant: the flame of a charcoal stove has the softly tenuous appearance of chiffon. Your second leads to philosophic reflection: 'a tousled sensibility is best' or 'what does it matter?—we're all Colonial servants, all insuperably white and money-making and child-breeding and ultimately irrelevant. If the Communists break the

Indo-China line. . . .' Past your third, glinting hotly in the
moonlight, the figure of a Malay girl appears: childlike,
feminine with enormous competence, reserved. Well,
after all, it's her country. What is she thinking? Did she
smile?

PART THREE

SQUIRE OF SUNGEI TENGAH

June–December 1951

CHAPTER 7

I Move to the Jungle

ONE afternoon ten days ago I went to have a talk with Ellis. There was something important I had to tell him. I started too early because I hadn't been able to sleep, and was glad to throw off my sarong, plunge my face into cold water and stiffen myself with trousers and shirt just back from the *dhobi* and immaculately glazed.

As I took the short cut down the steps at the back and then across the marshy valley, the huge pink and white edifice of the university flats began to block my view, rising in a succession of modernistic balconies from a daze of gravel. To the left stood the long row of garages, behind lay the even longer line of the servants' quarters. The atmosphere was tense with a privacy that must always be uncertain and jealously guarded, when several high-powered Professors have to live together: more so than ever now, since siesta muted every wireless and gramophone, and children must be neither seen nor heard if an angry memorandum were to be avoided. Between the conspicuous luxury of the façade and the real untidiness of family life, reticence lay interposed like a shadow and it was disconcerting to realize that from this shadowy altitude eyes even now looked out. For the flats dominated as much as they withdrew.

Ellis lives on the ground floor and so can be reached by a wrought-iron gate in the wall of his verandah, between the potted plants which never seem entirely serious as they would if he were a Professor and lived higher up. In fact one of the delights of visiting Ellis is precisely this incongruity of his, an incongruity which lies both in the degree to which he accepts luxury and the degree to which, failing superficially to belong, he nevertheless creates a kind of fastidiousness of the intellect and the spirit. From time to time you catch him smiling at the things around him, as though he had just emerged from his inner world and were discovering them anew, but this smile may be either *naïve* or cynical for it is impossible to distinguish the delight from the mockery. There was no reply now when the gate creaked and I called his name; my footsteps sounded hollow on the red tiles; I stood, no more than a yard inside his boundaries and hoping that to trespass on a verandah was not quite the same thing as intruding into a house, while I waited for the *amah* to arrive, very likely with her fingers laid against her lips.

But no *amah* came. Instead the flat began slowly to reveal its secrets, those curious off-notes which give it a quite different charm from the 'gracious living' intended by the architect. First, Ellis's large yellow dog glided towards me, a creature which seemingly never barks or bounds but ekes out a vapid existence as a purely aesthetic object, noble but exhausted, possessed of a hip disease and a romantically unpronounceable Welsh name. Then I noticed that Midge had re-covered the 'heavy furniture' in a particularly obdurate marmalade batik, expressive of her generous adventurous nature and of her theatrical interests, for she replenishes her husband's other-worldliness with a certain helpless, almost little-girlish, vivacity as though social life were something in which she 'dressed up'. Some toys, a make-up box and a black velvet cloak lay scattered on the sofa. And just then, when I felt like retreating before objects which the atmosphere of the place invested with so much significance, a very beautiful, very slim Chinese girl edged round the archway—the *amah's* fourteen year-old daughter—and beside her the daughter of the house staggered pompously into view, a child straight out of the Eighteenth Century, whose pale important face was made quaintly beautiful by a pair of amber-coloured eyes. Dog and girl and child had each the same quality of an independence that could not be trifled with; all were mannered in their different ways—difficult to pat the dog, impossible to cuddle the child; but nevertheless the silence was now broken, the girl gestured towards the bedrooms, the child called in some foreign language particular to itself, and suddenly I remembered that it was likely that Ellis was not only asleep but still in the process of one of his retreats, during which he constructs those semantic theorems of his and from which he emerges with a passion for nights at the Flying Club interspersed with bouts of Science Fiction. Was I waking him merely from his siesta, or from some trance on the meaning of meaning?

However, he seemed pleased to see me. He drifted sleepily through the archway, like some angular bird, clutching a flowered-silk dressing-gown about him; his thin legs and very white ankles looked stilted but elegant; his spectacles glittered both resignation and surprise.

'Ellis, I've really and finally made up my mind,' I told him when we had both sat down and he had gestured somewhat wearily for tea. 'I can't stay in my university quarters any longer. I've just got to move.'

He crossed his legs, so that one bedroom slipper began to dangle, pursed his lips and regarded my problem scientifically.

'How long is it that you've been here now?'

'Eight months. And I'm not getting anywhere. The machinery is beginning to clog!' I felt childish in my restlessness, especially when I saw his eyes flicker at the clumsy metaphor I had used. And, underneath, I knew that I had not really come to ask him for advice but to receive his confirmation—and incidentally to borrow his car.

'Of course . . .', he proceeded, running his hand across his brow and jerking his outstretched foot, 'there might be some questions as to where precisely you are hoping to *get*. And even, for that matter, why should you assume that it is your business to get anywhere. . . .'

'Yes, yes,' I agreed enthusiastically, glad to be hammered

at by logic. And I glanced round the room with a new confidence, feeling that the black and yellow official furniture, the toys and philosophic journals and dog-eared descriptions of space-travel and even Midge's exuberant batik, fitted into place, were withdrawn, that is, into Ellis's private but satisfactory world.

'It is not wholly impossible', he continued, 'that Singapore was produced for a different purpose than the satisfaction of your romantic ego. . . .' His eyes slid sideways and for a moment he looked as timid and coquettish as a young priest, drawing apart to contemplate a world of absolutes. But there are no absolutes for Ellis; at least his solitary speculations all show that life is absurd; the austerity of his inner logic forces him to make a practical exception of almost anyone. Besides, had he not written much romantic poetry in a mews in Paddington? 'However,' and I knew he was prepared to listen, 'you obviously have something up your sleeve?'

I told him of the last mad twists and turns in the development of the housing problem: my increasing exasperation with Ah Ting, the impossibility of entertaining anyone when the lavatory was the bottle neck through which my visitors had to squeeze, the peculiar clicking noise which now came from upstairs where the W.'s seemed to have set up a small factory for the manufacture of something or other—how their car made a grating clank as it came to rest under the only porch and how I had stood in my room listening (through the latticework) to the muted sounds of their very occasional dinner parties, terrifyingly quiet, mortifyingly considerate, as indeed they always were until I felt that I was living with ghosts. And then, I told him, arrangements had actually been made for me to move, not mere hopes of going into such and such a house when old So-and-so went on leave but a secure-sounding promise that I could have a pleasant, if small, two rooms and gallery further round the compound.

'In fact, the caretaker came to me the day before yester-day and told me to be ready to move next morning. And darn it, Ellis, I was frightfully well behaved. I told him that he was being very kind but maybe a bit premature—he mustn't move me without written authorization from the Committee! Luckily I did because yesterday evening the whole plan collapsed. Apparently the Bursar was just signing the authorization when Mrs. ——'s husband burst into his office. I've never met them but they live on the top floor of that house and Mrs. —— is said to be rather high and mighty. She wouldn't have me. Because of the monkey, she said. The result, amongst other things, was that R. felt I'd been let down and got so angry and sympathetic and bothered that he rushed out of the dark-ness at me last night, when I was crossing the playing-fields, and told me to get another promise from the Com-mittee in writing. And to demand that it be a whole house. I think he'd been protesting over the telephone for hours.'

'And yet', Ellis said with damning wisdom, 'I don't suppose you really expected, or even wanted, to move to as small a place as that.'

'It was partly the principle of the thing. . . .''

Before Ellis could wither me with his dry laugh, I told him of my house-hunting plans, of how I had wanted from the very first to live in the city and had asked people like Rosie and Terence for help.

'And, if I fail, there's something else. Something quite fantastic and wonderful and terrifying.'

So it was that I got round to mentioning the House, capitalized in my imagination already, which had been offered me several weeks ago by the family of one of my students. In the last resort, I had told myself, I could always move out to this house which I knew to represent everything that the sleek university did not: the shadowy abandoned dilapidated shape in the coconut grove beyond the rubber trees, comfortless, alluring.

'You've seen it?'

'Oh yes—and drunk Ovaltine, of all things, with an elderly relative in an attap cottage in the grounds. There are nine acres full of fruit trees. And snakes. And a Chinese village quite near. And no police-station within miles.'

I explained how delighted I had been, months before, when Ellis and Midge had first driven me into the countryside to the north of the island, up the Serangoon Road and then along the Tampenis Road to Changi. It wasn't the bathing at the end that attracted me but the vision from time to time through the coconut trees of the Malay and Chinese settlements: an acceptable untidiness and relaxedness, like a drowned childhood world. It was the vision I had had in Colombo. And as I spoke now to Ellis about it, improbable of attainment as it seemed, I felt the longing grow in me once more. I was far too nervous to live alone in what might be a Communist area—Towkay Lee had, in fact, warned me that I was likely to come into contact with the Communists when he approved his daughter's offer—but, if only I had the courage, I felt sure I should be happy.

'It will confirm your eccentricity,' Ellis warned and I knew that if Midge had been there she would have spoken more forcibly. 'Going native, you know. . . . People will think it odd.' He cast his eyes heavenward, as though taking in the layers of Professors above his ceiling.

'But one's eccentric there anyway! The other day I went out for a visit in Margaret's car. It was just as good as ever but extraordinarily unreal. I mean, how could one *possess* it? I stood on the balcony, which will be a very important part of the house if ever I do live there, and stared down at the sandy ground. I stamped through the rooms which echoed and occasionally shook at my tread. How could I furnish them? And then I walked to the beginning of the village where there's some sort of a school. I stood near the gate and crowds of children collected and jeered at me. It was all sticky yellow sunlight, working by itself.'

Ellis couldn't lend me his car for the house-hunting, since it was being repaired, and we soon spoke of other things. He was gently thrilled with the prospect of the long vacation. He would sit, he said, for hours and hours, and think. Yes, he was hoping to get down to another paper. He had also found a new kind of beer which was quite economical if you bought it in the case. He smiled secretly at the beer and the projected essay. I looked at the clean sharp slice of his room, the clean sharp slice of his balcony, and the ordered view beyond it, framed in concrete and brick and looking efficiently dark-green, as though seen through polaroid glasses. Two American cars passed each other, hooting musically.

'Yes, I've got to move. It's quite essential.'

'Essential?' Never were eyebrows raised higher, in amused astonishment at human folly. 'You don't know the meaning of the word. Nobody does. One day semantics will have changed everything—love, politics, criticism, everything will be stripped and new.' He laughed until his slipper tumbled to the floor.

And now, exactly ten days later, it has happened: I have moved. I am writing this by the light of a pressure lantern which dangles from a ring in the low ceiling overhead, stamping its rigid crystal glare upon walls in two shades of dingy green, while the distorted stump of a candle sheds a gentler light upon my paper, enabling me to cope if the lamp explodes or suddenly wavers and diminishes into smoke and flame. The lamp is far too hot and noisy to have on the table beside me. I am locked decisively, but not very firmly, into the upstairs sitting room of the Chinese house at Kampong Sungei Tengah. My sturdy little table of plaited rotan stands in the centre of a narrow emptiness, with no windows but six doors; over the double doors at each end of the corridor-like room are grilles through which a little air can penetrate from the heavy darkness outside, but the other doors lead into the pencil-thin bedrooms parallel with where I sit and now occupied by Rama (whom I persuaded to come out this evening) and my new friend, Gerald, who has decided to share the house with me. In fact, I shall have to sleep in here tonight, in one of the rotan chairs. But I would rather have Rama with me, as a sort of Asian ambassador and middleman should difficulties arise (should I be suspected of being a *pukka sahib*, for instance, or should it suddenly become a matter of life and death to be able to speak Malay), than I would a comfortable bed. It's nice of him to come out with his final exams so near.

I've never been grimier. We've been cooking this evening partly on the enormous 'range' downstairs in the courtyard, partly on one of those little Chinese stoves made out of a bucket lined with fire-brick, using bits of charcoal left in the range by its Japanese owners six years ago and sticks dragged in from the garden. We're still eating mostly out of tins, and drinking water brought out from the university in gin bottles, but even the dish-washing water has to be boiled since both wells are far from attractive. They're a good deal nearer a neighbour's pigsty than we are, on a lower level than the House, and both are shallow and full of weeds. The 'good' one has a wooden cover but when we lifted it some nameless complicated insect plopped into the darkness. In the 'bad' one a dead rat floated. There's rain-water somewhere at the back of the House but once it gets dark nobody's brave enough to search for it, especially as we're still deficient in lights, and the attap barn is as large as a summer theatre, with a gallery from which any sort of horror can be expected to leap.

Sweat pours down my neck, my hands are covered with blisters from trying to drive screws, and ridge-like welts from trying to pump the lamp; my stockinged feet are full of wood-dust which has been left in enormous quantities by large black wood-boring bees; my hair is streaked with cobwebs and fragments of mason-wasp nest, which fall down on you every time you open a door or close a shutter. Baby mosquitoes pattern the walls, apparently too astonished to bite, and in the darker corners flies with long trailing legs perform their sinister vagaries. We peered through the trapdoor in the ceiling this afternoon and found the roof full of bats. When I think of Ellis sitting over his Carlsberg lager, or Margaret telling her beads by the air-conditioning machine she has had recently installed, or R. mounting butterflies as he hears Dorothy's lines for her new play, I feel extraordinarily remote. Yet this is what I wanted. If only I didn't feel so nervous.

There *is* an old caretaker or handyman here, a relic I suppose of Towkay Lee's pre-war staff, but he speaks no English and is so frightened that he doesn't sleep in his shed at the side of the barn but a hundred or so yards away in a hen-house, to get comfort from the hens. Has he always done this, or is he doing it to keep out of trouble should our presence attract marauders? The explanation he gave Rama, in very halting Malay, was that the House is haunted and that he has heard 'strange noises' here. It immediately occurred to me that these noises might have had a less spiritual cause. It would be quite natural, after all, for a Communist cell or a secret society to make use of a building abandoned so long—and to resent its being no longer available. Even as I write, there is a rattle in the outbuildings and then a thud. . . .

I thought a good deal of this kind of problem when I left Ellis and started my house-hunt. It was easy enough to say 'I must find a nice Asian family to take me in', except that Asian families, including those of my students, are quite unfamiliar with the idea of white lodgers; they sleep in groups, it would seem, and their domestic life is so public as scarcely to admit the presence of a stranger. An aged relative snores behind a screen; a maid fits herself into a cupboard; children lie anywhere in rows. I soon found myself turning to Chinese hotels (too expensive) and then the Y.M.C.A. (too full). I had given a lecture at the Y. sometime before and I now renewed acquaintance with its manager, who had been 'in the bag' and amused me with his stories of the various types of tobacco smoked in the camps in Siam—Sikh's Beard and, even more horrible, Tamil's Armpit. He re-directed me to the hotels. There was a possibility I might have a room in the one I used to visit in Lavender Street, but what would the university authorities think of one of their lecturers living in a proscribed brothel area? So I spent an unpleasant morning touring the European boarding-houses, including the one in which I had hid during the riots: little nests of bored gentility, demanding fabulous sums from their civil-servant or army-wife guests. One married couple I know were charged nine hundred dollars, more than my entire salary, for a single room and a snippet of verandah.

I came across Jeremy and Rex again and for a short time there seemed a real possibility that I might take over Jeremy's room in a Chinese tenement in Albert Street. I went there with Rama, who was a great help during the search (he, Shaku and Ellis were the only people I had told of my decision to move), but we were soon disillusioned, not so much by the room as by a continuing uncertainty in the relationship of the two friends. Although Jeremy was said to have broken with Rex, the latter arrived soon after we did and it seemed pretty obvious that if Jeremy left he would move in. We had to climb up a succession of narrow flights of stairs, which wound in and out of the lower apartments, so that we were confronted by a series of families and shrines, the scent of joss-sticks accumulating as we struggled towards the attics under the roof. Here Jeremy now lived in one of a group of cubby-holes screened off from one another by walls of cardboard and brown paper no more than five feet high. The upper air was communal, wreathed in a dozen different smells. I could see into the farthest corners; a young couple was packed into the nearest paper box, a widow with three children fried something in the next, while a door gave access to a tap and perhaps a

5. 'A ghostliness out of its very solidity, as it glimmers at you from its palms' (*p. 192*)

lavatory on the roof. Jeremy had a nice window beside which he stood, naked except for a sarong, his plump white chest seeming to exude an irritating optimism. He turned down the radio when we came in. A sea of buckled red tiles heaved into the sky in which evening had begun to unloose its softer colours.

I couldn't help admiring him for having de-Europeanized himself so much, but no, this was not what I wanted. I remembered a wild night when I had holed up in somebody's room not far from here; remembered the broken trellises, the walls patched with newspapers and photos of American film stars, the filthy sheets smelling of sweat and cheap talc, and the morning sounds of hawking and spitting from every side followed by the shuffle of sandals. In contrast the House at Sungei Tengah took on a beautiful tranquility. It might be dangerous but it could at least be made clean. All I needed was someone to share it with me, for I knew that I hadn't the courage to live there alone.

It was at this juncture that I realized that a comparatively new friend, Gerald, might be willing to brave the jungle with me. We had been seeing a good deal of each other recently and, although he always talked as though he would be going back to England the next day, his plans never seemed to materialize. But then there was something particularly enigmatic about everything he did. He described himself as a 'refugee from Australia' and I gathered that he had gone out there, in despair of the Welfare State in general and a business-man stepfather in particular, with no more practical aim than that he had fallen in love with the Barrier Reef and was fond of botanizing and solitude. Mysteriously connected with the aristocracy, and possessed of a very marked if unorthodox, and often arrogant, character, he had soon tired of the strenuous life. His stepfather was supposed to have tricked him into returning by promising him a permanent release from the family business, only to pull a fast one on

M

him when he reached Singapore by sending him a further
letter in which he was threatened with no more money unless
he put his shoulder to the wheel. 'I adore money,' Gerald
explained, 'but I'm damned if I'm going to be black-
mailed. I shall stay here until they decide they really want
me.' How exactly he managed to live I don't quite know.
I think he pawned things. When I first met him he was
dressed in a very well-cut but rather dirty tropical suit,
demanded six stright gins in a row, reduced Singapore
society to nothing with a few withering high-pitched
comments, and told me he was sleeping on the floor of a
Chinese lawyer's house in Rangoon Road. 'I sleep with
the rats! They steeplechase all night over my poor under-
nourished frame. Only it's worse for the *baby*. They shove
it under their bed to sleep, although it's the son and heir,
and then make their beastly love above it. Of course I'm
truly grateful but I do loathe them—I hate all the
Chinese.' No wonder that when he first came to dinner
with me, Ah Ting looked scared. 'Do you have all your
work done by that horrid little boy?' It was characteristic,
however, that he added, 'He ought to be at school or
playing. . . .'

Anyway, Gerald has turned out to be a magnificent
mover and it didn't take me long to realize that his
intimidating manner covers all sorts of imaginative and
moral qualities. He has a deep love of animals and flowers
and arrived at the university flat yesterday morning, in a
taxi for which I had to pay, with one suitcase and two
dogs.

'I didn't know you had dogs,' I said to him as I lashed
the rotan furniture on to Margaret's car.

'They're rather sweet, aren't they? I thought they might
benefit from a change of surroundings, so I sort of
captured them.'

We took out the furniture first, the little there was of it,
and then made purchases in town, after which we had to
return the car to Margaret. Saucepans, food, some of the

bedding and all of the clothes, and of course Gerald's dogs and my monkey, would have to be taken by taxi. It was already getting late, so late indeed that we wondered whether we ought to start at all. We had a long conversation about it. At the end of the conversation there was only an hour before sunset. Suddenly, and very breathlessly, we went.

I got here first because I rode my military motorbicycle, a *Matchless* far too domineering for me, and illegal too, since I haven't dared to take the driving test and have simply thrown my learner plates away; once started, I knew it was essential not to stop and so I spluttered boyishly along the various legs of the eight-mile journey, up the hill past the reservoir and its attendant jungle, night seeming already to secrete itself in the dense damp foliage; through the market gardens and squatter huts of Braddell Road, where coolness and heat caressed my face in a series of lulls and puffs, mingled with the scent of flowering trees, damp earth, latex and pig-sties; then through Serangoon Village, with its traffic problems, and Tampenis Village where the sixth milestone reminded me that it would be soon time to turn off to the left, the coconut palms growing thicker, the stucco villas more and more widely placed; till, at last, turning by the pink Catholic church, I dipped and wound along the Ponggol Road, crossing one inlet and mangrove swamp and then another, with sampans in the rushes and black mud showing through the roots; accelerated through the thin parallel lines of *my* village, wobbled over wet rutted laterite, bumped over tree roots and leaves, dropped down the final ledge where the gate hung open, and arrived in the waste and stillness before my splintered red doors.

Evening hung grey in the House; every footstep echoed; the bits of furniture we had brought in the morning looked impractically forlorn. I climbed up to the balcony and waited, afraid of disturbing the bees, afraid to explore on my own. And then I saw Gerald's taxi nosing its way down through the rubber, as though first with unbelief and then with a more dreadful resignation and finality. The taxi-driver confirmed my fears.

'Bad house,' he said. 'You not want live here.' And left before we could find out what 'bad' meant.

We decided that our first necessity was light and so we started to unpack and assemble the chromium and scarlet pressure lamp, which we had bought that morning in Raffles Place, and which was, we understood, quite prodigiously powerful. We fitted the mantle, which drooped depressingly flat; we poured kerosene and methylated spirits; we struck matches and turned valves and furiously pumped. The mantle turned black and the flame of the spirits flickered and died. We read the instructions again and again, as the wind rose in the trees, but these contained, as we put it, an absolutely *basic* ambiguity. They told us to do things which just couldn't be done together. And, having put so much hope in this expensive lamp, we realized we had little else in reserve: a smoking storm-lantern, a tiny Chinese lamp more suitable to hang in front of a holy picture, and three candle butts.

Desperately we turned our attention to locks. Although the front doors closed quite firmly, there were so many others downstairs that it was clearly impossible to fortify the ground floor. Luckily there was a door at the bottom of the stairs. Gerald began hammering in a staple and bar. Then, the stairs defended, we realized that the back room was easily accessible from the broken courtyard wall or the neighbouring outhouse roofs. So we proceeded to fit a padlock on to the 'sitting room' doors, which were our second line of defence. It was nearly dark when we had finished—and there were still the doors onto the balcony. Furthermore, our padlock didn't work; the sitting room doors burst open anyway.

In the end we barricaded ourselves into the central room, drank soda water, ate sardines, rigged our mosquito nets temporarily, and tried to imagine that just this one room was fully lit. And all the time we listened. Tins rattled below us, something slid along the floor, something thudded or plopped. We began to feel dreadfully thirsty. Darkness surged through the House, edged with leaf-movements, the distant and then the nearby bark of dogs. No sooner had we got into our beds than a huge black bat circled the room with a muscular ripple. And there's no hurrying a tropical dawn, although sometimes a cock would crow from somewhere on the edge of my new, frightening domain.

And now I'm scaring myself again as I put this down. Today, however, compensated brilliantly for the horrors of last night. Early this morning we wandered through the estate, eating mangosteens, cheekoos and two delicious passion fruit whose pale suave shapes we discovered on the vine—the sort of fruit Hopkins would have liked, gushing a cool cloudiness punctuated by briskly fragile seeds. A small pineapple was growing on one of the plants along the path to the huts. Problems, in fact, look as though they might be no more than domestic and practical. We have hired a kerosene refrigerator (which was delivered today) but need a stove, a Government report on the better of the two wells, and a Boy.

As I rode to the university today to invigilate an exam, I felt its atmosphere closing round me like a tightening fist. All the relaxed gestures, the generosities, the living and soothing untidiness, lay behind me in Sungei Tengah.

CHAPTER 8

The House

W HEN I think what passes for a desirable prosperous house in a residential suburb in England I
cannot help laughing. Here is so different: as different as
Garbo from the latest Hollywood starlet, or a Dry Mar-
tini from a Coke, or being in love from 'having sex'. On
my balcony I feel that I have taken my stand, however
humbly and clumsily, with what is really important, so
that I can almost visualize the bad things sloughing off and
dropping away, the Tudoresque beams and leaded glass,
the panelled dens and cosy flounced bedrooms, the veneered
cocktail cabinets and chromium ashtrays and porcelain
nudes and rustic animals, indeed the whole mass and weight
of standard objects and stereotyped attitudes, seemingly
hugged ever tighter by my former fellow-countrymen as the
Welfare State spreads wider and wider its shoddy felicity.

A house has two natures: it is shelter—the rain beating
on the roof, the wind howling in the chimney—and it is
spirit, the projection of the personality of others, the
achievement of a personality for itself. As the first it is
cave and, beyond cave, womb: as the second, it so orders
and refines itself that it becomes something almost immaterial, an essence or idea. Although it expresses both
body and mind, it is limited by no particular instance of
either, for it confronts not one single year, nor even one
lifetime, but the whole stream of Time itself as it is
humanized into History. Every house should have in it
the power to recall barn and shed, outlining boldly the
minimum reasons for its existence; but every house,
remembering these things, should keep about it the ghost
of Euclid and the abstract proportions until its lines and
balances invite the eye to see more than is actually present

in the brick and stone. Since beauty is not just any expressive waywardness but relations, and significant distortions, within a traditional framework, a house may sink gracefully into beauty simply by growing old—at least Age brings out the essential human irony in its design and definition. The note of possessiveness, the pitch of certainty, eventually crack, and an old house, perhaps quite ordinary when newly built, is now revealed as holding in a fearful, a constantly trembling, equilibrium the part of it that would fall back to barn, shed and cave, and the other part that would dematerialize itself into no more than a romantic dream. This—I tell myself, pacing upon the balcony—is one of the truths about Sungei Tengah.

Relaxed from practical worries, for the university term is soon over and the immense summer vacation stretches ahead, I feel myself withdrawn by the house into a more timeless, certainly a more orderly pattern, a pattern which, although not entirely believable, is nevertheless far happier than the restless vacuum of the previous months. The House seems to hold within its supererogatory spaciousness, for it is after all too big to be either furnished or fulfilled by us, those various domestic moments in which Gerald and I fit book-shelves out of hairy local planks and bricks dug up in the garden, or paint the dark-green walls in the traditional Chinese blue-grey with the traditional brush or besom; it seems to accept our gifts of potted plants and creepers for the balcony, from whose ceiling we also suspend a large ceremonial canvas fish and on whose table we are later to place a bronze dragon, reputably Ming, as a grown-up might accept the toys a child deposits in its hands; there are, inevitably, moments when we resent the passivity of this existence and attempt rather brusquely to dominate our parent shade, just as there are times when the helplessness in our new found peace crystallizes itself, as it might during a love-affair, into the reflection that this is the peak of our tropical life, that we are now having our moment, and that ever afterwards we

shall look back to the days when we were the squires of
Sungei Tengah. Furthermore, and more practically, we
have no lease. . . .

It is a product of the House's overshadowing influence
that the various ways in which we start to inhabit it all
partake, once fear subsides, of an equal sense of adventure. There seems scarcely any difference in value, or even
any logical sequence, between one and another; to discover a bathing place at Ponggol, where a pale silky sea
nibbles the coconut husks, has an exact equivalence with
the purchase of beer and cigarettes, speaking for the first
time in the Teo'chiu dialect, from one of the local stores,
or the bringing home from Tampenis market of our first
opalescent squid; even my substitution of an old car,
actually an ex-Japanese taxi, for the incongruously athletic
motor-bicycle has, despite its far greater usefulness, no
primacy over the dragon or the canvas fish. Although we
gradually settle down and improve our comfort, until much
time can be spent in conversation, writing, and the generation of theories about almost anything, there has been a
sense of well-being and comfort almost from the first.

It was on the third day, I think, that we bought the
primus stove. Disillusioned by our experience with the
lamp, we had first thought of something that worked
quietly with oil and had searched happily and fruitlessly
any number of hardware stores at the Sixth Milestone, all
exactly the same, lined with bowls and plates and glass jars
and flowered teapots, hung with painted tin lamps and
sticky parasols, and floored, except for an alley, with more
crockery together with buckets and tubs. Some of the
domestic ware in these shops still retains its dynastic
simplicity. At last we went to the place where the workings of the pressure lamp had been explained to us, and
here we bought a stove, sister product to the lamp, for
sixteen dollars. This time we insisted on a demonstration.

'Let's see. You *open* screw. Odd. That's the opposite of
what you do with the lamp. Oh yes, the methylated spirit

in the same sort of jigger. Wait for it to be nearly burned up. Then pump. . . .'

Pump briskly, fiercely, furiously, until prickly heat stings your neck and chest and shoulders, but pump! And suddenly the top, which blushes red and spouts a wavering popping flame, becomes a collar of blue dots. Close the tap. Stop pumping? No, no, pump some more. Blue collar is confirmed, re-inforced. Charcoal and bramble miseries are, perhaps, over. 'Terima-kasi. Thank you very much. Keep it for us. We will be back in a minute.'

We went to the grocery shop where Chinese sit un-expectedly on stools, drinking Dog's Head Guinness. It's the nearest thing to a local. We drank Guinness and looked at the life of the street; nearby were large flat baskets full of yellow ducklings, which sell at forty-five cents each, and across the way a man was noisily hacking and planing wood into coffins. The proprietress opened her refrigerator and thrust fruit at us, practically forcing it into our mouths. It was fat fibrous fruit, studded with warts, which tasted of lemon and cream. We drank our Guinness in between mouthfuls of this custard apple and a boy went by making a sharp tenor sound by tapping a piece of wood with a stick. In the distance ragged Tamils scaled a clump of coconut palms to prepare the morning's brew of toddy.

Back home, we lit our stove after much trouble with the draught from an approaching thunderstorm. We kept putting it in different corners and locking it in, so that it was too dark to see. We propped it on a table and then on a chair, by a window and then far from a window, on the floor in the centre of the room and on the floor in a corner. We treated it gingerly, as befitted a devil, and at last we knelt before it as though it had been a god. Feet of flame leaped from it, yellow and untidy, and then it grew sullen and stertorous and apoplectic and its knob went red. But, in the end, it started.

It was around this time that Gerald and I had a long conversation on the servant-problem, one of the first of a series of similar conversations for which we clearly possess both a talent and a need, having lived bottled-up for so long, and which can be delivered as explosively as we like, since nobody in the neighbourhood is capable of understanding a word of what we are saying. I have sometimes wondered what one of the local squatters must think, supposing him to awake one night and peer out of his lattice, when he sees the two *hoong-mo* on the distant balcony, pacing and gesticulating, hurling cigarettes into the darkness and only pausing angrily to pump the lamp, while all around the forest is splashed momentarily with bars of light, although it is already two or three in the morning. It is impossible that he should understand English, let alone some violently argued point about the ambiguity of the word *Romanticism*, or the pros and cons of poetic analysis. Yet English is not entirely alien to the village. One night, having grown particularly exasperated at Gerald's dogmatic way of arguing and having drunk a whole bottle of that resinous *Ng Kah Pee*, which is the nearest thing to Snake Wine that I can tolerate for more than a glass, I seized one of the minute ikon-lamps and stole into the darkness, terrified of real snakes but determined on reaching the village, *my* village as I most strongly felt it then. It was completely silent and I walked into its middle, before sitting down on the ground. Nevertheless some yellow light leaked through a carefully barred door and to my surprise this was accompanied by the sound of a muted radio, giving a staccato idiomatic account of a boxing match in America. Someone must know English awfully well.

Our conversation seems scarcely to have ended—we had gone back, I remember, to the university flat I still kept on, to have baths—when a boy was standing below the balcony, talking to us in a cheery matter-of-fact way and obviously feeling out the ground. Like Ah Ting, he was also very young; unlike him, he had the scrawny build and blunt cocky manners of someone, very much the peasant, who wants to make his way in the world by becoming an errand boy, and perhaps eventually a mechanic. His singlet was grimy and too big for him; it slouched away from his bony chest. His dark blue shorts had none of the primness of Ah Ting's. His rather Jewish face had the look of an engaging talking-horse, and he began to stutter as he grew excited; he was inclined to gesticulate with his hands, flinging his weight on one jutting hip, so that he looked as though he were in the Mile End Road trying to sell you a tie, ingratiating and yet vaguely shrewish. Surely we had seen his house? He lived two hundred yards away, just over the *jalan*. 'I am Catlic schoolboy,' he said.

This was Leng, who soon began to work for us in the afternoons when school was over. Having given him a camp-cot and a picture of Our Lady of Fatima, we also succeeded in persuading him to sleep in at night. We thought he would be content with a little room at the near end of the annexe but he insisted on coming upstairs, in fact he demanded a mosquito net, stating that he had one at home, and he was displeased when I gave him the camp-cot instead of one of the *rotan* beds. As a matter of fact, he *does* have a net at home, for I have been there several times, but it is a bit of filthy cobweb, riddled with holes, and behind it lie the planks he shares with his brother and, sometimes, his grandmother. The hen-roost is less than a yard away.

Now he runs the household as though it were a boy-scout camp, hurls plates piled with soggy rice and an indecipherable wriggle of dried very salt prawns onto the table, retreats singing 'Oh where are you going, my pretty maid?' *fortissimo*, and has to be called back again and again. 'The butter, Leng . . . and another knife . . . and you've forgotten the sweet potatoes, haven't you?' None of these requests make him in the least surprised or apologetic. He answers with a raucous series of O.K.s and produces the object demanded with an air of triumph. 'A knife? you want a knife? O.K. I give it you. Here is a very nice knife.' And the knife clatters on the table, for he is enormously clumsy. Then, dinner over, he spreads his homework on the only table—his homework seems to consist either of sums or very elaborate lettering exercises —or relaxes in one of the two armchairs, demanding to be entertained. I often find that Gerald has been victimized by Leng's avidity for useless knowledge, and that they are discussing how to play Sardines or whether the streets of New York are really paved with gold. Leng is clearly not an unmixed blessing, but the House interposes, the imaginative life is much more secure, and I have grown quite fond of him despite his clumsiness and laziness. If I open the door I can see him now, asleep on his cot with the rubbish still unemptied and a rat disappearing through the window, his face transformed into that of a young Buddha, and on the shelf above him his prayer book, his Honey and Flowers brilliantine, and his catapult.

It was not, however, Leng's ability to cook the various oddities we provided for him, including a hen purposely run over on the Ponggol Road and of a quite impenetrable toughness, which created his value; it was that, as soon as we got to know him, the area around the House ceased to be a silent and empty space, and became instead full of Aunts and Uncles, Cousins and Ancient Relatives and personalities of one kind and other, amongst whom Leng distributed his favourite epithets of Good-hearted (a great many) and Bad-hearted (only a few). Huts exist everywhere among the trees, often indistinguishable from the shelters built for hens or the storage of coconuts, and family relationships thread between them, as in the case of Leng's older grandmother who is trundled from one to another. Most of the families nearby seem to have no male head and no small-holding to provide them with subsistence; they keep, at most, a pig in addition to their hens and grow a few bananas or a little sugar-cane or tapioca; some of them have already been showing an interest in Chia, the brown dog left by our caretaker when he decamped, and Leng regards this sly animal as a prized dish, giving details of how he could be caught and killed. It is therefore all the more astonishing to see our neighbours—those younger, that is, than the bedraggled matriarchs—emerge from their hovels to pass under the balcony on their way to church. The men, who bicycle to jobs some miles away, are dressed in spotless white; the women twirl parasols and dangle babies; the children appear as beautifully cared for as the little boys and girls who are taken by their nannies to a party in England. They all show a dignified reserve. And, as they pass below us in their slow sensible way, as though required by parasols and babies and the very looseness and big sprawling patterns of their pyjamas to loiter a little, swaying gently together, they bow to us and we, in our turn, bow gravely to them.

Leng's immediate relatives were soon introduced, his mother would do our laundry, a sprightlier grandmother brought us fish and sprigs of 'Chinese vegetable' from the small local market, an uncle of eighteen paid a wordless social call. And then, one afternoon, the chief matriarch of all—his lop-sided pirate-eyed grandmother-in-chief— was dragging herself up the stairs, peering shrewdly into the corners of the almost bare rooms, and finally sitting in ragged state on the balcony. We both felt grateful and reverent in front of the great age which had cleaved its way into her body (she had, so it seemed, lost not only an eye but a breast, and her skin was so tightly drawn and intricately wrinkled that it became something outside herself, like a stain, *through* which you must look); like an old tree, whose pulp has long withered away, she outlined the limits of a particular, but not easily discernible, *space*; and it was from this dark spacious memory that she addressed us, in a series of Teo'-chiu croaks, to the effect that life was hard, death would come soon, some of her sons had disappointed her, the Japanese had destroyed the others, but Leng was alive, Leng was intelligent . . . she was glad we had become the protectors of Leng. And shortly afterwards my responsibility for Leng was confirmed when he asked me to sign a vaccination certificate, which had been given him at school, in the role of parent or guardian.

However, Leng was not the only child I had to deal with. Children, in fact, invaded the House. There was Leng's brother Kim, who couldn't make my typewriter write Chinese although he tried hard enough, and there was the nature child, Ah Tum, who brought us bulbuls' nests and once a baby bulbul, but I think the symbol for it all was a Tamil boy called Ambi who possessed what the poet described as 'a deep but dazzling darkness'. He didn't really know English but he disguised this fact with an extraordinarily cultured accent. The first time he approached me in the village, and began fondling one of the doors of my car, I asked him whether he would like to go to town on the following day and he turned up that very afternoon, beautiful in blue shirt and white shorts and socks, having hopelessly misunderstood me. I couldn't disappoint him, although I was very busy preparing a talk for Radio Malaya. It was a curious journey, because half the time he was flashing with smiles, and what smiles they were—triumphant processions along broad avenues, yachts sailing down shining straits—and the other half he was in tears. He would burst into tears quite suddenly, if anything in the least unexpected happened, if I left him for a moment to go into a shop or met someone with whom I had to carry on a few moments' conversation. I bought him a bag of peanuts to give to the monkeys in the Botanical Gardens, but we couldn't find the monkeys and so ate the peanuts ourselves. This seemed to calm him a little. It's difficult to be very intense when you are eating peanuts. After this, I saw nothing of him for at least two months. Then he was on the balcony again, wolfing mangosteens and tossing their rinds onto the ground below. It was then that he did a very strange thing. He jumped up, slid over to the balustrade, knelt down and gave a succession of firm but affectionate pats to the earth around the potted plants. He came back to his chair and sat rather awkwardly, smiling when he caught my eye, looking miserable when he didn't: a big boy dressed like a little one, although not in party clothes this time. Then, after some preliminary wriggling, he was again propelled out of the chair and once more the soil was being pressed down and smoothed. Twice he did this and then disappeared. On the occasion of our third meeting he introduced a variation by suddenly running out of the room and beginning to wash the teacups. Even then he wouldn't stay. After this I didn't see him again until the day we were leaving for our week in Malacca, when he came up to us at the bus stop, shook hands, burst into floods of tears and escaped down the village street.

I have never understood what he meant by all this, and there was no time for a further query: the yellow mosquito bus plunged to a stop by the attap shelter used by the Travelling Dispensary on its weekly visits; we jumped aboard; the red laterite road to the House, the screen of tapioca, the fat floppy banana plants, were all sucked back into the distance and there was no sign of Ambi in the squat arcaded village. I suppose he liked us—perhaps liked us very much, needed us very badly, but we haven't seen him since and it is difficult to know.

It is always difficult to know during these months when we hang suspended on our balcony in the coconut grove. The children contribute their often ghostly presence, to which each adds some individual sign. Leng, the most articulate, will suddenly reveal a streak of poetry. Finding sand in my socks he approaches me gravely with the remark, 'I shall have to tell the Master of the Sea that you have stolen some of his gold!' Once he finds a huge fig leaf and invites me to sail with him in it to the island of Pulau Ubin. Osman, the Malay youth who helps me to pick my crop of aromatic velvety cheekoos (really a sort of guava), is no less ready with that one personal gesture which seems to sum everything up once and for all. One day I take him swimming. The tide is high, the water pearl-coloured. I notice that he stays very close to the shore and am at first afraid that he may be bored. But when I go to investigate I find that he has made a little mountain of sand under the water, decorated with shells and tufted with a green sprig, and that he is now trying to guide some minute fish into this paradise with his hands. . . .

Such are the pictures which steal into the House, as light might steal into one of those old solid cameras, or as the children themselves steal during the otherwise motionless afternoons, or as the spider-lilies press their faces through the wooden bars of the annexe windows. And the House itself is box-like, old only because of the weather and the war: a cream-coloured concrete square that you see over the dead leaves of the rubber, with the shifting perspectives of the thin trees about you, and overhead the rinsed and scattered light; pushed forward by the thatched outbuildings, themselves scarcely discernible in the undergrowth, and establishing itself in a square solid way, as you walk along Jalan Seranggong Ketchil, past the pigsties and the incinerator, and look left down the gentle slope of the path to the stone gate-posts and the big wire gate—your mind in a daze of heat and orange-coloured sand as you enter the shallow gloom of the rubber, pause by some sad little tree bleeding latex into its cracked cup, notice how the play of leaves above you is echoed by a flock of newly-hatched chickens scurrying over the ground; below you, then, the House, in its un-likely situation and at its oddly oblique angle, neither welcoming you nor turning you away but staring out over nothing in particular, seems to create a ghostliness out of its very solidity, as it glimmers at you from its palms. A blind man looks like that, with an intensity that turns out to be patience, at nothing in particular.

Beyond the rubber and through the gate you come out into the larger proportions of the coconut grove. Each palm has its own individuality, each is eccentric in its personal way, for none of them is ever quite straight and their lithe mast-like qualities are always mixed with untidiness at the bottom and extravagance at the top. If in one place they manage to march on each side of a path, with a grey-green dignity, in another they withdraw, at mad angles, from a bald patch of ground. The space in front of the house is overgrown but sketchy, a number of the shrubs look as though they could do with a good wash; your over-all impression may be of dead leaves and chicken wire, somebody's sow rampaging under the rambutans, a mangy dog slinking off through the spider-lilies and any number of trespassing hens. Here is the porch. The big double-doors are dark red and splintered; a cheap padlock secures them from outside, without quite closing the gap; it is only from inside that they groan romantically and give an appearance of strength as they fasten with an immense wooden bar which clangs through the house as it falls into place. They are decorated with four Chinese characters in gold, two to a door. THE HOLY GHOST THE SHINING LIGHT is what the legend says and this note of piety is echoed in a sepia metal plaque of the Virgin above the entrance, for the House was at one time the home of a group of Sisters of Mercy, but whether it was used as convent, school or rest-house I still don't know. (The bath would have been splendid for a school— ten or fifteen children could, without exaggeration, have been bathed in its porridge-coloured depths at the same time.) More obscure is the reason for two granite blocks on each side of the House. These blocks are carved and though the design is very hard to decipher by day I have found that the headlights of a car throw them into relief; deer on one block, on the other a bird flying down to feed its young. But what occasioned the setting up of the blocks I cannot discover. Certain grooves on the upper surface seem to rule out one's first guess that they were used to mount horses. Nevertheless the idea still persists and I imagine some remote Squire of Sungei Tengah, a sensitive

N

young moon-face perhaps or a fabulously stout tow-kay of the chase, leaving his porch for a crocodile hunt in the Ponggol River or the pursuit of wild boar in the Seletar wastes. Pythons and hamadryads would not be beneath his attention. A stirrup cup of *samsoo*, the blowing of a Chinese pipe, and off he would go surrounded by the ancestors of the dogs that surround us: Chia, Brindle, the asthmatic Lord Rosebery, and those formidably bouncing rockinghorse dogs who daily invade the estate with intent to do Chia harm.

Enter those double doors, whose edges crackle to your touch, and you are at once in the heart of the House. There are no preliminaries whatever. There is just a great stone-floored room, as long and wide as the main building itself, and completely empty except for an elaborate oval table, now in two pieces and propped up against one of the walls, and (oddly enough) a small built-in bookcase with glass doors and a trace of lacquer between the glass. You go in, admire space and chill, and there is nothing for you to do but go out again, through the opposite doors. Yet in that moment you have experienced the atmosphere, smelt the smell, heard the noises—looked up at the ceiling and seen it was pale blue, given a second glance and noticed a largish hole which is part of the floor of my bedroom. (Leng, of course, cannot resist the temptation to sweep dust through this hole.) You have been watched by six barred windows and two paint-choked grilles and you have felt the shadows and the dusts and the cobwebs about you. 'A good place for a banquet—or for storing sacks of flour. This is where he interviews his retainers—or buries his bodies.' And then your eyes are drawn down the vista, across the courtyard and through the barn, to the view into the garden. But everywhere here is garden, and nowhere is garden complete. Everywhere is tropical mixture of garden and waste. Here, though, in the big room, the tropics are subdued as they should be, not by cutting down the undergrowth and letting in the full treacherous light as the Europeans do with their jerry-built modernities, but by good thick walls and narrow shuttered windows. You spend only a moment in the room, no doubt, but during that moment you feel the House yawn, with the automatic yawn of the Ages, and you feel that you must stand very still, still as a rock, because the stillness of the House is precious and it is so easy for you to find yourself no more than an odd noise in it. (You make the noise; the House replies with a deep tenor *sound*, answering in the accents of Eternity.) You had better be a beggar here than a brightly-dressed *mem sahib*, full of exclamations (but wait until she asks for the lavatory). There are beggarly things about: a fishy stain on a windowsill where one of the pi dogs pulled down the morning's fish before we could get to it; a smell in the courtyard which suggests that the pedantry with which Lengs talks of 'relieving myself' and 'passing urine' does not apply to the locale of the act; a rat or two whom agility and long practice have made almost air-borne. . . .

One day, in fact, a beggarly dog came here to die, shambling in unseen from the green daze of the *lallang*, hiding out at first in a dark corner of the barn, but climbing after breakfast the next morning to the upper storey and curling its horribly tortured body under one of the low rotan beds: Gerald's bed, of course, as though it knew him already. In the jollity of early morning there was suddenly this sickening stench, right in the most private part of the house, and there he lay, half-eaten with disease before our eyes, no part of him not suffering with equal patience, one long disaster from tail to ear, and knowing it in his last mournful look of apology.

You are now in the courtyard which lies between the concrete main house and the thatched annexes. Ferns grow in the damp walls, moss sprouts between the bricks of the floor. But the courtyard is unorthodox; the central part is built over by a projection of the upper storey (once our kitchen and now our dining room and Leng's sleeping quarters) and to the right is the original kitchen, a sort of shadowy verandah open only on the interior side. The farther end of this cavernous and unpromising looking kitchen gives onto the bathroom which is parallel to the beginning of the attap barn. Here is the huge concrete bath, eight feet by five, and nowadays served only by a rain pipe from the roof which debouches raggedly in the middle air over it—or, of course, by buckets from the well. And in the outer wall are no less than three prim little lavatories, Pre-Raphaelite in appearance, their doors filled with amber-tinted glass. All are quite unusable. It was in the middle lavatory that the bees finally decided to swarm.

The outbuildings are cool and dark. The walls are bare brittle wood, the criss-cross lattices splintered and peeling, and the wooden bars on the windows would not impede an intruder for long. Look up, the steep roof is windowless and shadowy but the pleated attap, the colour of cinnamon, glows neatly and ingeniously through. There is an upstairs gallery whose floor and balustrade are obviously unsafe. The doors at the back are left open during the day. They frame a patch of moist yellow light presided over by a blowsy banana plant which bears grotesque fruit, a foot long, perhaps four inches wide, brown in colour and tasting of porridge. Outside the windows are beds of spider-lilies.

This part of the House, Tudor-Gauguin-Dutch, with its decay and gayness, its shadow and space, will always, I think, remain unpossessed. One walks through it, a trifle uncomfortably, because one isn't a child wanting to play hide and seek. There is a sort of giddiness of ownership, though, walking (most probably in bare feet) over the red floor until one gets to the rubbish and dirt that rats or the dogs have rooted out from a refuse box by the doorway, or is discomforted to find the gleaming tiles crossed by migrations of ants, so that one begins to look upon it all as a responsibility and says angrily and breathlessly, as one emerges into the heat, 'I must get Leng to clean up properly. The rubbish must be buried. There must be

plans and energy. Authority must be asserted.' And a
large red ant crawls up one's ankle.

Attached to these outbuildings is another attap shed
marked Cook House in chalk; a relic, I suppose of the
Sisters of Mercy. As a matter of fact there is a good deal
written upon the walls: characters dating from the Occupation, when a Japanese ran a chicken farm here, refer to
some distant order for *Cheap rice twelve people, medium
rice eight people, best rice five people, tidy up seven people* but
by the Cook House, where the janitor lived when we first
arrived, there is the following line from a Chinese poem—

When my lover is gone and the almond trees are in flower....

Just the one line, no more, scribbled in the darkest
part of the barn, broken off perhaps when a strangely
literate coolie was called to order, or itself the expression of an inner resistance to Japanese overlordship—
these words add to the House their perspective of feeling and language, wander innocently and helplessly
through by-ways which may be beneath the attention of
the exterior legend, THE HOLY GHOST THE SHINING
LIGHT, and now rise from the shadows to taunt us with
their meaning. Are we to find in them some hint, even
here, of the 'paradox' and 'dialectic tension' which are now
so fashionable in the poetry of the West, some hint of
Eliot's hyacinth girl and hyacinth garden, and of the
cruellest month when Spring reminds us of things that
other people have desired? Or is there, in their juxta-
position of loss and natural promise, no more than the
continuous lotus-eating acceptance, the happy dazed sus-
pension in a life without firm demarcation, and bereft of
seasonal change, which now and then makes us grow
restless, and attempt to dominate a place in which we are
so quietly cradled? What we do and say is often a good
deal larger than life: we make speeches at each other
during our balcony evenings, and I at least have plenty to
drink. Counterbalancing this Elizabethanism of action

and thought is the general fluidity with which life answers us; the 'squire's' determined stride and peremptory gestures are really no more than tentative sun-drenched ambles into frivolity and untidiness, accompanied perhaps by nervous little bows or waves to the tenants he passes; he feels himself at least superficially irrelevant (a ghost returning to childhood or a friendly clown) because what he 'belongs to' is not the surface picture of poverty, politics, pig-keeping, and so on, but a 'deeper reality', and anyway he isn't sure how he wants to belong. You can't become a functioning member of the community, but you can imagine yourself *hiding* in its attractive foreignness, *intuitively understanding* the primitiveness or innocence or vitality of which you feel it to be the expression, and *drowning* in an atmosphere where aesthetic stimulation suggests deep significance. And then, as a reaction, you may try to be masterful and domineering. The House is thoroughly sane, of course; it can even be a corrective to one's more fantastic flights, if only because it has to be looked after and helped to keep alive; inside it we may be lords but, as it magnifies our voices, it changes them, caricatures our enthusiasm, puts hysteria into our violence, makes loneliness sound like a knell. Only sometimes are we poets.

Imagine for a moment the situation on the balcony. It is a little world in the air, entangled with the trees, thrust into no particular view or direction. Beneath it lies the sandy right-of-way to the squatter huts. Here we come to look, and be looked at. Here we are both critics watching the stage and actors pacing upon it, and of course neither. And it is here that I tell myself that I am alive and in Asia and that there is meaning to what I see and that I love this meaning. Then there is a great rattle and Kim rushes by, ringing his bell. Did I experience—possess that? Or does Kim exist only in some far wider and far remoter totality, inherited from years ago, in which I have no responsibility, while his present actions function merely as images? As I wonder, I notice again a thickening cloud of very

small bees in the air beyond the balustrade. Another
swarm to be warded off, with paper alight on the ends of
broom handles, before they choose the balcony roof. One
of those deceptively mild utterances . . . but of what?
'Something deeply known as in poetry, where meaning
doesn't matter.' Perhaps one needs something more tangible and active than that in real life, I think, beginning
again the Elizabethanism of 'getting across'—but what I do
is to fetch a broom handle, and wave lighted paper, and if I
am really being dominant when I do these things (if this is
different from reverie), I am alas too preoccupied to notice.

Upstairs double doors close gravely, decisively, excluding Leng when his home-work and occupancy of the one
table become a burden, or his Catholic propaganda proceeds too long at too breakneck a pace. Outside the gates,
he can set his rat-traps, pee, and pray. The bedroom doors
(there are two to a room) have despite their cruder work-
manship a smooth light action, which lends itself to chinks
and obliquities; they open to a whisper, close like a finger
placed against the lips; you enter your bedroom as though
you retreated into your own thoughts, for your shut door
has the spiritual force of a silence; it is scarcely physical
since it doesn't lock. I fall asleep amongst the rough edges
of books I have taken under the mosquito net, not so much
to read thoroughly as to admire for their incongruous
juxtapositions: *Peter Pan And Wendy* side by side with
Death in Venice and an engineering manual by my father
on winding-engines. As the pressure-lamp stutters and
smokes, reminding me that it is time to put it out, I find
myself examining the small volume on Aubrey Beardsley
which my father gave my mother, *having first torn out two
of the illustrations.* And would my artistic great-uncle have
ever dreamt that his album of water-colours of Ben Nevis
and Cader Idris should one day be used to pin down a pile
of shirts from the force of a tropical sumatra?

I like the House best at twilight. It is grey enough to be
almost cool. It lives then by being perspectives, diagonals,

shadows; lives in open doorways, half closed windows and
the spaces of shining (although dirty) floor. I look with
delight at my open doors. They are static only in the most
theatrical way, like perfectly trained servants in prepared
positions around a table: green doors, and darker green
on green, with a faint efficient bit of shine on them where
they catch the light, a briskness like a badge, and open at
angles—so absolutely at one particular angle that their
stillness is the condensation, or the beautiful nervous
equilibrium, of movement, and they are engaged in a
ceremony, they are preparing something, waiting for
someone to come in; running from them are angles of
shadow with a shine there too, a soft brightness. Their
very geometry in its expectancy seems to give off light,
but it is crepuscular light, light reflected in dark water.

And as often when one concentrates there is an unexpected note—the reminder from outside that one is not
self-sufficient, which, taken rightly, may open up a whole
new perspective. The dining-room windows are rarely
closed, and windows are so uncommon in this country
anyway, that I have forgotten that the top panes are,
rather horridly, of blue-green glass. A cool dim eye peers
in or, more truly, holds back the light within its confines.
And beside it, for the other portion is open, there is a
mass of foliage, darkly, wetly glowing: *bambusa vulgaris*, a
cheekoo tree, rambutans. The leaves are strangely still:
violently still, as though their soul had come back and
stood behind them.

One night, when the pressure-lamp has been left for
safety in the courtyard, we come home to find its base
deep in a ring of flying ants, their wings the colour of
maple sugar or pale mink, crowding towards the light
with only a few actually flying about it, so that I can stroke
a mass of them gently. A hundred pairs of wings make a
single feather, perhaps ten thousand all the plumes beneath my hand. When one moves the light they follow
and quickly form again into a whispering circle.

CHAPTER 9

The Silence of Ah Tum

ONE day the coconut grove is sprinkled with pigeon orchids. These small white flowers, aerial and shy, float from the shaggy mangosteens with a tentative pallor more suitable to an English spring than the exotic East. In this they are typical of Malaya, whose light itself is a paradox, tyrannous, all-pervasive, and yet at the same time absent-minded and dreaming, as though it let the landscape pour through moist hands without bothering to make a collection or even a list. Interesting, strange things come to you singly. After a year of having seen no snakes at all you just miss stepping on a particularly large and poisonous one—and that in a suburban street. You find *one* scorpion only, mysteriously afloat in your cup of tea, followed weeks or months later by *one* pitcher plant or colony of flying-foxes (bits of umbrella blown to pieces in a blasted tree) or wild-pig or mouse-deer. All the rest have got themselves lost in the vacuous sunshine. And people themselves share in this. Parts of them seem to get lost, too, so that they smile vividly but do not speak, or perform unexplained and enigmatic acts of kindness, or get thoroughly muddled as to whether they are anti-British nationalists or not.

The pigeon-orchids are a case in point, because they look as though they had lost the sinister orchid fleshiness and virtuosity altogether, and we have to convince ourselves that they are at least trying to be voluptuous, that their mild cadenza belongs somehow to the passion-drunk tone poems of the Nineteenth Century, and that they have some faint affinity with *Les Fleurs du Mal*. We pull down a great bramble of them, at least twenty feet long, which we twine in and out of the balcony of the House. Within twenty-four hours all the orchids are dead, but then so are those left on the trees. And nothing really exotic has happened—or, rather, what has happened has been the emergence, after a considerable interval, of Ah Tum. His delicate figure, refined into obliquity, again appears on the path below and his catapult makes the leaves of the big tree tinkle and snap like breaking glass.

Ah Tum is said to be eleven years old. He has become the principal figure amongst the children who bring the life of the village to our doorstep and then up the stairs, who watch us as we lie in bed or have to be evicted from the doorless bathroom, not because he is as noisily friendly as the others (rather the reverse) but because he is in some way very different from his companions. He is shy, for one thing, but this shyness of his is neither the timidity of the little girls nor the emotionalism of Ambi, whose behaviour always embodied some unexpressed want; it is an animal shyness mixed with a kind of independence far beyond his years, and it is something he carries with him wherever he goes so that, even when he is being friendly and playful, he is still as nervous—no, as high-pitched— as a flower. All his movements have the elegance of a taut independence adjusting itself to the world around it. His normal position is tentative, on a slant; he reaches out, draws back. Since he is naturally very graceful, this reticence gives him an air of spiritual delicacy, as though he hesitated on aerial thresholds while the rest of us blundered away in our basements. But what interests me particularly is that he remains Chinese, without having recourse to the usual Chinese forms of charm. To find the Chinese attractive, really attractive, is one of the things I want to do while I live in the House.

This probably needs some explanation, since it is one of those elaborate personal indulgences which life here allows one time for, and since it plays its part in the story of these months. First, then, there's sensuousness, mostly visual: I like people and things for the way they look. But

liking them is dangerous, demanding contacts and action
and leading often to disappointment, and so it seems to me
that I tend to scurry back with my visual images to my
cell, where I reproduce the object of experience along my
nerves, performing an inner act upon myself; more than
touch, this is a kind of muscular embodiment. And then,
to spiritualize what is appropriated in this vivid but lonely
fashion, I turn my experience into a symbol and, since
symbols last when impressions fade and die, I approach
the world again with a whole set of imaginative preconceptions. One of these is that something 'strange' and
'difficult' is better than something pleasantly ordinary.
Thus, with regard to the native races, I have the traditional British liking for the Malays: some of them are very
beautiful (the visual sense); they have a distinctive vivacity within an encompassing, seemingly amoral, laziness
and grace (this appeals to one's own physical make-up);
they are supposed to be 'primitive' and 'childlike' (which
is consistent with one's symbolism). On the other hand,
the Chinese are primarily attractive because they require
an effort, both in the sense that the British like them less
and in the further sense that their solidarity and reserve,
externalized in a kind of 'water-proofing' and sexlessness,
make few demands. The Malays are obvious, amenable,
in technicolour, almost anyone's suburban dream; over
the Chinese, on the other hand, one's baffled symbolism,
taunted but not entirely fulfilled by one's visual sense,
casts an atmosphere of mystery.

When Leng looks like a young Buddha he is markedly
'strange', because it is an effort to see this quality in him;
when Kim develops the chubby Chinese baby into the gay
young Chinese tough, he is not 'strange' at all, although
the finished product will probably be so. What is remarkable about Ah Tum is that he is neither 'strange' in the
Leng way (gawky ugliness taking on very occasional
beauty, as though re-absorbed into the Chinese past) nor
is he just childish and puppyish in the manner of Kim;

he is the most aesthetically acceptable of the Chinese I know, not because he is 'easy' but because he transposes their strangeness into something much closer to my imaginative preconceptions, although still very mysterious. If this makes any sense, it may show why I romanticize him. In any case, it is natural that we should associate him with the jungle in which he spends so much of his time, with the sandy glade which leads, as Leng puts it, *inside* past our balcony and along which various little girls also pass, with pink parasols and red plastic handbags, spotlessly clean, fervently shy, as they return from school to the hovels they share with the pigs and the hens.

I call out to him from my position on the balcony. He looks up in his quizzical way, his eyes slanting under the soft curve of his fringe. For a moment he drifts below me, shoulder-high in his leafy preoccupation, so that I can imagine his eliding with the tree, or floating up into its dense glossy foliage. With his bare brown shoulders and delicately articulated shoulder-blades and arms, he is surprisingly frail—and, unlike the little girls, dirty. Then he is propelled away, dwindling back over the dead leaves of the path, self-absorbed, indifferent, possibly hostile.

I call Gerald.

'Tum-tum was here. He saw me and trailed off. I wonder why he doesn't like us. Surely he can't be afraid?' But Gerald repeats the few abrupt secessions and disentanglements in the affair of Tum in a voice expert in disillusion. 'He wouldn't come back in the car from the *wayang*. He left us after the movies. He hasn't brought us any bee-eaters or stick insects for days.'

'But we went to his house, at least I think it was his house . . .,' I persist, as though the mere effort were neighbourly—I am conscious, as so often during our balcony conversations, that there isn't much point in being logical, just as it doesn't matter very much what an athlete says when he has won a race or what is murmured amongst the flowers by a sick-bed: the dramatic fact is all that counts, and the dramatic fact to us is that we are being absorbed day by day into the coconut grove. In the green context of this existence our words have a new passivity. They are responses to what has happened to us deeply even when they point out that nothing at all has happened on the surface.

'He wasn't there. There were boys hiding in all the trees but not Ah Tum.' Scarcely listening, I see only the picture of that recent stumble—not far, surely not more than five hundred yards, but nonetheless infinitely *inside*: two sweating white figures, part priests, part clowns, moving through the pressure of eyes under the untidy sunlight, barked at by dogs of only apparent ferocity, scattering carpets of hens at their approach, with the land-scape around them tumbled, frivolous, intimate, like the beds on which one romped as children. The walk had quite ridiculously the sense of daring, and yet it wasn't just daring because in some way one already belonged.

There is, however, a possible reason for Ah Tum's staying away and, as his figure vanishes among the trees, this reason draws me back to the time about two weeks ago when we were coming across him quite often. It is con-nected with the wild flowers growing all over the estate and began, appropriately enough, with an attempt not only to understand them more fully but to relate them to him; its danger may have lain in the fact that a metaphor must not be confused with its original, that symbolism must not turn back again to re-arrange the objects given it by experience. Art is all very well but behind art is much lonely sensuality and dreaming; to make life like art involves, quite beyond a contrivance which can grow arid, a violence and ruthlessness which may end up as actually insensitive. And if an attempt was then made not merely to draw from Tum a secret he was perhaps unaware of possessing, but to smother him with secrets of one's own, the other Chinese boys, reacting on their part to what they sensed as being dramatic and exciting, tended to push him away from the group by ridiculing the 'strange-ness' in his beauty.

I remember the way Kim jeered when he showed me a small bird cupped in his fingers; although the bird chirped merrily, he shouted again and again, 'It will die! It will die!' This note of ridicule, although it now masked admiration, we often heard when Ah Tum stood at the fringe of the group and was seized upon by voices and hands. It was as though the children expected something miraculous to happen, dared it to happen, and hid their disappointment when Tum's hand slid into his ragged shirt to produce no animal, no small glossy dragon, but simply to scratch, by a triumphant coarseness. Yet when-ever he decided to do something in his quiet way, they always followed him more noisily and clumsily; they rolled coconuts along the ground, aimed their catapults at each other, offered food to the dog they really wished only to eat; by the time they were fully absorbed, Tum was al-ready thinking of doing something else, which usually meant that he was excusing himself. Unexpectedly he would utter a few shrill words and then turn helplessly towards us. Leng might explain 'Ah Tum say he must go now make pig-sty for his Auntie', or, 'Ah Tum velly sorry but he need pass urine' or even, 'Ah Tum bad boy—go village buy siglets,' and, whatever Leng said, Ah Tum would listen with a look of charming perplexity, his head tilted, a deprecatory smile just visible on his face.

On the day I am thinking about I was determined to make notes on the flowers in the grove. I felt depressed, as often before, by my inability really to *see* things, and blamed an introspective analytical nature together with the frivolous quality of the light. So I made forays into the garden, returned with a sprig of something, cursed the ants on its stalk and leaves, and placed it on the table where I could look at it properly. I was encouraged by the fact that I had tried this method with our first live squid, and it had seemed to work. After a little I began to write:

'*The Passion Flower*—cosmetic tiger. A skirt of minutely spotted tongues over scallops of green, a ring of claws beaded in purple but very near to the base the beads are almost red—centipedes' legs, the legs of baby lobsters—then a lantern of these claws which flow out, round themselves and curve in again like the shape of a bowl but each claw has a twist and their tops twist and wrinkle from left to right—they are purple to violet, tops faintly yellow, at the base the white and reddish beads are regular, then the red becomes purple and mingles with the white and has a soft puckered wrinkled texture like the cheeks of old ladies; inside it is a deep striped bowl full of rich scent of the order of frangipani, a little like night-scented stock, a little like clematis, and this scent is also in the smooth yellow fruit, with its water-drop shape, a pale suave fruit, which gushes into one's mouth a pulp full of thin brittle seeds for the teeth to crack. Inside the flower it is the dome of an opera house, the chandelier of four green prongs spotted with red to which are attached cream boat-shapes, hat-shapes, and between them a yellow ball from which spring three legs with cloven hoofs in red dust and yellow velvet. Botanical words for all this? My American dictionary dares to speak of the fruit as, of all things, the *maypop*. ... The passion is not the mingling of our misty limbs but Christ's.'

For the sensitive plant I took some paper with me and walked down the path to where a patch was to be found. Here I scribbled: '*The Sensitive Plant* and a common enough weed, as ubiquitous as neurosis. Like most sensitives the stalk is *thorned*. At a touch the segments of the long thin leaves shut together and the stalk that bears them bows to the earth, a very mechanical obeisance. The closed leaves, the oval ends of the segments lying neatly over each other, suggest the body of a grasshopper. The flower is a ball of violet threads, like the bloom of a pink; the threads are silky to the touch and each one is pointed with a brilliant spot of pollen; at the base, where they are packed together, their colour is salmon pink. The seed pods grow in a bunch, four separate oval seeds in a pod, and the pods are cactus-like and hairy. The modesty of the plant lasts about five minutes. Its dusty overpunctual intermittences take place at the sides of roads and forest paths and in the sandy patches under the palm trees.'

It was then that I realised that I was being watched. Ah Tum glimmered behind the jack-fruit tree and as I rather self-consciously kicked the timid leaves, he rolled the tree's single enormous fruit in his hands, laying his cheek against the tree trunk. For once we both appeared to be happily aimless in the same way; although I was far from thinking myself aimless, I probably appeared so to him. He followed me to the spider-lilies. These I didn't have to observe, because there were many in the House, but I noticed again their crinkled parachutes of white silk, with six ribs hardening and coarsening into white, yellow and then waxy green stanchions, until a worm of orange pollen dangled at each tip. I noticed how eagerly they burst from their tubes and how this upward thrust was balanced by six grooved and fluted out-riders of the same pure white as the parachute, which separated themselves from the stalk just below it and were less transparent, striped satin to its silk. Meanwhile Ah Tum looked down in perplexity at the swooping uplifted shapes, moving one foot from side to side. They had the intense searching look of Pre-Raphaelite women and corrected their often languid stance in the last few inches, long-necked, full-faced. Only here and there a flower drooped, with its tendrils curved beneath it, or actually kissed the ground, burying itself in a deep curtsy of spread entangled fronds. And now it seemed to me that my watching the flowers attentively and peacefully became a kind of tribute to Ah Tum, who was himself so much more oblique than the lilies' thrust and fall, but who shared with them their delicacy, the aura of nervousness given them by their out-riding tendrils: a tribute in the sense that I was looking outside myself, respectfully, and waiting and being aimless.

Of course this moment of tranquillity had to be broken. I snapped a stalk, began to pick the flowers. I indicated to Ah Tum that he might like to do the same. And so it was as flower-pickers that we moved on from the lilies to the hibiscus, across the marshy part of the estate where the mangosteens stand, rugged old trees, covered with moss and given, by the green dabs at the base of their fruit, the appearance of having hundreds of eyes. Already I began to feel that Ah Tum wanted to withdraw. He carried his lilies in front of him, holding them with both hands as though searching for a place to put them down, and he smiled with more than usual incredulity when I started on the hibiscus. Perhaps he thought it silly to pick such a common weed. Yet its five petals are crinkled and striated flame, fanning out from the neck to etiolated fringes, and brushing against each other so that they give the flower a twist, suggesting that it is beginning to spin. When I looked over my shoulder, I saw that he had shifted the lilies to one side and that his hand was reaching out towards a flower so slowly and uncertainly that it seemed impossible that he would pick it. I hoped that he had found some creature hiding in the hedge, which he was attempting to capture. But no, it looked as though he didn't dare to touch the flame-coloured bloom. However it was weak flame, as smooth and waxy to the fingers as crayon on paper. And underneath the red was ashen, the crinkles a definite fluting and branching, a darker shade of silver-red against the lighter, with the spiral more clearly revealed. On top the crimson and pink were slurred, the petals had minute breaks in them and rubbed dusty places; at the neck of the petal was a smooth abrupt downward chute, with a dead slick lacquer.

And then it was, for I had been moving rather fast out of a feeling that I must draw Tum with me lest he fade altogether, that we found ourselves by Leng's well where, since it was now beginning to be evening, Leng and Kim were about to wash. This made a sudden break. They rushed towards us, to where Ah Tum stood shrinking below his load of flowers, their voices sharp and cruel in the greying light. 'Ah Tum! He your servant now Sah? He velly nice flower-boy now, Sah? He smelling of velly pretty flowers!' They danced round him as his smile grew pale and worried, his body swayed and sharpened. Was he really annoyed? It was impossible not to join in the dance. Suddenly, on an impulse, I stretched out an hibiscus and laid it against his unusually brown cheek. Immediately Leng shrieked at the top of his voice, 'Ah Tum is a Malay! Ah Tum is really a Malay!'—and it is certainly true, although the red flower confirmed it, that part of Ah Tum's attraction lies in the darker colour of his skin. But no Chinese wants to be told that he resembles a Malay and I, for my part, felt at that moment a more familiar tension as the Malay charm seemed to fall, like the colour of blood, across Ah Tum's face.

Remembering this incident, I scarcely expect to see him again today, but a few minutes later he has returned and is once more standing beneath the tree. Gerald says, 'Well, at least our tree seems to have the best birds,' and then, looking over the balustrade, 'but surely that isn't Tum— that couldn't be Tum.' And I reply that I think it is, a foolish answer because I am inwardly certain, except for the difficulty in ever being factual about ghostliness: in what sense is Ah Tum *real* to us anyway? So we call Leng and Leng says immediately yes, of course it's Ah Tum, which he pronounces half with affectionate contempt and half with the sound of trumpets and triumph, as he usually does: the *Ah* much gentler than the quick decisive final syllable which, having achieved its drumbeat, surrenders itself into all the amusingly tender connotations of *Tum*. So that its very fierceness—and we think of Ah Tum as a miniature Thoreau, a nature child—surrenders as it bursts upon the ear, and is affectionate. And our

English play with it, making it Tum-tum, is at once a rattle of the kettledrums and a pat upon the back.

Leng, who has no grace at all except for his whimsy, shouts *Lie* meaning *Come* and to our amazement Tum enters the House, slips into the House obliquely, hesitantly, as he used to do a couple of weeks or more ago. 'Tum is coming,' says Leng. There is a bird noise in the hollow of the house, and steps: Tum advances, but only I feel sure to hang back from doorway to doorway, or to float out beyond us to the balustrade, staring into the tree, one leg drawn back, as though we had all whispered him, or as though we had checked him on our breath.

But Gerald insists. 'Whatever Leng says it's not the same Tum. He's older, or wiser, or something. He's had a shock. It's probably all the movies.'

The picture of Ah Tum in imaginative distress at the movies holds my attention for I have seen him there several times and I understand that he is a constant picture-goer. Not that the Overseas C ema, newly arrived in the kampong, is particularly corrupting. A screen has been set up in the heart of a coconut grove, in the open air of course, and one sits on rough wooden benches in an enclosure of patched multi-coloured canvas while a smoky beam of light, frequently intermittent, throws upon the dark air above the heads of numerous children—or draws out from the forest itself—a series of Chinese costume dramas, usually in a dialect that hardly anybody understands. But I can imagine Tum bewitched by the visions in front of him, the girls dressed up as boys and fighting and singing in an intense ritual way, the marauders leaping from the roofs upon their victims and —above everything else—the wizards and counter-wizards with their inexplicable magic. Who is good and who is bad in a world where everything seems so unfair— why should one old man in venerable whiskers be preferable to another no less patriarchally hirsute—why should the sympathetic-looking Tartar be blinded so excruciatingly because an old gentleman, engaged in a kind of High Mass, suddenly fires a minute arrow at an effigy on the wall beside him? Somebody is always throwing something, it's all a bit like baseball or cricket, and the things thrown (a brooch, an amulet, a bronze snake or a jug) writhe and twist on the screen, as a diver does in slow motion, and then produce those pale scratchy aureoles and rays one sees in an early Siennese painting, reducing the victim to a tiny figure crouched in a jug or sending him off across the sky on the back of a rigidly-tottering stork or dragon. Quite often two magic objects, thrown by opposing sides, meet and oscillate in mid-air and I imagine Ah Tum watching them with a sense of hopeless ambiguity, never before experienced. Or does he, in his role of nature child, see in the scattered light of the screen, and its waving shadows, a continuation beyond sunset of the swaying and twinkling foliage he has watched so often for a bee-eater or a bulbul, enjoying now a deeper intimacy than he has heretofore known, till the massed leaves take on the shapes of the spirits that he had guessed inhabited them, and breathe at him with a mysterious life?

Certainly he seems a little more at ease now for he withdraws to Leng's room behind the refrigerator where he finds the extremely childish book which Leng uses to learn how to write Chinese. He studies the pictures of five and six year-olds in their nursery gambols, he lies down on the camp cot and reads, he wriggles his toes. And then, incredibly, he begins to sing. Tum's high thin singing drifts through the house and we look at each other in amazement.

About this time Leng comes out onto the balcony.

'Tum is singing,' he says with an amused snort.

'Yes, Tum-tum is singing. It's quite extraordinary,' we agree.

And now I can dare to ask more questions about him, since the imagined breach seems to have healed.

'Is he a Catholic?'

'Yes.'

'A good Catholic—does he for instance go often to confession?'

'Ah Tum not go very often. He knows bad boys.'

'How d'you mean bad boys?'

'Use bad words.'

'And what are his other crimes?'

'He gamble very much. He make plenty money.'

'But he looks frightfully poor.'

'He spend on refreshment'—which is Leng's word for the ubiquitous orange pop which decorates the soggy wooden tables outside the wayangs and rises in fly-spotted tiers at the back of the Muslim shops.

Now it is that Tum, who scarcely becomes any easier to 'talk to', begins to haunt the house for he accepts an invitation to go swimming, and develops a passion for the water. The first time, when we are all undressing as quickly as possible, for it is high tide and the water is deep and clear, I notice him hesitate in his most marginal way, with his head held on one side, full of perplexity. His hand is on the belt of his filthy shorts. Kim rushes in, plump and aggressive; Tum watches, half-smiling. Then he divests himself quickly of his shorts and is, unlike the others, naked. But he has no body—or, rather, like many children, he has only a back. His back has form and grace, as though (to copy Wordsworth and Vaughan) it is upon his walking slowly away from childhood that there plays the celestial light. His chest and stomach are undifferentiated, a slight slippery curve to which bad food has contributed; in front he is all unformed, all action, moving towards his shape which he has not yet found; but this sense of his being bodiless does not make him unphysical. It is just that the flesh is still part of the light and the water, akin to fish, butterfly, flower, not yet insuperably and opposingly *man*— and it is known in the deep water-world of consciousness, as a thing is known in music or poetry, perhaps because its incompleteness attracts all the surrounding mysteries.

Certainly Tum takes to the water, flopping, almost
aquaplaning on its bright surface: fish-like, like a fish
enraptured with light. He buries himself in the water,
swims below it, and then stands again, all shoulders and
head, and talks shrilly with his new vivacity, his eyes no
longer oblique, in a kind of water-sophistication. The
front of his body draws him onto the water, as action,
slithering and flopping forward, but his back quivers
above it. Beyond him, across the Straits, lie the bandit-
infested mountains of Johore. We begin to play a game,
swimming down into the green ginger light and, navi-
gating, as his face takes on some of its former perplexity,
the pale arch of his legs. He splashes us in return. And
then Kim wants me to float on my back so that he can
use me for a raft, his hands on my shoulders, his round
cheerful face puffing above my chest. His polished thighs
thud against mine. A few moments later, in this syrupy
peach-coloured sea where anything can happen, anything
dissolve back into childhood and irresponsibility, I am Ah
Tum's raft and he is in my arms, briefly, with a touch of
quicksilver. But a more silvery splash, vivid as magnesium,
is caused by the panic of a shoal of tiny fish at the nearness
of our bodies, fish that dance up the precipice of our skin
and spray sparkling to each side, while closer to the shore
a newt-like creature skips out of the water and perches in
a leaning tree, an animal entirely wonderful and strange,
commenting on our play with the bright indiscretion of a
hiccough.

CHAPTER 10

The Chinese Babies

A CHINESE Theatre or *wayang* is a noisy colourful affair, set up in the depths of a coconut-grove, some open space behind the shop-houses, or directly beside the street so that the traffic is slowed for miles: colourful not only because the actors wear vermilion paint on their faces and gesticulate in front of rippling sheets of tinsel but also for its alleys of eating stalls, garlanded with mauve and white squid and spotted with orange-pop bottles under the buzz of the pressure-lanterns, and for its outlying fortune-tellers and sellers of pictures and books. It was here that I bought my two coloured prints. A long row of these prints was pegged up on a clothes line and appeared to be of great interest to a crowd of small boys.

Picture five babies upon a couch. The couch is a voluptuous milky blue, indefinite as to general shape but intricately ruffled. Each ruffle is a tree root, a snake, the groin of a mountain glacially highlit. The sky is blue-black at the edges. It softens to peacock, produces a barrel-shaped cushion, embroidered with crimson hearts and laced with yellow and green, and fades into the sumptuous anarchy of the couch. Precisely one third of the way across the picture the foreground intervenes in the shape of an occasional table, pedestalled vase and flowers. Dahlias? Roses? Mythical? Tissue paper? At least pink—no, two pink, two red, one white, amongst a profusion of foliage. Rampant foliage. On the vase a sage in a red garment appears to brood, a knotty staff in his hand, his cranium bald and distorted, at his feet a stork and a spotted deer. To each side the children sprawl and romp.

Each child is lighter skinned than a Chinese baby would normally be, each has identical black hair, smooth at the sides and dimly fuzzy in front; the mouths of all five are in various degrees open, and lacquered, and glistening, with sticky highlights on the lower lips, and all wear a variety of satin under-garment, a toga, a frock, or a little cache-sexe, opulently folded, luxuriously bulging or hanging to expose a plump armpit and minute nipple. The red, green, yellow and strawberry garments only set off the milky effulgence of the babies' skin with its violet and brown shadows, complacent creases and portly glows. But of course the faces, and especially the eyes, are the thing. It is not enough to say that the eyes *shine*, that the babies are delighted with life and smiling as they trail their clouds of glory.

> *Happy those early days when I*
> *Shined in my angel infancy . . .*

They gleam, glitter—they lick their lips. They have seen something far more desirable than the enormous peaches that strew the bed, and which two are grasping. One leans forward with the confidential leer of a black market operator clinching a deal. Two more thrust out their hands. Another, with a finger in his mouth, slyly ponders. Theirs is the world of a continuous plenitude of stolen sweets, a Garden of Eden ingeniously and joyously plundered without the least threat of reprisal. The flames of eternal damnation serve merely to invigorate them to a Renoir glow. They are gay agnostics, sybarites bathed in the light of '. . . ces époques nues dont Phoebus se plaisait à dorer les statues'. They are crooks without guilt, business men who need never fear stomach ulcers or heart-disease. They are older than the peaches amongst which they sit, and their lunar landscape is satin and silk. They are, in technicolour, the Id itself.

> *I'll have them fly to India for gold,*
> *Ransack the ocean for orient pearl,*
> *And search all corners of the new-found world*
> *For pleasant fruits and princely delicates*

is their cry, or rather the order they give to the grocer, and when they plan a party they echo Marlowe again, not forgetting Gaveston's wink of contrivance:

> *Therefore I'll have Italian masks by night,*
> *Sweet speeches, comedies, and pleasing shows....*

You can gather that the picture isn't realistic. Nevertheless it does relate at two points to the truth of Chinese life in Singapore. These babies *do* look a bit like some of the younger business men or *towkays*; they have something of the smooth tough uniformity which, like a kind of hygienic water-proofing, impersonal, cold, practical as rubber, protects the middle generation of Chinese who tend to look monotonously like errand boys or jovial monks, according to the size of their incomes. And I have seen in a photographer's window an enormous photograph of a completely naked baby, folds and folds of fat set squarely in front of the camera, which reminded me of my paper babies' complacency. It had, of course, the self-righteous air of one conscious of being smothered in love (its mother no doubt called it little toad or little pig and put a girlish ring in its ear to ward off the evil spirits), and so there was something missing. It lacked independence: the true piratical glitter.

The other picture represents, I think, what would happen to my Id-babies if they were miraculously to recover their innocence, or perhaps it shows a half-way state between real infancy and the black market paradise. The joy is rowdier, the props more numerous, the participants larger in number, but something has gone.

Eight babies disport themselves in a surrealist landscape which consists of a very small crag (with wild duck), some rocks (partially covered by a pink bedspread), a wave (erupting from nowhere and little more than a splash of threadbare foam), some ferns and a sprig, and two enormous tusked fish (out of Turner and Woolworth's). The children, mostly in playsuits of reasonably orthodox

pattern, ride the fish or—disappointingly—merely sprawl
on the uncomfortable shore and rocks. One has a model
boat, one has a ball. Their bodies are darker, pinker (a
truer hint of hellfire?—via our mortal fallibilities, a
tendency to heat rash or blushing easily), their hair is
rather self-consciously fluffed and marcelled, they look a
great deal younger and they are far more aware of their
public. They stare out of the picture and wave. Though
roguish, they want the approval of the grownups. This is
in contrast to the Id-babies, who are quite happy by themselves, with the exception of the one who looks as though
he were trying to sell you his sister. And a few testicular
peaches are no longer enough; there must be an elaborate
fantasy of the fish, there must be arduousness, while the
Id-babies are contented with their cushy-job and love-
nest *ménage*. 'This is fun but you can take me home soon,'
the eight babies say. One is ready to go almost immediately. He has the I-want-to-be-adopted look. A pudgy
hand resting on the red, blue and yellow stripes of the ball,
his face is faintly tilted, with wistfulness, and his eyes come
near to expressing a mute appeal. Furthermore the hair
on his head, or rather the damp fur which on the heads of
his playmates is so meticulously crimped and waved into
the semblance of hair, and then encouraged to effervesce
into tufts and fringes, is for once naturally untidy. It
doesn't look as though it had been plaited by a fetichist
out of the droppings left on a dressing-table in an hotel
bedroom. This Peter Pan really needs a nanny. And the
boy directly in front of him, the one who appears to be
scraping his belly on the reverse side of some very jagged
rock over which his naked torso leans, with his hands
plunged in the bed spread—will he not, in a moment or
two, ask to be taken to the lavatory?

The point seems to be that there is an uncomfortable
tension to this second picture. It has something to do with
the general tone: the colours are bright but too muzzy; the
babies' skins have a hot pinkness which does not emanate

from within but seems superimposed as though they had been dusted with coloured chalk; their strongly patterned play-suits (one in green has actually a brown bunny on the hip) are slipping off their shoulders, pinching them, getting in the way, while the spivs of the previous picture wear their oleaginous satin with an air. It's the difference between a *décolleté* and a bad fit, between the seductive and the untidy, between Rubens and an advertisement for Baby Talc. And then again the tension can be seen in the fixity and hardness and clumsiness of the objects displayed, as compared with the delirious but unconvincing romp of the children. The huge fish leap into the air, brandishing their tusks, rolling their wet circular eyes— but they are hollow, and surely more than half celluloid. Two babies mount the fish in the centre, which is at once in the sky and the water and half submerged in the mud; he is caught at the focal point of discrepancy, where sky and sea and land fail to make any satisfactory connection, and not without reason he appears to be rolling over on his side, desperate certainly, possibly dying.

> *For infants time is like a humming shell*
> *Heard between sleep and sleep, wherein the shores*
> *Foam-fringed, wind-fluted of the strange earth dwell*
> *And the sea's cavernous hunger faintly roars,*

writes Cecil Day Lewis of childhood, and there can be no doubt that the womb and phallic archetypes make their presence felt here, but the effect of the picture is not to celebrate childhood but unconsciously to satirize it. The fish is more like that dolphin 'red, dead and broken' which provides the final image for Rilke's *Birth Of Venus* than it is an emissary of Atlantis or of those simpler days when Triton blew his wreathèd horn; bringing 'the eternal note of sadness in', and especially of sexual sadness, it reminds one of an early Thomas poem:

> *Where once the waters of your face*
> *Spun to my screws, your dry ghost blows,*

> *The dead turns up its eye;*
> *Where once the mermen through the ice*
> *Pushed up their hair, the dry wind steers*
> *Through salt and root and roe.*

> *Invisible, your clocking tides*
> *Break on the lovebeds of the weeds;*
> *The weed of love's left dry;*
> *There round about your stones the shades*
> *Of children go who, from their voids,*
> *Cry to the dolphined sea.*

For the dolphin is dead. At least, it is turning into a toy, an image for poetry, a thing to dream about.

So it is that I take this second group of babies to represent the perils of romanticism. They have two worlds, which don't quite fit, and they are already beginning to be self-conscious about both of them, and not only about them but about their very status as children. They are so anxious to appear to be having a good time. But the sea of faith, suffused with a sexuality which had no need to be precise, is becoming limited as they play on its shore; put one way, you can say that the fish begin to smell of the case-history as they loll grotesquely against their meagre splash of foam—they are simplified but obsessive, like the images in a day-dream; put in a less Freudian way, the picture can be seen as showing the birth of a discontinuity between life and the imagination, and all the bewilderment and hurt and inefficiency and private nastiness which such a discontinuity can involve. For the wave and its fish will come less and less often, indeed the wave is already suspiciously slight and hysterical; the playthings will grow more and more solid and ordinary and out-grown. Shades of the prison-house. . . . It's then that the fun will begin. Which is reality, the monsters I used to play with or the solid objects at my feet? Or neither? Shall I romanticize the domestic side of things (the adult equivalent of boat and ball) like Wordsworth, or shall I have strange and terrible dreams like Coleridge, and then be guilty as Coleridge is in his *Pains of Sleep*, and cry out that I want to be adopted, like the little boy who turns out of the picture so appealingly:

> *To be beloved is all I need*
> *And whom I love I love indeed.*

The artist saw the problem when he provided these Super-Ego Babies with their schizophrenic sea-scape. A bedspread on a rock? Pure Dali. She is older than the rocks amongst which she sits. Poor Leonardo.

And these pictures, pinned up on the wall near the Javanese masks and the old sarong in blue and white—the last flutter of Wilde's blue china, I tell myself—are a taunt and a perversity. Am I the worst of snobs, so certain of my taste that I am prepared to run the risk of being misunderstood? For my visitors are troubled. 'Good Lord, why on earth do you hang things like that?' ask some. Pale young colonial men, graduates of technical colleges, brought up on the W.E.A. and the Arts Council, who have read all the appropriate Penguins and Pelicans, giggle at them mirthlessly, while their wives, in sensible flowery gym-tunics, look maternally hurt. 'Horrors, aren't they!' they add, pinning me into my eccentric niche. 'I don't see how you can live with them. I don't really.' And they think of their reproductions of Mt. St. Victoire and the Sunflowers in neat pale frames, under whose mild utterance they will offer you, as they talk of their trip to Europe (Provence so sunny and interesting, the sunflowers so cheerful and brave), a 'glass of wine' which turns out to be a thimble-full from the bottle of Cinzano they keep, reverently laid on its side, in the deepest recesses of their refrigerator. But others—colonial wives of some standing, freckled and sanded and bleached into responsibility, collectors of camphor-wood chests and wrought-iron silhouettes, Chinese brocade and Trengganu silver, but always abashed by any real sign of native life—will glimmer up at them with 'How very interesting! How vital! Awfully clever of you to find things like that.' So it is that the Babies corrupt us all. For I, too, am not sure whether I like them or, rather, for what I like them. 'Significant vulgarity,' suggests a pompous self. 'Jokes about Peter Pan and Christopher Robin,' says one more likeable. 'Some of the colour is quite attractive,' whispers a tremulous voice, adding, 'against that wall anyway,' as a gesture towards the velvets and columns, the bodies and battles and varnishes of the distant, the admirably ordered, the suspiciously western World of Art.

And then, when I have worked the whole thing out, some Chinese arrive and tell me that my Babies are loaded with religious symbolism. These Chinese are off-hand with them at first. Someone notices that the pictures were manufactured in Shanghai. This interests them because Shanghai is in China, and China, to which they have never been, is a mixture of fairytale and legend (a sort of subsidiary childhood to be 'remembered' in terms of stories told them as children) and an impressive culture (which has hardly touched them here in Malaya) and of course the challenge, the pressure, the excitement of Communism. There are some characters on one of the pictures too and these they decipher, laughing, but with the respect they always give to their written language, so much so that one hears of coolie women collecting old bits of newspaper lying in the street for fear that it should be desecrated. The pictures are invitations to longevity and fertility, they tell me; in a house they might be expected to have a magical effect. The old sage means long life, and so does the elongated vase on which he is depicted. The number of the peaches is chosen deliberately. They are, in fact, the seven Celestial Peaches stolen from Heaven by the redoubtable Monkey God—as Prometheus stole fire? And the Babies, whether satanic or sentimental, are there to encourage large families and plenty of sons.

But, hearing their explanation, and there is much more of which they are not so certain, I have an unreasonable desire not to accept it—not to give in, as a journalist would have to do, to the dictatorship of fact. What are facts in Malaya compared with anybody's desire to create something, to make something new? And, above all, to be personal. So I still look upon my Babies as spivs and cissies. The Super-Ego lot will probably make a dreadful mess of their lives. They will write poems to birds that are not birds, fish that are not fish, lights that never were on sea or land; they will take to drink or laudanum or abstract theories or mystical cults, because the real disgusts them even as it slyly and surreptitiously attracts; they will be sentimentalists in love, reactionaries in politics, egoists always. The Id gang, on the other hand, will have excellent digestions and incomes to suit. For they *belong*. Their clear outlines and cool ivory skins dominate the luxurious surroundings from which they emerge. They are Apollonian, for Nature has produced them as her finest flower, they have no need to regret or to worry, and they would never term life a battle. Longevity they may not in all cases attain, but their sex lives will be strenuous and protracted and their offspring numerous. A rosy proliferation of bastards, in fact, for the oleographs of the future.

CHAPTER 11

The Balcony

I WRITE at nights, using a rotan table on the balcony, lighting myself with the second and far more formid- able lamp; the brochure says that it is pure brass under the chromium, and that its shade ('usually of an orange red colour') is artistically designed, and that it is much in use in Asia and the Middle East. Since it dispenses terrific heat, so much so that the air palpitates above it and all the insects within sight rush to an immediate death, this last attribute is surprising. An Arctic setting would be more suitable.

This brochure is an interesting affair; its cover has a fiery glow, the first page is simple and hearty, technical- ities begin in a mood of bright optimism, arrows point melodramatically at illustrations where an artistically *fainéant* hand turns screws and fondles plungers, and it is only under the heading *Maintenance and Repair* that the machine begins to disintegrate (like Kafka's in the penal colony) into a series of nipples, gaskets, packing glands and bushings. Fearsome things can happen to it, its mantle turn black, its valve-stem develop a leak, its whole top burst into flames—hardly a night passes without this last occurring. By the final two pages it is spread out neatly all over the paper in an atmosphere of truculent technicality: completely unglamorous, dissected, skeletal.

Distance expires, Time has no meaning, and we occupy a tree-house in a fairy tale from which any part of the globe seems equally remote or equally near, and almost any century. The landscape has shut down; palms click their fronds together; if it is damp, bullfrogs twang; a succession of enamelled green beetles fly in from the dark- ness, eventually collide with the wall and fall to the boards where the dog snaps them up; sometimes, though, it is a soft filmy thing Leng calls 'a shit beetle' and this the dog refuses to touch. The balcony is melodramatically bright and hot, detached from the Malayan countryside and turned outward across seas and centuries, towards some impossibly bright future, some impossibly romantic evocation of the past. We join galloping shadows; effervesce with the lamp; our figures leap, vastly magnified, from the trees around us. And Gerald, describing the Italian setting in which he would really like this house, suddenly blurts out, 'My God, what happens if one dies here—I mean, is there a crematorium, or does one lie in all this awful *virulence* and rot?' only to find that a praying mantis has settled on his arm, like a piece of animated wire-sculpture, and now turns its cool globular eyes towards him, so that he has to burst out laughing.

But night is also, especially for me, the background to expeditions far more aggressive and Rabelaisian than any attempt to 'get across' with the kampong children, expeditions which start guiltily and blearily as the old car noses its weak headlamps into what seems like an impenetrable darkness of swamp and narrow road, but which gather speed and a kind of tight edgy confidence when the arclights of the arterial highway are gained, after which they dart, or more truly drag themselves, from stall to stall and bar to bar, with sometimes a mild collision which nobody seems to notice, or a leaking radiator pipe to be swaddled in an old scarf, a broken spring to be conveniently forgotten, a fight to be avoided, a new den to be explored, until I find myself driving the waiter at the Rendezvous (who lives at the other side of the village) home in the small hours. And climbing to the balcony then, with the extraordinary peace of the grove closing around, is to be universally and timelessly fiery or melancholic or bitter or just sleepy. Drink creates its palace without benefit of geography. The balcony does no more than re-inforce those great truths, those overwhelmingly

P

acute and sad comments on one's own life, which drinking
normally produces. The sensitive life belongs to Sungei
Tengah's day; the grandiloquent one to its nights. And in
a moment of what seems like brilliant generosity one may
then shout, as one grips the balcony rail and stares in a
megalomaniac way at one's silent acres, that 'Everybody
here, I mean all the Europeans here, are at least indi-
vidualists. We're all in the same boat and it isn't just a
boat, anyway, it's a bloody great pirate ship!'

How is one to live, though—not now but later? Where
is there left for one to go to? Mauritius, Madagascar, the
Gold Coast, perhaps Cyprus . . . will any of them be
suitable for the assertive life, the receptive life, as they
alternate here at Sungei Tengah? The more brutal note
brings Canada in, the whole four thousand miles of it, all
railways and geographical loneliness and a sort of half-
repressed heroism, with the clotted self-conscious cities
full of nationalistic culture and the very deft, rather conservative, accumulation of money, and underneath an
automatic well-fed innocence, like the bloom on skin:
aggression is a virtue there, every young man is dynamic,
every girl vital. But there are other reasons why Canada
should appear over the edge of the balcony; the tropics
demand their opposite, palms call forth images of ice and
snow, and this not only because the modern mind enjoys
a paradox and likes to see different kinds of experience
wrestling together; rather because behind the difference
there lies a dreaming similarity, for to have lived in two
foreign lands suggests that one has done something with
one's life, and yet in both, experience has not been tar-
nished with over-familiarity. In both, experience has been
like a series of metaphors, expressive of a reality one has
imagined, if only dimly, that one felt. In Canada especially, where almost anyone who 'writes' is sooner or later
claimed equally as 'Canadian' or 'important'—if not
indeed 'great'—it was possible to have a sense of the
country as one's own particular secret, one's idiosyncratic

private hunting ground. Assertion, and heaven knows writers and artists bickered with each other, occurred within this lulling atmosphere of knowing the country's magic, even if you didn't know, and didn't want to know, its common-sense. The foreigner who feels that he secretly belongs . . . the projection into the outside world of meanings which are either, according to his mood, absolutely basic or monotonously irritatingly personal . . . such things belong very much to these balcony evenings when I often wonder whether I should return to Canada, although I don't usually see them as clearly as this. It's rather that I clear a space in my mind and this space soon hums and fizzes with images.

Chief among these are the incidents of my last year there, when I lived in the basement of a rooming-house in a squalid but central quarter of Montreal, sharing my sitting-room with an enormous furnace, screened off in a corner. It seems right that I should summon to this balcony, where I am as happy as I have been for years, the figure of my landlord of those days, Mr. Leopold Shaughnessy, together with his long-suffering French-Canadian wife. There was no balcony then. There was, instead, a clothes-line that sometimes dipped from the level of their windows above me into sight of my own and one day I found a black brassiere and black lace panties tapping against the pane, emblems as I thought of intense sophistication and obviously, if surprisingly, belonging to Shauny's rather deaf sister-in-law, Mariette. When I told Mrs. Shauny how pleased I was to think this rather depressed girl had such inclinations towards gaiety, she replied 'Oh no. Mariette is still in mourning for poor Maman.'

Ribaldries of this kind, plentifully supplied by Canada, would be welcomed by the thousand or so Chinese who are at this moment packing a new *wayang* which came yesterday to the estate next to mine, and whose gongs and lanterns splash through the intervening trees. It is an equally robust voice which tells the story of how, at Saint

Sauveur des Monts where I lived for a year in a ski-chalet, a drunken tourist fell into a drift at the back of his hotel while fumbling for the lavatory. It was the coldest night of the year but quite still, with a beautiful moon. Hours later, when the son of the house went to the back stoop to bring in some skis, his eyes were attracted by a glittering object. He reached out for it and snapped it off. Just before tossing it away, something made him observe it more closely. It was a crystal hand. A more likely story is that told of a ski-instructor I myself knew quite well, a wooden red-faced man whose look of large stupidity was said to indicate sexual prowess. He was notorious for chasing American heiresses and finally married a very young one. A week later he was back in one of his haunts, with a *whisky blanc* in front of him, and in one hand a lawyer's letter, in the other a pair of falsies. 'It was no good either ways,' he said. And who more robust than that old friend of mine, the cement-manufacturer in Nova Scotia, who wrote little left-wing essays to advertise his product in the local paper and who loved nothing better than to entertain members of the Canadian Mounted Police while silently chuckling at the hammer-and-sickle motif he had concealed within his home-made dado? Or, to turn from the country to the town, what more fantastic than the gesture of a highly-placed and intelligent woman I knew, an expert on juvenile delinquency, who went out with me one night, took me home for coffee and then, in a flurry of nerves and romantic impulses, jumped into her studio couch while still wearing a black taffeta cocktail dress, pulled the cover over her, and then smiled at me wildly? Canada is not only a robust country; it is, like the U.S.A., curiously *basic*; men like Shaughnessy have a vitality akin to that of puppets, which themselves remind one of the appearance, if not of the dramatic roles, of the actors in a *wayang*.

Yes, Shauny was an excitable friendly little ostrich of a man, a dabbler in politics and a character to a large number of friends. He was enormously impressed with me because of my academic position; I was always 'The Professor' and 'Professor Pat'. Never can a landlord have given away so much beer. At least once a week a party developed in the front parlour by about three o'clock and continued raucously, indecently, monotonously, until Shauny retired with one or two pals into the kitchen for dinner. In the early stages I would hear him at the telephone in the hall ordering another case of Molson's beer, or expostulating at the grocer's delay, or telling some friend from the Income Tax Department (where he worked) or the Department of Veterans' Affairs to 'come on over'. Later, when his spectacles hung crooked on his scarlet face and his trousers drooped from his braces— argument and mimicry and urination being all to blame— he would ring up his favourite Cabinet Minister in Ottawa, using a special official voice, very grand and peremptory to telephone operators and secretaries but alas! far too loud. Meanwhile the pals for whom there wasn't room at the sink in the hallway trooped and stumbled down the stairs to my lavatory. Often they would open my door by mistake.

Nowhere was proof against Shaughnessy's cannibalistic hospitality. I remember a series of staccato taps on the door, polite but insistent—a hoarse whisper, 'Professor Pat, are you there?'—the appearance of a conspiratorial ostrich face: 'Come up and have a quart with the boys. There's someone who wants to meet you, Professor Pat!' And of course one couldn't get out of this without a struggle.

I was always introduced into these meetings with great ceremony, and appealed to as an authority on international affairs, the dollar problem or the improvement of Montreal traffic regulations (all subjects that were taken seriously to the point, at times, of blows) but I could never believe that Shaughnessy's heterogeneous guests shared his enthusiasm. Apart from their capacity, which was immense, I found them almost pathologically dull. They shouted, and were dull. They appealed to one in private asides, and were duller. They talked about sex, and were dullest of all. No one listened for more than a moment to anyone else. There was some attention, I recall, when Shaughnessy drifted from a meandering discussion of 'nice babies . . . D'you want a nice French baby, Professor Pat?' to a tirade against masturbation. His acts of mimicry were much appreciated. He had been an orderly in the Medical Corps and could be very funny about physical examinations.

The morning after one of these parties I would often be called on the telephone by an assistant of mine who was extremely efficient in organizing the Freshman English course. I myself had no lecture before ten but she was obviously an early riser. When I staggered upstairs to the phone, which occupied a dark corner by the Shaughnessys' kitchen-bedroom, it was only to find the door beside me open just sufficiently for a long arm to reach out and place a quart of Molson's on the ledge by my hand. A quart looked enormous at that hour of the morning. Resting my head against the wall, with my nose pressed for support against the top of the mouthpiece, I tried to sound intelligent and serene, but Shauny's present unnerved me. He always respected my privacy when I was telephoning, but he could never get into his head the fact that more beer in the morning did *not* dispel my hangover. So he thrust, pointed, winked, without actually speaking.

And then one day the quart did not appear and there was an air of whispering solemnity about the house. Instead of going to work, Shauny made various departures; the front door kept on banging; voices sounded low and continuous for long stretches at a time in the back room. Later Shauny started calling up the gang.

'It's Eddie,' he said hoarsely. 'You know what's happened to Eddie? The poor bastard's dead. Blooming well fell off a bridge and killed himself.'

When I heard this news, I don't think I was entirely surprised. It so often happens that an odd character you have been observing, or a peculiar situation in which you have been involved, yields eventually some dramatic fact in which all you have been only half-aware of becomes nakedly summed up. You get to expect the absolutely typical remark, the moment when caricature achieves dignity, the point of the anecdote. Sometimes no doubt you anticipate it yourself and try to lead your characters into the position where they will have to express it. One of the guilts of the 'writer' comes from his sense of being a sort of spy, secretly observing what he also participates in, and noting with satisfaction the successive clicks with which the story fits into a pattern, for there is likely to be more than one, and one day's humorous ending may give way to a symbol on the next, and later to a real tragedy.

Eddie Duncan was, as I see it now, a super-normal example of the Shaughnessy gang. In other words, he was a misfit. He had neither marital nor social status, substituting cynicism and bitterness for the one and memories of the war, in which he had been a captain, for the other. It's not particularly easy to make social judgements transatlantically, for the middle-class norm is spread very wide and commented upon very little, and its symbol of business success always gets entangled with that preoccupation with masculinity which requires its members to be one of the boys. Eddie was obviously a cut above most of the others; the Irish lawyer might be better educated but he was a drunk—the French Canadian Major perhaps betrayed his lack or loss of caste by associating so much with English-speaking Canadians; the others, the policeman, the clerk, the janitor from next door, were clearly without much ambition or, so far as I could see, brains; but Eddie held quite a responsible position in a Government Department, drew a good salary and was always prosperously dressed in a double-breasted suit, white shirt and gay American-style tie. He was a well-built solid looking man of about thirty-five, reasonably attractive in a bullish way, and he had the indefinable look of the Canadian about him—a sort of minimum gentility and toughness, a bit wooden, a bit coarse, as though (but I don't think I can hit it off) an advertisement for gents' underwear had been copied not quite accurately in sand. You looked at his carefully parted rather too wavy hair, and at his little moustache, and at his powerful shoulders in the drape-cut suit, and you thought, 'Yes, I have seen you before instructing your son in the mysteries of Easi-Supportex shorts—but no, you were not quite the same.' Compared to him, though, the others in the dark little front parlour, with its tinted statuettes, empty pearl and pink convoluted vases, and two framed oleographs, one of a girl languishing beneath a niagara of hair, the other inevitably of a stag bemused with a forest of antlers, were more obviously riff-raff.

'Go on, Shauny, show us what happened,' the thin little clerk would ask for the hundredth time. And Shaughnessy, top fly-buttons undone and braces slipping from narrow shoulders, would take each part in turn, clamping his toothless mouth and contorting his body into a series of jerky angles, so that both protagonists, the recruit and the doctor, seemed equally puppet-like.

'Bend ovah!' was the climax of the story. As he came to it, Shauny grew almost hysterical with excitement.

'So the poor beggar bends over, you see, and the Doctor, well he's pretty browned off because the guy's so goldarned timid, so he just lets out with his boot . . .' to explain which Shauny, who had been crouched in suffering tentative submission, leapt high into the air, clutching his behind.

Eddie alone would be relatively indifferent to the story, which was altogether too humorous and childish for him. He would listen for the ring of the door-bell and the arrival of another case of beer from the shop at the corner;

a boy would drag it over the deep ice-ruts on an improvised sledge; suddenly he would appear in the room, in
his wind breaker and tasselled toque, with little sticks of
ice slithering off his mittens; if he was old enough,
Shauny in his execrable French would insist on his drinking some.

'Avez un glass avec les boys!' he would say. 'Take a
pew and donnez-yourself de la bière pour warmez-vous,
you poor bastard.'

And the boy would grin as his eyes sought those of all
the men in the room. Then he'd toss off the glass expertly
and run a huge red hand over his lips.

'Pas mal bien,' he would say in a *patois* almost as
curious.

Eddie drank heavily and for a long time I disliked him
a great deal. He was really foul-mouthed, full of self-pity,
continually re-directing the conversation to his obsession
with sex. It was he who prompted the lawyer to his wild
involved explanation of the significance of the prostate
gland and his extraordinary stories of couples locked by
hysteria in the act of intercourse; he, too, was usually the
butt of Shaughnessy's sudden purity tirades. The others
respected him, but with a hint of caution and pity; I think
they realized that Eddie could be really violent and that
his misery was a genuine intellectual thing (once or twice
he got into fights while still in the parlour, and he was the
only member of the group to produce dirty postcards at
one of the sessions). When women were present, which
was very rarely, they flirted with him more than any of the
others and he responded with a bickering jeering tenderness, making passes too quickly and then relapsing into
sulks.

'You behave yourself with Lucille,' Shauny would
caution him. 'She's a real nice baby, a real nice respectable
French baby, never been touched by no —— —— bastard like you, everything above board and O.K. with her,
isn't that right, Lucille? Go on, Professor Pat, you tell

him. Professor Pat knows Lucille is no low nasty son of a bitch, like you act she was, because he's a genuine Oxford-trained gentleman of the old school and I tell you Eddie he won't stand much of your nonsense around here!'

'If that girl's a lady I'm Peter Pan, that's what I am.'

All this could get very tedious and for a time I tried to avoid being in the room when Eddie was. But later, I started talking quietly to Eddie, refusing to take offence at anything he said—and he said a good deal, for he had a deep mistrust of my 'limey education'—with the result that eventually I was looked upon as a soothing influence. In fact, to be Eddie's guardian was the one thing I achieved off my own bat at Shaughnessy's parties. It got so that he expected me to sit next to him.

We talked a good deal of amateur psychiatry. I chose this subject deliberately because I knew how fascinating it was to Canadians, especially Montrealers: odd emotions could be recognized and permitted if they were seen as problems, with the possibility of a cure; psychiatry also seemed to have the effect of flattering a shy defensive individual (and most Canadians are defensive and shy) into a sense of his own importance, rather as though it provided him with a personality; once at his ease, Eddie was glad to release some of those tensions which seem to underlie so much of Canadian life. I learnt of his aggressively puritanical father, his boyish escapades (he had belonged for a time to a fascinatingly organized and ritualized group of schoolboy burglars), his great friendship during the war, 'he was a lovely guy but he went and died on me,' and his rows and lusts with the typists in the office. An Englishman would have had a more complicated past, richly decorated with his own individuality and capable of being absorbed to a considerable extent into the cultural framework around him; an Indian or Malay would still have much of his neurosis in common with his race or creed as an almost tribal thing; but Eddie as a Canadian couldn't be eccentric in the English sense, or run amok like a Malay—he had to be naked. And this nakedness of his began to be endearing. I decided to ask him what he saw in Shaughnessy's parties.

'After all, Eddie, you can't say this is a very exciting bunch. And nothing ever happens except drink and arguments.'

But Eddie seemed shocked at my criticism.

'Hell, Professor, Shauny is an old friend of mine and generous to a fault. All us boys like Shauny. He's a bit of a fool at times but he's got what it takes—he'd help anybody that was a buddy of his with his last f——g dollar.'

However my query must have made him think for at the next party, which was the last he was ever to attend, he suggested that we go out together later in the evening.

'Say, Professor, how about you showing me some of the high-tone places where the long-hairs hang out?' was the way he put it, although he usually retired with the Shaughnessys when he wasn't so drunk that they sent him home.

I explained to him that there was nothing I would have liked better, except that I didn't know the toney places at all, if it hadn't been for a previous arrangement about a movie. He was very insistent for he even followed me down to the basement flat to make the demand again.

'Let's stay together,' he said. 'Let's stay together and talk.'

This time I think I noticed a call for rescue but it was very noisy at the bottom of the stairs, for the Irish lawyer came banging out of the lavatory at that moment, and besides my guest for the evening had chosen just this moment to arrive. Eddie blundered away. Later I heard him talking in the Shaughnessys' room.

He had fallen off a bridge, landed on the ice, crawled for some distance in what might have been an attempt to save himself and finally disappeared where the current was strong and the ice surface was thin and broken. He had crawled in the wrong direction. This was important

because everybody seemed anxious, in the bewildered
vulgarly excited turmoil after his death, to prove that he
had committed suicide; it was as though violence in itself
wasn't enough and there must also be sin and a scapegoat;
at least Shauny and his friends were curiously inadequate,
I thought, about the tragedy. On a superficial plane they
acted as though tragedy was a thing they could not understand and from which they derived gossip, a shock, a
thrill, some cheap dramatics. More deeply, they wanted
to make Eddie's death realer, perhaps, by making it
morally significant. Of course they never said this but it
seemed to underlie what was otherwise a terrifying desire
for sensationalism.

Violence is of course a feature of Canadian life. In
nature it is predominant, the message of the fierce sum-
mers with their black-flies and thunderstorms, forest fires
and droughts, and of the bitter winters when the icicles
hang five feet long from the eaves and the nails snap in the
wooden houses at night. The much-admired Fall colours
are evidence of violent decay; the Spring muskegs, seeth-
ing with flies, of violent rebirth. The Group of Seven
school of painters has caught the savage poster-like scenes
that make up so much, but by no means all, of the
Canadian landscape. But in Canadians themselves the
theme of violence is usually repressed in favour of a queer
undecided ordinariness and ugliness—undecided because
no-one has yet felt that the pattern is finally appropriate
and national, if indeed a pattern exists at all; everyone
seems to be biding their time, holding themselves in,
concentrating on *not* being English, *not* being American,
and this held-back violence expresses itself at its freest in
ice-hockey, at its ugliest in the pathologically bleak interior of a Montreal tavern, at its nastiest in juvenile crime,
at its most bewildered in politics, at its most nationalistic
or precious in literature and art. Nobody prepared from
outside to dismiss Eddie as a colonial (and he was certainly
provincial in many ways) can hope to understand the

tensions bearing down on him, as the ice-cap is felt to bear down on the heads of those who inhabit the horizontal strip at its base. Eddie wasn't born to be just a man, any more than any Canadian is born to be just a man; he was born to be a Canadian, which meant that he had to be very proud of something which nobody had ever conclusively shown him to exist at all.

I don't say that I saw it all like this at the time. It is one of the privileges of a tropical balcony to make generalizations, to grip the balustrade, stare into the warm dark silence (for the *wayang* is now over) and conclude, 'Of course, that was how it really was. It all fits into place now.' One has a huge sense of the significance of everything: one's life, one's two foreign countries, all the tough things that turned out to be tremulous, and all the tremulous things that one still fights for so toughly. And it seems possible, as the shadows plunge through the trees, as one's bid for security surrounds one with this successful pool of light—the dogs and monkey asleep, Gerald sleeping, and Leng—that in a year or two one will be able to go to Cyprus or Madagascar. Somewhere foreign enough to belong to.

But in the morning the balcony is less assertive, less angular, mixed with an outside world which treats it tenderly, enchantingly, but in which action is restricted. Men, for instance, come to pick the coconut crop.

All day they go about their business. Some of them have enormously long poles, the sections lashed together, with a short knife fastened on top. With these they grope into the tops of the trees, feeling their way towards the clusters of ripe fruit, for not all the coconuts are ready, and doing some damage in the process. You see them at a little distance from the tree, with the slender pole at an angle swaying and poking. When the knife is around the right stalk, they jerk and pull; there is a smashing noise, and perhaps only a great bladed leaf falls out of the tree, but most often it is five or six green husks plunging through the air, thudding on the ground, bouncing up again and rolling in all directions. The men never seem to be hit, the coconuts always fall slightly in front of them but, once on the ground, they perform all sorts of jolly eccentricities. And the grove, that had seemed to us so static, so almost wholly a picture postcard, comes alive and reveals the precipitous nature of air, the irregularity and clumsiness of earth—the coconuts are fallen angels turned to gnomes, the brilliant disaster recovers itself as a practical joke.

Boys gather the fruit in round baskets carried in the usual way, one on each side of the body with a stick to support them laid across the shoulders, and one lot is piled by the passion fruit, where a husker stands ready. He builds himself a palm-leaf roof against the sun, buries the shaft of a sharp pointed knife or prong into the earth and for hours and hours tears the thick husks off, using his left hand to bring the husk down on the knife and his right to pull the fibres after the incision. Three separate plunges of husk on knife are necessary, sometimes more, and each operation involves considerable pulling and wrenching. He is a tall bony man in singlet and wide brown shorts; his eyes set far apart, his cheeks sunken, a tuft of hair falls over his seamed forehead—he looks in fact like a great stark neutral boy.

About noon these coolies take their *makan*. They fetch leaves from a certain tree and mix these with their rice, gobbling their food quickly, the bowls held close to their lips. Towards dusk lorries arrive to be loaded with both fruit and husks. The rhythmical counting sounds like a chant as each man tosses a coconut onto the pile: easy, sad, rather acrid with the succession of Chinese tones. An elderly man, vaguely elegant despite his clumsy tunic and sateen trousers, must be the *towkay* who has bought the crop from Mr. Lee. The men are soon finished. They wipe chest and armpits with coconut fibres and are ready to go.

Other visitors are more expected. There is Beda Lim who arrives importantly in a Press car when it is still early in the morning and Leng's slapdash breakfast has only just been pushed to one side, in order that the shaving mirror can be balanced on a pile of books; he is now a cub reporter, having left the university without a degree, and he wishes to interview me, no, to get me to write an article, but on what he is not sure. Perhaps the Missing Diplomats? Perhaps the Student Detainees? Perhaps . . . but his eye has strayed to the biscuit tin (it doesn't contain biscuits), to a book from the library , to the *collages* we have pasted out of old copies of *Life* and hung on the walls. How artistic it is here! How romantic! And, of course, bohemian. He leaves in a cloud of good-wishes, for the car must not be kept waiting, having commissioned an article at a very good price and having bestowed a last speculative glance on our decorations. I work very hard at the article but his editor refuses to pay; he had no right to ask for it. I open the Sunday edition of his newspaper and there is the photograph of an immense *collage* designed and executed by Beda Lim, who contributes an analytic description. He's deliciously *naïve*, as optimistic and distracted as a bumble-bee, and yet there's a solid serious human being inside—he's always serious about the right things. Or nearly always. As he goes down the stairs, he apologizes for not inviting me to a party (he calls it a soirée) which is being held by a group of Chinese journalists the same evening 'at a place where the girls let you fondle them. I'd ask you to come but I think you would find it a little embarrassing. They use pretty strong language. They use one word in particular all the time.'

And then it is Gung-wu who is on the balcony, and of course Shaku, and a promising schoolboy called Edwin who bicycles all the way out with his latest poem, *Cosmic Leech*, and after him there is the superbly named Miss Hedwig Aroozoo. They all seem a little astonished to find me here. They give me the feeling that they are city slickers and I am a country cousin. They must know about houses like these, they must even have lived in them, but they are too sophisticated to admit it. Hardly anyone admits to quite knowing the address, or even the name of the village. Once here, however, they deluge me with talk of politics and literature and European conventions and sex. It turns out that Gung-wu was taken up in quite a big way by Radio Malaya as soon as term ended but that the experience has not been entirely happy. First he discovered colour discrimination in the lift of the Cathay Building where the radio station has temporary quarters —in its way a delightful setting for this group of inspired amateurs; you may be having a drink with one of them in the first floor bar when he suddenly jumps up with, 'My God, I almost forgot to put the station on the air!' or 'Excuse me for a moment, I've got to read the News.' It is difficult, anyway, to imagine the beautifully pale Gung-wu as *coloured*. When he acted with me months ago in the university production of *Antigone*, he was my son Haemon and we played a long scene together, I thought of him as made of crystal faintly suffused with pink: he was so delicately poised, so nervously sharp and clear, with so precise and yet compelling a diction, that it was like being the father of a yacht or a race-horse. And then, after the colour problem, he was assigned the task of translating Orwell's *Animal Farm* into Chinese, which seems a stupidly abrupt demand on his political innocence, for do not highly-placed police officers woo him with presents of the best modern literature, hoping that Cyril Connolly or Graham Greene will keep him on the right side of the fence? He is not a Communist but that doesn't mean that he is willing to take part in violent anti-Communist propaganda. More recently he has been doing film-work up north in the Federation. He enjoyed most the opportunity this gave him of talking to surrendered bandits, whom he seems rather loosely to admire, perhaps because any young man finds a revolutionary exciting, especially when the

6. 'With sampans in the rushes and black mud shining through the mangrove roots' (*p. 179*)

revolutionary turns out to be of middle-class origin and with artistic interests. Gung-wu's bandits were graduates of the better high-schools, loyal, idealistic, enormously ingenious in taking poetry and the stage with them into the jungle, and yet, admiring them, he seems to see no discrepancy in the fact that they are now leading police patrols back to the hideouts of their former colleagues. Of course it's a confusing business: do we not fight the *bandits* with a plane we call the *brigand*? Gung-wu's attitude is a frightening example of that response to sheer *fact* which is a species of *tida apah*, of the ethical irresponsibility caused by having been kept under so long. Someone rebels—that is exciting and courageous, if misguided; someone surrenders—that is exciting too, and may be strategic in a more sophisticated way; both are symptoms of the 'malady' of British rule, significant as facts if not as operations of the will.

Generally speaking, Gung-wu and I now understand each other much better. There was a night some time ago when much beer was drunk and a poem was written, while the other students sang themselves to sleep in their rotan chairs with the *Foggy, Foggy Dew*. Candles guttered on the floor, a joss-stick burned, Gung-wu lay flat on his stomach writing and I sat facing him, waiting for the result with particular eagerness, since it was addressed to me. It was very obscure, too obscure to be grasped so late in the night, and I mislaid it the next day. Was it critical or appreciative? I don't know. But it created some bond, some recognition that two would-be poets from different countries should have something to say to each other, and that such a thing could be said elegantly and obscurely amongst the guttering candles, with Arthur Lim and Yong Thaw Hong almost asleep in their chairs.

If Gung-wu is still very much the brilliant juvenile, Hedwig has that almost *grande dame* poise and serenity which is so characteristic of Asian women, especially when they are on their own; where Gung-wu's nationalism may strike one at times as no more than a chip on his shoulder, Hedwig's is worn as a mark of good breeding, a civilized discrimination and sympathy, which provides so to speak a vista back from her very obvious intelligence (some people regard her as a blue-stocking) to her equally strong, and charming, femininity. She never dogmatizes. The glint of her spectacles melts into a giggle or a smile. She lives with her parents in a house that is a forest of holy pictures and yet she is an especial friend, and confidante, of the left-wing James Puthucheary, whom the police allow to send her long poems under the belief, or so she claims delightedly, that she has a romantic interest in him. She tells me now that her leftist parody of the *Waste Land*, originally written for one of my tutorials, has been very much mutilated before being broadcast from Kuala Lumpur and she describes the shock to literary circles recently caused by the gentle Augustine Goh Sin Tub's having written a poem which includes the monosyllable 's——t'! This is at least better, we both laughingly agree, than the equally gentle Lim Thean Soo's lyric printed in *The New Cauldron* last year:

> *So comely a bob of hair*
> *Her head did fittingly wear.*
> *The flowered dress at which I would stare*
> *Enwraped her delicate body fair . . . etc., etc.*

—better, that is, to have Gung-wu's adolescent, 'The moon, impure as ever, like tea-leaves' than Hashim Sultan's 'Once a beauty I met, an office girl in Singapore. . . .'

This innocence and effervescent experimentation, which inevitably seeks for expression in Western forms, so that even now a man as tough as James echoes W. H. Auden from his prison, leads us to discuss my recent visit to the Student Detainees. It was all disconcertingly like a picnic; the launch from the clinical-sounding Master Attendant's pier, the light-drenched progress across the harbour, the island with the Malay village on stilts, and then the prison island with its beautiful cricket field and air of lackadaisical smartness. We carried the delicacies of the Cold Storage in baskets and the magazines we took with us included *Life* and *Time*; our revolutionary friends were to eat chocolate biscuits and open tins of 'Leicestershire Mushrooms'—they would be able to stare at Rita Hayworth and Zsa Zsa Gabor, after the bevy of detectives had had a wonderful time paging through all this glossy journalism. We met the students in the Cricket Pavilion, below an oleograph of the Royal Family and an English lesson partially erased from the blackboard. They trooped in looking very well and rather too intensely gay. Yes, it was true that they had formed themselves into a university of their own—James was the Professor of Political Science but had been demoted from the position of Assistant Cook. Their menus were nationalistic, in the sense that each culture had to be represented. And sex, oh dear yes! was a terrible problem. As James chatted to me across the table, I couldn't forget that it was just possible that I might have been able to save him and the others from arrest. Hadn't an extraordinarily indiscreet, or perhaps an intentionally provocative, detective told me at a cocktail party nearly a year ago that he thought James was 'harmless' but that 'They' intended swooping down on the Medical College in the Christmas vacation? The detective had hoped that I would exert what influence I had over James, and I had certainly told him that my sympathy didn't extend to acid-throwing and ambush, that I wasn't a Communist, while he had tended to play down his sympathies with the left. Nevertheless there he was, untried after all these months; a first-class prisoner, as all the students were first-class prisoners, but a prisoner just the same.

Hedwig agrees with me now about the unreality of the island's atmosphere, about how extraordinary it is to see the other prisoners, the proletariat, winding down in their pyjamas and white shirts and shorts, so inconsequentially

young-looking and from a distance girlish, to crouch on
one side of the railing around the cricket field while their
black-clad mothers crouch on the other, with double-
saucepans of food in their hands. I tell her how Masood
Bin Ali, almost in tears at the sight, gestured to the thin
line of Singapore across the yellow water. 'What is it
now?' he asked. 'Nothing but trash. . . .'

'I don't suppose that you agreed.'

'Would you, wholeheartedly I mean? There's more
to it than politics.'

'Including, of course, Shaku. . . .'

But Shaku is not as pleased with the house as I had
hoped, perhaps because it is too near to home and not
bleak in her favourite Yorkshire way, but she is as talkative and charming as ever. As we drink the gritty kampong coffee and munch the dusty kampong biscuits, I
notice a strange more baroque twist to her beauty, an
oddness and staginess, and realize that part of her hair
has an exotic fiery sheen. She has peroxided it by mistake.
'I do assure you, Mr. Anderson, that all I wanted was a
remedy for dandruff. However, I must have helped myself too *liberalee* to the bottle my girl friend provided. Do
you find the result nauseating?' As a matter of fact I don't,
especially since a moment or two later a storm approaches
us; we hear the rain whipping through the trees, drum-
ming closer and closer; thunder growls and a great wind
is sucked through the house, which whinnies and creaks;
a more witch-like Shaku is quite appropriate now, her
small face tilted to the storm.

Compared with Hedwig and Gung-wu, our rare European visitors present a different problem. It is they who
should appreciate the house and the dream that is lived
in it. Their job is to see the non-political side of our
pioneering. But, although we have had some pleasant
times, exploring the estate, bathing at Ponggol, collecting
coconuts and fruit for our guests, minor problems have
over-shadowed the major one. One difficulty has been the

bees, which always decide to start swarming when parents and children are assembled on the balcony, and luncheon is—if one dares use so grand a word—laid.

'Oh dear, these ghastly bees,' says Gerald. 'I must apologize for them, although I think they're quite harmless.'

'They're going away—they're going into the tree,' I add, as Leng's approaching footsteps shake the house.

'Many bees,' says Leng, with a plate of tinned ham and cucumber in each hand and a look of having no idea whatever where to place them, as though they were a gift to the cosmos.

'I don't think they're a swarm,' a polite guest ventures. 'They're probably attracted by some tree in bloom.'

'Bees coming in,' Leng says with all the dullness of fact. And then, a sadistic gleam in his eyes, 'You must kill. You must burn with kerosene.'

'I do think they *are* concentrating a little . . .,' says the polite guest while a child or two looks tearful.

But suddenly there is a shriek from his wife.

'Darling, our car's on fire.'

For somebody has thrown a cigarette down from the balcony and it is now burning merrily on the roof of the Vauxhall parked below.

If it isn't the bees, it's the sanitary arrangements. Let Gerald take charge once more:

'It's too awful,' he begins, embarrassment making him look excited and conspiratorial, for if he is to make a bridge at all it must be an intimate one. 'But there's nowhere but that big tree over there, the one like an umbrella with the glossy leaves. Inside it's quite private.'

And the guest disappears bravely while we all look away, to avoid seeing her (a man doesn't matter) as she crosses the path and hesitates for a moment, wondering at what point to enter the immense dome. A hen flies out, squawking.

It is this primitive drawback which sometimes reconciles

me to the fact that D. seems determined not to come out here, although I am sure R. would like to. I made the suggestion the other day and she immediately flung any number of obstacles in its path. As a matter of fact, I thought I was getting on with her better only a few weeks ago. When I called on departmental business, she poured me out some beer in one of those pewter tankards which are ranged according to height on her side board, marching up and marching down between the wrought-iron candelabrum with its coloured candles and the silver and blue brocade curtain over the archway into the bedrooms, and then asked me to hear her latest part. She plays a lunatic who gives an outburst on sex from a landing back stage. 'The very flies do lecher in my sight' sort of thing, in a dressing gown and a flood of grey hair. But now our relations seem to have sagged again. Yet I respect her as an emotional power-house, am intrigued by her, feel rejected without giving up my interest.

There is to be no D. then—but there *was* Bunny. Bunny is our name for an elderly art-mistress who looks like a powder-puff or a cuddly toy, lisps brightly in the manner of a Victorian child, presses her face as close to one's own as possible, and entangles one in a spiritual down in which sexiness and hygienic good-fellowship struggle for emergence. Both would be jolly, smelling of a good soap. But it's a toss-up whether her symbol is fun in the bathroom or frolic in the bed. She takes herself very seriously as a painter. When she asked us to dinner, she sat with Gerald on the sofa and left her businessman husband to me. We talked, they whispered. Our talk grew more manly, until it smelled of cigars; their whispers became so confidential that they seemed about to turn into Peter and Wendy. As though she hadn't hooked Gerald sufficiently, she gleamed an additional naughtiness. 'Tell me. Do you think I'm a bit niffy? Are you sure? Are you sure I'm not just a wee bit offensive?' It took a long time for Gerald to grasp what *niffy* meant. When he had gone

red and reassured her with a giggle, she tried again. She
asked him into the bedroom to see her Balinese carving.
'I'm sure you'll think it interesting. You don't mind?
You're certain you don't mind? Good. The others won't
object if we leave them—just for a jiffy—will they?' Head
to one side, she searched our faces. 'No of course not.
They're deep in talk.' She minced off and you could almost
see a big blue sash, with a bow at the back. Gerald, whom
she would have been astonished to know had described
her as being 'vulgar but with a sort of Kraft-Ebbing
charm'—he was certainly grateful for the sympathy she
offered—followed her. When she had closed the door, she
held out both her hands. 'I can see you are dreadfully
unhappy. Let us be friends.'

By the time she came out to Sungei Tengah, I was
thoroughly disillusioned and Gerald was growing scep-
tical of her ability to understand. He had treated her
confidence seriously but he felt even then that he didn't
have the emotional security to make an adequate response.
One or two things since had shaken him. Such was her
offer to paint his portrait as soon as they were 'really and
truly *en rapport*'—it was to be only a 'spiritual likeness, of
course'. Now we did rather a dreadful thing. The previous
night I had been on a party and a drunken sailor had
brought brandy back to the house. The brandy had been
poured out into very strong drinks but not finished. So
Bunny was given a surprisingly (for us) glossy drink, with
ice-cubes and ginger-ale and even a slice of lemon. She
sipped it coyly. 'I think your house is . . .' she paused,
fluttered a hand, 'splendid. A little unusual but that is to
be expected and only makes it more fun. I call it a jolly
place to live. And this drink is yummy.' I stared at the
brandy and then across the balustrade at the soon-to-be-
jolly tree.

And then it is night again on the balcony and the
Seventh Moon is growing full. Huge flying foxes come
down from the north and the blue air is full of the sound

of guns. The other day I saw a boy carrying one of these bats on the beach at Ponggol. The shot had disfigured it so that it looked very strange: a wound in a furcoat wrapped up in a camera.

'Why are they such fools? Why don't they fly higher— or very much lower so that they are shielded by the trees?' Gerald asks, and I find him standing at various windows in turn, gripping the bars, his face sharp and pale in the moonlight. 'Isn't there some way we could drive them off?' But Leng of course is boyishly excited. He discusses guns and the tastiness of bat soup. He describes how the hunters capture a wounded bat, pinion it to the ground with a stick through its wings and wait for others to answer its call for help.

The sky is marbled, with clear stretches. The moon hangs in a circle of golden fur, then clear and liquid, then eaten by an angrier cloud. The bats fly slowly and firmly, now one, two, three, a group of five. . . . Our own rambutan harvest is not quite ready but there must be ripe fruit further south. I remember one moonlight night when smaller bats than these came into the tree outside my window at the university, filling the air with their fuss and twitter and with the peppery sound of husks falling to the ground. And I have seen, just once, a colony of foxes in a dead tree; its branches were black with them, fantastically dishevelled.

One night men drive up in an old car. They shout in Chinese. 'Oh God, what do these creatures want?' gasps Gerald. I can see that he is preparing to hide. Leng says they are asking permission to shoot on our place. The 'old ladee' up the road has directed them here and now we have a discussion as to which old lady this is, and is she a relative or friend of Towkay Lee? 'What right have they, what right?' The filthy old lady with the goitre and the balding head who drags the palm fronds, rusty and sharp as scabs, away through the gates? Or the lady who strolls, screaming, in front of an obscene carpet of hens? But, somehow, we know we are defeated. Our position as tenants is far too insecure for us to be able to intervene. To Gerald at least this denouement will be nothing new. His eyes fill with tears. 'If only it would get really cloudy they might be safe.'

The intruders' car, stocky with purpose, bumps down the path and Gerald, in purple shirt and chequered sarong, hangs over the balustrade. He is preparing himself for some sacrifice which will be more than a gesture to him. In a moment, despite my warnings, he runs downstairs and disappears along the grove—barefooted despite hook-worm, centipedes and kraits—in the hope that his shadowy presence may somehow deter the hunters, that they may be afraid of shooting him and consequently desist. But this is only a signal for Leng to run off too.

There are loud bangs. Shot patters over our roof. Faced by this desecration I feel something even more treacherous in the air which condenses itself most easily into the question: how long are we going to be allowed to stay? For often now there is a sense of strain around Mr. Lee's visits. Both of us feel inclined to hide ourselves away as though somehow we were illegal. We have successfully lived here—will they envy us our success? And yet we have lived oddly, with strange paintings on the walls and a good deal of 'un-European' untidiness—do they resent this sort of thing? Our rare conversations with Mr. Lee are courtly and affectionate, little nervous islands of almost super-civilization which he seems to appreciate, but most of his visits ignore us completely; his huge American car, packed with wife and children, bumps down the path to the hut of the Elderly Relative. Is he planning to give the House to Teo'chiu refugees from Swatow? Why did a group of nuns imperiously invade us the other day, marching into the House and discussing, with American accents, the previous uses of everything?

And now, I feel, Gerald will be even more aware of our isolation amongst the 'cruel Chinese'.

Finally we decide to abandon the House for the evening. We drive to the movies, past a Malay film at Tampenis and an Indian film at Paya Lebar, into the heart of the town. The moonlight is answered fiercely by yellow fires on Serangoon Road. The Chinese are burning paper-money for the use of the spirits.

PART FOUR

EPILOGUE IN BLUE AND WHITE STRIPED PYJAMAS

Spring 1952

Epilogue

I WAS propped up in a hospital bed when Shaku came to see me. Months had passed. Gerald was gone; I had resigned from the university, not without misgivings which I knew would grow and grow as the months and years went by, but in what seemed at times no more than a fit of romantic revulsion, another gesture in a life that was becoming all gestures, and my resignation had been accepted; as for the House, it had been first requisitioned by its owner (which we at least expected) and then, some time afterwards, there came the incredible and wounding news that it had been lent to another European of my acquaintance. Although a nice man, he showed from the first that he did not appreciate it as we had done. Once more I lived at the university and once more Ah Ting was my servant. An air of finality, of epilogue, possessed these days and I would often wonder whether I should have resigned at all. There was so much to do in Malaya, so much that could only be done by a real friend of the students, provided he could be calmer and more settled. To leave them might be suspiciously like a betrayal. . . . But the staccato blows of change meant little to me that hot afternoon in April, for I had been drinking Tio Pepe and had then fallen asleep.

To my left the Shanghai doors opened onto a corridor bisecting the surgical wing. Through the gap at the bottom I could see patients being wheeled to the theatre or clinic, the thin black legs of a nurse from Madras, shadows restless in the private room across the way. A scarlet hump went by on a trolley, suggesting triumph or gore; a tray of medicines rattled by in the opposite direction, and every medicine was the colour of sleep. The

Chinese orderlies giggled silently from room to room, making gnome-like appearances through the doors, telling you what to do in sign language, squeaking encouragement and sighing apology, for they had no English and there weren't nearly enough nurses to go round. I was well enough now to stagger in the mornings to the bath and there a diplomatic gnome bathed me, to a succession of titters, while my strange-feeling body responded to warmth and light. My body seemed to me a gift which I had been granted for a second time.

To my right two sets of doors gave onto a wide gallery. Unlike the central corridors, which were always busy, this seemed devoted to the spaciousness and indolence of disease; from it disease looked out upon the world with its blank dignified exhausted face, watching the timeless sunlight pour down into the court but really fixed, as during a sea-voyage, upon some thin horizon of the mind; the very whiteness of the sheets suggested they were snow-drifts deposited by an alpine loneliness in which memories of childhood and irresponsibility fused with imaginative flights, so that the heat of the hospital, over-crowded as it was and open on all sides to the air, could not be felt sensuously but was a recollection of summer fields and seas, caused by the gleam of sunlight on snow. The practical noises of the place invaded my room by way of the corridor; the gallery yielded quite other and more terrible sounds; here too the patients loitered, the stoicism and level-headedness of the Chinese transformed by their blue and white pyjamas into an appearance of gaiety, to which the sexlessness of their large smooth bodies gave a further accent of childishness, with the result that they seemed schoolboys waiting for a dormitory feast to begin, or products of some indolent Sunday morning, comfortably alone with wives in whom they no longer took much sensual interest.

This alfresco air was the most that could be offered in the way of ordinary life. On one side of it stretched the

resigned snowdrifts of sleep and waking dream; on the
other, the automatism with which the various diseases
asserted themselves. A deep-voiced shouting and anger
occurred throughout the night, repeating a few words in a
highly cultured accent—*No, no, no*! was one phrase,
magisterially delivered but often followed by an additional
No! of a more querulous and hopeless character; *Tell me
what you mean, man* was another; while once or twice the
unknown, and anyway unconscious voice, barked out
with *I object, I object very strongly*. A groan concluded it,
either releasing the tension and allowing the patient to
sleep, or only to be repeated a moment later as the prelude
to another cycle. Very different were the sharp bubblings
and whoops flipping out of the restless silence like so many
irrepressible fish, of the Chinese hero of the anti-Japanese
resistance who lay dying in the room next to mine. I soon
found that the bass voice belonged to a frail, elderly Tamil
school-teacher who lay, with a number of other second-
class patients, in a ward improvised from part of the
gallery. He sent his apologies, Sister told me; he didn't
want to be a nuisance. Perhaps the Japanese had bullied
him like that, or perhaps that was the way he disciplined
his pupils. The inheritance of a hundred years of arguing
with the British may have played its part.

Such noises belonged chiefly to the night. Then one
might lie sleepless for hours—I didn't find it incongruous
that I had been given a pile of ballet magazines to read,
and that I often picked one up after midnight, for those
immaterial bodies seemed at home in hospital. Girls floated
by on whiffs of ether, pierrots formed themselves out of
the black and white of sheets and iron bedstead, and a
devil in tights turned out to be a rubber syringe. But
sleep was not restricted to the hours of darkness; it
washed through the hospital in the daytime as well,
touching now one bed and now another; it pushed before
it long dazing lines of foam, themselves balletic, and the
philosophic calm with which one remembered and

analysed one's life, astonished oneself with the acuteness of one's perceptions or simply contemplated one's 'wound', could quickly crumble into sheer laziness. Not that my room looked lazy. No less than two bedside tables swung over my bed: one piled with Civil Service exams (Conrad, Maugham, and 'What do you consider to be the task of the film in Malaya?'), the other thick with books, tins of cigarettes, and apples and oranges brought by Ah Ting. More fruit, much more, rotted in the cupboards. On a shelf in the wardrobe lay the unpleasant little bundle of bloodstained shirt and vest, soggy identity card, Gerald's crumpled letter.

Shaku arrived early. No other visitors trooped down the central corridor. She had a 'woman watching by a death-bed' look. I decided to tease her by keeping her in suspense as to the story of my accident. Besides, I hadn't had the chance of talking to anybody all day.

'I'm so glad you didn't bring fruit,' I told her when, the wings of her personality folded, she proffered a round tin of Players with much the same gesture she had used when making a gift to the Goddess Kali in Tagore's *Sacrifice*. 'Flowers are different,' I went on 'but they would be too cliché a present from you. In any case you despise most of the tropical varieties.'

'Oh no, there are several kinds I'm quite fond of.' But her voice lacked the usual conviction. She expected to be impressed, not to chatter. On the other hand, if there was chattering to be done, it was up to her to play her part if only to prevent me from tiring myself. 'Gardenias are so clean and fresh. . . .' And she gestured towards some remembered dance, whose romantic suffering she had forgotten, for Shaku nearly always suffered at dances and on two separate occasions I had seen her faint. 'But orchids are horribly sinister and fleshy, like spiders!'

'What I was going to say is that I have never really enjoyed fruit. I've always wanted to. I've read about lovers eating cherries together and picking wild strawberries in

... dream world of having homes, furniture and ke... and children where ... be indeed, to fill... with... complaints for money...... the bryan woman... ... hope and respect... a fiasco...

"Children began to invade the house," Joe... bitter tears...

7. 'A crazy world of flaring lamps, far too much beer and children whose business it was to flirt with Europeans for money'—the beggar woman here tried to get me a Boy (*p. 281*)

'Children began to invade the house' (*p. 190*)   *Crown copyrig*

the morning dew, and of how voluptuous a peach can be, but somehow I've never quite realized that sort of thing in real life. I've been scared. . . .'

'Scared?' She twisted one small hand in the other and looked up from under downcast lashes as though searching my face for signs of imminent decomposition.

'Scared enough to have a theory about it. It was the same thing with summer—in fact the theory fitted them both. You see I loved a phrase like "high summer" or "mid-summer's eve" but I couldn't help feeling that I wasn't quite up to them.' A European Sister looked in through the open door and smiled. Turning towards her, Shaku grew more beautiful and poised in profile, although the movement itself was agitated, as though she feared she might be sent away; there was still the faintest peroxide shine to her hair. 'Yes, summer had a competence and completeness and a kind of oldness and sadness in its very innocence which seemed to belong to athletes and lovers and other nice inarticulate people, who were natural and therefore knew how to belong. But in summer I was always thinking of autumn, almost as though I wanted to get it over with. To become literary and reflective and safe.'

'I expect you invented the theory first and then . . cultivated the feelings,' Shaku broke in, unconvinced. 'Are you sure you're comfortable?'

'Yes, perfectly comfortable. You mustn't fuss over me.'

'I'm not fussing. I'm not an especially fussy person. But I *have* come to enquire after your health.'

'In a minute.' I paused, amused at my ability to dominate her but very glad to have her alone, to keep her suspended over conventional attitudes which she was the the last person to wish to exploit for more than a few moments. 'And fruit—well, fruit had even more immediacy than summer: a sharpness, a sourness, an air of having to be consummated, and hence all the possibilities of disillusion. Or shall we say a mixture of art and emptiness?

It's quite different with steak or pork-chops. You *eat* them. You plough into them and chew and bite your way for a considerable length of time. But a fruit is a unit in itself—a beautiful object—and when you put it into your mouth you have to have a complete experience, at least you want to. Not only do you destroy it but as you do so it yields you its essence, which is a pale clean thing and can taste very pure and ghostly. So you say it's sour or un-ripe or avoid it altogether because you're afraid of missing the true essential experience!'

'I've seen you eating mangosteens by the dozen! And rambutans,' she added, for accuracy's sake.

'Exactly. Because in the tropics it's always summer and there's a great deal of fruit—very good reasons for my coming here, to try again.'

'And disprove your theory?'

'I suppose so. . . .' The conversation suddenly became sad, especially with Shaku sitting opposite me, being so attentive and kind and innocent; the dull shadow of self-hood lay over it, a romanticism, an inadequacy; one wanted to explain things and then, when one did, one seemed to be letting oneself and everybody else down. I saw a way to switch my line of talk, so that it was closer to pure teasing. I told her that cigarettes were the right gift for me, that Europeans were puritans who couldn't really enjoy fruit because they were too introspective, too conscious of their own nerves and fantasies and too anxious to punish themselves; I spoke of the awful un-wanted virginity of the European soul, completely differ-ent from innocence, because innocence is touched and hurt by the outside world while puritanism prejudges everything and can only hurt itself; and then I attempted to link these ideas with individualism and art and art's loneliness, borrowing heavily from Thomas Mann. Smok-ing, I told her, is the artist's solitary vice, which stimu-lates his voracious nervous system; he sucks life in, he puffs life out—but are those elaborate patterns forming in his lungs, those grey clouds expelled to dissolve in the air, are they life at all? Virginia Woolf writing books that smell of Turkish cigarettes! And nowhere the Big Bang of real fact, to clear the analysing, digesting, distorting smoke away and make a space, like a woman naked at a window!

'Are you sure it's all right for you to talk?' asked Shaku, from the edge of her chair, with her handbag grasped in both hands and her eyes flickering with worry.

'Yes, yes. Besides, you're supposed to imagine that you are visiting some bedridden old philosopher or that a king is holding a *lit de justice* especially for you. Didn't Thomas Hobbes discourse from his bed, writing notes on the sheets and even on the skin of his own body? And Archimedes. . . .'

'He was in his *bath*,' Shaku blurted, education getting the better of reticence.

'Well, you should see me in my bath here—or I suppose you really shouldn't, but you can imagine what it's like with a tiny Chinese scrubbing me.' Shaku smiled for the first time, her maternal Eastern soul being appealed to.

'But you're so heavy!'—that recognition of sheer physical fact which, taking weight as evidence of virility and discounting all the aesthetic disadvantages, is so flatteringly offered by small races.

'You make me positively and definitely glad that I don't smoke,' Shaku added, with that mounting emphasis of hers.

'I make myself want one of the cigarettes you brought me,' I replied, turning too exuberantly towards the tin on the bedside table, and being rewarded with a spasm of pain. She caught my grimace.

'Does it . . .'—*it* being still unspecified by my flow of nonsense, and hence to be suddenly remarked now as a vague grim shadow—'does it hurt very much? Are you in pain?'

'My ribs hurt when I move quickly or cough. Apart

from that, I'm strictly convalescent. I'm still the rival of Richard Widmark for your attractions.'

'I gave up Widmark years ago. You know that perfectly well. As a matter of fact—but you'll laugh if I tell you. . . .'

'I couldn't laugh, it hurts too much.' I could see that I was in for one of Shaku's quick changes of mood for vitality was pressing through embarrassment all over her face. The child-guardian of an over-size subconscious, she had a habit of reminding me that I was her academic superior before letting some jungle creature through.

'I dreamed last night that we were married.' The significance of a dream, together with its respectable ancestry in the Romantic Movement, quickly erased the incipient giggle from her voice. She spoke slowly and then gazed in front of her with large solemn eyes. Embarrassment ushered in problem; problem would quickly disintegrate as discussion darted about.

'Was it fun?' I made myself more comfortable on the bed, which was the kind that winds up, changing the natural sprawl of the body into a moral landscape of valleys and peaks. With head and knees occupying the prominent positions, sensuousness drained away into the shallows, fading amongst the white sheets. To tell the truth, I had never been quite sure how fond of me Shaku was. The Tropics, with their atmosphere of symbolism-or-nothing, made it less imperative to know. In a poem, she was my child bride. 'Was it so much fun that you can't tell me about it? Or did you try to reform me or something?'

'Well, it didn't go on for very long, exactly—the dream, I mean. There was a castle. . . .'

'My dear Shaku, there always a castle where you're concerned. I bet there were daffodils. And a lark singing his little heart out. And a Turkey carpet onto which the sunlight threw the pattern of diamond-shaped window panes.'

'As a matter of fact,' she interrupted me, 'I was worried about having to leave my cat.'

'Couldn't it have come on the honeymoon, too?'

'No, it was ill,' she looked up and then burst out, in a kind of exasperation, 'Don't question me so closely. A dream doesn't have to be logical.'

'But the cat sounds distinctly Freudian.'

'I assure you, Mr. Anderson, the cat was basically of no importance at all!'

'And now,' I said, 'you're pleased. You're not a widow. I'm still alive in a drowsy sort of way.'

'I wouldn't call you drowsy.'

'Drunk, then?'

Once more she played the game with a sweeping gesture. 'I don't deny that you may have . . . *partaken* of that bottle of *liquid refreshment* by your side . . . but I don't think your *intellectual powers* have suffered to any extent.'

'Shaku, you're marvellous. Have some?'

'A small portion, please.'

'We'll drink to my recovery.'

'And your book.'

'Oh dear, my book. . . . We'll drink to the part you play in it—the dusky young tigress leaping onto the pillion of the first Eurasian motor-bicycle that comes along —the siren of the Mount Rosie Women's Hostel reciting Byron under the palm-trees as she waits for her demon lover to arrive, dismount, fall on his knees and present her with his Economics Notes. Meanwhile her aristocratic white husband has suffered a fearful accident. . . .'

'Yes, tell me what happened.' I had got round to it at last. It would be easier to explain to her than to R. 'The students are criticizing Beda Lim. They say he should have stood and fought—they say he was cowardly to run away.'

Beda had been re-admitted to the university after all.

'But he didn't run away. It was I who ran. He behaved with perfect propriety. I have got very fond of Beda

recently—we go out a lot together, you know—and I
don't think anything nicer has happened to me in Singapore than the time we got his setting of that love poem of
Auden's sung by a Shanghai male tart at the Savoy. Art in
the midst of squalor. It was wonderful. It's been played
at the Monico, too, and I shan't be surprised if it's
rendered one day by full orchestra at the Carlton. Beda
pushes it hard enough. He isn't reticent with it as he was
with that other poem he wrote to his French girl-friend.
You know the story?'

'I don't think so.'

'Beda got to know this exceedingly nice girl and he took
photographs of her—it was towards the end of his camera
phase—and when he had developed them, he wrote a
poem on the envelope before handing it to the girl. It's
completely typical of Beda that, having read in *Time
Magazine* of the current fashion for Renaissance calli-
graphy, he printed the poem with immense care in a sort
of semi-archaic hand. It was so neat and black that the girl
thought it was print, and didn't bother to read it. I was
with him. He had to tell her. It was quite embarrassing as
the poem was, like most products of the University of
Malaya, extremely romantic.'

'I thought he left you to fight alone.'

'I didn't fight. What happened was that Beda and I
went to the open-air eatingplace in Bugis Street after we
had wandered through several bars—it was quite late,
fairly crowded, with the usual assortment of soldiers and
people slumming, painted little girls zithering and singing
away, and the young men from the Savoy gossiping
with the girls from the Airview—and we sat down at my
favourite group of tables, the one served by the stall which
cooks the best food—you've been there with me—and
ordered beer. As a matter of fact. . . .'

'Was there an air of tension?' she broke in.

'Not in the least. But, as I was just going to say, there
was one thing: we were short of money, not that we'd spent

much, and I boasted to Beda how easy it was to get people
to stand you drinks. Memories of my rare but exciting
cadging days in Bloomsbury prompted me to it—or was
it just thirst? So I sort of encouraged people to join our
party, and succeeded in snatching one perfectly respectable little seaman from his loneliness. The beer problem
was solved right away, as it turned out, because some
Norwegians already at the table left most of theirs, and we
had two bottles already. But if I showed my wicked
cadging side—the side Gerald loathes—as he's probably
told you—Beda's worst flaw was stimulated, if you can
stimulate a flaw. He became *naïve*. He saw that I had
snatched someone, so he thought he could snatch too. But
as he thought of snatching, his mind drifted naturally to
women. There was the usual cluster of bedraggled tarts at
a table to our left. Portly matrons with their faces looking
mauve under their powder, who do their best to combine
Victorian busts with shapeless sarongs. Beda joined them,
and I bet Eliot's bit about 'promise of pneumatic bliss'
was running through his mind—or was it young Stephen
Dedalus swooning into the arms of a Dublin floosy? But
he didn't come back with one of them. He came back with
Albert Snood. . . .'

'Isn't that a character in Dickens?'

'I shouldn't be surprised if it were, but there was nothing Dickensian about this man. I was busy talking to my
seaman. Then I turned in his direction, with no idea
except to be pleasant. And it happened. The next thing I
knew he had pulled a piece of broken glass out of his
pocket, and begun waving it in the air. It was the lower
half of one of those beer goblets, I think, with a nice
jagged edge. . . . Five minutes later I was out cold. When
I came to my senses I found myself in a coffee shop—the
one that stays open all night—with the blood dripping all
over me.'

'But why? Did you quarrel or something?'

'To tell you the truth I had no idea what happened

until the day before yesterday. There was just an eerie blank. Then I found that my enemy had been rounded up and had made a statement, in which he claimed that I had insulted him in the oddest way. He was in civvies, you see, so I naturally asked him what he did—was he a soldier or an airman or anything like that? He replied that he did nothing. I imagine I thought this evasiveness was part of a game, for I certainly missed the dangerous paranoiac note. I said, jokingly, "If you live in Singapore and do nothing, you must be either a spiv or a Communist agent." That started him. I had called him a Communist. Would I please accompany him to the police-station, bringing with me the documents that proved my charge?'

'He must have been crazy!'

'It was a nasty situation, partly because it was so odd. He was waving the broken glass but otherwise he didn't seem violently angry. He still sat hunched over the table, a short thickset man with a large pale rugged face, and mumbled on and on and on. I did absolutely everything to placate him. So did the others. But he got neither better nor worse, and there seemed as though there'd be no end to it. Finally, after I had apologized and explained at least ten times, I got bored, raised my voice, declared the matter closed—and walked away. He came after me. I found myself trapped, with my back to a wall. Then nothing. . . .'

'And were you hurt very badly?'

'Two broken ribs and a fractured jaw. This cut on my lip as well. Plus, I suppose, the indignity. Lecturers are not supposed to get involved in such Hogarthian scenes. And I'm afraid there will be more publicity as the Army insists I prosecute. If I don't they'll subpoena me through the civil courts. Anyway, have some more sherry. The Frazers brought it.' The novelist Shamus Frazer and his beautiful wife were among the most interesting people in the colony.

Shaku declined the sherry. She looked impressed, as

only she can. Recovering herself, she asked—'You're looked after well here, I suppose?'

'Oh yes, it's a sort of idyll but a dreadfully un-adult one.' I indicated a formal basket of flowers which one of my First Year students had sent me and which, to be faintly original and daring, I had suspended in mid-air. 'People treat me as though I were properly and nobly ill, when everyone must secretly feel that I have been foolish, and that this is a judgement upon me for my escapades in the past. You know the way my mind works. I'm quite prepared to see myself as a victim of the struggle of capital letter things, Art and Life, but even I can only achieve this with wry smiles and irony—I couldn't consider my position on this bed as anything but ludicrous.'

'To the students,' Shaku answered with great deliberation, 'you are something of a hero.'

'Well I'm not. I'm a clown—or a naughty boy hiding in a cupboard—or an anti-social bee in the centre of a flower. To come back to what I was saying before, this is a cigarette-smoke world of shapes in the air and passive reverie. I wanted to be drowned in the tropics. How do I end up? Flat on my back in bed. The dreamer's paradise, with sickness as the dreamer's excuse! A lovely masochistic muddle is all that I've got and, saying this, I add the one missing note of self-pity. Thank God Gerald isn't here —I doubt if he would have consented to come and see me.'

'But you were saying you wanted some sort of violence, what you called a big bang . . .,' Shaku observed, 'and now you speak of drowning. I think you use too many metaphors.'

'Didn't you tell me that a dream can't be logical? When Snood hit me, it may have been a big bang—for somebody else, reading a novel. But what did it do to me? It gave me a week of enforced reverie, some anxious disgust, and any number of tins of cigarettes.'

'Well, at least, you always claimed that you wanted to be involved and not just an observer and now you are.'

'More involved than with you? I'd rather have your dream than a dozen fights.'

'And perhaps you'll be more careful now,' Shaku went on, with a faint tightening of her voluptuously childish lips. 'I tell you I have been positively horrified to see how tired and grey you looked when you came into the canteen some mornings to get your breakfast. You need to eat. Not just to drink ginger-beer and aspirins.'

'You're trying to reform me, which is what all women are supposed to do.'

'You'll be going away soon and then I shan't be able to *presume* any more. I shall be very sad.' It took only a second for Shaku's eyes to fill with tears and when they did so she looked down into her lap, where her small brown hands lay abandoned. A faint wind stirred along the verandah. The ornamental basket of flowers swayed in the air before us.

'So shall I. And I know, in fact I've told everybody, how much I shall regret Malaya. But I can't see,' I went on, feeling a queer need to be definite and angry—'I can't see a blaze of reality behind our relationship. It's too charming and hopeless. What can we do?'

Shaku didn't answer. Solemnity had become more than she could handle, as it so often did; her role was that of a student listening to an exposition; my question was rhetorical.

'There's something literary about the tropics, something nostalgic and false. In between daydreams and dramatics a whole area of life is missed. Perhaps you are too much part of myself to be an answer. . . .'

When Shakuntala had gone—and Masood and Pat Wong, who came after her—I settled down for the evening. I got carefully out of bed and paid a visit to the second class ward, where I had spent my first two nights. It was only a few yards away, in what had once been a verandah to the surgical wing. The patients were the same: a Public Works Department Chinese, middle-aged and angular, with an amputated toe and the habit of sleeping at night while *sitting on the edge of his bed*; a European policeman, the rather self-conscious possessor of enlarged testicles; three boys thrown in abandon on beds by the window. Talking to them, and stimulated by their remarks on the progress I was making, I felt a desire to climb out and lose myself in the city again. The noise of traffic drifted through the palm trees. But I went back to my room to correct some more exam papers and found the Chinese youth who had taken to visiting me already there, anxious to recount the latest dressings he had done and to bemoan his failure in the Cambridge.

Night falls quickly in a hospital. Soon my reading light was the only one left on. I picked up a book and opened it at a photograph of Robert Helpman as Hamlet. Then *Les Sylphides*, white and delicate as the frangipani petals on the lawn outside my university flat; then *The Red Shoes*, bold as the hibiscus in the hedges at Sungei Tengah. Suddenly a voice rang out. *Tell me what you mean, man*, it cried, sinking a moment later to a restless *No, no*! Very soon it would be echoed, I knew, by the curious gaiety, the dreadful impersonal *élan*, of those whoops and gurgles which came from the room next to mine.

Shortly after this conversation with Shaku I was able to leave the hospital. The last, strangest period of all began.

But it won't be easy to describe, least of all in terms of the relative culture and detachment expected from a first person, who can be sick and unfortunate provided he is unselfish and brave, and whose introspections must always be governed by a high ratio of outside objects and events, unless he is to be the X of a case-history or have a rare Dostoievskian talent for the confessional. What happened? is the question that prose has to answer, together with How? and Why?—and if the elements are especially curious, if the mood is self-pitying and the instances grotesque, prose has the excellent habit of transposing a disastrously painful 'I' into a carefully-studied 'He' or 'She'; as for poetry, it alone can deal with that vast area of life in which nothing much happens at all. An Alka-seltzer tablet dissolved in lime-juice . . . the thickening smear of blood on a dining-room table, removing the polish even as it glued bits of paper into the grain of the wood . . . the presence of small wasps . . . a lost razor, stolen by a monkey and found buried in leaves in the gutter of a flat roof . . . and, amongst these trivia, death itself, in an epidemic or an atrociously painful disease, striking amongst my friends.

Day after day the ancient Hillman sat on the gravel outside my windows, lop-sided because a tire had gone flat, unstartable because the battery needed changing (and that was a borrowed battery, too), filling with leaves, blistering with heat, rusting under the rare but torrential rain. Children played round it and inside it lived a cat. This was a marmalade-coloured animal, scrawny and ill-smelling, which curled up on the seat where Leng and Ah Tum had ridden, and Gerald had flirted with Shaku, and the monkey had chattered at Gung-wu's imaginative flights. There the Ming dragon had rested in its jagged severity—bought on the same day as the car and pre-sented as excitedly to Leng whose response had been, 'You pay plentee dollars this thing? I think it broken. I think you take have mended and then be O.K. for souvenir.' And, of course, bathing-trunks and towels, library books, plants and flowers of every description.

Dragging myself out of bed late in the morning or early in the afternoon (lectures had given way to exams, exams were corrected and handed in) and wandering blindly through my huge hot rooms (for now, when it was far too late, the whole house was mine) I would peer out of one of the windows in a secretive guilty way (I felt a trespasser in this new expansiveness, already monkey-soiled) and there the car stood, symbol of power, mobility, freedom, symbol of 'the wild night drives' of the past, but quite unable to move. And just as the greater space and possibility offered me by the house were blocked back by heat and lassitude, for the upper rooms were actually hotter than the ground floor, while the intenser light showed up the impersonality of the decoration, so the car still possessed a decrepit and rakish glitter as it sprawled drunkenly below me, as though dismissed by a sudden flurry of jacaranda petals blown against its windscreen. The thought of doing anything about it was enough to drive me back to bed, where I would lie for hours with aspirins, alka-seltzer tablets and lime-juice beside me, aware perhaps on the fringes of my shallow sleep that the people next door, who had been very kind to me and of whom I was quite fond, were going on leave but unable to make any motion towards them, to help as they carried their luggage to the taxi I now heard drive up, or to say good-bye, and only getting up when someone came to the door, shouted my name or insistently rang the bell, in order to hide in the dining-room or the bathroom, amongst the ants and the bees (for Ah Ting had gone, and the place was in disorder). Once or twice indeed, with the moral support of a student, I did make some effort but when the idea came to me, after several weeks of despair, that it was possible to start a car with the crank, I no sooner got the motor running and began to edge forward than I found that a tyre had gone flat, and the prospect of having this mended—especially as there was now no spare wheel—seemed altogether too improbable. Ridiculous as it may sound, I became convinced that the car belonged to another period separated from me by an immense gulf of time, in which my accident took on a mysterious dividing role, and I often thought it appropriate that almost the last ride I had taken in it was on the eve of Gerald's departure, when we had driven out in the moonlight to the Sungei Tengah house, finding it deserted and apparently very much more decrepit, with a great wash of spider-lilies at its sides and back. Evidently my European rival lived there no more.

Yet the car had only recently been decarbonized and its engine was in better order than ever before. 'A little energy, the expenditure of a few dollars—less than you spent on a couple of evenings' drinking—' I can hear you say, 'and you would have been driving merrily about, completing your record of Singapore.' But here there must enter another element of the grotesque—an objective one. There was something hideously the matter with the car. You could never be sure that its left front wheel was not going to come off. A fugitive wheel is the most un-nerving of accidents, at once ludicrous and dangerous. When it first happened to me, at two in the morning between the Capitol cinema and the *padang* (the most public and sophisticated of places, full of traffic lights and zebra crossings, although completely deserted) I was taken completely by surprise. I drove to a stop, rather slowly and gracefully, on three wheels and an axle, leaving a long scratch behind me. I found my wheel two hundred yards away and rolled it back to rest by the crippled car. And I then embarked on an extraordinary adventure which involved first an hysterical visit to Beach Road Police Station (the focal point in the riots of two years before); second, a long wait amongst the Malay constables in a backroom; third, my suddenly losing my temper and demanding, with an arrogance never before dreamed of, that I be put in touch with the Colonial Secretary at once; fourth, instead of my prompt arrest, a sudden wave of friendly activity in my direction, with the result that two jeep-loads of Malays accompanied me to the car, mended it, and then insisted on hiding it in the Station over-night so that the Traffic Police should not meddle with it, and perhaps investigate its state of repair, or the sanity of its owner. And yet, no sooner had I fetched the car back next day than the wheel once more raced off by itself. This time a garage repaired it—but not convincingly. There was something radically wrong with the hub.

So it was that, during those last unforgettable weeks, I gave up all hope of using the car again and tried instead to sell it, as I was selling the radio and my bits and pieces of rotan furniture. Six hundred dollars, then five, four, three, two. . . . A Chinese student seemed interested: a queer cocky little man, who had been a missionary or a schoolmaster, and wrote Methodist poetry à la Mrs. Hemans, and was very glib about the beauties of Nature. After weeks of negotiation he came one afternoon with his friends. They didn't ring, having evidently decided to inspect the car first, and I heard their feet on the gravel and their high sharp voices, as I hid behind the shutters. They rattled, tapped, pushed, and then I heard them giggle as their voices ebbed away. I don't think the student ever spoke to me again. My attention switched to a European I met in a bar, a pale sombre man in some sort of minor business capacity, who seemed to drink without enjoyment and to visit dives without much conviction. Early one morning he arrived at my house, announcing mournfully that he had been out all night and that he wanted to give me a cheque for the car right away. I was paralysed with hangover and hardly took in what he was saying. I drifted brokenly towards him, hitching my clothes round me, and warding off the screaming figure of Chi-chi—and he hung about, dazed and haggard, but with petulant certainties slipping out of the corners of his mouth. I told him I didn't think it fair to let him have the car before we were both certain that the transfer would be allowed—I foresaw endless difficulties with the Traffic Department, wrongly as it appeared later—and in the end he wandered off to get some sleep. The next day I got a curt little note saying that 'in view of my unco-operative attitude' he had decided 'not to proceed with the purchase'. I had hoped it was a letter from Gerald as I saw it lying there on the tiles below the netting, when I lumbered down the stairs with the exclamatory figure of Chi-chi in front of me, arms flying into the air, head aureoled with light. 'Don't touch,' I had shouted but the monkey already gripped it in his teeth and looked at me now over his shoulder, fear and mischief in perfect equilibrium, like some master of irrelevance determined that the marginal, the superfluous, the vaguely irritating—the spots before one's eyes, the scampering below the wainscot—should be carefully re-erected in the centre of my world. 'But Chi-chi, Chi-chi, this is too much,' I could have cried. 'You have already destroyed an entire packet of Lucky Strike cigarettes, upset a half-empty bottle of stale beer, and stained the floorboards in three places with your sweet-smelling but corrosive pee!'

So, when I looked at the car, it was not only its immobility which worried me but also the problem of whether I should ever be able to get rid of it all.

One seemed to take an endless time getting taxis, for the students' telephone was always occupied and the only other ones were in the heart of the university, in the tiny common-room beside the air-mail editions of *The Times*, or in R.'s office itself, and I had for months regarded these almost as out of bounds. Typewriters hammered away under the Moorish arches; Eurasian sub-clerks might pounce on you with some embarrassing financial query or show by their very politeness that they knew your resignation had finished you, that you were all washed-up, drained of power; each day larger and larger cars seemed to drive up outside the main entrance and park in blazing droves between kerbs so white that you could almost *hear* their colour, with the shriek of chalk on a blackboard, flowers so hot that they shrilled like burglar alarms, gravel so clean that it resembled broken glass. Half way to my office my freshly-laundered shirt would be sticking to my chest, for the *amah* had shrunk it as assiduously as she had starched it; my belt bit into my belly; my Kwong-wu trousers were momentarily as stiff as canvas, shining with glaze from the iron, bleached from grey to a streaky white, and yet ready to disintegrate within a couple of hours to the baggiest of over-alls. By the time I had got via my office to the canteen I felt absurdly hot, like chocolate dissolving inside its pseudo-elegant wrapper. And there were no taxis available—or, if there were, there was no certainty that they would arrive, or arrive at the right place. It was this atmosphere, not only of heat and emptiness but of the busy continuance of a life to which I had grown eccentrically irrelevant, that made me stumble so hysterically round the campus in search of R. when I was told that my electric light was about to be cut off. I was told this by a young man in official buff uniform who had already made several attempts to get into the house—he had come early in the morning and rung the bell for seemingly hours and hours, but I hadn't got up to see who it was, for I had scarcely thought of him as anything more practical than a mystery and a torturer—and, although it turned out to be a mistake, I found this sudden demand, without warning as it was, one of the most serious confirmations of my illegality. I had, in fact, burst into tears. . . . Nevertheless movements out of the compound had to be made, if only to get food for Chi-chi.

I got into the habit of buying him cut-rate papayas, already slimy to the touch, when I was drinking late at night—for not even the difficulty over taxis prevented me from continuing to go out once it became cool—and sometimes, having left the shopping till too late, I brought him back cooked Chinese vegetables wrapped up in a dried banana-leaf. These were always elegant little parcels, tied with raffia so that you could twirl them on your finger but increasingly warm and limp, and I don't think Chi-chi really approved of them. It was while I was holding one of these parcels, guilty that I had not got something more suitable but at the same time relieved that I hadn't forgotten him altogether, that I was told of the death of Ali. I was sitting on a wooden stool outside Abdul's hole in the wall in Albert Street, so late at night that the Chinese cafés had already closed, when Yousouf came down the road to tell me. Ali, whom I had thought of sometime inviting to become my Boy, had died quite suddenly 'of a heart attack' at the age of fifteen. No longer would he wait on me at table in the Muslim restaurant, whose name I could never remember, smiling more and more broadly as I intoned my invariable order: Satu chicken curry, satu mutton, satu dahl, satu vegetable, satu salàd, duar chapati, satu Anchor besar! No more would I watch him as he crossed over to the bar, inevitably run by Chinese and as brightly anonymous as the remainder of the big room was human and dirty, with that curious Malay stolidity of his, grave and yet frivolous, as though tough-ness must perpetually divagate *below the level of conscious personality* into the coquetry of a child. And, as I heard the news which couldn't for a moment sound real and hence was capable of being immediately tragic—it had a sort of dream validity which didn't demand as yet any protective worry or depression—I became conscious of the city around me, no longer that of night-life but of night itself, ashen rather than dark, full of crumbling plaster walls and rats scampering over pieces of paper. It seemed that the world must slough off the dramatic opposition between pressure-lamps and shadows and go, as it were, bald into dawn.

But after this news about Ali, death took possession of the day as well, seeming to breed in the light, and I remembered that question Gerald had asked on the bal-cony in Sungei Tengah months before: could you get your body burnt if you died instead of surrendering it to the steaming soil? For it was now that Masood bin Ali was struck by a headache which kept him silent and non-commital for days, moving from one corner of the public-rooms to another, in an attempt I suppose not to relin-quish the sense of his friends, of discussion and politics, coffee, lecture-notes and the distant sound of ping-pong, all things to whose enjoyment he had dedicated his grave dark eyes and which he had achieved, as so few Malays ever did, from some remote rural background in Upper Johore. Finally he was taken to the hospital, and at first to a public ward, where his headache was diagnosed as meningitis. I learned from Gung-wu that he had been terrified to go, dreading an operation; perhaps, under his sophisticated exterior, there lay some primitive fear. Sophisticated he certainly was, or rather looked, and I had been interested to see how successful he was becoming with European women, for I had often wondered when the students would begin to think of themselves in this way, not of course that Masood was 'dark' and 'elemental' as some of the others might conceivably have been thought; there was something courteous and knightly about him; he was rather dazed, if anything, by the progress he was making and perhaps he realized that it separated him, as did his personal beauty which was not in the least conventionally Malay, from his family and culture. He could have leaped straight from the canteen to the pages of *Vogue*. Instead he died. Gung-wu wrote him a poem, and Gung-wu and Beda prepared an obituary for one of whose phrases I was responsible, ascribing to him 'a grave and limpid charm', which was certainly a fair description of those nocturnal melancholy eyes, like the greatly magnified eyes of an insect, and that dusky olive face quietly smiling or bowing with great dignity above the restrained but willowy body. I have a photograph of him, taken by Beda, in which he leans back against an arch on the campus, with his profile very close to the camera while the distant landscape, slightly out of focus, appears to be a plain of tumbled hot ash as though it prefigured already the headache and fever which were so soon to engulf him. And not only him, for at the time of his death a polio epidemic was raging, several children were taken ill, and one of the newest lecturers died within a few days. Yet there was no sympathetic relaxation of the heat; it wasn't an atmosphere at all appropriate to death unless, as I began to feel, death was the secret that had always hidden behind the idiotic gaiety and emptiness, in which case it lost importance, was no more than a rip in the glazed paper with its coloured photograph, and thus a final confirmation of the failure of personality.

I thought, then, of the death-houses I had visited in Sago Lane. What could be more atrocious to the eyes of western personality than these places, facing each other across the cramped street, in which the dying lay on their beds on the first floor, knowing that beneath them their companions of yesterday were stretched out in the morgue, under paper sheets inscribed with prayers, and hearing and smelling the business of death continuously carried on in the street outside—the brass-bands, the groups of professional mourners, the great wheels of frangipani? I remembered the cadaverous torso of a Chinese, all dull stringy varnish, outlined against the small window as he sat on his bed—and another Chinese who lay on his side as he occasionally dabbed an enormous growth on his neck with a damp towel. The hot light from the window shrank back exhausted from the lean ribs and long emaciated arms of the one, while what glimmering remained in the darker parts of the room seemed almost an exudation of the body of the other, and of those like him, who lay in restless stoicism, sweating their vapours and their poisons into dirty towels and rumpled sheets. Outside, the frangipani were no longer the European's garden blossoms but the death-flowers of the Chinese, strident and cloying; they in their turn linked up in my mind with the chalky or bluish plaster of Chinatown, the repetitious red characters on the arcades, the thin gold in the jewellers' shops, the fake gold in people's mouths; and death was something the light did, with a careless grin, to people who were unable to say 'I', who wore shorts like boys and seemed incapable of love, and built those piles of money which had no other conclusion than to be knocked down. . . .

(A prejudiced view: in handling this kind of past, the

end of something, there is a positive fear of re-living it. I notice how my paragraphs become more and more formal, more and more heavily framed, as though I just had to put the past to bed. And then, from the artificial stillness in which nightmare can be gathered, a wilder note suddenly sounds. Perhaps there has to be a tug-of-war like this: a series of plate-glass windows, an occasional opening door, probably in an unexpected part of the street. . . .)

After death, punishment: the unfortunate Albert Snood was given sixty days and reduced to the ranks. Grotesquerie was rampant here. The preliminary hearing, at which my assailant and I found each other with a single old-school major in between, was well under way in the Hall, and all sorts of embarrassing details were being gone into, before a pale figure appeared round a curtain, looking very shocked, and I realized that *an exam was taking place* on the other side! We then moved to the dining room of my house where Chi-chi watched us, whooping from a transom. I got so fed-up with the stupidity of the sergeant, and the chill legality of the officer in charge, that I ended up by helping Snood with his defence—not that he had one. The Court Martial itself was equally dreary. The defending Counsel, who announced with a grim smile that he usually prosecuted, was actually unaware that his client had confessed, and hence began a long argument as to the likelihood of my having had a heart-attack, or tripped over something. He then described my remark as being the most insulting that could be made to a British Soldier on a War Front, etc. I replied that I hadn't made the remark directly—it had been preceded by an *if*.

'Besides,' I went on, 'if I were to describe you as either Hitler or Betty Grable, would you *have* to decide that I had called you a Nazi?' I got a laugh for this.

The defending Counsel had a dramatic line of talk, anyway. Referring to the moment when Snood came up to hit me he said:

'So you turned, did you, like a rat in a trap?'

'I hope I didn't look too rat-like,' was the only answer I could think of at the moment.

'Just a minute. I want to get this clear,' he went on, weighing a pencil in the palm of this hand like some experienced barrister who would toss it into the air as a climax to his questions. 'Having insulted the defendant and realizing that he very properly resented your remarks, you decided to make yourself scarce rather than stand up to him *man to man*. You took to your heels?'

'I left, yes.'

'Did you see him hit you?'

'I suppose so. I can't remember.'

'There seems, if I may say so, a great deal about that evening that you can't remember.'

Fortunately there wasn't much of this sort of thing, and I spent a good deal of time explaining the lay-out of Bugis Street to the tribunal. They even wanted me to draw them a map.

In the course of the affair I learnt that Snood was about to be prosecuted on an even more serious charge. We then went off to luncheon in the Mess, and it was such an awful meal, and the atmosphere of the camp so oppressive, that I could hardly blame any officer, let alone any Other Rank, for going berserk. All I could think was that I had been impressed by the Judge Advocate stifling in his wig, and that I was grateful no reporters had been present. Not that this prevented the *Straits Times* from giving an account later, when the verdict was confirmed, which must have been based entirely on hearsay.

Compared with finality, any attempt at renewed life was tentative and hysterical. I did give a dinner-party, as soon as the whole house was mine, when Ah Ting was still with me. And at almost the last moment I determined to carry out a plan I had long thought of (since it *was* my house and I had a positive *right* to be myself) by putting on, as a sort of tropical evening dress, my dark blue sarong instead of black trousers. It wasn't quite long enough and I had to do a lot of adjusting before it really covered my ankles, and I didn't feel too happy when I exposed myself for the first time to Ah Ting and an additional youth I had borrowed from Margaret, but I persisted in the fantasy and received my guests with my ape on my shoulder, my Chinese purse at my waist, and a sort of rustling nakedness round my bottom half. Gerald would not have approved of this, of course, but the dinner itself was decently unpretentious in his manner. I had filled the dining room with tropical greenery amongst which candles peered out. I served only sherry before it. Afterwards, when we went upstairs, there were two bottles of gin.

Not everything was perfect, for the dissonant off-note of those days had to come in. Ah Ting forgot the celery. I found it weeks later in the refrigerator, abandoned ever since the kerosene gave out. Withered and ashen, it drooped under a cloud of flies. Ah Ting also forgot to give me my raspberries and ice-cream (he had been misled by the fact that there were less dessert-plates than people) so I chewed olives and made conversation with the air of someone who prefers the salt of wit to the silence of gluttony. Later on some students came in, and then Shaku. Later still, when we had started on the second bottle of gin, I myself produced the wrong note by sitting on the sofa with Shaku and kissing her at last. They were hopeless violent kisses; perhaps our real mutual affection, together with my respect for her and her own radiant romanticism (which defended her innocence far more than timidity or coldness would have done), required that we should play our love scene in the centre of the stage; afterwards, when Shaku used to come round to help me with the house work, this explosion seemed to have granted us the privileges of domesticity. But it was not until I had said goodbye to her for the last time that she presumed to use, in a note she sent me accompanying the present of a dagger, the christian name she had had engraved upon it. 'Mr. Anderson,' she would begin, right up to the end, 'Mr. Anderson, you know what the students are saying? They are saying that when you go, you are going to put to sleep your dog, your monkey and me....'

Less successful than the very minor pass I made at Shaku was my last attempt to open that gate whose scarcely-defined presence has appeared so often during this recital, creaking open upon a neat modern cul-de-sac when it should have given softly upon a gentle glade. Once more I began to search for a Boy. Ah Ting's father was ill and, shortly after the dinner party, he left. I thought I could save money by keeping the house empty of servants. After all Allan Painter had done without one for months. Nevertheless dirt accumulated and, as my energy diminished, I became obsessed with the thought that the place was dreadfully untidy, especially at the back, where dogs persistently raided the dustbin and Chi-chi's papaya rotted in a halo of ants. Then, too, the Cold Storage left the dog's piece of heart on the dining-room table; a bloody smear appeared; the marmalade cat got to it before I could, leaving a trail of tissue paper and blood. Practical reasons thus came to the aid of imaginative ones and often after midnight at Bugis Street I would think of capturing someone amongst the wildest Chinese, as a series of young boys with shaggy hair, stalwart bodies and expressions far more ferocious and attractive than those of the normal European-trained servant, bowed in front of me, cleaning my shoes, or marched away with my cigarettes dangling from their lips. A third Chinese servant was simply asking for difficulty, especially when the Malays were so adaptable; but difficulty had always attracted me and the very cohesion and foreignness of the Chinese made them in a way more challenging than the conventionally-exotic Malays; perhaps the street-urchin class would produce the kind of primitive loyalty I was looking for. With Beda Lim as my interpreter, I began

making inquiries of the beggar woman who always came
to my table. Negotiations were started and future meetings arranged, aborted through the language difficulty,
missed. The whole thing was a crazy idea in a crazy world
of flaring lamps, far too much beer, and children whose
business was to flirt with Europeans for money: little
girls tarted up till they were part dolls, part whores, and
singing 'Kelantan, Kelantan!' to zither-like instruments
while the bedraggled harpy figures of their mothers
watched them from the shadows; little boys whose racket
was certainly not sexual but whose jeering laughing eyes
caught one's own across the forests of bottles, 'Siglet!
siglet!'

One day I realized that the negotiations, half-hearted
at any time earlier than one's fifth Anchor, had taken
effect. The beggar woman was coming, bringing with her
a Boy. They arrived in the middle of the afternoon. It was
with a dreadful distinctness that I heard them and realized
that others would hear them, too, as I lay flat on my back
in bed, with all the shutters closed. I got up and peeped
at them through the slats. No doubt my caution was
elaborate but I had the feeling that the afternoon was so
glaring and still, and my house so nakedly deserted, that
any movement of mine would create a discernible shadow
and sound—a something upon which they could pounce.
There were two women, a trishaw and driver, a vague disgruntled blot which must be the Boy. It wasn't easy to
look through the shutters, by the way. You could pick up
shapes and little else. What mattered to me was my folly
in ever inviting them, the very idea of 'introducing into
the university' a servant recommended by 'a notorious
beggar woman' who would very likely be 'a criminal or at
least diseased'. Guilt shook me. I went back to bed. For a
time voices chirruped, at the sides, at the back, then there
was silence. I got up to see if they had gone away. Not a
bit of it. The trishaw was drawn into the hedge, the little
group sat on the stone coping at the entrance to the drive,

beyond the frangipani trees. Again a phrase came ready-made to mind. They were 'camping out on my doorstep'.

In the end I dressed, seized a five dollar bill, dashed into their midst in a cloud of English, Malay and sign language, and persuaded them that I was immediately leaving for England. 'Jalan England, Jalan England' I shouted, pointing in the direction of Margaret's house and the Library and shoving the bill into the beggar's fingers. For a moment only the boy's eyes met mine. I have seldom seen a stonier face. 'Finish, all finish!' I added, throwing up my hands. 'Thank you. Goodbye.' And I walked quickly back to the house. . . . Yet oddly enough, I *did* have a Malay youth working for me in the late afternoons during my last two weeks. He was called Hassan and he wore a yellow singlet under his shirt and silver-buckled shoes. He used to get into the bath in order to clean it and, as he bicycled away, he was all waves and smiles and friendship. He had every reason to be pleased for not only did he over-charge me but I couldn't resist supplementing his pay. 'For Hari Raya,' I said, putting my arm round his shoulders. He was my first and only Malay servant but, what with his dressing up for the Naval Cadets and his septic tonsils and his forgetting to come, he only appeared about five times and then not for more than a couple of hours.

The incident of the beggar woman confirmed my gro-tesqueness. Midge and Ellis had warned me that once you resigned you no longer mattered, while, when you left, it was as though you were dead or had never existed at all. My accident had turned me into an indiscretion, an in-delicate joke. No European entered into the spirit of the thing, either to see it as Rabelaisian or to realize how up-setting it actually was. 'I hope you are quite recovered,' they might say, as though I had had a bout of fever, and thus turn my night life into something unspeakable. For my part I now found myself quite nervous when I went out; new incidents were on the point of developing several times; people seemed deliberately to attach themselves to me and then suddenly to turn nasty, so that I began to wonder if my judgement had gone sour or if nervousness had changed my manner.

This isolation only brought me closer to the students who saw me now, I suppose, more as an equal. Shaku did my house-work, Beda Lim came out with me at night, but at least a dozen others were helpful in different ways and one day a big party was thrown for me in the Botanics. They couldn't have chosen a better place. We sat at marble-topped tables outside the little pavilion, began with monkey-nuts and ended with ice-cream. Turbans glimmered under the trees (Jamit wore his pink one) and cheongsams flitted across the grass (not a costume I really like but I must admit Suat Hong looked as pretty in hers as Siok Lim did in a blouse and skirt). Cameras clicked. I made a speech. Afterwards the university paper reprinted this, together with editorial comment, which must have displeased a number of people. Even Margaret was shocked. 'I think it's a bit undiplomatic of them. Professor —— leaves after twenty years devoted service and he gets scarcely a mention. You resign and are given no less than *three* photographs.'

One day Nadeswaren came to see me, eyes very bright, talk hurried and difficult to follow.

'Don't tell anyone but I have been handing in blank papers in all my exams. I have spent the time scribbling—crazy ideas—thoughts, ambitions, bits of poetry—anything. I felt I must think things out, my brain has been in a whirl for days, but I am getting somewhere, nearer the Truth, nearer the true way to learn. Everyone thought I was a big-shot but I wasn't honest with myself, I didn't really read or understand anything, I just thought education was mugging. . . . Now I know. I have a feeling of power.'

I was quite worried about him and checked up with his friends. In the end I came to believe that his 'break-down' was really a healthy attempt to break through the dreary academic pattern. His vitality didn't peter out in hysterics. He went round looking more and more radiant. Later, when he helped me clean out the house, I presented him with a pair of voluptuously coloured trousers which Gerald had left behind.

As Nades grew Dostoievskian, the politically-minded X sank into bitter silence over his coffee in the canteen. A State Scholar from Johore, he had grown to resent the provision in his contract which required him to join the Civil Service for five years after graduation.

'I sit all day drinking one coffee after another,' he said. 'What else is there to do? Life here is too unreal. Too many restrictions, too much fear, no political expression. Just playing around with dead ideas.' He smiled helplessly, his dark Tamil eyes no longer snapping behind his spectacles. 'I think I shall go home to Batu Pahat where I can study.'

'But you can study here.'

'There are no books—not the books I need. I want to study History . . . and Economics . . . in a scientific way.'

'Whatever your political views, I'm sure *they* would like you to get a degree,' I said, using the argument Jowett had used to Hopkins!

He was contemptuous in his reply. 'If you mean the Communists, they have no interest in this place.'

'I do mean the Communists.'

He smiled, sunk into himself, not even responding to Gung-wu who joined us and offered the help of the Student Union. Later I heard he had gone.

'But what will he do in Batu Pahat? It's a tiny place, wired-in, under the shadow of mountains. Will he go into the jungle?'

'He went because one of his parents was ill,' I was told.

'No, that was a blind. He told me he would make an excuse like that. He has gone to be a revolutionary!'

'I think his father telegraphed him,' was the vague,

seemingly apathetic reply. Another in the endless stream of don't-know, can't-say, couldn't-care-less.

Then one day all the students were gone and the canteen was closed. I should have expected this, but it came as a shock. No more food, or cigarettes, or aspirins. No more conversation. Nowhere to go. I had no car and couldn't expect to use taxis for all my meals and necessities.

Without my Asian allies, I felt incapable of facing the emptiness of quadrangle and arcade, gravel sweep and tidy lawn, the slightness of the foliage—the suburban simper (for I still tried to arm myself with words to describe it), the purely technical flash (as when a pram went by, priggish and burning). It was, I told myself, a world of tin-foil and tissue paper: hot as a birdcage, bright as magnesium, powerless as ash. It was . . . but the click of words falling into place still left me empty and anxious; my House was a toy I no longer had the energy to play with, as well as a prison; it was better to go downstairs, to the old abandoned room, and stand by the barred windows remembering how I had told Ah Ting when I had first employed him, 'They'll never get me to stay in this house,' and mutely calling for help as I gripped the bars.

Help came in the person of Allan Painter, who invited me to spend my last days with him. He now lived four miles away, at the top of a steep hill running up from Bukit Timah Road, sharing his house with an old hand at Malaya who ran the household with great efficiency and who told many diverting stories of life before the war. Allan's life was as self-contained and whimsical as ever; he sipped his brandy, read his French novels, wrote bits of Firbank-like observation on bits of paper, and occasionally sallied forth on his motor-bicycle in search of conversation and girls. I remember one slender creature whom we nicknamed the insect-girl, for she looked incredibly delicate in her green dress and we thought she must have chlorophyl in her veins instead of blood. Her hair was cut in a fringe, her cheek-bones high and prominent, her eyes soft but expressionless.

Allan now thought of me as 'a nice kind of phoney'. He sensed, I suppose, my lack of academic training in English and my habit of intoxicating myself with words, in which I found security and strength.

'I suppose you're not such a bad type of Empire-builder, really,' he told me. 'You adore hero-worship and like to enthuse the young. Since you see everything more than life-size, including yourself, you need the wide open spaces.'

'I know I'm beginning to realize how muddled my attitude to Malaya has been. Or at least how emotional and basically conservative. Childhood plus sex—what I'm after is a Garden of Eden.'

Allan is not a talker and we soon drifted to a more congenial topic: how to phrase 'I like you, would you like to come to bed with me?' in the Bazaar Malay retailed in a primer for mems.

When Allan fell ill with flu, I went back to the university, caught flu myself within four days of sailing, and lay marooned and terrified in my bedroom. It so happened that the bitch was on heat—the Cold Storage man left the door open—dogs wandered through the house all night, panting, slobbering, growling at each other, but never other than mournful—the next day, when I had driven them out, they still provided an odd farewell committee—an obscene comment, as I saw it then, on a dreamer's and romantic's house—I was without food and almost without cigarettes and my view of life was tinged with fever and anxiety lest I should miss the boat. Besides, I still had to do most of my packing and I hadn't yet completed the sale of my insurance. Hassan was ill too.

The last day came: an endless taxi-ride from bank to insurance company, from one government office to another. Early in the morning, as I abandoned object after object into the hands of Hassan and his friend Suki, until they stood under heaps of cushions, gramophone records, saucepans and books, Suki said to me, with his wry smile.

'You married? You getting married, yes? You Professor London University now? I think you want wife?' To which I responded by shoving Volume Two of the *Anatomy of Melancholy* into a gap in his multifarious load. But it was not Hassan or Suki but an unexpectedly rediscovered Osman who accompanied me to fulfil the vow I had made to Gerald that I should have the dog electrocuted at the Animal Infirmary before I left. Osman was growing taller and his face had a sulkier more adolescent appearance than before, but he still affected his *petit gamin* attire, abbreviated clothes which only shyness prevented from vanishing altogether. I haven't the least idea what he thought about it all. I only know that he was gentle, silent, completely lacking in vulgarity, and that I valued him.

In the early afternoon my taxi drove away from the university for the last time. I hugged Chi-chi and handed him over to the small boy of whom he had grown fond, little thinking that neither the boy nor his parents would ever let me know what had happened to him. I shuddered at the untidiness of the house—but Hassan had promised to return in the evening to clean it up. I didn't look back as we drove off. I knew perfectly well how much I should regret Malaya and how often my mind would return to it in imagination, to make a fresh start under more favourable circumstances and to calculate how different things would have been if I had immediately found a house, or even a room, of my own. Still departure was dramatic and had its gaiety. It was with gaiety that I imagined myself encircling all my friends (and that evening, the sailing being delayed, some of the students were once again taking me out on a party), with the Malay phrase that meant 'Lost to the eye but remembered in the heart'. As I sat at the majolica bar of the Italian liner, scribbling a note to Gerald who was busy flat-hunting in London, it was this phrase that I sent back to Shaku and Gung-wu, to Beda and Ratnam, to Allan, R. and Margaret, to cocky Leng and weeping Ambi and the distant foliage-flecked figure of Ah Tum:

HILANG DI MATTA DI HATI JANGAN